Spencer Hill Press

Contact: Spencer Hill Press, PO Box 247, Contoocook, NH 03229, USA

Please visit our website at www.spencerhillpress.com

First Edition: June 2013.

Pickett, Michelle K. 1971
PODs : a novel / by Michelle Pickett − 1st ed.
p. cm.
Summary:
Teenage girl survives the virus that destroys civilization only to find that the danger doesn't stop with the end of the world.

Cover design and interior layout: K. Kaynak.

ISBN 978-1-937053-28-4 (paperback)
ISBN 978-1-937053-29-1 (e-book)

Printed in the United States of America

PODs

Michelle Pickett

SPENCER HILL PRESS

Also by Michelle Pickett

Milayna
March 2014

The Infected: A PODs Novel
Fall 2014

In loving memory of my dad,
Michael Lewis Hayes
March 12, 1944 to January 28, 2013

Always Loved.

Before

Nothing is as far away as one minute ago.

~ Jim Bishop

Chapter 1 : Learning

I walked in the front door just minutes before dinner to find my parents huddled in front of the television set.

"Hey." They either didn't hear me or decided to ignore me. "I'm home," I said, louder.

"Turn it off, turn it off," my mom whispered.

"I'm trying…"

"Change the channel…for cryin' out loud, give it to me!" My mom grabbed the remote out of my dad's hand and turned off the television.

They both jumped away from the TV, my mom smoothing invisible wrinkles out of her clothes.

"Hey, sweetie, we didn't hear you come in." My dad gave me a forced smile.

"Yeah, I got that. What's up?"

"Nothing," they said in unison.

That was clue number one that something was wrong.

My mom recovered first. "How was the mall?"

"Oh, you know, I was with Bridget. She loves dressing me up like an overgrown Barbie doll." I flipped my blonde hair over my shoulder and rolled my eyes. "I think it's the hair. The rest of me looks like Skipper—short, skinny and no boobs."

My mom laughed, the sound loud in the small room. But even with her piercing laughter, the room seemed quiet—

the kind of quiet that buzzes under the surface of the noise everyone makes to hide the huge elephant sitting in the middle of the floor.

"What's up?" I watched them look at each other, and then at me.

"Nothing, Eva. Why?" my dad answered.

"You're both acting funny."

"Well, don't all teenagers think their parents act funny?" He put his arm around my shoulders. "We're having your favorite for dinner tonight."

"Ugh. How many times do I need to tell you liver doesn't taste like chicken? I believed that when I was five. Now I know the difference."

"No liver tonight. How does pizza sound?"

"Truthfully? Pizza on a Tuesday night sounds like something's wrong. We never have pizza on Tuesdays."

Okay, what's up with these two?

"We don't?" Mom asked.

"No. Dad says it's a weekend meal."

"Your dad says a lot of things us girls should ignore."

My dad frowned. "I'm standing right here. I can hear you."

"I know." My mom grabbed the plates out of the cupboard.

Pizza on a Tuesday—that was clue number two that something was really wrong.

Clue number three came the next day at school. Everyone was talking about the news report. I didn't think much of it. There'd always been theories about the end of the world, but we were all still around. So I tried to ignore the gossip and get through the day. But, as usual, nothing happened to anyone under thirty in Sandy Shores, Texas without Bridget knowing.

Bridget set her Diet Coke down on the lunch table with a thud. "I can't believe you didn't see it."

"Why?"

"Hello, like, it's end-of-the-world stuff!"

"Lemme guess. Jake told Alexa who told Bryce who told you—"

"Don't knock the rumor mill, Eva. Jonathan asked you to prom just like I said he would."

"Sorry, sorry. Far be it from me to interrupt the flow of journalistic mediocrity."

Actually, Bridget's rumor mill is pretty accurate. It's almost like having a psychic on speed-dial.

"Ha, ha. So how did you manage to stay away from television all night? It was on every channel."

"Well, for starters, I actually did my homework." Bridget rolled her eyes. "And my parents ordered pizza and declared it family game night. We didn't have the television on last night."

"That proves my theory."

"What?"

"Parents of only children are more protective," Bridget said matter-of-factly, flinging her hand in the air before letting it slap the tabletop.

"I think others have had the same theory, Bridget."

"Yeah, but your parents proved it last night. They were shielding you from the news. That's why you had family torture night—"

"Game night, and it wasn't torture. It was kinda fun."

"How many game nights have you had?"

"Truthfully, it's the first one I can think of," I admitted.

"Well, there you go."

Yeah. I wasn't exactly sure where I was going, but Bridget had a point. One of the biggest news events of the year, if not the decade, was on television and I was eating pepperoni pizza and playing Scrabble with my parents. I hadn't even known we owned a Scrabble board.

Bridget was right, of course. My parents *were* shielding me. I guess they didn't factor in the high school's raging gossip-mongers. I knew not to take things churned out from the rumor mill at face value, but hearing them made me even more curious why everyone was panicking—and why my parents wanted to keep it from me.

Clue four: A very little thing, with life-changing significance.

The man on TV was balding. What little hair he had was gray—not a nice-looking silver or even white, but a dull, lifeless gray. Depressing. Ugly. He was the person who told me my life was going to drastically change—the man with the ugly gray hair.

He read his lines from a teleprompter, his eyes roaming from one end of the screen to the other. He read the words with perfect pitch. The blonde reporter—"eye candy," my dad called her—sat next to him smiling and nodding.

Stop bouncing your head. You look like a bobblehead. Aren't you listening? Don't you see the same words on the teleprompter...or are they too big for your limited vocabulary? Stop smiling!

"The virus has no name. Scientists call it HHC6984, or simply 'the virus.' A person can be infected for days, perhaps a week or more, before showing symptoms. Once the symptoms surface, it's already too late. Death is certain and swift. From the onset of the first symptom to the patient's inevitable death is a span of two to five days.

"The virus is resistant to every antibiotic and antiviral medication we know of. It is highly contagious, although how it's transmitted remains a mystery.

"If a cure isn't found, it will not only turn into a pandemic, but will likely infect most of the human population by year's end. Scientists are not optimistic about finding a cure," the man with the lifeless, gray hair reported. The blonde bimbo beside him still smiled. I sat on the floor in front of the television, a Coke in one hand and the remote in the other, trying to wrap my brain around what I'd just heard.

A virus? A teeny, tiny virus is going to wipe humans off the face of the earth? Well, why not?

Everyone knew it was coming. We just didn't know how or when. Call it the apocalypse, Armageddon, the end-of-life-as-we-know-it, extinction, whatever you want. Something like it killed the dinosaurs, why not us? Maybe it was our time to go—to hand over the earth to the next wave of inhabitants.

Several scientists had predicted it would be an asteroid, like the one that'd killed the dinosaurs. Only a few people thought it'd be a tiny bug—something too small for the naked eye to see—a virus so lethal people were dead before they knew they were infected. A virus that was killing people so quickly there was no need to name it something memorable—there'd be no one left to remember it.

"What are you doing?"

I jumped up at the sound of my dad's voice. My Coke sloshed over the rim of the can, the sticky liquid dripping from my hand onto the beige carpet. I spun around, an apology on my lips, when it dawned on me—I wasn't doing anything wrong. I was watching the news.

"I'm watching pay-per-view porn. Oh, wait, that was yesterday. Today I'm learning of my impending death from the stupid news reporter and the blonde idiot sitting next to him. I mean, it's not like my parents knew but decided not to tell me themselves. Pizza and game night on a Tuesday—I knew something was wrong."

"Eva, I'm sorry. We needed time to process the information ourselves," my dad told me. "Your mom and I planned to talk with you today."

I dropped onto a chair at the kitchen table. The room was decorated in reds and whites—it seemed too cheery now, with my mom's strawberry knick-knacks everywhere—a strawberry cookie jar, salt and pepper shakers, and placemats. I wrapped one of the placemats around my finger while I sat at the table with my dad.

"What's gonna happen, Dad?" I asked, cold fear clutching at my heart.

"I don't know. The scientists and doctors are working on a cure. They could find one any day—"

"But the news said they weren't hopeful."

"I know, but remember, penicillin was discovered by accident. So who knows what they can find in the next few months? We just have to wait and have a little patience."

The waiting lasted a week. The dead were piling up in every country—including parts of the U.S.—the bodies burned in an attempt to kill the virus before it could infect anyone else. The sight of burning corpses heaped in large mounds like grotesque firewood filled the cable news channels. I pictured faces of people I knew and loved on the burning bodies and it made my stomach heave and bile rise in my throat. Those lifeless shells had been living, vibrant people. Now they were nothing more than charred bone. My heart skipped painfully in my chest.

Doctors and scientists were still clueless. They didn't know the virus's origin or how it was transmitted, and they weren't any closer to a cure than they had been a week ago. The only progress they'd made was they were now able to locate the infected cells before symptoms surfaced. So now, people not only were going to die from the virus, they knew a week ahead of time.

Great.

In an attempt to contain the virus, most air travel had been suspended, and the sky became empty—an eerie silence. When the sound of jets came, it was usually from small military aircraft. Most countries had closed their borders, and some had declared martial law. The television had played nothing but reports of the virus and its impact since the news had first broken. So it surprised us when the news broadcast was interrupted and the waving American flag, the presidential seal superimposed on it, filled the screen.

My parents and I were sitting at the table eating dinner together, something we'd started doing after the first reports of the virus. From the TV in the living room, a newscaster announced, "We now go to the White House, where the President has called an emergency press conference." The three of us exchanged looks as we stood, our chairs scraping against the tiled floor. We moved to sit in front of the television and waited to hear from the President.

Maybe a cure's been found. Or a vaccine.

Chapter 2 : Raffle

Wednesday

The President walked to his place behind the podium. His face looked haggard and worn. Dark circles surrounded his dull eyes, adding years to his age. My throat constricted and my stomach roiled as I waited to hear what I prayed would be good news.

"My fellow Americans," he began. The blood rushed behind my ears and I had to strain to hear him. He talked about the many deaths, the failure to find a cure, and the fact that the virus was moving through the populations of every country quickly.

"It's lethal and seemingly unstoppable. In an effort to save as many people as possible I'm authorizing the use of the Populace Obliteration Defense, also known as the POD system. The POD system is a series of underground habitats designed to provide protection from an Extinction Level Event, such as a meteor, nuclear blast, and the like. That's the good news.

"The bad news is, even with the use of the PODs, most of the population will die from the lethal virus, because, unfortunately, there isn't enough room in the habitats for everyone."

I watched him speak and was amazed at his poise. He relayed the information to the country like he was giving stats on a football game. There was no emotion in his voice, no sympathy for those who had been, and would be, lost. Every hair was in place, his tie perfectly tied, a flag pin adorning his lapel. Gold cuff links twinkled when he gestured with his hands.

He doesn't have to worry. He has his spot in a POD.

"Congress and I have come up with what we believe is the fairest course of action—a raffle. Each eligible person's social security number will be entered into a database—"

"Mr. President, Mr. President!" reporters shouted over each other.

"Yes?" He pointed at a woman with bottle-blonde hair.

"Geez, she has so much lip gloss on it looks like she just ate a greasy hamburger."

"Shush, Eva," my mom said, waving her hand at me without looking away from the screen.

"Who is deemed *eligible* and who isn't? Shouldn't all citizens have the same right?"

"In an ideal world everyone could be saved. In an ideal world we wouldn't have to make such decisions. This is not an ideal world.

"Those who are considered ineligible for the raffle include anyone with a criminal record. Anyone who is in poor health now, or who has a degenerative disease that may cause further health risks in the future will also be ineligible. We have prepared a document listing the full eligibility criteria."

"I stole a candy bar from the grocery store when I was five. Does that mean I'm ineligible?" I asked, only half-joking. "It wasn't even that good a candy bar."

"Eva, hush!" My mom's eyes never left the television.

I didn't particularly want to be quiet. When I was, I started thinking. And thinking was something I didn't want to do. I didn't want to think of the virus and all the people it had killed—and those it would kill.

I stared at the television, the images blurring as tears threatened to fall. I blinked them back. I was absentmindedly wringing my fingers, and my knuckles popped. My mom laid her hand gently over mine. I looked up at her. She smiled. I grabbed her hand and held it like I had when I was a little girl.

The briefing room bustled as reporters yelled to be heard over the shouts of their competitors. The President waited for the noise to stop before speaking again.

"Each eligible person's social security number will be entered into a computer. The computer will randomly select a list of social security numbers. Each of these people will have a space in the PODs.

"There are one hundred main PODs; each holds a hundred people. Essential government workers, scientists, engineers, medical and maintenance personnel will be housed in these main PODs. An additional ten thousand political, scientific, and military personnel will be housed at separate, undisclosed locations.

"Attached to the main PODs are fifty sub-PODs. Think of the arrangement like the spokes on a bike's wheel. Each sub-POD will hold ten people—the raffle winners. In total, the one hundred main PODs have five thousand sub-PODs."

A flurry of questions erupted. The President held up his hand to silence the crowd.

"I apologize, but I am not taking any further questions at this time. Please let me continue. Beyond the essential political, scientific, medical, military and maintenance personnel, fifty thousand openings remain. The only fair way to fill these openings is by blind raffle. This raffle will take place tomorrow night. Those chosen will be phoned and given instructions on when and where to meet their transport. By this time Friday, the first wave of POD occupants will begin their mandatory two-week quarantine.

"When the quarantine process is completed and people are deemed virus-free, they will be escorted to their assigned PODs and the next wave of selected individuals will begin their quarantine.

"The total timeframe from first wave to third is six weeks. The POD occupants will then be sealed in their assigned

PODs, where they will remain for one year, or until we are certain the virus is no longer a threat. That is all. Thank you."

The President was whisked off the stage by the Secret Service. The reporters grabbed for the documents that staffers handed out—packets outlining the government's course of action and the eligibility requirements for the raffle. The television shifted scenes and returned to the regular newscaster, who immediately started blathering about the President's speech.

All I could process were the numbers.

Only seventy thousand of us will live. Twenty thousand have already been chosen. That leaves fifty thousand openings for the raffle winners. The rest of us will be left to deal with the virus, left to die.

I could tell by my parents' strained looks they were thinking the same thing.

No one had thought it would come to this. Everyone assumed a cure would be found, or at least a treatment—something would be able to stop it. But it looked like a tiny virus *would* be the downfall of civilization.

Sometimes life's a bitch.

Thursday

The raffle was scheduled to begin at seven that night. At seven sharp my parents and I sat waiting in front of the television. We squeezed together on the couch, my mom on my right and my dad on my left. The television hung over the fireplace in front of us.

Even though the room was warm, my mom and I huddled under a fleece blanket. It acted as our shield, keeping the ugliness away. My mom's hand skimmed back and forth over the blanket on my knee in silent reassurance. My dad's arm stretched across the couch, his hand resting on my mom's shoulder. I was nestled, too warm, between their bodies.

Drops of sweat fell from beneath my hair and slithered down my back. I shivered involuntarily and my mother hugged me tighter to her.

We waited silently for the raffle to begin. I'm not sure exactly what we expected to see. I envisioned several scenarios. In one I saw a room-sized computer—complete with flashing lights and buzzers—spitting out social security numbers like cash from an ATM. Or maybe a small laptop would scroll number after number across the screen, while a small printer beside it captured each one on paper. Then another image would fly through my thoughts. A large digital display—like the arrival and departure screens at an airport—would show nine spinning columns. One by one they'd stop, revealing a number until all nine were showing, the word "live" or "die" flashing beside it.

Whatever I thought I'd see, it was definitely not what I saw—which was nothing. Absolutely nothing was broadcast. The selection was done behind closed doors. No cameras or reporters were allowed inside. The newscaster seemed just as surprised as we were and scrambled to fill time. He recapped the events leading up to the raffle, told us in mind-numbing detail everything we already knew. What he didn't tell us was the one thing we needed to know, but feared knowing at the same time—who was going to live and who was going to die.

Twenty minutes after seven the newscaster announced that the selection process had ended and the phone calls had begun. My heart was in my stomach as I waited to hear our phone ring. I was hopeful we'd be picked. My mom was a cardiac nurse and my dad a college professor; surely they'd be needed for rebuilding the country.

But the raffle is random. My parents' professions won't earn spaces in a POD.

An hour went by and our phones sat silent. My hope was waning. I paced the living room floor, staring at the black house phone—one minute begging it to ring, the next cursing it. I checked that my cell phone wasn't on silent—four times. My heart was beating so hard it hurt. My shirt stuck to my sweaty back, and wisps of hair stuck to my face.

The phone is gonna ring, it has to. We still have a chance. It'll take a long time to phone fifty thousand people.

I thought of a hundred possible reasons our phones hadn't rung, trying to reassure myself.

Two hours. My hope was gone. I knew the chances of our phone ringing had been slim to begin with, but as time ticked by so did our shots at places in the PODs. Despite the warm room, goosebumps covered my skin and my teeth chattered. The back of my throat burned as my stomach bile rose.

I grabbed my backpack off the floor behind the couch and pulled out one of my books, even though doing homework wasn't necessary. Either I was going to the PODs or I was going to die. Whichever it was, chemistry homework should have been the farthest thing from my mind, but I needed something, anything to distract me. I flopped back onto the couch and pulled a neon yellow highlighter across a passage in my notes, the tip squeaking against the page. My frayed nerves snapped.

"Can we please turn him off?" I yelled, slamming my book closed. "He's been blathering on all night long. He just says the same thing over and over and over. Please, shut it off."

My mom looked at me. I thought she was going to yell at me for being disrespectful by shouting. Instead she smiled sadly and nodded. "I'd rather read than listen to him, anyway."

"Thanks, Mom."

"And I've got papers to grade," my dad said. I guess he hadn't thought about the absurdity of grading papers any more than I had about doing homework.

Two hours, thirty-seven minutes.

My phone rang.

Chapter 3 : The Call

My mother bolted off the couch. My dad, who was coming back from the kitchen, stood with his hand poised over the flip top on a Coke can. I looked up from my chemistry homework, my pen dangling from my fingers. The three of us just stared at my cell phone. It rang twice. On the third ring I grabbed it.

"Hello?" My voice shook. My rational side told me not to get my hopes up. It was probably Bridget. But the side of me that still had hope said maybe, just maybe, it was them. We had a spot.

"Evangelina Mae Evans?"

"Y—yes. I'm Evangelina." I saw my mom grab Dad's arm. My dad dropped his Coke can. It hit the floor with a thud, fizz spraying out of the partially opened top. He absently patted my mom's hand. They both stared at me while the pale-brown foam sprayed across the living room.

"Your social security number was selected."

I was surprised at how calm I was. Maybe the brusque manner of the man on the phone helped me keep my cool. Maybe it was shock.

"Do you have a pen and paper?"

"Yes."

"Write this down. You'll report to Glendale High School in Glendale, Texas on Wednesday, the twenty-seventh, at eight

AM sharp. You'll leave for your quarantine period at that time. Bring your birth certificate, your social security card, and your belongings. Each occupant is allowed two suitcases—no more. Do you have any questions?"

"Yes," I said. "My family? They—"

"The social security number selected was yours. If anyone else in your family was chosen they will receive a phone call."

"Just me?"

"Yes. Any other questions?"

"No." My voice cracked and a lump formed in my throat.

"Goodbye." I heard the receiver click and the line go dead. I stood motionless, the phone still at my ear.

It wasn't until I heard my mother's quiet sobs that I put the phone down and looked at her and my father.

"You were picked?" my dad whispered.

"Yeah, but—"

"But nothing, Eva. You were picked!"

"But I can't...I can't..." I started to cry as the reality of what was happening hit me. I'd have to leave my parents. How could I be happy I had been chosen when they hadn't been?

I can't leave them to die.

"It's okay, Eva," my mom murmured, hugging me. She smoothed my hair while I cried against her shoulder. "We know you'd take us if you could; we know. But you have to understand, as parents we're overjoyed that our child was chosen. We'll be happy knowing you'll have a chance at a full life. Don't cry, Evangelina. This is wonderful news."

No, no, no, this isn't good news at all. How can I leave them knowing...

Friday

I only had two weeks to get ready before I left for quarantine. My mom insisted on a shopping spree. "Eva, you need a new wardrobe. You'll be down there a year, maybe more. You'll need clothes that will last."

"Somehow, I don't think we'll be having fashion shows down there, Mom. You don't need to buy me anything." Besides, going to the mall—or to any public place—was disturbing. Many people wore white surgical masks and latex gloves, and everyone avoided getting to close to other people. Not that there were many people to get close to—the place was nearly deserted, and several of the mall stores had their metal barriers down, their interiors dark. We still hadn't had any reported cases around Sandy Shores, but we knew it was only a matter of time.

"You never know," she said with a flick of her hand. "Stranger things have happened."

"Yeah? Name one," I said.

"I married your dad, didn't I?"

I burst out laughing.

"How about this?" My mom held up a purple hoodie with a cute design on the front. I loved it, but the logo told me that it was way out of our price range, especially for a hoodie.

"No, Mom, that's too much."

"Eva, it might be cold down there. You'll need some warm clothes."

"But it's too expensive—"

"I want you to have it. Humor me, okay?"

By the time I was done *humoring* my mother, she had bought out the mall. Jeans, t-shirts, sweat pants, hoodies, underclothes, shoes...was there anything left? She'd bought me over two dozen outfits, including clothing for both warm and cool weather. So, no matter what the temperature, I had something to wear. I wasn't sure I could fit everything in the two-suitcase limit.

When we got home my dad met us at the door. "Here, Eva, take these with you." He thrust two flashlights into my hands, with two large bags of batteries. "I hope there are enough batteries to last you the year. I got you one of these, too." He held up a metal case with a lock. It was big enough to fit my batteries, and whatever else I wanted to protect. "Hard telling what type of people you'll be around."

"Thanks, Dad," I said, tears clogging my throat—again.

I'm crying over flippin' batteries. Probably the last packages of batteries my dad will ever buy me.

Memories of Christmas mornings and birthday parties flashed through my mind. My dad was always on battery patrol, making sure anything that needed them had batteries. Now a flashlight would be the end. The realization that there'd be no new memories to share made the tears fall faster and an ache form deep in my chest.

That night the news showed the first wave of raffle winners leaving for their quarantine period. The newscaster babbled on and on about what was happening and what the raffle winners could expect when they arrived at the quarantine facility.

"I wonder if they're scared," I whispered.

My dad squeezed my shoulder. "I suppose they are."

"I'm not."

"No?" He angled his body on the couch to look at me.

"No. I'm sad. I'm just sad. Maybe I'll be scared when I have to leave."

I jumped when the newscast was interrupted. A man ran into the newsroom screaming, "The government did it! They caused Armageddon! It's their fault! AIDS, Ebola, and now the virus. They made them all."

"Security!" a man off-camera yelled. "Get him outta here."

Dressed in tattered, dirt-smeared clothing, the man ran to the camera, his unshaven face dirty and his thinning gray hair hanging in greasy strings. Grabbing the camera with both hands, he shook it back and forth. "The raffle was fixed. It was fixed! We didn't have a chance. Only the young ones. Only the young ones!" he screamed as security pulled him out of the room. "Save the books!" he yelled as the door closed.

"Well," the newscaster said, shuffling his papers. "I wonder what drug he was on," he joked. No one thought it was funny. We were too busy watching the little box over the reporter's right shoulder. It still played live footage of people climbing into the buses that would transport them to the quarantine facility.

Where are the older people? Where are the mothers, the fathers? Everyone is my age. Did anyone any older even have a chance? "The raffle was fixed...only the young ones," *the lunatic had screamed. Maybe he wasn't as crazy as he'd looked.*

Tuesday, eleven days to quarantine

My cell phone rang and I immediately reached for it, but I didn't press the talk button right away. I stared at the name illuminated on the screen. It was a call I'd been dreading, but I couldn't ignore her forever.

"Hey, Bridget."

"Hi. I've been trying to talk to you for days, but you never pick up. Why haven't you been in school?" She'd been crying. Her nose was snotty; I could hear the tissues brush against the receiver of the phone.

"I'm sorry. It's just been so weird." I felt bad that I hadn't made more of an effort to talk with her, to make sure she was all right. "My parents said I didn't have to go if I didn't want to. I can test out of my courses if things...well, if—"

"I can't believe it, Eva. We're gonna die." She started crying again. I didn't know what to say. *What do you say to someone who's just been given a death sentence?*

"I know."

She cried harder, and I couldn't understand what she said. I sat and listened and let her cry. What else could I do? I was her best friend. I cried with her, for her.

"Why aren't you more upset, Eva?" she asked when her sobs turned to hiccupped cries. She didn't wait for an answer. "You've always been the strong one. The practical one."

I was glad she couldn't see me. She'd have known right away. We'd been friends since grade school, there wasn't much I didn't tell her. There wasn't much point; she always seemed to know when I was hiding something. And I *was* hiding something—I hadn't told Bridget I'd been chosen. I don't know why. I guess I didn't want her to feel worse, or maybe it was because *I'd* feel worse. I was planning to tell her the night before I left, but I wasn't sure I'd tell her at all. I knew that was the coward's way out, but maybe I wasn't as strong as she gave me credit for.

Friday, eight days to quarantine

In the week since the first wave of chosen had left for quarantine, people had started questioning the validity of the raffle. Had it been fixed? If not, why didn't the people leaving show more of a mixture of ages?

Theories swarmed and scientists discussed the likelihood that a random drawing from such a large population pool would create a group formed entirely of teens and young adults.

I tried not to listen. I had my own theory.

"Convinced the government-sponsored raffle was rigged, citizens around the country are rioting, demanding a new raffle," a live news correspondent reported in front of city hall.

"We want one drawn in front of everyone. Not behind closed doors where Big Brother can manipulate the numbers," a middle-aged man told the correspondent. The man wore horn-rimmed glasses and a stained t-shirt with the word "raffle" hand painted inside a circle with a red slash mark across it.

The correspondent tipped the hand-held microphone back to speak into it. "Surely you must realize that even if another raffle was to take place the chances of getting a place in the POD system are astronomically against you. Your result would likely remain the same."

The man's face hardened, his eyebrows forming a slash above his eyes. He leaned into the reporter's face and muttered, "You were chosen. That's why you don't want another raffle."

"Actually, I wasn't chosen."

"Chosen! Chosen!" the man chanted, drawing the attention of the other rioters.

The mob converged on them, and the reporter stepped backward, bumping into her cameraman. The camera slipped and fell to the ground, filming hundreds of feet swarming the area where the reporter had stood.

I sucked in a breath, covering my mouth with my fist. I hadn't realized I was leaning toward the television until my mom pulled gently on my arm. I scooted back on the couch, my eyes still glued to the screen where the live feed had frozen on a distorted frame of chaos.

"What did they do to the reporter?" I shrieked, pointing at the screen.

"Eva—"

"They hate us!"

"They're scared."

I slumped against the back of the couch.

Of course they're scared. They know they're going to die.

I looked at my dad out of the corner of my eye and wondered how scared he was. I was scared for him.

Seconds later the studio anchor's face filled the screen. He picked up his report without hesitation, leaving everyone to worry and wonder about the fate of the correspondent and her cameraman.

"As riots rage, looters are taking whatever they can carry. And, as seen in this footage, they don't care who sees. Police have been unable to stop the looting, and store-owners are taking the law into their own hands. Gun-related deaths have soared, increasing by more than two hundred percent.

"Hoarding is commonplace, and with it, price gouging. A gallon of milk that would have cost three dollars before the raffle is selling for seven, even eight dollars. The greatest mark-ups are on canned goods and other non-perishables as people try to gather enough supplies to wait out the virus."

"Damn right I'm buying everything I can get my hands on. I'm gonna board up my house and wait out the virus. POD or no POD, I'm taking care of my own," one man said as he and his family left a grocery store with four carts loaded full of canned vegetables, soups, and fruit. The camera stayed on the carts. "...can't show our faces—if people know who we are, our neighbors might come steal our supplies."

"It's getting bad," my dad said. "I knew it would." He shook his head. "Neighbor against neighbor, friend against friend, families divided—all because of a little bug."

"In an attempt to quell the growing unrest, martial law is in effect as of today. The Army..." The newscaster still droned on, but my dad turned the television off.

"Eva Mae, I'll be glad to get you out of this and tucked safely in your POD." He patted me on the knee before standing and walking to the kitchen.

"But what about you? How am I supposed to just leave you here with all this going on?" I flung my arm toward the television.

"Don't worry about us, Eva—"

"Dad, remember our trips to Perch Lake? Remember the little cabin on the lake we rented from the old couple?"

"Yes. It was wonderful there."

"Let's go back. We could fish and hunt for food. The cabin is isolated. We'd be far from people—we could wait out the virus together. We'd be safe from the violence. Why are you shaking your head? We can pick berries and grow a garden… it'll work, Dad! Stop shaking your head!"

"Eva, you're going into the PODs. It's the only safe place there is and that's where I want you."

"What about what I want? I want to stay with you." I felt like stomping my foot, but forced it to stay still, reminding myself I wasn't two anymore.

"I know you do, but that isn't how this works. You go into the PODs and we stay here. That's the deal, Evangelina."

"Will you go to the lake? For me?" I held my breath as I watched my dad weighing the benefits of trying to survive holed up in a cabin in the woods for a year, fishing and hunting for food—neither of which he did well. At the jerky nod of his head the breath I was holding whooshed from my lungs and I threw myself into his arms, squeezing him. "Thank you, Daddy."

Thursday, forty-eight hours to quarantine

We had pizza again for dinner. My dad said he was in the mood for a heartburn-inducing pizza. My mom, who hated to cook, jumped at the chance for a night off.

I knew the truth. I was leaving the next day. Pizza was my favorite meal. It wasn't hard to figure out. We sat at the table eating pizza and playing Scrabble. We didn't turn the television on. It was nice not having to listen to the same news clips, the same stories, the conspiracy theories.

I took a bite out of a slice of pepperoni and double-cheese pizza, some of the cheese plopping on the table with a splat. I snatched it before my mom could wipe it up with her napkin.

"That's still good!"

"Evangelina, don't talk with food in your mouth."

I took another bite of pizza, the sauce and cheese oozing from the corners of my lips. "I'm really gonna miss this," I said around the huge bite.

My mom rolled her eyes. "Eva," she sighed. I looked at her and smiled.

That's how I spent my last night at home. Laughing, teasing, eating pizza and playing Scrabble with my parents. It was great, except for the giant pink elephant sitting in the middle of our Scrabble board. It would be the last family dinner, the last game of Scrabble, and the last night I'd ever spend with my parents.

The PODs

The future is an opaque mirror. Anyone who tries to look into it sees nothing but the dim outlines of an old and worried face.

~ Jim Bishop

Chapter 4 :
Leaving

Friday, twenty-four hours to quarantine

"We don't need to leave yet," I whispered, looking back through the front door at the home I'd never see again. "I think I'd better check my room one more time. I feel like there's something I've forgotten."

"Get in the car, Eva, please," my mom pleaded. "You haven't forgotten anything."

"No, just listen…we could rent a houseboat and stay at sea for a year. It would give the virus time to die off. It'd be like we were all in a POD. We'd just be on the water instead of underground."

"Eva, we've been through this. The POD system is your best chance. We'd never get enough food and fuel on a boat to last an entire year. Supplies are already running low. Grocery store shelves are empty—too many people are hoarding. Besides, we don't know the first thing about sailing. We'd sink the first day," my dad chuckled. I didn't think it was funny.

"Dad—"

"Evangelina." He only used my full name when he was frustrated with me. "Other people have had the same idea. What happens if someone sails around for a year and is a carrier of the virus? When they came back from their little jaunt around the world, they'd infect anyone who was left."

"That could happen anyway. You just said people are leaving—"

"No, I said people have the same idea. The government isn't letting them leave. Everyone stays on dry land to—"

"Die," I shouted. *Why won't they at least try? Then we could stay together.*

"No, contain the virus."

We'd been having the same conversations for days. My argument would change. Each day I'd try another scenario, another reason I shouldn't go to the PODs, but the end result remained the same. My parents were set on me going. They were convinced it was the only way I'd be safe.

"Get in the car, Eva Mae. I don't want you to be late," my dad told me.

I slid in the backseat, the gray leather soft and silky under me, and the smell of my dad's aftershave wafted over me. The Sonic cup I had promised to throw away still sat in the cup holder. Papers and textbooks filled the seat beside me, overflowing and littering the floor. My dad never was very organized. The backseat of his car served as his desk and filing cabinet, a mishmash of graded and ungraded papers swirling together.

My mom sat in the front seat next to my dad, silent and folded in on herself. He patted her knee before taking her hand in his. They held hands while my dad maneuvered the car through the neighborhood, toward the high school where I'd catch the bus to the quarantine area.

There has to be another way. Think, Eva, think…hurry. Make them let you stay.

The closer we came to the school, the harder it was for me to breathe. It felt like my sweater was choking me. I pulled it away from my neck. My hands were clammy, my heart raced, and my mind spun trying to think of a way to convince my parents it was better for me to stay with them than spend the next year underground like a human mole.

"Oh, my…damn."

My dad's voice tore me away from my thoughts. I looked at the scene around me. I'd expected news crews, families gathered to say goodbye to their loved ones, even a protestor or two, but I never expected such complete and utter chaos.

The National Guard had erected a makeshift fence around the school; it must have been twelve feet tall. Barbed wire curled around the top. Soldiers were stationed every few feet along the outside of the fence, rifles held across their chests, keeping news crews and protestors out.

There were hundreds of protestors swarming the area. Police and National Guard members dressed in riot gear tried to hold back the angry crowd for our car to pass through, but several protestors broke through and rushed our car.

They screamed and beat the car with homemade picket signs declaring the raffle a sham and demanding a new one. They yelled profanities at us, spitting at the car as we passed by. A mother in the crowed cried and held out her infant, begging me to take him with me.

I put my palm on the cool glass of the window, fingers splayed, tears rolling down my checks as I watched the sweet face of the infant disappear as we drove past.

More of the out-of-control crowd pushed through the police barriers. The cars in front of us inched forward, honking at the rioting people. Our car was forced to a stop. Rioters screamed at us as they climbed on the hood and trunk. Others pushed the car from the sides, rocking it back and forth.

A man stood outside my window. He looked through the glass with hate in his eyes. "The raffle was fixed! It should be my family leaving, not you!" Spittle hit the window, spewing out of his mouth as he shouted. It dripped down his chin and onto the front of his stained t-shirt.

I looked into his bloodshot eyes through the glass, and fear slithered down my spine. It was like seeing a car accident. I knew I shouldn't look, but I couldn't pull my gaze away. That seemed to infuriate him even more. He started hitting the glass with the handle of his picket sign, trying to break through. Still I watched, frozen.

"EVA!" my dad shouted. I jumped at his tone, looking away from the rioter as I glanced toward my dad. "Close your eyes!"

Just as he yelled to me, glass flew through the car. My mom screamed. I felt chunks of glass hit me as I jerked away from the window. The man I'd been staring at laughed. He reached in, his hand feeling back and forth for the door lock. Acting on impulse, I kicked his hand as hard as I could. Using the heel of my boot I smashed his hand over and over. My stomach churned as bright-red blood ran down his hand, dripping on the pile of my dad's crisp white papers.

I was still kicking his hand when I heard a *pop…pop…pop*. The man's body jerked before sliding down the side of the car and hitting the ground with a thud.

"Did they shoot him?" I screamed.

"Yes, but they're probably just rubber bullets. Police use them in riot situations," my dad shouted over the noise of the rioters.

I jumped, a small scream escaping my lips, when I heard more pops. Looking around, I saw police with riot shields and batons, forcing the people away from the waiting cars. Some officers used Tasers; others used huge cans of pepper spray. Slowly, the rioters were pushed back and the cars continued their trek to the high school. A trip that should have taken twenty minutes took nearly an hour.

"Name?" a soldier asked when our car pulled up to the fence surrounding the school.

"Evangelina Mae Evans," my dad answered.

"ID." The soldier held out his hand. He looked at my identification papers and social security card, comparing the information with what he had on his list. Satisfied, he handed my papers to my dad and walked away. He signaled and the gate opened just wide enough for my dad to drive through; it closed again as soon as the car was past.

"Seven thirty. Plenty of time for you to sign in and stow your things," my dad told me as we got out in the parking lot.

I nodded.

"Evangelina," my mother whispered. "Come here."

She held her arms out for me. I walked into them and she hugged me tight against her. I hadn't realized I'd been crying until then. The hot tears stung my face. I pulled back and looked at her shirt. It was smeared with blood.

"Let me clean you up, Eva," she murmured. She wiped the blood from my cheeks, pulling a few small pieces of glass out of the cuts.

"Miss? Do you need a medic?" a soldier asked.

I took a shuddering breath as a wave of dizziness hit me—I hated the sight of blood. "I don't think so."

"Fine. Take your belongings to the bus. You have fifteen minutes until boarding." I watched him walk away, weaving around families standing in tight little clusters.

"I hope the rest of the people aren't as chipper as he is," I muttered.

My dad chuckled. "Come on, let's get you to your bus."

The bus ride to the quarantine facility took more than ten hours. I was shoved against the window by my seatmate who slept almost the entire trip. He was a big guy, taking up most of the seat, and when he slept his body lolled to the side, wedging me against the metal side of the bus.

As we traveled, the air turned hot and dry, different than the humid, sticky climate of my coastal Texas hometown. The old school bus didn't have air conditioning and the small windows didn't let much air in. My seatmate's body heat didn't help. I was hot, thirsty, and had to pee in the worst way.

Wondering how much longer I'd be drooled on by the guy next to me, I strained my face against the window, looking for anything on the flat landscape.

That's when I saw them.

I don't know why I was surprised. I should've expected it after what had happened at the high school, but I hadn't. It was worse than at the school—rioters everywhere. They waved anti-raffle signs and signs cursing the "chosen."

The land around the quarantine area was flat, dry, and dusty. The people lining the road sat under makeshift tents to keep out of the sun. Some stood on top of their RVs waving their handmade signs; one burned an American flag.

I watched women holding their small children toward the bus, begging with tear-stained faces for us to take them. I wanted to reach out and snatch them out of their mothers' hands as we drove past. Several of the other people on the bus reached up and pushed their windows shut.

The National Guard at the quarantine site didn't allow people to get close enough to touch the bus. They were shot with rubber bullets or Tasered if they tried to cross the police line. Every time I heard the shot of the riot guns I jumped. My muscles ached from tensing them—waiting for the inevitable sound.

"Why are you crying?" A boy sitting in front of me looked at me like I'd grown another head. "They'd probably kill you and steal your place in the PODs if given the chance."

I shook my head, remembering what my dad had told me. "They're just scared," I said. After all, they were, essentially, the walking dead.

The rioters screamed and cursed us. They threw rocks and eggs as we drove by. An egg hit the window next to me, the slimy insides plopping against my head, matting my hair.

"Gross," the boy sitting next to me said.

I just looked at him and rolled my eyes.

Yeah, the egg is gross. And the drool coming out of your mouth and dripping on my leg while you slept, leaning on me, was glorious.

The bus stopped in a fenced area like the one at the high school. The crowd screamed and banged the fence posts with their crude, homemade picket signs. Some climbed on the fence, pulling at it like chimpanzees at the zoo.

"Stay seated until your name is called," a soldier yelled. "When you are called, grab your belongings and wait to be escorted into the building."

Oh please, call this guy's name. He needs to move before I shove him off the seat. I'm tired of being pinned against the side of the bus. I need some room.

Thankfully, my name was called soon after we stopped. I stood, stretched the kinks out of my muscles, and plowed through the massive body blocking me. Clambering over the other luggage that filled the aisle, I grabbed my two suitcases and stood in front of the bus. The one-story brick building was large but had no windows, only a single green door. I couldn't see the other sides, but I had a feeling there'd be no windows there, either—no glass for rioters to break through.

The soldier walked up from behind me, tapping my suitcase with his clipboard. "Follow me."

I shuffled into the brick building, guided by the same guardsman who'd ripped me away from my parents hours earlier…

"I love you," my mom said through her tears, her voice thick and trembling.

"I want to stay with you," I pleaded.

"Come here, kiddo." My dad, his face distorted with grief, folded me in a tight hug. He kissed the top of my head and told me he loved me and how proud he was of me. "I know, when this is over, you are going to do great things, Eva. You're a fighter. I love you so much."

A rough hand grabbed my arm, pulling me away from my dad. "Get on the bus," the male voice ordered, yelling to be heard over the crying of parents and children saying their final goodbyes.

"I'm not done saying goodbye…" He didn't let go, pulling me with him. My heels digging into the dirt, I tried to pull away. I needed one more hug, to hear them tell me they loved me and to tell them I loved them, too.

"MOM!" I screamed. "DAD!" Tears stained my face. The man thrust me toward the steps of the old, yellow school bus. I screamed one more time for my parents, telling them I loved them, reaching my arms out to them.

I could see my mom's body rock with the force of her cries. Tears ran down my father's face. "We love you, Evangelina," I heard them call just before the bus door closed.

It was the last thing I'd hear my parents say. It was the last image I'd have of them. I pressed my hand to the window of the bus, my head bowed as I sobbed. I didn't try to hide my tears. Everyone on the bus was crying for their families. We knew what awaited them.

Death.

I shook my head, trying to erase the horrible memory. I wanted to remember the good things about them, not saying goodbye.

Goodbyes are hard, but this one had been different. This wasn't a *goodbye, I'll see you in a month.* It was a permanent goodbye. I'd never see my parents again. The overwhelming sadness took over, like a black hole sucking me in. Fat, salty tears ran down my face, and I could feel my nose running. I swiped my arm across it. My eyes were swollen, my throat sore, and my chest tight.

I was alone. My parents were gone. No brothers or sisters. Just me—an orphan of the virus.

Chapter 5: Quarantine

Saturday, quarantine day one

"Hold out your arm," a burly nurse in a full hazmat suit told me. She swiped it with an alcohol pad and stuck the needle in without warning.

"Hey!" I rubbed the welt forming where she'd given me the shot.

A little warning would have been nice. Geez, this is going to be a long two weeks if all the nurses are as friendly as you.

"That's your first dose of birth control. You'll receive a booster every three months while in the PODs."

It's not like it's spring break, lady. I'm not looking to hook up with anyone.

After the friendly nurse gave me my shot and drew a disgusting amount of blood into little test tubes, I settled in and prepared myself for my two-week quarantine stay. The doctors would test and retest me for the virus. I knew from news reports that everyone had to go through quarantine before they were allowed in the PODs. There'd have been too many people if we all came at once, so people selected for the PODs arrived in staggered groups.

A thick packet of papers had been on my bed when I'd arrived in my quarantine observation room. It outlined what I could expect during quarantine, what would happen when my two-week stay was over, how the POD system was arranged, what to expect living in the PODs—going into mind-numbing detail that made my high school economics textbook exciting by comparison.

I quickly understood why my quarantine room was called an observation room. Everyone could see everything I did. The room was a box made of thick glass. Inside, I had a bed and a TV. The only privacy was in the bathroom in the far corner, which had curtains that ended a few inches from the floor. Additional curtains were bunched at each corner outside the glass; people inside had no way of closing them to get any privacy.

Beyond my glass walls, rows and rows of identical glass boxes extended in all directions, the glass becoming blue-green like pictures of glacier ice. Across the hall in front of my room was a girl my age. On either side of her were guys. Behind my room was another row of observation rooms. I stood in the middle of my room and turned in a slow circle. We were everywhere. The chosen—locked away in glass fishbowls while people behind surgical masks and hazmat suits waited and watched for us to show signs of the virus.

At the front of the room was a box inset in the glass where I'd insert my arm when it was time for my blood check. Thick rubber gloves hung limp from where they attached to the outer wall. Next to that was an airlock mechanism through which I received my daily MREs—meals ready to eat. The nurse opened the door on her side, inserted the meal and closed the door. The chamber was then filled with an antibacterial vapor, killing any germs that may have entered on the meal's container. When the vapor process was complete, the door in the observation room unlocked, allowing me to retrieve my meal. It happened four times a day—breakfast, lunch, dinner and a snack.

At least it was just me in the observation room. I wasn't ready to make nice with a stranger. My emotions were still too raw from the goodbye with my parents.

Quarantine, day two

I couldn't sleep. Day one and two merged, creating one long day. The lights had dimmed for several hours, but it never got fully dark. I'd never been particularly claustrophobic, so I hadn't been worried about quarantine. I knew I'd be in a small room. I was okay with that—I thought.

But scenarios tumbled over and over in my head.

What if there's a fire, a tornado, rioters break in, a flash flood, a meteor—okay, the last one probably won't happen, but still.

It was hard to breathe in the little room. I felt like I was suffocating; I couldn't get enough air. My blood pounded quick and hard against my temples.

"What happens if there's a fire?" I asked the nurse who poked my finger and filled the little tube with my blood. I tried really hard not to think about what she was doing. I hated getting my blood taken. I'd thought the little finger pricks would be easier. I was wrong.

"The sprinklers come on," she said. I swallowed back the bile that rose in my throat at the sight of my blood being squeezed into the tube.

Sprinklers...no kidding.

"I meant to us. We're locked in here. How would we get out?"

"Don't worry. There's nothing here to catch fire." She stuck a tiny, square Band-Aid on my finger, passed the sealed test tube through the decontamination airlock, and walked away.

Nothing to catch fire? Is she for real? With medical personnel like her there's no wonder we don't have a cure for the virus.

I walked to my bunk and fell across it, throwing my arm across my eyes and trying to forget that I was locked in a small room with no way out.

Quarantine, day three

The first two days of quarantine I'd concentrated on my little room, my memories, my fears. The world beyond my little cell hadn't really registered. But on day three I spent time looking at the world outside the glass walls.

I sat on the cold tile floor at the front of my observation room, watching the people in the other cells. When the girl across the hall met my eyes, I grabbed my notepad. In big letters I wrote my name across a page. I flattened it against the glass so the girl across the hall could read it. I saw her smile. She motioned for me to wait and ran to her bunk. She wrote across what looked like the back of a page from the briefing booklet, holding it up so I could read it.

"Kelly."

Finally. Someone to communicate with—sort of.

By the time the day ended I knew everyone's name in the rooms around mine. We'd even managed to play a game of charades. It was fun, and for a little while I forgot where I was and why.

Quarantine, day five

I jerked awake, sitting up in bed. My heart hammered in my chest, echoing the banging in my head. I strained to hear over the blood rushing behind my ears. Was it just a dream? No. No, I could definitely hear someone—a male voice.

"I'm not. The test is wrong!" The thick glass surrounding me muffled his pleading voice.

I couldn't tell where he was. Noises bounced around the quarantine facility's cement and glass walls. I peered into the hall. The yellow glow of the security lights shining on the green hallway floor gave the room an odd, yellowish-green haze.

The guy was still yelling, and the sound was getting louder. Shadows moved in the hallway, and my heart beat faster.

"Don't do this. Please don't do this. I'm not sick. The test is wrong. It's wrong." He was crying now.

I jumped back from the glass, sucking in a breath, as a person moved out of the shadows. Another person came into view; three people followed. Two of the three were medical personnel. The third, a guy about my age, was being wheeled down the hall inside a Plexiglas container. He sobbed, his feet flailing against the sides. I recognized him—his observation room had been four rooms to the right of mine on the same side of the hall.

The members of the medical team wore hazmat suits and breathing apparatuses. My hand flew to my mouth and I stumbled backward toward my bunk. He'd failed. His test results must have come back positive for the virus.

Someone else in a hazmat suit moved to the glass of my isolation room, staring at me through the unreadable facemask. I instinctively took another step backward, tripping and falling onto my bunk with a grunt. Once they moved beyond the end of the row, I couldn't see where they took the crying guy. His sobs grew fainter until I heard nothing but my own breathing.

I sat on the edge of my bed, my heart beating so fast it hurt my ribs. I pushed my hair out of my eyes with shaking hands. I shoved them under my thighs on the mattress and forced myself to take deep, cleansing breaths.

I sat on the bed for a few seconds, listening to my own overloud breathing and wondering what was happening to the boy, terrified that I'd be the next to be wheeled out in a plastic box. I ran into the bathroom, falling on my knees and sliding to the toilet before puking up the "tuna surprise" I'd forced myself to eat for dinner.

Hanging over the toilet bowl, I said a silent prayer that my blood tests were clear and I wouldn't be pulled out of bed in the middle of the night and hauled away to suffer God only knew what.

And then I said a prayer for the guy who *had* been.

Later that morning I was waiting at the glass wall when Kelly woke. She sat down across from me, dark circles ringing her eyes.

The boy? I wrote.

She nodded, her gaze darting to the room to the right of me. I turned and looked down the row of glass rooms. His was still empty. I was hoping that it was all a bad dream—that I'd wake up and he'd be there like he'd been every other morning.

I looked back to Kelly. She held up her notepad before quickly laying it in her lap.

Virus, she wrote.

Where is he?

DEAD.

My blood ran cold. I dropped my notepad and scrambled backward, kicking against the floor with my feet, scooting myself across the tile floor until I was jammed between the toilet and the curtained wall. The only place in the room I could be alone, just me and my tears. And my fear.

Quarantine, day seven

One week down, one week to go. I was counting the hours. At least I was trying to. There wasn't a clock in my observation room.

Quarantine was brutal. Since the first guy had been dragged out of the facility two days before, three more had been removed. Each time, the screaming and pleading had been horrible. I had lain in my bunk with the pillow over my ears to block it out.

PODs

Every morning I said a prayer of thanks that I'd made it through another night. My blood was clean…so far. Then I'd look around the other observation rooms and see who was missing.

The only things that made the days bearable were the few people I'd learned to communicate with since quarantine began. We'd write notes on our notepads and use hand signals. We'd even developed our own form of sign language. It helped pass the time and kept us from going insane from lack of personal contact, because the nurses sure weren't bubbly conversationalists. We affectionately called them Grumpy, Grumpier and Grumpiest.

Quarantine, day eight

I was lying in bed trying to fall asleep. It was always the worst time of day. Memories and fears suffocated me in the darkness.

Memories of my parents were especially vivid at night. I stared at the ceiling and watched them play across the white surface like it was a movie screen. Birthdays and Christmases were all good memories, but so were the dance recitals my parents had never missed. Even the soccer team I'd played on that never won a match—my parents had still been at every game, cheering from the sidelines. And when we'd made our first goal of the season they'd cheered the loudest and acted the craziest. I smiled through my tears thinking of that day. That had been the only goal we'd made that year. My dad had said that it was special because it was the only one. I was only in first grade, but even I knew we sucked.

I was still awake when a nurse pulled the curtain outside my room. I looked inside the rooms next to me; the curtains were pulled there, too.

I heard a commotion in the hallway. The boy in the room to my right was asleep, but the boy to my left, Brad, was awake. I looked at him. He shrugged. We walked to the wall and listened. I couldn't make out the noises. It sounded like scraping or scuffling. Whatever was making the noise was right in front of my room. My curtain moved back and forth. I backed away from the wall.

A scream pierced the darkness and I jumped.

"No, no, no!"

The hall quieted. The commotion outside my curtained wall stopped. I sucked in a deep breath and forced myself to walk back to the wall. Just as I reached the glass, something blew the curtain aside and I saw the wheels.

I turned and ran across the room to my bunk, my bare feet slapping against the cold tile floor. I scrambled under the blankets on my bed and pulled the pillow over my head, squeezing my eyes closed.

I knew what those wheels were attached to. And I didn't want to be anywhere near it.

I don't know when I finally fell asleep. I don't remember getting tired. I woke to the sound of the nurse calling my name through the intercom. It was time for my morning blood check.

I climbed out of bed, walked to the wall, stuck my hand inside the box and waited for her to prick my finger and take her share of my blood. It was in the middle of the blood test that I noticed the empty room.

"Where's Kelly?"

"Who?" the nurse asked.

"The girl who was in that room." I pointed at the room across from mine.

"You ask too many questions." She grabbed her supplies and walked away.

I dropped to the floor, staring at Kelly's room through the watery blur of tears.

PODs

My blood was still clean. All the tests coming back showed I was in good health. I started to relax. Fewer people were being pulled out of quarantine. I hoped that meant the rest of us were healthy and would finish our time without a problem.

I was sick of watching television. It was the only form of entertainment I had except for a few books, which I'd already finished reading. I'd even read through the PODs packet—twice. I had no human contact—since Kelly had been pulled from quarantine our group wasn't the same. Everyone seemed to want to keep to themselves. All that was left was television, with its constant coverage of the effects the virus—and the raffle—were having on the country.

There were new theories about the virus. Some people believed it was man-made and that's why it'd shown up so quickly. Scientists were baffled by the first cases, stunned at how quickly it had spread. Where it had originated was a mystery, how it was transmitted still unknown. It was an enigma.

"The military has been experimenting with germ warfare for decades!" The middle-aged man in the worn baseball cap gestured with wild hands at a reporter wearing a surgical mask. "They made this! Just like they did with AIDS! With Ebola! They made them all!"

I shut off the TV when the nurse arrived to take yet more blood. "May I have another book to read, please?"

"No. If anything from the outside that hasn't been properly prepared breaches your quarantine room, you'll be deemed a liability and banned from the POD system. We still don't know how the virus is transmitted. It may be possible to contract the virus through touching contaminated objects. If something were added to your room without being properly sterilized, you'd run the risk of contracting the virus."

I stuck my hand in the little box set into the glass wall. "There's nothing in the other rooms?"

"No." She slid the specimen box into the port on one side, the outer layer peeling away as she pushed it into place. The layers of sealed plastic prevented any contaminant from the outside world coming into contact with the air of my isolation room, and vice versa. Sliding her already-gloved hands into the permanent gloves on the other side of the box, she reached for the inner layer sealing the specimen container, which seemed to gasp as she broke the vacuum seal.

"What happens when someone is removed from the quarantine area?" I asked.

"They're replaced." The nurse lanced the side of my finger with a little metal stick, and then squeezed my finger until a fat drop of blood formed. She collected the sample with a thin glass tube. They took blood several times a day; I had little nicks and scabs on all of my fingers. I thought I ran the risk of them getting infected. Death by blood tests—that'd be ironic.

"How are they replaced?"

"You're always full of too many questions," she snapped. Usually the nurses wouldn't talk to me at all.

"You're the only person I've got to talk to."

"There's a waiting-list of extras—extra people to fill spots when someone is removed from quarantine."

"Why are people removed?"

"Either they are a carrier of the virus or they have another health issue that can't be dealt with in the PODs."

She placed the blood sample into the specimen container and wrapped a Band-Aid around my finger before pressing the inner seal onto the container and sliding the outer layer back in place as she removed it from the port.

Picking up her things, she looked at me. "All done. Lunch will be here shortly. That'll give you something to pass the time. It's spaghetti day."

I loathed spaghetti.

Quarantine, Day…something

"How many more days?" I asked the nurse. I'd nicknamed this one "Happy," since she was one of the few nice ones in the rotation. "Grumpy" had done the blood draw the night before.

"Just two more, sweetie," she answered.

I stood still while she drew my blood for the third time that day.

She wore a green hazmat suit and large, thick yellow gloves, and even behind the clear plastic, her face was covered by a white mask from her chin to the bottom of her eyes. Her hair was shoved into a green hat the same color as the suit. She looked like she was auditioning for the role of "Green Bean Number 1" in a school play.

The only way I could tell her apart from the other nurses was her voice, soft and soothing. She'd talk to me, called me "sweetie," even. The others just took my blood like greedy vampires.

"What day is it?" With no windows and no clock it was impossible to keep track of time. I guess it was preparation for the PODs. We'd be underground, so there might be no way of telling time or what day it was there, either.

"It's Wednesday morning," she answered. "There you go, Evangelina. You're all done for another eight hours."

I pulled my arm out of the hole and smiled. She'd used the vial marking pen to draw a smiley face on the bandage she put over the needle stick. She must've been a mother. She knew that even the littlest thing, like a hand-drawn smiley face on a bandage, made a bad day a little better. When she left, I peeled it off my finger and stuck it to a page in my journal, which was what I was now using my spiral notepad for. I wrote about the nurse and how she made me think of my mom.

Chapter 6 : Introductions

Day One

I finished quarantine and was moved to my new home—POD 78, sub-POD 29. According to the packet, all sub-PODs housed ten people, five female and five male.

Locked in an underground tuna can with strangers for an entire year? I sure hope we all get along.

After being sealed in a transport container that felt like a glass coffin, the techs wheeled me to the POD entrance and sealed the edges of the container to the doorframe before letting me out on a landing at the bottom of a small ramp. My suitcases were marked with large stickers declaring them "Decontaminated," along with chalk markings of "78/29" and what I assumed was today's date on both sides. In front of me, elevator doors stood open, and a tech wearing a hazmat suit stood inside waiting for me. We rode down the elevator—the slowest ride ever—and when the door finally opened I stepped out into a large central room, round with high ceilings and ringed with doors. The tech walked me to the door labeled "sub-POD 29." A red and white striped metal box was attached to the wall just beneath the sign; a glass panel revealed a red lever within, like an oversized fire alarm.

I walked down the metal corridor to the sub-POD I'd call home for the next year. The sound of my footfalls reverberated off the walls, and the grated walkway shimmied. I had to hold the railing to keep my balance.

Looking around, I saw the chute running from the main POD to the sub. According to the packet I'd received in quarantine, it worked like a bank teller's window. Open the door, insert what you wanted to send, close the door and push the button. Suction and air flow did the rest. We'd receive our weekly allotment of fresh fruit and vegetables through the chute, and our required blood test kits as well. Much like in quarantine, a disinfectant vapor would fill the chute before items were allowed to enter the sub-POD. The same was true for things we sent to the main POD. This was designed to eliminate contamination between PODs.

On my right, a water line ran to the sub-POD from the water supply in the main POD. With the treatment and filtering systems in the sub-POD, the water was recycled, but each sub-POD could receive additional water through this line, if necessary. Under the water pipes were several large metal tubes. I guessed that one was our electrical supply, another the internet cable—the packet said each sub-POD had its own wi-fi node—while the others were the air supply and carbon dioxide filtering systems. I wasn't sure how it all worked—I just prayed it did.

I hesitated when I reached the sub-POD door, biting my lip as something tightened in my chest. I'd spend the next year of my life—maybe longer—with my POD mates. What if we didn't get along? What if…? The tech escorting me grew impatient and pushed me through the circular door, shutting and locking it behind me.

I stood just inside the POD and looked around. There were already seven people there; I made eight. Two more and the POD would be full.

"Hi," I said to the others in the room.

I got a less-than-lackluster welcome. A pregnant girl sitting on the couch in the main living area smiled and said hello. She looked a few years older than me, with blonde hair a bit lighter than mine.

I guess there are nine people here. I sure hope the geniuses locking us down here have a plan for when that baby is born.

The dark-haired guy sitting against the wall with earbuds in his ears didn't hear me, or decided not to acknowledge me.

A boy and a girl about my age, both with laptops in front of them, sat at opposite ends of the table in the combo kitchen and dining area. The whole place was painted stark white—it looked very sterile and clean, even with the chocolate-colored carpet in the living area. The girl waved and said something in a language I didn't understand. When I didn't respond with anything more than a dumbfounded look, she smiled and said "Hi" in a thick accent. In my head I named her Friendly, because she'd offered me a nice welcome, even if I didn't understand most of it.

The stubble-faced, heavy-set boy sitting across from her looked up, his blue eyes boring into me as he drummed his fingers on the table. After a few seconds, he gave a disgusted sigh and returned to his computer.

Mr. Antisocial. This could be a really long year.

Sitting in a beanbag in the middle of the room was a boy with several facial piercings and tattoos; his blond hair was cut close to his head in a military style. He smiled in answer to my greeting, but didn't speak. I dubbed him Beanbag Guy—I thought "Piercings Dude" was too obvious.

A girl sat in a corner of the living area, crying. She looked younger than me, maybe twelve or thirteen, with a mocha complexion and her hair in tight braids. I named her Baby. Not because she was crying—I did enough of that myself— but because she was obviously the youngest.

Finally, there was a boy sitting against the wall, doodling in a notebook. Brown hair fell over his face. He didn't look up as I came in. I named him Doodle Boy.

I picked up my bags and walked to the hallway that led off the main room. I stuck my head in the first door and looked around. The room had the same white walls and brown carpeting as the main living space. Five beds—more like cots—filled the room, aligned perfectly from one end to the other. Only two were neatly made; one had a tangle of sheets and a pile of clothing that spilled onto the floor. What looked like two windows were set into the far wall—the curtain on one was pushed aside, revealing a glass pane that emitted a yellowish glow in a pale imitation of daylight.

"That's the guys' room," I heard someone say. I realized it was Doodle Boy. He still didn't look at me.

"Oh…sorry."

"The girls' room is at the end of the hall."

"Thanks," I said with a smile. My smile was wasted. He didn't look up from whatever he was doodling.

I walked down the hall, passing a bathroom and what looked to be a storage room before reaching what was apparently the girls' bedroom. I went inside and looked around. It was a mirror image of the boys' room, with one minor exception. There were only four beds—the fifth was a crib. The three girls who'd arrived before me had claimed their beds. On the bed closest to the wall was a box with my name on it. I flipped it open and found a laptop, the lid labeled with my name and the POD and sub-POD numbers.

Interesting.

Closing the box, I looked around for a place to store my things. Someone spoke behind me and I jumped. I turned around and Friendly's face was so close to mine our noses nearly touched.

I took a large step back. "Do you speak English?"

The girl raised her palms up and shrugged. "Little," she said before rattling something off in a language I didn't understand. This time it was my turn to shrug and smile.

Friendly started talking again; reaching under the bed, she pulled two drawers from the bed's base. She pointed at my bags and then the drawers. She reached around me to the headboard and pulled down the front. Inside were shelves and a clock reading the day and time.

So much for storage space.

I smiled. "Thank you."

"You're welcome," she said, her accent stretching out all the vowels.

She walked into the hall, motioning for me to follow her. When I didn't, she ducked back in and motioned to me again, I followed. She entered the bathroom, where she showed me a row of metal lockers—the kind they had in school. They were about four feet high and two feet wide—not a lot of space to store everything I'd need for the next year.

Each brown door had a name on a card in a slot. The girl pointed to a name and then herself. "Jai Li."

"Jah Li," I said, trying to say it like she had. She smiled and nodded.

"Jai Li."

I found my locker and pointed at it. It was labeled with my full name, Evangelina. She frowned and I laughed. I pulled a pen from my bag and scratched out the ending of my name, leaving only "Eva."

I pointed to my name, and then myself. "Eva."

She smiled. "Eva," she repeated.

"Jai Li," I said in return.

She giggled. I smiled at the sound. I'd just made my first friend. Of course, the only thing we could say to each other was our names, but maybe before this whole thing was over we'd find a way to connect.

She grabbed my hand and pulled me into the neighboring room. A stacked washer and dryer were next to the door, with a small washtub, a mop and broom, and other cleaning equipment. Beyond the laundry area, thick shelves held all the things we'd need for the year, like bins full of vitamins and shelf after shelf of neatly stacked MREs, each labeled with a POD resident's name and a date for consumption. I fingered a stack of MREs with my name across the top.

Someone's picked out what I'm going to eat every day for the next year of my life. How bizarre is that? How do they know I'm going to want lasagna on March 12th?

Additional shelves held things like toilet paper, shampoo, toothpaste, cleaning chemicals, and laundry detergent. I turned around in a circle, taking everything in. My head pounded looking at the supplies. A year's worth of my life sat on those shelves and all I could think was, what if they didn't buy the right flavor of toothpaste? My mom knew what kind to buy. But she wasn't there. And a quick glance at the shelf told me the right flavor of toothpaste wasn't there, either.

What an idiotic thing to think of, Eva. Get a grip.

Across from the laundry area was another small room, the door labeled "Waste." Inside was a trash compactor and a chute for our garbage.

After the tour, Jai Li and I wandered back into the living area. I stood in the middle of the room, uncertain what to do next…or for the next year.

"I'm Tiffany," a soft voice behind me said. I turned and found Pregnant Girl smiling at me from where she sat on the couch. She had a deep dimple in her right cheek.

"I'm Eva."

"Nice to meet you, Eva. Did Jai Li show you everything?"

"I think so."

"Well, there isn't much to show." She stood, her hand against her rounded belly. "We have a 1980s stereo—with a cassette player—and these." She pulled a sliding panel open on the wall that separated the bedrooms from the living area. There were shelves behind it—shelves full of book after book after book. There must have been hundreds, many of them yellowed with age.

"Well, that ought to keep us busy for a while."

"Yeah." She smiled again. "There are DVDs, but we haven't found a television to play them on yet, so we're just watching them on the laptops. One's probably stuffed in the storage room somewhere. We also have some board games and cards, and there are games on the laptops. They've set up a social media website on the POD-to-POD intranet, but so far no one's in the mood for chatting or games."

I nodded. I understood. Everyone was mourning the loss of someone, of everyone we'd ever known. For every one person in the PODs, there were thousands left topside. We'd all left people we loved up there.

I walked back to the bedroom. Thankfully, Jai Li didn't follow, and Tiffany eased back into her position on the couch. After spending two weeks without anyone to really talk to, I had thought I'd be chatty, but I didn't feel like being friendly. Thinking about the people left topside made something deep in my chest ache. My parents were up there.

I started unpacking my things. I reached in my suitcase, pulled out the too-cute-for-words-but-too-expensive purple hoodie my mom had insisted on buying me and started to cry. I slipped it over my head and finished unpacking while warm tears slid down my face.

That afternoon the last of our roommates showed up—a boy about seventeen or eighteen, tall and lanky, with dark mahogany skin.

"I'm Seth." He didn't stop to talk with anyone, just walked in the front door and through the POD to his bunk. That was okay. No one felt like talking much, anyway.

Just after Seth walked through the door, the tech locked it, just like he had after I'd arrived. But there was something else. We could hear the seal closing around the door. It sounded like a cat hissing. I hated the sound; knowing what was happening made me feel claustrophobic. I was stuck—we all were. We couldn't get out of the POD until that seal was broken…and that could only be done from the outside. It was like we were in a prison. I guess we were.

For the next two days, no one spoke to anyone else. Surprisingly, it was a comfortable silence, considering we were nine strangers.

I fingered the small photograph taped to the headboard of my bed. I stared at my mom's face; it blurred from my unshed tears. My head started to pound and my throat burned from trying to hold back a sob. I was starting to remember the good things about them rather than the last time I'd seen them. I didn't want that memory to mar the many, many happy ones I had. But the happy memories were painful, too.

Day Four

Seth and Earphone Guy lay on their beds, listening to music. Doodle Boy was still hovering over his journal. He was either writing or drawing—either way, he didn't look up, and he hadn't said anything since he'd told me where the girls' bedroom was. Mr. Antisocial stalked the POD with a scowl whenever he left his computer, and Baby still sat in the corner crying. Jai Li, while nice, didn't have much to say that the rest of us could understand. Tiffany moved back and forth from the couch to her bed, reading and sleeping. Occasionally I could hear sniffles and muffled crying from her side of the room. And Beanbag Guy hadn't left the beanbag since I'd arrived. He even slept in it.

I was pacing the kitchen, looking in cupboards and drawers, when Seth walked up to me.

"Hey."

"Hey, yourself," I said, grabbing the orange juice out of the double fridge and pouring a glass. It was made from a powder and had a weird aftertaste. "Want some?"

"Sure. Thanks."

"I'm Eva, by the way."

"I'm S—"

"Seth," we said in unison. I smiled.

"What do you think's going on up there?" I wasn't sure I wanted to know.

"People are still rioting and calling for a new raffle, convinced this one was fixed."

"What do you think?"

"About the raffle? Yeah, I have a feeling it was rigged." He shrugged one shoulder and drained his glass of juice. "Most people topside are sure it was. No one over the age of twenty-five was chosen, or anyone under twelve. The news is manipulating the facts, of course."

"Yeah, I didn't listen to their theories before I moved down here. I have my own."

"What's your theory?"

I jumped at the sound of his voice behind me. I got the slightest whiff of cologne when I turned to face him. I looked around the room and noticed our conversation had everyone's attention.

"What's your name, Doodle Boy? I don't feel like discussing anything with someone who's too rude to introduce himself."

He tried to hide a grin. "Doodle Boy?"

"Yeah, all you've done since I got here is sit against the wall, doodling in your notebook. So I nicknamed you Doodle Boy."

"Fair enough. My name is David."

"Nice to meet you, David. I'm Eva."

"So tell us about your theory, Eva. Why is everyone so upset about the raffle?" David asked.

I pulled out a chair and sat at the table. "Well, everyone is convinced it was fixed. Like Seth said, no one over the age of twenty-five was chosen. Children under the age of twelve were also left off the list. So it's obvious that age was a factor in who was selected, raffle or otherwise."

"They chose the young, healthy people," Seth said.

"Yeah, but my theory doesn't stop there. Seth, what was your best subject in school?"

"Math."

"And what was your grade point average?"

"Four-point-oh."

I nodded. So far my theory held up. "David? Tiffany?"

"Science and, yes, I carried a four point," David answered, resting his chin on his fist and elbow on the counter.

"My best subject was also science," Tiffany said, "I majored in biochemistry in college. Four-point-oh."

"I'm George." It was the first time Beanbag Guy spoke. "I was in college studying to be a nurse. I had a four-point-oh GPA, too—all through high school and college."

"I'm Aidan," Earphones Guy said quietly. "Computer science and networking. We had an honors track, so my GPA was a five-point-oh."

Our eyes moved to Antisocial Guy. We waited for his answer.

"Josh, and what the hell difference does it make?" Pieces of the pretzel he was eating spewed from his mouth.

"So here's my theory. If you wanted to rebuild a nation, you'd want young, healthy people, but also intelligent ones. After all, how could you build a great nation if it was filled with idiots? I would bet that if you polled the people who were chosen, you'd find they excelled in one subject or another. I carried a four-point-oh grade point average in school. I did well in all my courses, but I excelled in English."

"So how are you going to prove it?" Beanbag Guy— George—asked. He leaned forward in his beanbag.

I shrugged. "What difference does it make now? The PODs are sealed."

"Well, for what it's worth, it sounds like a pretty damn good theory." David moved back across the room and reclaimed his spot against the wall.

"Eva?"

"Yeah?"

"What was my nickname?" George asked with a grin.

I laughed.

Something banged in the tube by the now-sealed door. I jumped; the book I was reading fell to the floor.

"I'll get it." David walked over and opened a hatch in the tube, exposing a sealed plastic canister that he pulled out. The hatch closed with a small bang, and a chemical smell, which I recognized from quarantine, wafted through the room. "Time for blood check, everyone." He took the container over to the table.

"What?" My heart, still racing from the noise, took a nosedive when I heard the words "blood check."

"Blood check. We need to do it every two weeks. You'd just missed it when you came." Tiffany twisted off the lid and searched through the little packets until she found the one with her name on it. She grabbed the packet with my name and handed it to me.

"Open your packet and take out the card. It has your name and number on it. Grab the lancet, too. Then you just have to prick your finger and put a few drops of blood on the card. When you're done, seal it in the plastic bag with your name and number, and we'll reseal the container and send them all back to the main POD."

"I have to poke my own finger?" My palms started to sweat. I sank into one of the kitchen chairs, taking slow, deep, cleansing breaths to try and slow my racing heart. My fingers trembled trying to open the packet. It was bad enough having the nurses in quarantine draw my blood, but to do it myself...

Oh, this is so wrong. I hate the sight of blood, especially mine.

I watched Tiffany place the end of what looked like a fat pen against her skin. She pushed a button and the lancet-pen made a loud snap. She jerked a little, but didn't have any trouble squeezing out enough blood to cover the circle on the card.

I picked up the lancet-pen and twirled it in my fingers. It looked harmless—just a gray, plastic tube. I turned it upside down and peered in the hole where the little stinger was. I couldn't see anything inside.

"See?" Tiffany held up her lancet. The scalpel-looking thing stuck out. It was much bigger than the little needle I'd imagined it to be.

My insides swirled, and the room began tilting. There was no way I'd be able to stick my finger and squeeze out blood to fill the card. "Uh, Tiffany? Do you think you could do it for me?"

"Sure. Give me your finger."

I held out a finger. She opened the alcohol pad and wiped it. The smell of the alcohol made my head swim. The room was fading.

She held the lancet to my finger. I closed my eyes, squeezing them tightly. I braced myself. I heard a loud click and felt the metal cut my finger. It was more than a little stick.

Tiffany held my finger with one hand and squeezed with the other. Just the thought of what she was doing made me nauseous. I knew she was squeezing out dark red blood. I could picture it seeping into the card, filling the circle. The room tilted a little more. I felt off-balance. Tiffany's voice sounded far away.

"Eva, are you okay? We're all done."

"It's done?"

"Yep. You're good to go for another two weeks."

I have to go through this every two weeks? I groaned at the thought. The blood tests in quarantine hadn't been as bad as that.

Slowly, the room righted itself. I didn't feel quite so dizzy, but I didn't trust myself to get up. The room was still fading in and out.

I picked up the bloody card, trying not to look at it when I shoved it into the plastic bag. I sealed the bag and handed it to David, who looked at me with a grin. "You look white as a ghost, Eva." He dumped everyone's packets in the container, resealed the lid, and sent it back up the tube.

"Blood isn't my thing. Why do we have to do that? Are they still checking us for the virus?" I asked.

"I think part of it is to check our nutrition and vitamin levels. The other is to check for the virus. They don't know how long it can stay dormant in a host's body. If one of us turns out to be a carrier then…" David let his words trail off.

"Then what?"

"Well, I'm not sure, exactly, but I don't imagine it would be good."

"Jeez, think about it, would ya?" Josh made a cutting sound and slashed his thumb across his throat.

"Knock it off," Tiffany whispered through clenched teeth, her gaze landing on Baby.

Meals and blood check were the only times I'd seen her leave her corner. She didn't need Mr. Antisocial scaring her any more than she seemed to be.

"You saw people test positive for the virus in quarantine, didn't you, Eva?" Earphones Guy asked.

Kelly.

My voiced cracked when I tried to answer. I cleared my throat and tried again. "Yes."

"Do you know what happened to them?"

"I have a good idea, yes," I said.

"Well, I imagine it'll be the same here." Earphones Guy—Aidan—rubbed the back of his neck with his hand and blew out a long breath.

Chapter 7 : Redecorating

Month One

Tiffany and I sat at the table eating breakfast. We'd made it part of our daily routine.

"What are you staring at? Do I have cereal on my nose?" Tiffany brought her napkin up and wiped her face.

I laughed at her expression. "You just remind me of someone." She had so many mannerisms that reminded me of Bridget. It was bittersweet.

"Oh." She gave me a little smile. "I'm sorry."

Jai Li tugged on my sleeve to get my attention. She spent a lot of time with Tiffany and me, but it was hard creating a bond when we couldn't communicate very well. We'd been able to understand enough to know that Jai Li was the daughter of Chinese immigrants, but her English was stunted from only speaking Chinese at home. In California, she'd been in a private school, one that had been giving her a traditional Chinese education. But her English seemed to be limited to memorized words; she didn't put them together into sentences, and didn't seem to understand us when we did.

Still, we tried.

She pointed at the milk carton sitting on the table. The "milk" was some kind of ultra-pasteurized stuff that stayed good for years, but it tasted weird on its own. I only used it for cereal, whatever generic knock-off brand came in the air-tight bags of thick, blue-tinted plastic.

"Milk," I said slowly.

"Milk," Jai Li repeated.

"Water." I pointed to the glass in David's hand as he walked by. He held it out so Jai Li could see it before taking a long drink.

I smelled the faintest whisper of his scent as he walked by—citrus and patchouli.

Geez, he smells good.

"Water," she repeated, sticking her finger in the water pooling around the carton of milk from the condensation running down its sides.

"She's a quick learner. What level is she up to now?" Tiffany asked.

"We're almost finished with the first module." Jai Li's laptop had language software installed, and she sometimes asked me to help with her pronunciation as she progressed through the ESL—English as a second language—lessons. "That's like a year of language class in high school."

"I wonder why she doesn't try to teach us Mandarin."

"I don't know. Maybe because everyone here speaks English."

"Cereal," Jai Li said in her thick accent, pointing at the bag. I smiled and nodded. "Cereal."

"Baby." She lay her hand on Tiffany's protruding belly. "Oh!" She jerked her hand away, a funny look on her face.

"Baby," Tiffany pointed at her stomach. "Move." She wiggled her fingers around.

"I want to feel." I placed my hand across Tiffany's belly. Little ripples moved under my palm. Her skin tightened and loosened, stretched and relaxed under my hand. It felt odd. "Does it hurt?"

"Not really. Sometimes the kicking hurts, but the rolling like it's doing now doesn't hurt. Watch." She pulled up her t-shirt a little and pointed at her belly. "See it?"

I always wanted lots of kids. A big family to make up for the siblings I never had. Now I'll be happy to live long enough to have kids at all.

"Doesn't that feel weird?" I watched in awe as her stomach rippled with the baby's movements.

"Sort of, but I hardly notice it anymore."

"Well, it looks like something out of that *Alien* movie," I said, my eyes never leaving her belly. I reached out my hand again and felt the baby rolling beneath it. "Do you know what it is?"

"Nah, I didn't want to know. Had I known I'd be stuck down here when it was born, I would have found out so I could've told my parents. It's their first grandbaby." Her voice dropped to a whisper. "I wish I could tell them somehow." She rubbed her belly, staring at the floor. "Anyway, I also would have been able to buy boy or girl clothes. The poor kid is gonna be sick of green and yellow by the time it's two." She laughed, but there was sadness reflected in her eyes.

"Who knocked you up, anyway?" Josh called from the other side of the room.

I rolled my eyes and shot him a dirty look. "Geez, do you have a filter on that mouth?"

"No. Do you have a filter on your attitude?"

"My attitude is fine."

"Yeah, if high-and-mighty is your thing," he said.

I waved him off and looked at Tiffany. "So, how far along are you?"

"Middle of my second trimester—five months."

"And where are your parents?"

"Illinois."

"The baby's dad wasn't chosen?"

"The baby's dad was a colossal mistake. He didn't want anything to do with the baby and I don't want anything to do with him. I guess now I won't have to deal with him." Her smile was bitter.

"Sorry, I'm being too nosy."

"It's okay, Eva. You're not."

I smiled. I'd never really thought about what other people had to give up. Tiffany was not only going to be a single mother, but once she left the POD she wasn't going to have any help from her family when she needed it. They'd all be dead. Jai Li had given up being with people who could understand her, people she could talk to about her fears. George had given up nursing school, and Aidan had left three younger brothers behind—he had their picture up by his bed. Everyone had lost something, some more than others.

I looked over at Tiffany, trying to lighten the mood. "Did you bring toys?"

"Hmm?"

"For the baby. Did you bring toys?"

"Yeah, but I couldn't pack much. The baby's locker had some toys in it already, though."

Well, I guess the people who fixed the raffle aren't all bad.

"Is anyone as sick of the white walls as I am?"

We all stopped what we were doing and stared at Baby. I stood at the sink, pouring milk over my cereal. I wasn't paying attention and overfilled my bowl. Milk ran down my fingers and dripped in the sink. I threw some sliced strawberries on my cereal and rinsed the milk and sticky juice from the berries off my hands.

They were the first words we had heard out of Baby's mouth since entering the POD. She'd just sat in the corner and cried. Sometimes she drew in a notebook or read, but she never came out of the corner other than for meals, and although we'd tried to get her to talk, she'd never said a word.

"I hate them," she added.

"I don't particularly like them," I said. "My house had a lot of different colors in it. I don't think anything was white. I'm Ev—"

"Eva, yeah, I know. Actually, your name is Evangelina. Eva is your nickname. I like Evangelina better."

"Um, well, Evangelina was my grandma's name. It makes me think of her when I hear it."

"Well, I guess we're all going to have to put that aside now. We can't be running from names that remind us of someone else. We'd never find a name we liked, since everyone is dead."

"The kid's got a point," Seth said around a huge mouthful of cereal.

David was leaning on the counter, his chin resting on his fist. He shrugged a shoulder and nodded.

"I suppose you're right." I dried my hands on a towel. "Speaking of names, what's yours?"

"Katie."

"Well, it's nice to meet you, Katie."

"You too, Eva, Tiffany, Tiffany's baby, Jai Li, Josh, David, George, Seth, and Aidan."

"Seems you've been listening," David said.

"Just because one chooses not to speak doesn't mean they choose not to listen."

We all looked at her, dumbfounded. The statement sounded very profound for someone so young.

"I'm Katie. I'm thirteen. My best subject in school was art. I was in eighth grade and had an "A" average, like in your theory, Eva. I left my parents, grandparents and older sister behind. I think we're all caught up. Now, back to my original question—what about the walls?" Katie stood and brushed her pants off. She looked around the room, waiting for our answer.

"They could use some color," Tiffany agreed.

"Good!" Katie ran to her bunk. We could hear her rummaging around before coming back into the living area with boxes of pastels, markers, watercolors, and acrylic paints. "Let's get to work."

"Wait, what are you going to do?" Aidan looked at Katie, down at the paints and markers, and back to her again.

She smiled. "Redecorate."

I shook my head. "Katie, as much as I don't like the white walls, I don't want to use all your art supplies."

"Oh, that's okay. I have a ton more in my bunk." She stared at the pastels for a few seconds before selecting a handful and passing the box to me.

"All right, then. I suppose we're redecorating," I mumbled around bites of cereal.

I heard a chuckle behind me just before a hand reached around and took the pastel box from my hand. I smelled him before I turned to look at him. I already knew what I'd see— gray eyes. Not a dull, lifeless gray, but a shiny, silvery gray with just a hint of blue. Slowly, I turned and looked up. He shrugged. "Far be it from me not to give a girl what she wants," David said with a grin.

He walked off and sat down next to the boys' bedroom door. It was about the same place I'd first seen him doodling when I entered the POD.

I sat on the floor about ten feet from him, halfway between him and Katie. Tiffany sat adjacent to me at the wall separating the bedrooms and bath from the living area. George started his art masterpiece on the kitchen wall, Aidan and Seth in the hallway. Jai Li watched us like we'd gone insane. Maybe we had.

Josh sat on the couch and rolled his eyes. "Coloring on the walls. I guess the people who fixed the raffle *did* pick a bunch of children." A pile of candy wrappers littered the floor around his feet. Had he brought an entire suitcase filled with junk food?

"You're going to pick those up, right?" Tiffany frowned at the wrappers on the floor.

Josh shoved another little candy bar into his mouth and smirked at Tiffany as he flicked the wrapper on the floor.

Tiffany sighed, and I gritted my teeth. *We've all got to live with each other for a year. Can't he even try to make an effort to get along?*

"Two rules," Katie announced. "Keep it clean, and let's have some fun!"

I wasn't a very good artist. It ranked right up there with being a champion athlete...and the way I'd broken Molly Garner's nose last year—while running track—was testament to my talent as an athlete. So rather than draw something completely heinous and force everyone to look at it over the next year, I used a paintbrush to write words.

I wrote some of my favorite quotes. Tiffany stopped on her way to the bedroom and watched. "'*Some people drink from the fountain of knowledge, others gargle.*' Hmm, is that quote meant for Josh?"

From the couch, Josh frowned and flipped her off, then shoved earbuds in his ears and started nodding along to the beat of his music.

"Yeah," I said under my breath. "He's the gargling type."

"What other quotes do you have?" she asked, looking around me to see what else I had written. "'*When you were born, you cried and the world rejoiced. Live your life so that when you die, the world cries and you rejoice*' I like that one," Tiffany nodded.

I smiled. "It's a Cherokee proverb."

I also painted some random words like *peace, joy,* and *love.* I wrote whatever came to mind, like I would in my journal. I did most of it down at the floor level so it'd be hidden as much as possible by furniture, hoping someone with talent would draw something spectacular above to mask my mess below.

I was painting my favorite verse from the Bible—Psalms 118:24—when Josh came up behind me.

This is the day the Lord has made; let us rejoice and be glad in it.

"What's there to rejoice about, Eva? Huh? Everyone is either dead or dying and you want us to be all happy and stuff? That's kinda sick."

"Hey man," George said, "cool down. We all deal with things differently."

"I don't like her sanctimonious crap. I don't want to have to read it every day." He picked up a paintbrush covered in black paint and swiped it over the verse I'd just painted, the black swirling with the red I'd used, making a large, ugly splotch on the wall.

"Josh, you're a real—"

"It's okay, George. No big deal." I picked up the black paintbrush and blacked over the red and black mess Josh had made. I evened out the edges and made a black square. As soon as it dried, I took a piece of white chalk and wrote the verse on the black paint.

"There." I turned and looked at Josh with a smile. "If you paint over it again, I'll write it in permanent marker across your forehead when you're asleep."

"Bitch," he muttered under his breath.

"Spray hairspray over it," David said.

"What?"

"The hairspray will keep the chalk from smearing."

"Okay." I grabbed my hairspray from the bathroom and sprayed the wall. "Thanks." I smiled at David.

He shrugged, not looking away from his drawing. "No problem." David had drawn a sweeping mural across one entire wall of the living area. It was a forest filled with trees, their leaves colored red, yellow and orange. A figure—I couldn't tell if it was male or female—raked fallen leaves at the side of the road. The road wound through the hills of the landscape until it disappeared in the horizon, which held a large autumn sun.

"It's beautiful," I whispered. I didn't know I'd said it out loud until he turned and smiled. I could almost feel the chill of the autumn air, smell the leaves on the wet ground, hear them crunch under my feet.

"Thank you. Your border around the floor is…interesting."

"It's okay," I laughed. "You can call it horrible. I'm under no delusion that I'm an artist. You can paint over it if you want. I wish you would, actually."

He smiled but didn't answer. He was adding something to his mural and I stood on my tiptoes to look over his shoulder. When he was done, he dropped his arm to reveal another figure in the painting. The person sat cross-legged on the ground, reading a book.

"I wish I had your talent, David."

"I like that," he said with a small frown.

"What? That I think you're talented?"

"No. I like how my name sounds on your lips."

I felt the blush crawl up my body until my face burned with it. My breathing became shallow; I couldn't get enough air into my lungs. Why did that one little statement get me so... so...confused, elated, off-balance?

Seth rounded the corner and spied David's mural. "Whoa! That's wicked cool."

"What's cool?" Aidan asked from the hall.

"You gotta see what David's done. Get out here."

I took the distraction as my cue to make a quick exit. I didn't know what to say to David. It wouldn't be a good idea for any of us to become involved while we were living in the POD. If the relationship went sour, it would make our living arrangement worse than it already was. We already had Josh's attitude to deal with. We didn't need two people bitter from a break-up added to the mix. No, there was no way any of us should become romantically involved. None.

No relationships in the POD, Eva. Your rule. Not even if the guy smells as good and looks as yummy as David. Wow! Where did that come from? And how come I want to tell him that I liked the way his name felt crossing my lips?

I walked down the hall to my bedroom. Tiffany was there, trying to paint moons and stars on the ceiling above the baby's crib.

"Tiffany! What are you doing?"

"Decorating the ceiling. The baby won't have a mobile. This will at least give it something to look at."

I had a good idea, even for me. I went back into the living area and whispered to Katie what I wanted to do. She smiled and nodded.

I walked over to David, determined to ignore his earlier comment. "Would you help me and Katie?"

"Sure, Eva." He smiled.

Now I just had to get Tiffany out of the bedroom.

"Tiff? Come on, it's time for a break."

"'Kay."

She meandered into the kitchen, one hand pressed against her back and the other on her belly, and dropped onto a chair. "What's our MRE lunch for today? Is it spaghetti? Spaghetti? Or…gasp…spaghetti?"

"Have I told you how much I hate spaghetti?" I pushed my meal away.

"It's come up once or twice," she said with a laugh.

Tiffany ate her lunch before falling asleep on the couch. She slept most of the afternoon, giving David and Katie enough time to finish the mural around the crib.

"It's awesome. She's going to love it." I could hardly wait for her to wake up so we could show it to her.

"It's not too bad," David said with a small smile. "It's the best we could pull off with what we have to work with."

"I think it's beautiful."

"Oh, the baby, the baby, we must paint something beautiful for the illegitimate baby," I heard Josh whine behind me.

"Stay out of this, Josh," I said, not turning around.

"Don't worry, Evangelina. I don't want anything to do with the baby or your little surprise party for its mommy." He stuck his head in the bedroom and looked at the mural. "It's okay, I guess," he said, before returning to the dining area to stare at his laptop screen.

Finally, after what seemed like the longest nap ever, Tiffany woke up. She made her way to the bathroom and we all snuck into the bedroom, giggling like little kids. When she opened the door from the bathroom I called, "Hey, Tiff? Can you come in here a sec?"

When she walked through the door and saw us all standing there, she looked wary. "Uh, what's going on?"

"We got you and the baby a gift. Well, some of us did the work, but the others supervised." I smiled.

David chuckled behind me.

We shuffled to the side, revealing Katie and David's mural of a summer's day—the sun shining, birds flying in the sapphire sky, a little stream bubbling over some small stones as it made its way toward the horizon. A large oak tree stood in the center, a swing hanging from one branch. Flowers dotted the lush, green grass, and butterflies danced among them. The ceiling was midnight blue, edged in silver-gray clouds and filled with stars and a crescent moon.

"Thank you," Tiffany said between tears. "It's beautiful."

I put an arm around her shoulders. "Well, we aren't able to give you a baby shower, so we decided to give you and the baby this. Everyone painted something, except Josh. I wasn't able to paint much, but it was my idea and they did relent and let me paint my own initials in the corner."

"Yeah, and even that was pressing her artistic ability to its breaking point."

"Very funny, David. Anyway, we thought it would give the baby something to look forward to after the POD is opened. Fresh air, wide open spaces…"

"Thank you. I don't know what to say. It really is beautiful."

"Here." David thrust a paintbrush at her. "I thought you might want to paint something on the mural, too."

Tiffany looked at the paintbrush and shook her head. "I don't want to do anything to mess it up."

"Then just do a butterfly or flower. Write a message to the baby in a corner. Do anything you want, but do something. It should be from all of us, including you."

Holding the paintbrush next to the wall, Tiffany bit her bottom lip. "Okay," she said slowly, "I'll paint a butterfly." She dipped the tip of the paintbrush in orange paint and took her time, mimicking the butterflies Katie had painted. "And I want to write something."

"Whatever you want," David told her.

She squatted down, wobbling from one side to another as she tried to keep her balance, but gave up after a few seconds and plopped onto the floor. "I'll probably never be able to get up again," she laughed.

She chewed on her fingernail, thinking of the perfect message to write to her child, taking her time, getting it just right…

One day you'll run and jump and swing in a field much like this one. I can't wait to watch you and hear your giggles. I can't imagine loving a person more than I do you.

Love Always, Mommy

By the time the day was over and all the finishing touches done, a lot of the walls had been covered in paintings and pastel drawings. George drew fruits and vegetables along the walls in the kitchen and I doodled in places it would be hard for people to see if I messed up. There was still a lot of white space to cover up, but we decided to save that for another day.

Month Two

After our day of redecorating, we spent more time doing things together. We played cards and board games. Aidan found the television in the back corner of the linen closet, and we decided we needed a movie night to celebrate.

"What are we celebrating?" Aidan asked.

"Who cares?" Katie said with a giggle. "Hurry up, Aidan." She handed him the cables to hook up the DVD player.

"I thought your best subject was computer science and networking, Aidan. Seems like you'd be able to hook up a DVD player," Josh said with a belch.

Aidan opened his mouth to say something. Instead he let out a frustrated sigh and muttered something under his breath that made Katie break out in a fit of giggles.

Once the television and DVD player were hooked up and working, we gathered in the living area, jostling for the best spots in front of the television. Aidan had found a horror movie and everyone was excited to watch it—except me.

I sat on the floor with a scratchy blanket pulled up to my eyes. Josh plopped down next to me and yanked part of the blanket over himself. He rested his hand on my knee. I scooted over as far as I could, pulling the blanket with me.

"What? Untouchable?"

"No, the blanket's too small for two people," I said, trying to keep my voice neutral.

"Too good for me?" he said with a smirk.

Yes. I don't like selfish jerks. "No," I said, trying to give him a sincere smile. It was hard.

"If you don't wanna share, go get another one."

"Get your own." I jerked the blanket away, sitting on the edges so he couldn't get under it.

When the movie started I held my blanket with both hands, covering my face—one side slightly lower than the other so I could peek over the top. I knew it was coming. The stupid lady was going into the dark basement alone. It was quiet. She walked further into the creepy room. I held my breath. I waited, my heart beating faster. My hands hurt from clutching the blanket. The lady stood in the darkest corner...of course the killer was going to jump out at her. I braced myself. The blanket ready to cover my eyes...

"AHH!" Aidan yelled, tickling my side. I screamed and jumped up. He thought it was hilarious—the others did, too.

"Aidan, you're a jerk," I said, scowling.

I'd had enough scary movies for the night. Going into the bedroom, I climbed on my bunk. The hinges squeaked as I pulled open the cupboard in the headboard and grabbed a book. I'd just opened the novel when a shadow fell over the page. Expecting Katie or Tiffany, I was surprised to see David.

"Hey," I said, trying to remember how to breathe like a normal person. But every time I took a breath I smelled him and he smelled beyond amazing and that was a problem—at least for me.

"Not much of a horror fan?" He tried to hide a grin and ran his hand through his hair. I watched the silky strands sift through his fingers.

"What clued you in?" I was surprised my voice didn't shake, since my insides were.

"Well, you held a blanket up to your eyes the minute the movie started playing."

I laughed. "Yeah, I did."

"You're reading." He rubbed his hands up and down the sides of his thighs.

"Mm-hmm, I do that sometimes."

He chuckled. "I just thought you'd want some company. I mean, you are all the way down the darkened hall by yourself…"

"Ha-ha, David."

"Eva, I…" He waved off his words. "I'll let you get back to your book. See you tomorrow." He smiled and walked out the door.

What was that?

Butterflies the size of softballs flew around in my stomach. I tried to shoo them away. No romances in the POD. It didn't matter that he made my insides swirl out of place every time he was in my line of sight, smell radius or general vicinity— and, since we were locked in the same tin can, he was at least within one of those all the time.

"Eva, move your person!" Seth yelled.

"I'm trying. She won't go where I want her to."

"You're gonna get killed…"

"Well, then help me!" I yelled.

The five guys seemed to have no problem maneuvering their virtual men in the stupid video game. They had them running all over the screen. My person stood in place twirling around and around. She wouldn't cooperate.

"Your avatar is as stubborn as you are, Eva," Seth laughed.

I heard David chuckle behind me. "Ugh, I'm done," I said when virtual me got killed for the millionth time. "Let's play Wii Bowling." I knew they wouldn't. They were too involved with their little virtual friends running here and there.

"Eva, face it. Gaming is not your thing."

"I told you. I suck at all things sports-related…even virtual ones. Except bowling on the Wii. Come on. You know you want to…"

No answer. It was just as well. The last time we'd been bowling, my little hand thingy had slipped and flown backward, hitting David in the eye. But I had bowled my best game.

"Hey, guys, did you know we have video chat on these things?" Katie tilted her laptop to show us.

"Cool. Who's the guy?" I asked with a smile. It seemed Katie had already made a new friend.

"Cameron, but he goes by Cam. He's in sub-POD Twelve. We've been talking a lot," she said, blushing.

"Hi Cam," I said, waving at the screen.

A young kid, around fourteen, smiled and waved. He never took his eyes off Katie.

"Ah, young love," David said, walking behind me and looking at the screen. Katie's blush grew deeper.

I grabbed my laptop and opened the intranet.

"You looking for a boyfriend, too?" David asked with a grin.

"I guess so. No one will let me play videogames."

"Because you suck," Josh called.

"I might as well see if someone wants to chat," I said, ignoring Josh.

"You know," Josh came up behind me, "If you're looking for someone to hook up with, I could help with the boyfriend thing." He put his sweaty hands on my shoulders and massaged them with sausage-like fingers.

"Ah, no thanks," I said, moving forward, out of his reach. "I'm not looking for a relationship in the PODs." That was partly true. If David's hands had been massaging me...well, that would have been a different story entirely.

"Who said anything about a relationship? I'm just looking to hook up. Lemme know when you change your mind. All the other girls are too young, too pregnant, or too ethnic for me." Josh went back to the game.

David chuckled behind me. "Tough decision, huh? Turning down Mr. Commitment."

"Yeah, my heart's breaking."

Chapter 8 :
Homework

Month *Three*

The fun had to end sometime.

The chute running from the main POD to our sub-POD had only been used for our fruit and veggie delivery, birth control boosters for the three girls who needed them, and our blood checks, so the thing was only used once a week—until...

Thump.

It can't be our fruits and vegetables. They came this morning.

"I'll get it!" Katie ran to the chute like a child on Christmas morning. She opened the hatch and pulled out the container. A few seconds after she'd closed the hatch, we heard another container arrive, this one landing with a deep thump that made us jump. Then another thudded in. And another. By the fifth arrival, we'd all gathered to see.

"What is it?" Aidan called to Katie, who'd taken the first container to the table to unseal it.

"Books and stuff."

"Uh-oh," I muttered.

"There's a letter. 'School begins tomorrow. Each of you will be assigned a course guide designed to prepare you in a certain subject. Packets addressed to each POD occupant accompany this memo. Please find the envelope with your name on it and review the contents carefully. Books will be sent via the chute by the end of the day. Links for your online courses will be uploaded via the intranet later today. All class assignments will be completed online via the POD intranet. Please complete the orientation course before you begin your assigned course schedules. Instructions on how to upload your assignments are included in the packets you just received. Please review each item carefully,'" Katie read.

David held out a canister to me. "Evangelina?"

I pulled several books from the canister. The large paperbacks still held the curl of the round container. "Thanks. I guess."

"'Evangelina.' That's pretty."

"Thank you." I smiled. He returned my smile, and that made me smile wider, like an idiot.

"So? What'd ya get?" Aidan asked.

"A bunch of English crap."

Another large boom made me jump. Another set of books had arrived. The chute continued banging—making us all jump every time—until everyone had their books. Conveniently, each person's course work was in a subject he or she had excelled at in school. *I guess my theory was right about that.*

We compared notes. Tiffany had biochemistry, with a lot of pharmacology stuff; it looked like they had a career track in mind for her. David also had science materials. George received several nursing textbooks.

Aidan didn't get any books. "My stuff's comp-sci, so it's all online. What'd you get, Seth?"

"Math."

"What?" Josh threw the electrical engineering texts he'd received. The books scattered across the floor. "They think they can just choose our lives for us? Screw that!" He stalked off to the boys' dorm room.

We looked up to watch him go, and went back to looking at our books.

"They're building on our strengths," David murmured.

"Yup," Aidan agreed. "This is going to be so much fun. Much better than playing videogames, watching DVDs and hanging out online with pretty girls in the other PODs all day."

David chuckled. "Yeah, a barrel of laughs."

We each found spaces where we could look over our books and coursework. Tiffany sat on the couch and George in his beanbag, which had moved from the center of the room to the side of the couch—the side Tiffany was on.

I went to the girls' bedroom, letting the heavy stack of books fall on my bunk before I sat down beside them. I looked at the pile and sighed.

I had worried about how we'd spend our time in the POD, how we'd keep from getting so bored we'd want to pull our hair out strand by strand. My worries were over.

"Hey, Eva, whatcha wanna play?"

"Nah, not tonight, guys. I'm going to look over this stuff and see what type of torture is waiting for me."

"C'mon, don't go all bookworm on us," Seth held up the deck of cards. "We could play hearts again, if you wanted."

I shook my head. "Sorry, guys."

Seth, Aidan, and I had gotten into the habit of playing cards after dinner. Others would join us occasionally, but the three of us played nearly every night. Looking at the books and the thickness of my coursework packet, I was afraid those days were gone.

Passing the guy's bedroom, I saw David and George sitting on their bunks, going through their packets. George had a deep frown, which worried me, mainly because he had so many piercings it was hard to read his expressions. So the fact that I could tell he was frowning couldn't be a good thing. David's face was neutral. I couldn't tell if he was deep in thought or daydreaming.

I called as I walked by. "That bad, huh, George?"

"Worse."

Great.

I sat on my bunk and opened the cellophane seal around one stack of books. It held a dictionary, a thesaurus, and the thickest book on grammar and punctuation I'd ever seen. In the pile thrown across my bed was a book on Shakespeare—I had to laugh at that, since I'd been studying Hamlet just before the virus hit—two books on business communication, another book on literature, and finally, a teaching textbook. The teaching book scared me—I'd never considered being a teacher. In fact, I'd considered everything *but* teaching. I hoped the book wasn't a sign.

"It's not real, you know."

I jumped at his voice. "What?"

"The window. It isn't real," David said.

"Oh, I didn't realize I was looking at it. Daydreaming, I guess."

The white curtain—the designers must have loved the color white—over the glass had a smudge of green paint from when we'd decorated. At night the light within darkened, helping us keep our sense of time. The clocks fastened in each bed's headboard not only told us the time, but also the day and date. Between the two we felt we had some normalcy, at least where time was concerned.

"They're a nice touch," I said with a smile.

"Mm-hmm." He gestured to my bed. "Can I?"

"Sure." My heart rate increased.

"So, what did Santa put in your stocking?" I looked at him stupidly. "The books? What'd you get?"

"Oh, right, the books. Um, just as I guessed. My strongest subject is...was...English. The books all have to do with English and literature."

"What's that one? The one you're holding."

"It's the ugly duckling of the bunch. It's a book on teaching."

"Teaching, huh? I could see you as a teacher. You're really good with Jai Li."

"I suppose."

"Not sold on the idea, I see." He smiled.

"Not really. It isn't what I would have chosen. Then again, I didn't have any great plan, anyway. Maybe it's just as well they chose for me. It's funny—I was studying Shakespeare in school, just before the virus. I remember thinking I'd never use it in my day-to-day life because I wasn't going to be an English teacher or librarian." I laughed at the memory. "Seems the government has other ideas. What about you? What was in your little bag of tricks?"

"A bunch of science books. The main focus seems to be on Earth science, biology, and marine biology. I'm not sure what to make of it. Maybe they'll try me on all three and then decide which I'll focus on."

"What grade were you in? Or were you in college?" I asked. I didn't know much about David. None of us did. He seemed to listen more than he spoke.

"I was a senior."

"Ah. I was a junior."

"So you're seventeen?"

I nodded. "And you?"

"Eighteen. Actually, my birthday was the night before I left for quarantine."

"I'm sorry."

"Well, it is what it is." He shrugged one shoulder. "Where are you from, Evangelina?"

"Ugh, please call me Eva. I'm from Texas. You?"

"Michigan. Is your family Italian?"

"No, why?"

"Evangelina just sounds like an Italian name. I was curious."

He was curious about me? I wasn't sure if that was a good thing or a bad one. I kept reminding myself that relationships in the PODs weren't a good idea. But he smelled so good. And his eyes—gray, almost silver. I'd never seen eyes that color. I couldn't help but look into their depths. They were hypnotizing.

"Where?" I asked, and he gave me a puzzled look. "Where in Michigan are you from?"

"Oh, Lansing. It's right about…"

He stopped talking when I started laughing. He looked confused and I laughed harder. He chuckled and raised a brow.

"I'm sorry." I tried to force myself to stop laughing. I couldn't. I started giggling again. Taking in two big gulps of air, I stopped long enough to tell him, "I didn't know anyone really did that."

"What?"

"Point to their hand to show where they live…" I was laughing harder now.

"Yes, we do." He grabbed my hand and pointed at my palm. "And I lived right there."

He must have realized I'd stopped laughing. He looked up. I'm not sure what expression he saw on my face. He made small circles on my palm with his finger. It tickled and my first instinct was to pull away, but then he'd stop touching me. And I didn't want him to stop.

"Well, I guess I should go. I hear homework calling my name." Slowly, he let go of my hand.

"Oh." I wasn't ready for him to leave. "David?"

"Yeah?" he turned halfway toward me, one hand on the doorjamb, the other in the pocket of his jeans. He looked so good, my breath hitched in my throat.

Keep your mouth shut, Eva. This isn't a good idea.

"Do you want to bring your books in here? We can compare our torture," I said.

He disappointed me by walking away without answering. I stared at the door, surprised. Not because he didn't want to study together, that was fine. But that he'd leave without answering me. That didn't seem to be something he'd do. But, I didn't know him well enough to assume anything.

I'd just started flipping through the course packet when he walked back into the room.

"Do you want me to sit on the floor?"

"You can sit on the bed."

He raised his eyebrows and looked over my bed. Books and pens littered it from one end to the other.

"Oh, sorry." I scooped up a bunch of stuff and dropped it on the floor, leaving room for him on the end.

We sat in silence for a while, flipping through books. The only sound was the ruffling pages and the occasional squeak of a highlighter against a paper. It was a companionable silence, not strained or uncomfortable.

I grabbed my calendar and started writing what assignment was due each day. Out of the corner of my eye, I saw him watching me.

"What?" I asked, not looking up.

"Nothing. I thought I was the only one who did that. I generally have more about my assignment due dates on my calendar than anything resembling a social life."

"I find that hard to believe." I groaned inwardly. *Did I really say that out loud?*

"Why?"

"I just don't see you as the guy without a following, that's all. You're more, you know, the *it* guy."

Ugh, shut up before you embarrass yourself any more.

"The *it* guy?"

"Yeah, the guy every girl in the school wants to date. My school had an *it* guy every year. I just don't see your calendar filled only with assignment due dates. Dates with girls, yeah, but not dates with assignments." I looked up at him.

A small smile tugged at his lips. "No, I was far from being the *it* guy. And, yes, my calendar was full of due dates rather than girl dates."

"Well, my calendar is going to be overflowing with due dates from everything they want done." I tried to change the subject with the least amount of embarrassment.

"Mine, too. However, I could manage a date or two in there somewhere. Maybe a study session tomorrow after dinner? Same place?"

My stomach fell somewhere in the vicinity of my toes. "Sure."

"Great, I'll bring the lemonade. I have to go. There's a couple of kids who won't stop yammering. I can't get anything done." He smiled. "See you tomorrow, Eva."

"G'night, David."

Katie walked in as David was leaving. She sat on my bed, clutching her laptop to her chest.

"What's up?" I asked.

"Cam is in my science class," she gushed. "We'll get to hang out together in that chat room, too." She flopped backward.

I laughed. "You like him, huh?"

"He's the best. I wish we'd been assigned the same POD. He could have taken Josh's place."

I laughed. Yeah, we all wished someone could've taken Josh's place.

Chapter 9:
Faith

School in the PODs was about twice as much work as high school had been—maybe because they knew we didn't have anything else to do: no extracurriculars, no social lives, no family commitments. And the more assignments I finished, the more I realized I was being groomed to be a teacher, especially when they started having me create lesson plans. I was pretty sure they wanted me to teach English, but I'd also been given social studies, art history, women's history, and world literature. Thankfully, they didn't include math.

David's packets had been pared down to Earth science and marine biology, which made him happy. "Maybe I'll go home to Michigan, see the Great Lakes again. I'm sure there'll be work there."

"I wonder what the virus will do to the animals," I said, frowning. "Will there even be anything left? I mean, the scientists knew so little about it. They didn't know if it would infect animals, marine life, plant life—"

"Eva, let's get through our POD stay first. Then we'll worry about the toll it's taken up top, okay?" David reached out and rubbed my hand. My body immediately reacted to his touch.

Since our first study date, we'd studied together every evening after dinner. We talked a little, laughed a lot, and somehow got some work done in between. The first few days, I felt awkward. I didn't know him well and we talked very little, focusing on our work. Eventually we talked more, and I grew more comfortable around him. Then it all changed.

The air became electrified when he was near. My heart raced, and the awkward feeling was back. It took me a day or two to realize what my heart already knew. I liked him—a lot more than I should. It was more than just two friends getting together to study.

At least it was for me.

David showed no change in his behavior, which disappointed me, even though I kept reminding myself that a romance in the PODs was a very bad idea. I was falling for David and I could tell myself it wasn't a good idea over and over again—my heart wasn't listening.

When he reached out and stroked my hand, my skin tingled, goosebumps slid up my arm, and I could feel the heat of a blush spread across my face. Maybe he recognized the signs, maybe not. His hand moved away much too soon.

"It's late. I should go." David said as he gathered his things and stood.

I flipped through the pages of my book to keep my hand moving and resist the urge to grab his.

"I guess I can finish this tomorrow morning." I said, trying to keep the disappointment out of my voice.

"Eva…" He sighed and looked at the floor, resting his forehead against the doorframe.

I waited for him to finish, for him to say what I'd hope he'd say. I was gripping my pen so hard my fingernails dug into my palm.

He shook his head before looking at me. "I'll see you tomorrow."

"Okay." I wasn't ready for him to leave our peaceful cocoon, but I didn't know what to say to make him stay. If we went in the living area the others would be there. We wouldn't be able to talk.

"David?"

"Yeah?"

"Stay."

He ran his fingers through his hair and took a half step back into the room. He frowned and turned toward the door. Gripping the doorframe, he said, "I'll see you tomorrow, Evangelina. Same time, same place."

"Sure," I answered with a small smile.

My face burned with embarrassment, and I was glad no one was in the room to hear his rejection, see the red-hot blush covering my face. Tears pressed against the back of my eyes. I took a deep breath and looked up at the ceiling, blinking furiously. It was a trick Bridget had taught me. *"If you don't want to cry, look up at the ceiling and blink, and the urge will pass."*

It didn't.

I wasn't sure what the jumble of emotions filling me meant, but it was more than a typical schoolgirl crush. I'd had those, and whatever I was feeling for David wasn't one.

None of us were typical teenagers anymore—that reality had ended the day we'd gotten on those grimy yellow school buses. Leaving our families, our friends—everyone we'd ever known and loved—was hard enough. Leaving them to die was quite different. We'd had to grow up quickly. We weren't at summer camp; we were fighting to stay alive—to keep the human race from extinction. That was a lot to bear.

Another reason I knew it wasn't a crush—a crush is like a match to gasoline; it flares quickly. David and I had been studying together every night for a month. The feelings I had for him had only been an issue for a week, give or take a day. My feelings were from getting to know him—his dreams, wants, and fears. It went beyond a physical attraction.

And that's why I knew I had a problem.

Someone plopped on the mattress next to me, interrupting my thoughts.

"What are we studying tonight? I saw Loverboy leave and thought you and I could get some time together."

Ugh, how do I get rid of him? "I was just about to quit for the night, Josh." I closed my book, hoping he'd take the hint.

"So you'll study with him, but not with me?"

Yup, you got it. "Ah, like I said. Just quitting for the night."

"I thought you didn't want a romance in the POD, Eva." He scooted closer to me. I could smell his breath and wondered when he'd last brushed his teeth.

"I don't."

"Sure looks like you're getting cozy with David." His voice was hard.

"We're just friends. Not that it concerns you."

"It concerns everyone in the POD if you're going to go flaunting it around."

"I'm not flaunting anything!"

"Come on, Eva. Let's play." I jumped at the sound of Tiffany's voice.

"What?" *Thank the Lord. I don't care what we're playing.*

"Canasta. Come on, I need a partner. It's girls against the guys."

"Oh, we are taking Seth and Aidan down," I said with a laugh, joining her in the hall.

"Seth isn't playing. He has too much work to do. David's taking his place."

"David?"

Tiffany nodded. She didn't notice the blush that made my cheeks burn and the way my hands started to tremble. Or if she did, she didn't mention it.

Aidan and David were already waiting at the kitchen table. I took my seat across from Tiffany and tried not to look at anyone but her. My mind scrambled to find a way out of playing, but I'd already told Tiffany I would. It would make things more awkward between David and me if I made excuses not to play. Yeah, like it wasn't already awkward.

Aidan made a show out of shuffling the cards. Every time he fanned them together I jumped at the sound.

"Cut the deck. Eva!"

"Oh, right. Sorry." Aidan gave me a funny look before taking back the cards and dealing them.

"What are we playing, again?"

"Canasta. Do you know how to play?" David asked.

"Yeah, it's big up north. My parents play with some friends of theirs every week." I didn't look at him when I answered, staring at my cards like my eyes were superglued to them.

"When were you up north?"

"I wasn't. My parent's friends are from somewhere in Wisconsin. They taught them how. I fill in sometimes, if they need a fourth. At least I did."

"Ah."

"Are we gonna play cards or twenty questions?" Aidan looked between David and me.

"I guess we'll play cards, Aidan. I'm not sure you can count to twenty."

"Ha-ha, very funny, Eva."

We played cards until none of us could keep our eyes open. The girls beat the guys, of course. Not once, but every game we played. We were officially crowned Queens of Canasta.

As soon as the last game was over, Aidan took off for bed.

Tiffany started to straighten up.

I took the cards from her hands. "Go to bed, Tiff. I'll clean up."

"It's okay."

"You're exhausted, and it's not good for you or the baby. Go."

"Thanks, Eva."

I stayed up to pick up the cards and snack wrappers. I turned, a stack of snack wrappers in my hands, and came face-to-face with David.

I sucked in a breath, startled. "I'd thought you'd gone to bed."

"I didn't want to leave you with all the mess to clean up." He took the wrappers and placed them in the trash, and I grabbed the dishtowel and started to wipe down the table. "Eva?"

"Hmm?"

"Why did you ask me to stay earlier?"

The dishtowel stilled, my arm still outstretched to reach the other side of the table. I stood there trying to find an answer that wouldn't embarrass us both. "Uh, I guess…I mean…I wanted to keep talking with you."

He closed the distance between us. I turned and looked at him. His face held an odd expression, his gray eyes darkened. He reached up and tucked a stray lock of hair behind my ear before brushing my cheek with his thumb. My skin tingled.

I thought he was going to kiss me. Every cell in my body tensed, waiting for him to lean in. I pleaded in my head, but of course he didn't hear me. And he didn't lean in to kiss me. Instead, his hand fell away from my face.

"It's really late. The kitchen's clean; the rest can wait until tomorrow. C'mon, let's go to bed."

I turned out the lights and followed him to the opening of the little hallway that led to the bedrooms. Pausing at the door to his room, he ran the tips of his fingers up my arm, just a whisper of a caress. I could feel the blush wash across my face and wondered if he saw it. Did he know what his touch did to me? Did mine do the same to him? "Good night, Evangelina. Sleep well."

Well, crap, there's no way on God's green earth I'll get any sleep after that. What was that, anyway? Is he trying to torture me? Because it's working. I'm in so much trouble.

Month Four

Two days later, at four PM, Tiffany had the first contraction. She told me not to tell anyone. It was probably nothing anyway. Stupidly, I agreed. By six o'clock they were coming every five minutes and Tiffany was in pain—a lot of it. She couldn't stay quiet any longer. With each contraction she held her belly, trying not to moan.

"Do your breathing exercises. Like on TV," Katie said.

"Screw my breathing," Tiffany snapped. She got up and paced, and I walked through the POD with her. When the contractions came I'd rub her back and shoulders like I'd seen on TV—apparently the source of everything we knew about childbirth—trying to keep her relaxed, but I could feel her muscles tighten. Sometimes she'd lean against the wall, her head lying on her arm, massaging her large belly as it squeezed the breath out of her. Other times she'd lean on me—her arms on my shoulders, her full weight pushing down on me, her fingernails biting into my skin. I thought I'd crumple under the weight, but I stood and let her lean on me as the contractions pummeled her from the inside out.

She was walking the hallway when I ran into the main living area. "David, call the main POD and tell them the baby is coming. Tiffany needs a doctor."

"Don't leave me, Eva." Tiffany's voice was slurred with pain.

"I'm not. I'm right here." I put her arm around my shoulder. She leaned heavily on me as we walked to her bed.

Josh walked by the door. "What's going on?"

"The baby's coming."

"Oh." He shrugged. "Try to keep the screaming down."

Ass.

"I'm going to see about the doctor. I'll be right back," I told Tiffany when we got to the bed.

Tiffany nodded and I bolted to the door, flying around the corner. David was coming from the other direction. My feet skidded out from under me when I tried to stop.

I caught myself with my hand before I completely embarrassed myself by falling on my butt. "What did they say? Are they sending a doctor, or do they want her to go to the main POD?"

"They didn't say anything."

"What do you mean, 'they didn't say anything?'"

"I mean no one answered. They didn't say anything."

I just stared at him, trying to think of what to say, my mouth opening and closing like a fish. Tiffany cried out from the bedroom down the hall. My mind spun, my fingers drumming a rhythm against my leg as I thought of what I should do.

I ran to the sliding doors where the games and books were kept. Flinging the doors open, I furiously scanned the titles of the books. I couldn't find the ones I wanted. Desperate, I started clearing shelves. One by one I picked up the books, looked quickly at the titles, and threw them aside.

My mountain of discarded books growing rapidly, David crouched beside me. "What are you looking for?" Ignoring him—and the looks I was getting from the others in the room—I continued throwing books on top of the pile. "Evangelina." I stopped and looked at him. "What are you looking for?"

"There are a couple of pregnancy books in here. Maybe some of them have sections on emergency home births," I said, going back to throwing discarded books on the pile. "Okay, okay, here they are."

I scanned the table of contents in the first one for the chapter I needed, and then did the most frantic speed-reading of my life. Looking up, I saw no one was doing anything. They were just sitting there staring at me while Tiffany cried in pain from the other room.

"Aidan, find as many cotton towels as you can and iron them."

"Iron them?"

"Just do it! I don't have time to tell you all why. George, find some string—shoelace, something that can be used to tie off the umbilical cord, and get ready. You've got a baby to deliver. David, keep calling the main POD. Seth, look in that baby crap in the closet and find one of these," I twirled the book so he could see the photo of the nasal aspirator.

"A turkey baster?"

"Smaller, but yeah, kinda. Katie, uh, boil water. We can use it to sterilize stuff."

I looked up when I felt a hand on my arm. Jai Li pointed to the book, "Baby?"

"Yes."

She ran down the hall.

"Here," I tossed one of the other pregnancy books to David. "Look through that and see if there's anything else we need." I took off back toward the bedroom. "And keep trying to get someone to answer in the main POD," I yelled over my shoulder.

I found Jai Li in the bathroom washing her hands. She pointed for me to do the same. We lathered on thick layers of soap, scrubbing thoroughly. When we finished, we went to Tiffany. Katie was there, adjusting a pillow.

Jai Li yelled Josh's name. He stuck his head in the door, but wouldn't come in the room. "Get...um, garbage..." she slid her hands back and forth, "bag. Many bags."

Josh looked at Katie. "Get garbage bags, kid." He walked away.

Useless.

Katie ran down the hall and rummaged through the kitchen, opening cabinets and slamming them shut. She came back with a fistful of garbage bags.

I watched as Jai Li spread a garbage bag at the foot of the bed, covering the floor. She lifted the sheet under Tiffany and covered the bed's mattress with another bag. She placed the third under Tiffany, covering it with a towel.

Jai Li yelled David's name. She said something so fast no one understood her. "Wet cloth," she repeated slowly. David brought a damp washcloth to the door, holding it out toward Katie. Jai Li motioned for her to lay it across Tiffany's forehead.

Tiffany groaned as something gushed out onto the bags. I scanned the pregnancy book, trying to figure out what that meant...

Oh, her water broke. Things can move faster now. Great. We need slower—until a doctor comes—not faster.

"David!"

"I'm here," I heard him say from the hall. "They still aren't picking up."

"Towels and the turkey baster," George called, holding the items in his outstretched hand from outside the doorframe.

Katie ran over and grabbed the towels and the small nasal aspirator, handing them to me. I was across from Jai Li at Tiffany's feet, the pregnancy book at the foot of the bed.

"Baby coming," Jai Li said.

No kidding!

Jai Li gestured to the nasal aspirator in my hand. Pointing at Tiffany, she said, "head out," she mimicked using the aspirator. "Body out." She met my eyes. "You do."

I understood what she was saying. Between the diagram in the book and the directions Jai Li was trying to give, I knew what needed to be done…kind of.

"We need that string!" I couldn't remember who I'd told to get it. "George, come help me," I yelled.

"Here's the string, Eva." David reached into the room.

"George, get in here and help us!" I yelled.

"I can't."

"You were in nursing school! We need your help."

"We never got to the part about delivering babies."

"George, we really need your help!"

"I really can't, Eva. I don't know…I haven't done this before."

"And you think we have?" I muttered something about men being useless and heard David chuckle from where he stood outside the door with the rest of the guys.

I scanned down the page. *Water breaking…active labor… mother may feel need to push…* "Tiffany, are you ready to push?" I tried to keep my voice calm and soothing. The book said if I panicked, she'd panic. The last thing I wanted was for her to start panicking, because I was secretly doing enough for both of us.

Jai Li tilted her head, studying the illustration in the book for several seconds, and then motioned for Tiffany to scoot down. Jai Li took one leg and gestured to Katie to take the other. After another glance at the diagram, together they pushed Tiffany's knees toward her chest.

Which left only one person to… "No, no, no," I shook my head. "Jai Li, you do it."

She shook her head.

Tiffany started moaning as another contraction hit, and I saw something…start to come out. I read the page once more, trying to keep the shaking out of my voice. "Okay, Tiff, on the next contraction, you need to push hard. Inhale deeply and let the breath out slowly while you count to ten."

Her inhale sounded more like a whimper. After a couple of breaths, she moaned. "Here comes another."

"Okay. Inhale…one…two…three. You're doing great, keep pushing. Inhale again and push."

Amniotic fluid and blood dripped on the plastic bag covering the floor; my hands and Tiffany's legs were splattered with it.

Oh, gross, gross, gross.

"Jai Li?" I motioned to the blood. She smiled and nodded.

Normal, okay, at least something about this birth is normal.

"It hurts, it hurts, it hurts."

"I know, keep pushing. Jai Li!" I pointed as the thing I'd seen before emerged even more. I didn't know if what I was seeing was what I thought it was.

"Head," Jai Li said with a smile.

That's what I was afraid she'd say. I groaned silently. Sweat ran down my back and my hands trembled. The main POD still hadn't answered our calls for help, and the baby was coming now—with or without a doctor. It was just me, a thirteen-year-old kid, and a teenager who barely spoke English but who somehow seemed to know the basics of labor and delivery. We made an odd team, but that was who was going to deliver Tiffany's baby, because even though I was silently willing it to stay put until a doctor came, the head kept sliding forward.

"Tiffany, your baby has lots of hair. It's blonde, the same color as yours. Push hard, it's almost over."

A sickening suction sound filled the room. I watched as the head slipped through the birth canal. Jai Li gestured at the aspirator in my hand, and I did my best to clear the baby's airways like the book showed. I said a prayer that I had done a good job of it. The rest of the baby's wet, slippery body slid into my hands.

It was perfect. A miniature person…with a huge set of lungs. It didn't take long for it to take its first breath and scream. It was loud, robust and healthy. I quickly wiped as much goo and blood off as I could before laying the baby on Tiffany's chest like I'd seen in movies. And, like in most movies, the four of us were crying.

"Someone write down the date and time," I yelled to the guys standing in the hallway.

I checked the book for the next steps. After waiting for the umbilical cord to stop pulsing, I tied the string around it in two places, like in the illustration. Using scissors, I tried to cut through the cord; it was tough and rubbery and I had to work at cutting through with the dull blades.

Once the final cut had been made, I lifted the baby and wrapped it in a blanket before placing it back in Tiffany's arms. "The book says you should nurse now, Tiffany, that it'll help expel the placenta." *Eew.*

With the help of Jai Li, Tiffany turned the baby into position, its little mouth already searching for its first meal. Katie tucked a blanket around Tiffany's legs.

I gathered up the bloody towels and bedding in one of the garbage bags. "Guys, did you write down the time and date? Tiffany will want to know."

"I wrote it down. Is Tiffany all right?" George asked.

I looked up. Tiffany gazed down at her newborn baby nursing, a wide smile on her sweat-soaked face, her hair matted to her head, her cheeks rosy.

"She's great, George."

"Eva?"

"Yeah?"

"Is it a boy or a girl?"

"Oh! I didn't look. Just a second." I lifted the blanket and looked. Leaning over, I whispered in Tiffany's ear. She was the mom. It seemed only fair for her to be the first to know.

Grabbing a towel, I wiped more blood and gelatinous goo from my hands and arms. In the hall, I smiled at the guys lining the wall. "It's a girl."

"They're okay?" George asked, looking at the stuff on my shirt.

"Yes, they're great. Everything is picked up and she's covered, if you want to go in."

"Okay," George said. *Are George and Tiffany the only people in the POD unaware of his crush on her?*

"Eva, you did—"

"Give me a minute." I rushed to the bathroom. I didn't even get a chance to close the door before I puked. Everything had moved so fast, I hadn't had time to think about it. But the baby was born and healthy. Tiffany was out of pain…and my hands were covered in goo and blood.

David ducked his head in. "You okay?"

"I don't do well with blood."

He laughed. I slammed the door.

"You did a great job, Evangelina." I heard him say from the other side.

Chapter 10 : Cut-Off

After getting sick again, I climbed in the shower and watched as Tiffany's blood mixed with the water, turning it from bright red to pink before disappearing down the drain. The automatic shut-off kicked in after four minutes, the system's way of conserving water. I slid the handle back to "on"—I didn't feel anywhere near clean enough.

I'd never seen a baby born before, and I'd definitely never delivered a baby. It'd scared me. She'd been in a lot of pain, her body convulsing and face distorting from the force of it. What if something had gone wrong? There was no doctor, no medication, no hospital. Was this how it would be from now on—our only medical care coming from clueless teenagers following diagrams in books?

I thought of my parents, my friends. What kind of care were they receiving? Were they getting medication to keep them comfortable? Or were they suffering?

So many emotions bombarded me at once—I felt as if I'd suffocate under their force. There was too much to think about, too much to worry about. I slid down the white-tiled wall and cried as I watched the pink, bloody water circle down the drain. My tears disappeared in the shower spray. The shut-off kicked in again. I turned the water back on.

I heard David call to me, asking if I was okay. Still I cried. Katie knocked on the door and said Tiffany was asking for me. I sat in the shower and cried under the prickly spray until the water pressure dropped to a trickle and was so cold my teeth chattered. Unable to stand the cold, I heaved myself up from the floor, dried the tears from my face and took a deep breath.

I won't cry again. I'm one of the few lucky ones—no one said it'd be easy.

"Geez, I didn't think you'd ever get out of there. I gotta take a leak." Josh knocked me into the wall as he rushed into the bathroom.

"Excuse me," I muttered.

"What are you going to name her?" I'd pulled Katie's cot up next to Tiffany's, and I lay there watching the baby sleep between us. With her perfect little fingers wrapped around one of mine, I rubbed across her hand with my thumb. Her skin was so soft and pale, I could see little blue veins just underneath.

By the time I'd had my shower and dried my hair, Tiffany had already cleaned up the baby, dressed her in a tiny yellow onesie, changed her own clothes, and gotten George to put a sheet on the crib. Jai Li had finished changing the sheets on Tiffany's bed, so she was able to rest and recover without having to deal with all the grossness.

"I don't know. I have a few ideas, but I was sure she'd be a boy. I had a boy's name picked out. I was going to name her after my grandfather."

"So what are your favorite choices?"

"I was thinking…Evangelina Faith. That's my favorite. I think it's only fitting that she be named after the person who delivered her and, I hope, will be her godmother. As for Faith, we all need a little faith right now, so it seems appropriate."

I looked down at the baby's pudgy face. She was perfect. A little tuft of curly blonde hair, rosy cheeks—I could hear her soft sighs as she slept.

"I don't know what to say, Tiffany. Of course I'll be her godmother. But you really don't need to name her after me. I mean, wouldn't you rather name her after your mother or someone in your family?"

"Nah, my mom's name is Kitty. I'm just not feeling that. My grandmother's name is Maude. I was never going to name the baby after any of the women in my family, and her... father," she swallowed hard and her eyes glimmered. "His family wouldn't acknowledge her. They don't deserve any part of her," she said through clenched teeth.

I felt little Evangelina's body squirm. Her fingers tightened around mine and I heard her sucking in her sleep, her little pink lips moving in and out.

"You know she'll be in kindergarten before she can say her own name, right? Probably fifth grade before she can spell it." I smiled.

Tiffany laughed. "Yeah, it's a mouthful. I was thinking of calling her Faith."

I nodded. "She's beautiful."

"Thank you, Eva. For everything." She leaned over and kissed my cheek.

Month Five

Study. Sleep. Eat. Study some more. Repeat.

Sometimes we'd find time to actually do something fun, like play a videogame or watch a movie, but for the most part our books and computers—and the never-ending assignments—became our daily routine.

For our five-month anniversary in the POD, we'd decided to declare a "no study" day. We were going to make some popcorn and watch movies and play videogames all day long. They even were going to let me play again.

Tiffany lounged on the couch holding the baby, George next to her in a beanbag. I sat on the floor next to George, Katie on my other side. Everyone else flopped around the television on the chocolate-colored rug.

David walked into the living area from the hallway and looked around. His eyes fell on Katie. "Hey, kid, scoot over."

"Why? There's a whole room."

"Because I have dibs."

"Dibs? On what?"

"Eva. Now move."

Katie stood, stomped to an open beanbag, and plopped down so hard I thought it would burst, spewing whatever was inside across the room. David sat down next to me, stretching his long legs out in front of him. He folded his hands behind his head, propping them against the couch.

I tried really hard not to look at him. To keep my eyes from darting in his direction, I focused them on a small white piece of lint. It shone bright against the brown carpeting. I concentrated on the lint, telling my eyes not to look to my left. They didn't listen. I took a quick peek at him from under my lashes. He was looking at me and grinned.

I quickly looked away, wondering what he'd meant when he'd told Katie to move because he *had dibs* on me. I spent the entire first half of the movie dissecting what he'd said and done. The second half of the movie I spent worrying what I'd say or do when the movie was over. As it turned out, I didn't need to worry. As soon as the movie was over, the guys started playing a videogame, their little mini-me avatars running here and there on the screen. What they were supposed to do I still hadn't figured out.

Katie and I moved to the table. I was playing Tetris, the one videogame installed on the laptop I was actually pretty good at. Katie was videochatting with Cam again, something that happened several times a day.

Katie screamed.

I jumped up, knocking my chair over. "What's wrong?"

"Something's wrong with Cam!"

I went around the table to see. On the laptop screen, panicked people ran to the door of their POD. One guy fell to his knees; a girl my age covered her mouth with her hand. They grew silent, listening. I strained to hear…the crunching, crushing sounds.

"Cam?" David yelled. "What's going on?"

"I don't know," Cam came back to the screen. Tears ran down his stricken face. "There's a loud crunching outside. It sounds like it's in the corridor."

"Take the computer over there so we can hear," David said.

The picture on the screen bounced as Cam carried the computer to the door of the POD. At the first loud crack, I jumped, and Katie let out a little scream and grabbed my hand. It sounded like someone had let off a pack of firecrackers just inches from us.

"What is it?" I whispered.

David shook his head.

"Cam! What's happening?" Katie screamed, tears running down her face. The video picture froze. "Cam!"

"The air's stopped." His whisper came through a second before the picture started moving again.

"There's no water!" I heard a woman shriek in the background.

"They're cutting us off!" a boy cried.

The lights in their POD went out. The picture froze again, but we could still hear the cries of the people in the POD.

Katie sobbed Cam's name.

"Katie," Cam's voice quivered. "I'm scared."

The connection died.

My breath hitched in my throat. Tears stung behind my eyes; the lump in my throat made taking a breath hard.

"Cam!" Katie wailed. She threw herself at me and I hugged her close. "What happened, Eva?"

"I don't know."

David checked her computer, entering an online classroom with an active chat. It worked fine. He video-conferenced a friend in another POD. It worked fine. He clicked the icon to video-conference Cam. He got an error message—*contact not recognized*. He looked at me, his face grim as he came to my side.

"Sit down, Eva," David murmured in my ear. With a hand on the small of my back he guided Katie and me to the couch.

I sat next to Tiffany as she clutched her baby to her chest, her face pale. Katie leaned against me. I put my arm around her, stroking her hair as she cried. "What happened, Eva?"

"I don't know, sweetie."

David typed furiously, his brow furrowed. Then he leaned back and stared at the screen for a moment before getting up and walking away from the computer.

"What happened?" I looked at David. "They shut off that POD, didn't they?" In my head I could still hear the metal crunching as the tunnel that led from the main POD to the sub-POD was crushed. I could still see the fear on Cam's face, hear the screaming and crying of the other residents.

Without power from the main POD, the sub-PODs had no air, electricity, or water. Too far underground to dig their way out—especially with the access tunnel crushed—they'd slowly lose oxygen and suffocate. Or maybe they'd die from dehydration first. It didn't matter. The people in that POD had just lost their lifeline…and with it, their lives.

"They must have broken a rule…"

"Shut up, Josh! Those are *people*. It could've been us." I snapped. *What an ass.*

"But it wasn't," David said, his voice soothing.

"What's the big deal? We didn't know those people," Josh said, still playing his videogame.

"I knew them," Katie whispered, tears and mucus running down her face.

I turned toward Josh, furious. "But it could have been us. It could be the next time. Who here is up to date with their coursework?" No one answered, and I got louder. "Well, if you aren't current with your assignments, you damn well better get off your rears and get working on them! We can't give the main POD *any* reason to shut us off. From now on, we stay current on our coursework, we don't complain about our MREs, even if we get the nasty spaghetti three nights in a row, and we keep kissing their lily-white butts until we can get out of here."

"Eva—"

"That includes you, David. I *know* you aren't current in your coursework."

So instead of relaxing, we spent our five-month anniversary in the POD doing homework and saying prayers for the poor people in Cam's POD. They would have been better off staying topside—at least a person infected with the virus died quickly. The same couldn't be said about slow suffocation in the dark—buried alive.

David sat at the end of my bed, the same spot he occupied every night after dinner. I looked at him. His brow was furrowed and he bit his lower lip. He always looked that way when he was concentrating.

"It isn't the schoolwork, you know," he said quietly.

"What?"

"The reason they shut off that POD. It wasn't because of the schoolwork. It didn't matter if they had all their assignments uploaded on time. It didn't matter if they'd followed the water usage limits. It had nothing to do with any of that." He turned and looked at me, his face grim.

"Okay, then what?"

"The blood tests."

"What about them?" I sighed in frustration.

"One—or all—of them…tested positive for the virus. It's marked in one of the databases I found. Cam and at least two of the others in his POD had been classified 'Exposed.'"

I slowly crawled off my bed and closed the bedroom door. I shoved the books out of the way and sat down next to him.

"What do you mean? Surely they aren't still testing for that. I thought part of the blood tests were for nutrition," I whispered.

"They don't know how long the virus can lay dormant before the carrier shows symptoms. You know that. They knew squat about it."

He reached out and twirled a lock of my hair around his finger before sliding it behind my ear, making me shiver in response. His hand skimmed my cheek, his eyes following it. The pad of his thumb ran over my lips, and they parted slightly, a sigh escaping between them. His hand fell away and his eyes looked into mine.

"Eva—"

"We really need to get to work. I have a lot to do before I'm done." I'm not sure how I kept my voice from quivering. My insides were—they had melted when he touched me, and I couldn't remember why a romance in the POD wouldn't be a good thing. When he touched me, when I smelled him, when I looked into his silvery gray eyes, I forgot all the reasons we shouldn't be together.

"Yeah, I have a lot to do, too," he said, frowning.

"David? Should we tell the others?"

"George, Seth, and Aidan already figured it out. I don't know about Jai Li and Josh. If Tiffany and Katie don't know already I wouldn't tell them. It would upset Katie even more, and Tiff doesn't need the added stress worrying would cause. She has enough to worry about with the baby."

I nodded, but it felt wrong not to be upfront with each other. I wouldn't want them hiding information from me if the situation were reversed.

David and I finished our work and went into the kitchen area. We sat next to each other at the table, looking at a crossword, our heads so close I could smell his minty breath. Katie laid her hand on my arm. Her eyes were red and swollen, and she was still making little hiccup cries.

"Do you really think someone got kicked off because they were late on their coursework?" Katie asked me.

My eyes darted to David before I answered. I didn't want to lie to her, so I said, "I don't know. But we all should make sure ours are done by the due dates." I smiled, trying to reassure her.

"Mine's done." She turned and shuffled into the corner she'd occupied for the first few weeks of living in the POD. For the next week, she drew, worked on her coursework, and cried. She didn't speak. She didn't acknowledge us.

Chapter 11 : More

I bolted upright in bed. The bed sheets were tangled around my feet, my white and brown comforter kicked to the floor. Another nightmare—I'd been having them since Cam's POD had been shut off two weeks ago. Most nights I saw the faces of the people, that horrible moment when they realized what was happening and began to scream, but sometimes I dreamed our POD had been shut off.

I slipped a sweatshirt over my head and padded down the hall to the living area. I turned the corner and my breath hitched in my throat. David sat in front of his laptop at the kitchen table, his back facing me—his well-defined, muscular and very naked back. I felt a million butterflies swarm in my stomach.

Surely it's illegal for him to look that good.

I took a big lungful of air and walked toward him. "What are you doing up so early? Or haven't you been to bed yet?" I asked, groaning inwardly when I got close enough that I could smell him—patchouli and citrus.

Is he torturing me on purpose?

I was close enough to touch him. I fisted my hands at my sides to keep my fingers from reaching out and trailing along his back muscles. My fingers had little minds of their own and it was a fight keeping them under control, mainly because

I wanted them to glide against his skin…to feel the muscles beneath…

Oh, gads, I'm a train wreck!

He flinched at the sound of my voice, snapping his laptop shut. Looking over his shoulder, he smiled. "You look beautiful in the morning, Eva. Your blonde hair messy and falling around your face, your eyes—not quite blue, but not quite green—sparkling in the morning sun…or the simulation of the sun," he said with a crooked grin.

"Stop joking around. What were you just looking at?" I'd seen the picture on his laptop before he'd shut it. People running around their POD, a look of terror in their eyes. I reached out and opened the lid of his computer. My arm brushed against his, sending goosebumps racing across my skin. I had to concentrate to remember what I was asking about.

The screen was nothing but static. "They cut off another one? Who?"

I let go of his computer and started to pull my hand away. He grabbed it, folding it into his own, threading our fingers together. He grazed his lips over my knuckles.

Oh. Wow. Do that again.

My insides swirled out of place and did things I'd only read about in my mother's racy romance novels.

"Yes. Someone I know from class. You don't know him. And who says I'm joking?"

"What?" He was difficult to understand on a good day, but that early in the morning, seeing him in nothing more than blue pajama bottoms, his lips moving against my fingers as he talked, it was nearly impossible.

"You told me to stop joking around. I wasn't joking."

My heart was beating so hard and fast in my chest, I was sure he could hear it.

I pinched the bridge of my nose between my fingers. My fingernails bit into my flesh.

Say something, Eva! Do Something—anything. Just…something.

"So…" I started, only to be interrupted by my yawn. *Except yawn, idiot! Kiss him…wait…what?* "What's your theory on the

PODs being cut off? Do you think there's that many people testing positive for the—"

He stood, turned toward me, cupped his hand around the back of my neck and pulled my lips to his. That shut me up. Shock slammed into me, quickly giving way to pleasure, and pleasure to urgency.

I wrapped my arms around his neck, threading my fingers through his silky hair. David's hand moved from the back of my neck to cup my cheek, his thumb caressing my skin. The other one moved to the small of my back, pulling me tighter against him.

He kissed me long, deep. It was sinfully erotic feeling his bare skin under my fingers. When he tore his lips away, he looked in my eyes. My first instinct was to turn away, but both his hands cupped my cheeks. He bent his head and grazed his lips over mine before looking at me again.

"I've wanted to do that since the first day I saw you. And each day I've known you it's been harder and harder not to."

"Well, what took you so long?"

He laughed before dipping his head again, leisurely exploring my mouth and lips with his tongue. I moaned when it darted quickly between my lips; his answering groan made me feel sexy, womanly. He wanted me as much as I wanted him.

He put his hands on my shoulders and pushed me away, taking a step backward. "Eva, I...we can't."

Disappointment smacked me, and I took a step back. Embarrassment heated my cheeks and I took a deep breath before I looked up at him. My hands shook as I reached up to put my hair behind my ear.

"Yeah...um...we shouldn't. A romance in the POD is a horrible idea. If it went south we'd be stuck looking at each other every day. It isn't a good idea," I shook my head. "No. Not a good idea." I said what the rational side of my brain told me to. It wasn't a good idea to get involved while we were living in the POD. Afterward, if he was interested, I'd be all for it. Well, truth be told, I was all for it now.

"Uh, that isn't what I was going to say."

"Then what?"

"No, you're right. A POD romance is a horrible idea."

My heart sank. I don't know why. He was just repeating what I'd said. He was agreeing with me. Why did it disappoint me?

"What are you two yapping about out here?" Seth walked out of the bedroom rubbing his eyes. "You're gonna wake the whole POD up."

"They cut off another POD," I said, thankful for the distraction.

"Huh. That makes three that we know of."

"Three?" I turned to David. "When was number two?"

"The day before yesterday."

"And you didn't tell anyone? Don't you think we all need to know?"

"Aidan and Seth know because they were online when someone mentioned it. We didn't say anything to anyone else because I was hoping it would be the last and we wouldn't have to worry about it happening again."

"And those are just the ones we've heard about. Hard telling how many others may have been let loose," Seth added.

I groaned at the thought. At least three sub-PODs gone, the people left to die agonizing, terrifying deaths.

"I can't believe you didn't tell us, David." I said through clenched teeth before walking down the hall to my bedroom.

"Eva, wait," he called after me just before I heard him snap, "Idiot," at Seth.

I closed the bedroom door with a soft click, shutting him out, and leaned my back against it.

What next? We've already dealt with the loss of our families, our friends, and our old lives. After dealing with quarantine, being sealed in a small space with a bunch of strangers, and being told what jobs we'd be doing for the rest of our lives, now we have to worry about this? We feared the virus, but now we also have to fear the very thing that was supposed to save us from it.

"Eva," he whispered outside the bedroom door. "I'm sorry. Please, come out."

He's another thing that's changed. From an awkward friendship, to a one-sided attraction, to a mind-numbing first kiss…and now, all I feel is anger. Anger that he's hiding things from the POD, from me.

"Eva? Please."

I reached for the doorknob. My hand hesitated over it. The fingers of my other hand rested on my bottom lip, which was still sensitive from his kiss…wanting more.

What will happen if I open the door? Will he kiss me again? Do I want him to now that I know he hid information from me—from the entire POD?

I dropped my hand and turned from the door, climbing into bed.

Month Six

"I hate Scrabble," I said with a grimace.

"You're an English genius." I snorted a laugh when George said the word 'genius.' "You must kill at Scrabble."

"Nope, I can't spell to save my life."

"Then how do you do so well in English?"

"Spellcheck. If I hadn't had spellcheck I would've failed. Besides, well, Scrabble was the last game I played with my parents. We had pizza and played Scrabble the night before I left. It's…it's a reminder of them. I remember the good times, like the laughter and teasing that night. But I also remember the horrible parts, like…like watching my parents get smaller and smaller through the dirty windows of the bus as it drove away. It's odd how things can change so drastically in just a day."

Tiffany laid her hand on my arm, giving it a light squeeze. She smiled sadly.

Josh sighed and rolled his eyes. "Oh, please. Stop your freakin' whining."

"Don't pay attention to him, Eva," Aidan said. "We all know how messed up things can get in just a day."

Katie picked up the Scrabble board, placed it in its box, and then stood on tiptoe to place the box on the top shelf, out of sight. "Boggle?" she asked quietly.

"Yeah, Boggle sounds great," I whispered.

David walked toward the table, and I said a little prayer that he'd keep walking. I never had been very lucky. "Do you need a fourth?"

"Sure, Dav——"

"Nope. Boggle doesn't require teams. The three of us are just fine. Thank you very much."

Tiffany's eyebrows rose at my tone. Katie, who'd been grabbing a pen and paper for David, froze and looked at me.

"Eva, can I talk with you for a minute?"

"I'm busy."

"Tiffany and Katie won't mind. They can play a game while we're talking."

"I don't mind," Tiffany agreed with a smirk. I kicked her under the table. I hadn't told her about David's kiss, but she'd guessed.

"Fine." I tromped down the hall toward our bedroom, where I could yell at him without the whole POD hearing. He followed close behind.

Halfway down the hall he reached out and grabbed my wrist, jerking me to a stop. I whirled around to face him. His free hand grabbed my other wrist, holding my hands above my head, pinning them to the wall behind me. He leaned forward and kissed me hard, his tongue gliding between my lips.

I turned my head—intending to yell, tell him all the reasons we shouldn't do what we were doing, all the reasons I didn't want to—but his lips followed mine and, instead of telling him all the things I'd rehearsed, I kissed him back.

He let go of my wrists, but kept his hands against the wall on either side of me. I knew I could push him away if I wanted. My brain told me I should leave. His kiss told me to stay. Instead of pushing him away, my hands gripped his shirt and pulled him to me.

He groaned deep in his throat when I sighed in pleasure. I wrapped one hand in his shirt and threaded the other one into his hair. He let his hands drop from the wall to frame my face.

"Oh!" Jai Li gasped.

Startled, I tried to pull away from David, but he wrapped his arm around my waist and held me to him.

"Kiss," she said in her heavy accent.

"Yes, Jai Li, 'kiss,'" I whispered. My breathing was heavy and I felt my heart beating a staccato against my ribs.

"Love." She grinned.

I opened my mouth to answer. I'm not sure exactly what I would've said.

David answered before I had a chance. "Yes." He looked into my eyes, his thumb moving gently over my bottom lip. "I think it is."

I forgot how to breathe. "I—"

"Goodbye," Jai Li said. I'd forgotten she was there. "Kiss, kiss," she said, waving her hands, telling us to finish what she'd interrupted.

"David—"

"Don't. Don't say anything. I don't want you to say it until you know for sure. Just because I said it—well, Jai Li said it for me," he chuckled, "doesn't mean I want you to say it back to be polite. And I definitely don't want to hear you deny it."

The room seemed to tilt to one side and then the other, like I'd been twirling around in circles and was dizzy. I opened my mouth to say something, but couldn't seem to put a coherent thought together.

Did David just tell me he loves me? He loves me? David…loves me. David, Greek-god handsome…no…underwear-model sexy…no…Greek-god underwear-model sexy David loves me. Oh wow. There is going to be so much kissing!

A warmth started building in my chest and spread throughout my body; even though I was warm, my skin was covered in goosebumps.

I had to concentrate on what David was saying, "I know what you said about a relationship down here not being a good idea—"

Yeah, I take that all back. I think a relationship down here is a great idea.

"—and you're probably right. But I don't give a damn about the POD. I don't care where we are or where we end up. I just want you to be mine. I don't want to wait until we're out of here."

My heart twirled and did a nosedive into my toes before springing back into place. I could hardly breathe. I had to remind myself how. I pulled him to me and kissed him slowly, exploring his mouth, tracing his lips with the tip of my tongue, losing myself in his taste, in his smell. Our lips never leaving each other's, we stumbled into the bedroom. David kicked the door closed with his foot before we fell across my bed. I lifted his pullover, running my fingers over his bare skin. He ground out a curse between his teeth. He unbuttoned my shirt, his fingers shaking so violently he ripped the last two open. He skimmed the tips of his fingers over my skin, dipping just below the lacy edges of my bra. I shivered and felt more warmth growing in the pit of my stomach.

"Eva," he whispered and rolled over on his back next to me. He threw his arm over his eyes.

"I know. We aren't alone."

"No, we aren't." He let out a long breath. Standing, he opened the drawer under my bed and pulled out the purple hoodie. "Here, put this on. You can't go out there with two buttons torn off your shirt. It looks like something you'd read about in a racy romance novel. The bodice-ripping rogue out to defile the innocent damsel...or something like that," he said, laughing.

"Okay, bodice-ripper, but that's not what I want." I smiled and took the hoodie from him. I threw it back in the drawer and pulled my shirt closed, covering myself. Crossing to his bedroom, I opened the drawer under his bunk.

"What are you doing?"

I pulled out his U of M sweatshirt. I pushed the shirt I was wearing off my shoulders and let it pool around me on the bed. David cleared his throat and turned his back to me.

"What?"

"I'm just…giving you some privacy." His voice sounded strained.

"David, two minutes ago you had your hands all over me. Seeing me slip out of one shirt and into another isn't a big deal."

"Yeah, well, you aren't a guy. We're not good at window shopping. If I can't have it, I don't want to torture myself by looking at it."

I laughed.

"I like that."

"What?" I asked.

"The sound of your laugh."

I smiled at him. I didn't know what to say in response. Did I tell him I liked that he liked my laugh?

"I like that, too."

I blew out a breath. "What?"

"When I compliment you your face turns red. You don't try to act shy and timid. You don't have to—your face shows me. You don't act coy or play hard to get. Your racing heart tells me everything I need to know. And I love how you look wearing my favorite sweatshirt," he said, grabbing the front and pulling me to him. "You realize if you go out there wearing that it'll be like you're wearing a neon sign. Everyone will know, Eva."

"I think they already do. And…I want them to know. I don't want to wait, either. POD or no POD, I want to be with you."

He smiled his crooked smile and nodded once. He took my hand in his and we walked back into the main living area. Seth and Aidan didn't pay any attention to us. They were involved in a battle of galactic proportions on some videogame. George looked up from his packet of schoolwork. He raised one pierced eyebrow, but didn't say anything. Everyone was quiet, politely giving us our privacy…except Katie.

"What were you guys doing? You took so long."

"Just talking," I said.

"Then why do you have David's shirt on?" she asked.

I shrugged. "I was cold."

David coughed to hide his laughter. We both knew I was far from cold.

Josh gave us a scathing look.

Chapter 12 :
Josh

Month Seven

"Do you two have to do that now?" Josh snapped. He glared at us over the screen of his laptop.

David and I were each walking on treadmills, talking and laughing. By that point, we were eating together, doing homework together, exercising together. He even tolerated playing Wii Bowling with me. *Inseparable.*

"What?" David asked.

"Giggle like that. You sound ridiculous, and the treadmills squeak."

"Are we bothering you, George?" David called.

George sat in his beanbag in the corner of the room studying. "Not bothering me."

"You're the only one with a problem, Josh. Besides, you're just sitting there making a nuisance of yourself online. You can go in the other room and do that." David didn't look at him.

Tiffany came in, the baby in her arms. "Hey, has anyone heard anything about the villages?"

"No, what—" I took a breath. "What about them?" Trying to keep up with David's pace was making me winded. David hadn't even broken a sweat.

"There's a rumor online that the government is setting up villages throughout the country; when we get out of here we'll be assigned to villages."

"I haven't heard anything, Tiff. I thought we'd all be in one area." I lowered the setting on my treadmill to extra, extra slow.

"Geez, you people are stupid. Of course they'll be separating people into villages," Josh snapped.

I took another deep breath. "I hate to ask you this, but why?"

Josh huffed and rolled his eyes. "They have to make villages near resources. The resources we need aren't all in one area. We'll need to disperse and set up communities according to the resources available."

"There aren't that many of us. They can't spread us out too much." Tiffany bounced baby Faith on her shoulder.

"They'll do whatever they want to."

I frowned. Josh had a point. We were at the mercy of the government.

"Now take your lovebird crap to another room; you're making me sick." He flicked his hand toward David and me.

"Stop eating in the living area, Josh! Geez, you're a slob. Look at the crumbs you're getting everywhere," Tiffany said.

"Well you're a—"

George turned a page in his textbook, not looking up. "Choose your next words *very* carefully."

"Whatever," Josh took another huge bite, intentionally dribbling bits of food. Crumbs landed on his t-shirt and the strip of hairy belly that was exposed where it rode up. I shook my head. If anyone needed to be on the treadmill, it was Josh.

"Where'd you hear about the villages, Tiffany?" I asked.

"Oh, people online are talking about it."

"Well, there are about seventy thousand survivors in the POD system. If they made one village in every state, that would only be villages of roughly...um," I tried to figure out the math.

"Fourteen hundred people, give or take a few," David said, working through the problem in his head. He bumped up the speed on his treadmill to a jog.

"Show-off," I said, smiling.

He shrugged and grinned at me.

"Ick," Josh scowled as he stomped to the bedroom.

"Great. Now we'll have crumbs all over our carpeting," George muttered.

David laughed. "Small communities," he said.

"Yeah, I doubt they'll spread us out at all, but if they do they'll keep the communities large enough to sustain themselves." I switched off my treadmill and stepped down.

"I guess we'll find out in a few months," Tiffany said, patting Faith's back and going back into the bedroom.

Month Eight

I was folding laundry in the bedroom when I heard someone behind me. I turned and groaned.

"What do you want, Josh?"

He didn't answer as he came toward me, his face hard. I took a step back, bumping into the wall behind me.

Grabbing me by the wrist, he leaned his face so close to me I could smell his ever-present body odor and see the flecks of dandruff in his hair. I wrinkled my nose, trying to block out the offending stench.

"What are you doing?" I shook his hand off my wrist. He placed his hands on the wall on either side of my face.

"I didn't think you wanted a POD romance, Eva."

"I didn't."

"And David?"

"Is none of your business." I tried to push past him. He leaned in closer.

"Does David share?" he whispered.

"What?"

He leaned his head forward, tilting it, lowering his lips toward mine. I clamped my lips together and put my hand over my mouth, as I pushed off the wall and tried to duck under his arm. He grabbed me around the waist. *Not even if Josh were the last guy on Earth...*

"What's going on?" David's voice came from behind Josh.

Josh flinched. "A misunderstanding," he said with a shrug. "Isn't that right, Eva?"

I looked into Josh's pale blue eyes and wanted nothing more than to give David permission to hit Josh—I knew that's what he was waiting for. But I didn't.

"Yeah. A big misunderstanding."

"You're sure?" David looked at me, his brows raised in question. I nodded. "Let's make sure it doesn't happen again, or the outcome may be different." David slapped Josh on the back and smiled.

"Most definitely." Josh left the room.

"Why'd you lie for him, Eva?" David asked, turning toward me and looking annoyed.

"Fighting won't do any good with him, David. Besides, nothing happened. He's all talk. I'm going to take a quick shower. Don't do anything—I'm fine. I don't want you going out there and starting anything while I'm in the shower. Promise me."

He nodded.

I only used my allotted four minutes of showering water, but it never got more than lukewarm. I dried off and slipped into a pair of sweatpants and a t-shirt. David was leaning against the wall across from the bathroom when I opened the door.

"Have you been standing there the entire time?"

"Mm-hmm. You told me not to go out there."

I laughed. "That isn't exactly what I said, David." He pushed off the wall and guided me backward until we were both standing in the bathroom. Reaching behind him, he closed and locked the door. He never took his eyes off my face.

He dipped his head and kissed me, rubbing his hands up and down my arms. "You're freezing. You need to warm up. Sit down."

I sat at the little counter wedged between the linen closet and the bathtub. It looked like it had been put there as an afterthought. David plugged the hair dryer into the socket. He made a face, turning the dryer around, looking for the power switch.

"It's on the bottom of the handle."

He smiled. "I knew that. I was just making sure you were paying attention. How do you do this? Do you brush and dry, or just blow it around?"

I laughed. "Give it here, I'll do it." I reached for the hair dryer, and he lifted it over his head.

"No."

I stared at him before shrugging. "Okay…just brush it straight and dry it."

He flipped the power on and ran the brush through my hair, blowing the warm air across it. I watched him in the mirror. His brow was furrowed, the same look he made when he was really concentrating on his coursework or on his art. He worked slowly, brushing my hair with gentle strokes. I closed my eyes and let the feeling relax me. I was disappointed when I realized I needed him to stop.

Standing up, I pulled the plug out of the wall. Looking at him in the mirror, I shook my head, trying to find the words to express the feelings, physical and emotional, I had. I wasn't sure what they meant, so how was I supposed to communicate them to him?

"David, I…"

He took me by the shoulders and turned me around to face him. He lowered his lips, moving them over mine. Dropping the hair dryer on the floor, he reached around my waist and lifted me on top of the vanity, our lips never leaving one another's.

Our breathing increased. I could feel his heart hammering against his chest, and a small portion of my brain gloated that his physical response to me was as great as mine to him.

I pushed my hands under his shirt, running my fingernails across his skin. He grabbed the hem of my t-shirt and pulled it up—and I pushed it down, jerking away.

"David, I can't."

He didn't answer. His hands gripped the counter on either side of me. His head bowed. "I'm sorry. I didn't mean—"

"Don't say that." Tears pressed the back of my eyes, pushing their way out. One ran down my cheek. I swiped it away angrily. I didn't want to cry.

"What?"

"Don't say you're sorry. Think it, but please don't say it. I'm not."

"Geez, Eva. Can't you see? I'm not sorry about that. I'm sorry our living arrangement isn't different. That I can't take you out on a real date. Instead, I maul you in the bathroom." He ran his hand down his face in frustration. "I'm not sorry I kissed you."

"Are you guys coming out or what? It's the only bathroom in this thing, you know," Aidan yelled outside the door.

I smiled. David groaned.

David opened the door and elbowed Aidan in the ribs. "You're a moron."

"What? I have to go." Aidan smirked as he closed the door behind him.

David sat on my bed, his back against the headboard, his legs stretched out in front of him. I was lying sideways, curled up with my head in his lap as he twirled a lock of my hair around one of his fingers. The feeling sent jolts of electricity through my body.

"So where'd you learn how to blow-dry a girl's hair? Oh, wait. If this is an ex-girlfriend story, I don't want to know," I teased.

"No, I've never dried a girlfriend's hair until tonight."

Girlfriend? I guess I am. I'm David's girlfriend. He's my boyfriend. Yeah, I like the sound of that.

The thought made me extraordinarily happy, and I had to push down the giggle I felt bubbling up. "So? Where'd you learn it?"

"I have two younger sisters. Eight and six. I dried their hair sometimes to help my mom out."

"I'm sorry, David. I shouldn't have pried."

What's it like to have a sister? Six years old—she's just a baby! It must have been hell for him to leave them.

"It's okay. We've all lost people we love. It's better to talk about it than bottle it up, don't you think? I mean, mourning can only go on so long before it eats you up. We all need to focus on the happy times. At least that's what I keep telling myself."

"Yeah, that's what I tell myself, too. What—"

"Emily and Hannah."

"Pretty names."

"What about you?"

"I don't have any brothers or sisters. It was just me and my parents."

I always wanted a brother or sister. I'm glad now I don't have one—it's one less person to leave behind.

"And does thinking about the good memories help?"

"Not yet," I admitted.

I wish it did.

"Me, neither."

Chapter 13 : Electricity

Month Nine

"You want to go on a picnic?" David asked me.

"Yes. Can you break us out of here?"

"No, but I can manage a picnic, and maybe even some alone time." He grabbed the quilt off his bed.

Threading his fingers through mine, he pulled me behind him to the storage room, where he pulled his wet clothes out of the washer and stuffed them into the dryer before turning it on.

"I didn't know we were doing laundry," I teased.

He gave me a smile. "Hush."

David turned on the washer, stuffed it full of clothes, and dumped detergent in the tub.

What the heck is he doing?

Then he spread his quilt on the floor, grabbed our MREs off the shelf and laid them on the blanket with two bottles of water. After shoving the rubber doorstop under the door— making it next to impossible for anyone to push it open from the other side—he plopped down on the quilt and looked at me expectantly.

"Sit down, Eva." He patted a spot next to him.

"Okay." I lowered myself down next to him and watched him open our MREs, laying them out in front of us on the quilt like a gourmet feast.

"There. How's this?"

"As far as picnics go? It's definitely a first for me."

"Yeah, the laundry area probably isn't the most romantic place to have a picnic, but it has three things that make it the best room in the house…or POD, whatever."

"And what are they?"

"First, it's my laundry day, so no one will be in here. Second, the washer and dryer drown out the noise of the others, so we can talk without them interrupting or hearing everything we say."

"And the third?" I asked.

"You're here."

Heat crept across my face. It felt like I had a thousand butterflies flying in my stomach.

"You're blushing." David turned toward me, putting one leg over mine until he was on all fours above my legs. Looking in my eyes, he tilted his head and kissed me slowly. I closed my eyes and let myself get lost in his kiss. I wrapped my arms around his neck. Leaning back, I pulled him down with me.

Pulling his shirt over his head, I whispered, "Shouldn't you wash this?" Then, I flicked open the button on his jeans, slipping my fingers just inside the waistband. "And these?" I sucked in a sharp breath when he kissed behind my ear, sending shockwaves of pleasure through my body.

"Eva," he murmured in my ear, his breath making my hair flutter against my skin. "Don't tempt me."

"I think you're the one tempting me. You brought me in here, blocked the door, turned on the white-noise machinery. Why was that? Just to eat?" I teased him with a grin.

He rolled off me and threw his arm over his eyes. I scooted down and moved his arm around me. We lay on our backs on the floor, looking at the ceiling.

"You ever think of what things would be like without the virus?" he asked.

"A lot. Why?"

"If the virus hadn't hit we might never have met."

"I know," I said, running my fingers through his hair.

"If there's one good thing that comes from this whole thing, it's that I met you, Eva."

I rose on my elbow and kissed him. "I feel the same way."

"I'm glad we're together."

"Me, too." I kissed him again. *Will I ever get my fill of his kisses? Each one feels like the first, curls my toes, and makes my insides melt.*

The lights went out. From the living area, we heard Katie scream. George, Aidan and Seth talked over each other, their voices growing more and more frantic as the seconds ticked by.

Cold fear stabbed through me, and I gasped. *They're cutting us off!* "David?"

"I don't know," he said.

We got up and felt our way out of the laundry room. Without any windows the inside of the POD was pitch-black. I wasn't particularly claustrophobic, but the dark felt like it was bearing down on me, making it hard to breathe.

We'd lost electricity in the entire POD. *Buried alive.* I clutched David's hand tighter, feeling him squeeze back.

The baby cried from somewhere in the POD. I could hear Tiffany trying to soothe her.

"George?" Tiffany called.

"Stay there, Tiff." He bumped into me trying to find his way through the blackness. "Sorry."

The baby and Katie kept crying—I wanted to join them.

Katie was hysterical. "They're cutting us off!"

"No—" I started, feeling my way around the furniture to where I heard her voice. With every hesitant step, I listened for the sound we all dreaded, the crunch that sealed the passage...

"Yes! They are! This is what happened to Cam! The lights went out, and then he was gone. We're gonna die!"

"No, Katie." She jumped when my hand found her arm. I leaned down to put my face somewhere near hers. "Listen! There are no sounds outside. If they were cutting us off, we'd hear it. Remember how loud it was? We'd hear it. They aren't cutting us off. There's just a problem with the electricity."

"There wasn't anything like this scheduled," David whispered in my ear.

I held Katie's hand as we made our way to our bedroom. I grabbed my laptop off my bed. Seeing the light cast by the screen made it a little easier to breathe.

"I have two flashlights in my bunk," I said.

After aiming my laptop at my headboard cabinet, we found my flashlights and the stash of batteries.

Thank you, Dad! You'll never know how much we needed these flashlights.

We found two more flashlights in the storage closet. We set one of the lights up in the living area, where we gathered close and cast anxious glances at the sealed door, still listening for the sound that would mean our deaths.

We heard nothing.

"So, what's going on? Did we blow a fuse?" Tiffany asked.

"There's no fuse box in here," Josh said.

David put his arm around me.

Josh gave the arm a pointed look, and then rolled his eyes. "Then what?"

"How the hell am I supposed to know?" he snapped.

"Don't start right now. We don't need you being…snappish." Tiffany said.

"Maybe I can find the electrical panel." Josh grabbed the flashlight off the table. I snapped another one on to take its place.

"It must be behind the cupboards. That's where the conduit enters the POD," Seth pointed into the dark toward the kitchen.

Josh scoffed. "No kidding."

Seth groaned. "Can I punch him now?"

David chuckled. "He's the electronics whiz. Let him fix the electricity first, and then have at it."

"You know, you two idiots can do this yourselves," Josh said, climbing on a chair to peer into the upper cabinets.

"Yeah, because we're the only ones who use the electricity. You don't use any. Ass."

"David…" I shook my head.

A metallic bang from the kitchen made us all jump. "Found it. I need something I can use as a screwdriver."

"What about a screwdriver?" Aidan asked with a grin. He held up a small toolbox. "This was in the storage room."

Aidan opened the box, lifting out a hammer, plumber's putty, and a small container filled with a variety of nails and screws as he rummaged. "Flathead or Phillips?" he asked.

"Flat."

Josh snatched the tool from his hand without so much as a *thank you*. We all seemed to stop breathing as he undid what he assumed was the box where the electricity came into the POD. *Hmm—maybe he'll electrocute himself and we won't have to deal with him anymore.*

Shame on you, Eva.

"Eva," Josh called, and I winced.

"What?" David answered for me.

"I need someone to look in the toolbox and see if there are any wire caps and electrical tape."

"Here," David said, passing the items to Josh.

He worked for what seemed like an eternity. Drops of sweat slithered down my back. I jumped at every little noise, waiting for the crunching sound. The longer we waited, the more convinced I became Katie was right, that our POD had been cut off. My stomach twisted and I had to take deep, cleansing breaths to keep from becoming as hysterical as Katie.

I moved to the sink and turned on the tap, taking a shuddering breath when the water came out. *The air supply is still flowing. The water system is still on. They didn't cut us off; it's just a glitch in one part of the system, a fluke.*

As long as the water and air flow remained, I could convince myself we were safe—that we weren't going to die a horrible, agonizing death.

The lights flickered on and we all sighed, only for them to go out again. That happened two more times before the lights came on and stayed on. Josh eased himself down from the cupboard and jumped off the chair.

"It was just some loose wiring. Probably made in China or wherever she's from," he said, jerking his thumb toward Jai Li.

"You're a jerk," I said.

"Probably made in America," Jai Li said with an evil grin. Everyone laughed—except Josh.

Josh sneered. "Well, I'd say you guys all owe me. I'll take everyone's allotted microwave popcorn this week."

"Wait! We *owe* you?" Aidan asked. "How do you figure?"

Josh shrugged. "You'd be sitting in the dark if it wasn't for me."

"No one owes you squat," Seth said. "If you hadn't fixed it, you'd be sitting in the dark with the rest of us. I'd say fixing it benefitted you as much as it did us. Get over yourself."

"And you're not getting my popcorn," Katie said, walking into the bedroom.

"Brat," Josh called after her. She flipped him the bird. I had to cover my mouth to stifle a laugh.

Month Ten

My eyelids felt heavy, like someone was pressing them down, and gritty sand was rough behind my eyes. But I didn't want to go to sleep, not yet. I wanted to talk to David. We stayed up as late as we could and talked every night. We sometimes fell asleep together in the living area. Of course, "sleeping together" meant actual sleeping. It wasn't a cute euphemism for something else—we weren't alone in the POD.

Some nights we talked about silly things.

"Favorite color?"

"Red, you?"

"Black."

"David, black isn't a color."

"Technically—"

"Okay, sorry I said anything. Um, favorite movie?"

"*The Exorcist.* Spinning heads get me every time. You?"

"I don't think I have one."

"You have to have a favorite movie—"

"If black can be your favorite color, then I don't have a favorite movie. First kiss?"

He grinned. "Ah, a gentleman would never kiss and tell."

"You don't remember her name, do you?"

"Okay, I don't remember her name. It was the fourth grade! You?"

"You don't really want to know who my first kiss was. You just want me to tell you you're the best I've had."

"Of course."

And other nights we talked about serious things, some sad and some happy.

"What did you plan to do after graduation, before the virus?"

"College. I was hoping to figure out the next step while I was there," I admitted. "You?"

"Veterinarian."

"David? Do you think anyone survived?"

"I don't know. But if my family survived, I can't wait for them to meet you. They'll love you."

"Mine, too."

We never ran out of things to ask or tell each other. It was my favorite time of day—the only time David and I had any semblance of "alone time."

When we couldn't keep our eyes open any longer, we'd fall asleep, usually with me on the couch and David on the floor next to me.

"I didn't think you'd ever wake up!" Katie squealed when I opened my eyes one morning.

"What's wrong?" I asked around a yawn.

"Nothing. It's all right. Look!"

She pointed to the wall to the left of the couch, which held one of the few remaining white spots left in the POD. Since the day we'd first started filling them with paintings and pastel drawings we had added a little at a time, and the walls were almost covered.

Someone had added another picture on the wall to the left of the sofa. I looked at it. Then I looked some more. It was done in red and black—flowers and hearts intertwined in a circle, with words in the center. My gaze locked on the words. Did he really draw that? Does he really feel so strongly that he'd put it there for everyone to see?

"He did it while you were sleeping. When I got up he was painting it." Katie bounced with excitement.

"Where is he?"

"Shower. Isn't the painting wonderful? I hope I find someone as romantic as he is. You're lucky, Eva."

"I know." I smiled, still looking at the newest artwork on the POD wall.

"You like it?" he asked quietly from the doorway.

"Yes."

"It isn't too much?"

"Well, I guess some might think it's a little over the top. I happen to think it's just what the wall needed." I stood and walked to him. I threaded my fingers through his hair, still wet from the shower. Our lips touched, just grazing each other's. "Thank you."

"Anything for you, Eva."

"And if I said I wanted you?"

"I'd say '*silly Evangelina, you already have me,*'" he answered, tickling my lips when his moved against them.

"Oh. My. Gosh. Get a room, would ya?" Seth headed into the kitchen, smirking.

Josh brushed past us, filling the room with the scent of the unwashed. "You've got to be kidding me! *'David loves Eva.'* Who wrote that crap on the wall? We know, we know—you're in love. We don't need to read about it. Now that's all I'm gonna see when I eat."

"Then find somewhere else to eat," I snapped.

David chuckled. "You wanted her—I got her."

Josh glowered.

"Whatever." He shoved a spoonful of cereal into his mouth.

"You *got* me?" I whispered in David's ear.

He tightened his arm around my waist. "Yup."

I shook my head, smiling. "Actually, I think I had a little bit of a say in the whole thing."

David laughed. "Whatever you want to believe. Bottom line, you love me." He quickly kissed the tip of my nose before smiling at me. His smile dared me to disagree.

The thing was…he was right.

Month Twelve

"Do you think they'll keep us together?" Katie asked, biting her lip.

"What do you mean?" I asked, watching Faith crawl through the living room. Her chubby legs shuffled across the carpeting, her arms so fat her elbows disappeared in the rolls.

"I heard they're making camps, like little villages. The people from the PODs will be assigned to camps. Everyone's talking about it online. Do you think they'll keep everyone from our POD together?"

"Well, I don't know, but if it's true I'm sure they'll keep us together. Why else would they put us in the same sub-POD?"

"I hope they do. I'm not ready to start over again."

I smiled and gave her a quick hug. "Me, neither."

Tiffany scooped up the baby from the floor and bounced her on her knee, smiling at her giggles. Drool dripped from Faith's mouth as she chewed on her fingers. Tiffany reached over to pick up the tiny nail clippers, and in that millisecond of distraction the baby flung her hand out and grabbed Josh's cup. Juice spilled down his shirt.

"Dammit!" he shouted, bolting upright from the couch.

"Sorry—" Tiffany started.

"Keep that little brat away from me!" Josh yelled.

Faith started to cry.

"Great, now we have to listen to her wail for an hour. That's just fantastic." He stomped into the bedroom.

I got up and sat down next to Tiffany, grabbing a baby wipe to dab at the spattering of juice on the couch. "Don't worry about him. He's an ass. Isn't he, Faith? You dumped that juice on purpose, didn't you, huh? Smart little girl."

The baby stopped crying, and gave me a dimpled little grin. Tiffany laughed.

I smiled and patted Tiffany's shoulder.

Her eyes grew serious. "She doesn't bother you, does she? When she cries and stuff?"

I shook my head. "No. You know we all love her."

"I keep thinking about how she's my only family now. My parents won't ever get to meet her. She'll never know her grandparents. They would've doted on her."

I reached over and gave her hand a squeeze. "We're each other's family now, and she is going to be spoiled rotten. And after we get out, we—"

A loud thud by the door made me jump. The chute. "Oh!" I made a silly face at the baby. "What's that? Huh? What'd they send us?"

I walked over with a cold dread congealing in my belly. It was too early for another blood check. No one was expecting more books; we were still in the middle of the current batch of classes. According to the gossip online, it had been weeks since any POD had been cut off from the main, but it was never far from my mind...from anyone's.

My fingers shook as I reached out to open the hatch. Grabbing the cool steel handle, I took a breath to steady myself. "You're being silly, Eva," I whispered.

The door slid open quietly. The acrid disinfectant smell hit me, taking my breath for an instant. I pulled out the container, which felt empty.

I unsealed the lid and reached in, feeling paper. It glided across my finger at the wrong angle. I jerked my hand back and looked at the deep paper cut. "That can't be a good sign," I murmured.

"What?" David asked behind me before wrapping his arms around my waist and kissing the back of my neck.

"Oh, nothing. We got something from the main POD." I reached in and snatched the red paper out of the basket. "It says there's another systems check later today. What does that make? Three this week?"

"Something like that."

"I wonder what system needs checking three times in a week," I said, squeezing a paper towel over my cut finger so I didn't have to look at the grotesque red ooze. "And why are they sending this message through the chute? They could've just e-mailed it out."

"Don't get paranoid, Eva. Things need checking." He turned me around and pressed me against the wall, the chute's handle digging into my back. He leaned down and his mouth moved over mine. My insides did cartwheels and butterflies flew around, tickling in some private places.

I planted my hands on his chest and gently pushed him away. "Are you trying to distract me?"

"Is it working?"

"Yeah, kinda." I smiled. I loved the taste of him. "It's been a year that we've been down here, David."

"I know. It still doesn't mean anything is wrong." He bent his head and kissed me lightly.

"Why do you think we haven't heard anything about getting out of here?"

"Have I told you you're a worrywart?"

"Yeah, yeah."

Month Fourteen

It was the day the last assignments for the current batch of courses were due—our final exams for the modules. We uploaded them through the online classrooms and waited for the next batch of books and course assignments. Additional MREs arrived weekly to supplement our dwindling supplies. But when the container shot down the chute that day, hitting the metal wall with a loud clang, it was empty except for our blood test kits.

We pricked our fingers, completed the tests, and tossed them inside like usual, except for Josh, who left his bloody gauze and lancet on the kitchen table.

Tiffany made a face. "Gross. Clean up after yourself."

"It's just a little blood. You clean it up." He flicked his hand, dismissing her.

"I don't want to go anywhere near your bodily fluids."

"Just pick it up, man. Why do you have to make everything so difficult?" George sighed.

"Fine." Josh stomped over to the table and swiped the items into the garbage.

"Thank you."

Josh grunted in reply.

After our blood work was completed, we hung out, waiting for the new coursework. It never came. Everyone seemed relieved. I was worried.

"Maybe we've just finished it all," Katie said. "We've been down here more than a year. They probably only brought enough materials for a year and that's it."

"You're probably right, kiddo." I didn't believe it for a second.

Month Fifteen
    It happened.

The PODs Open

It may be hard for an egg to turn into a bird: it would be a jolly sight harder for it to learn to fly while remaining an egg. We are like eggs at present. And you cannot go on indefinitely being just an ordinary, decent egg. We must be hatched or go bad.

~ C.S. Lewis

Chapter 14: Freedom

"**W**ho ate all the damn strawberries?" Aidan yelled. "I was saving them for my cereal."

"I did. Use the banana," Josh said.

"A banana isn't a strawberry. I marked the container with my name. You're a jerk—"

The container hit the metal wall of the chute with a crack. I always jumped when it did that. I hated it. It reminded me of the banging and crunching we'd heard when Cam's sub-POD was cut off from the main.

"It's not time for our blood checks," I said.

"Maybe it's strawberries. I'd really like some strawberries... Josh," Aidan said, an edge to his voice.

"Drop dead," Josh replied, never looking up from his computer.

David got up from the table where we were having breakfast. Taking the container from the chute, he pulled a manila envelope out of the basket.

He dumped the contents on the table for everyone to see. Inside were ten name badges, one for each of us. Our photos—except Faith's—and names were printed on one side; the other had barcodes. David scanned the label on the envelope, his face growing pale.

"What's it say, David?" I whispered.

"'*The seals to each sub-POD will be broken tomorrow morning. Do not attempt to leave your sub-POD. Officers will give residents directions and escort them to their appropriate area topside.*' That's all it says."

"It's over," Tiffany murmured, pulling the baby close.

"Hot damn! Finally, I'm free of this tin can," Josh jumped up and hurried to the guys' bedroom.

Well, at least Josh is happy. Why aren't the rest of us? I thought we'd be excited. But instead everyone looks…anxious. What will we find up there? What has the world become?

"Well, guess we should start packing up our stuff," Aidan said.

"Yeah, I guess so," Seth agreed, rising slowly from his seat, rubbing his hands up and down his thighs.

One by one, everyone walked to their sleeping areas and started packing their belongings—except me. I sat in the living room alone, flicking the corner of my name badge with my fingernail. The lanyard wound so tightly around my fingers they turned red.

My insides were quivering, jittery. Something wasn't right. For fifteen months we'd all looked forward to the moment we could leave, but now that the time was here it felt…wrong.

I longed to feel the warmth of the sun on my face, to see it shine brightly in the blue sky instead of the simulated light of the POD windows. I wanted to feel cool blades of grass beneath my bare feet, the autumn rain on my face. I was happy at the thought of hearing birds chirping in the trees early in the morning, and the songs of crickets and bullfrogs at night. But no matter how much I looked forward to those things, I couldn't stop worrying. Something was going to happen to shatter our happy little family. I could feel it in my gut. It twisted and churned in my stomach, like a tumor growing until it made breathing difficult.

Standing, I scrunched my toes in the chocolate-colored carpeting and stretched, trying to shake off the uneasy feeling. I walked toward the girls' bedroom to pack, turning my badge over and over in my hands, when I saw it. In the lower left hand corner I saw a label—A23S2. I remembered the conversation I'd had with Katie.

"Do you think they'll keep us together?" she'd asked me.

I had told her they would. At the time I'd believed it.

"David?"

"In the bedroom."

"Can I see your ID badge?"

He handed it to me and continued to throw his things in his suitcases. I held them together, a lump forming in my throat.

A48S1.

They didn't match.

I handed his badge back to him and went down the hall to the girls' bedroom.

"Tiffany, can I see your and Faith's badges?"

"Sure. What's up?"

"I'm not sure."

Faith babbled happily in her crib, playing with a toy. I smiled and tickled her under her chin, then wiping the drool on my pant leg. She grinned at me. Tiffany stopped packing and handed me their IDs.

I looked closely, reading and rereading the information.

A45S9 on both. Tiffany's and Faith's matched. Mine and theirs didn't.

My heart dropped. That's when I knew. "Oh, no," I whispered.

I looked at Katie's—A03S10. Ours didn't match, but hers and Jai Li's did.

"Crap, crap, crap. They can't do this." I wasn't aware I'd said it out loud until David touched my elbow.

"What's wrong?"

"Nothi—"

"Eva, don't say *nothing*. I know you. Something is wrong."

I swallowed hard. "Uh, can you just help me get everyone into the living area, please? I promise I'll tell you."

"Sure."

When we'd all assembled in the living area I showed everyone the numbers on their badges.

"So?" George asked.

"So, what's your number, George?"

"A23S2."

"That matches mine. David, what's your number?"

"No."

"David?"

"No. I'm not...they aren't separating us."

"What's your number?" I asked him again.

"A48S1."

"That matches mine," Seth said.

"Mine and the baby's match," Tiffany whispered.

"Yeah. That's when I knew for sure. They wouldn't separate a mother and her baby. They wouldn't care if the rest of us were separated." I said quietly, bouncing when I fell on the couch next to David. His feet were spread and his elbows rested on his knees. He bowed his head, looking at the plastic badge. He knew as well as I did. The numbers had something to do with where we'd be going. Ours didn't match.

"They can't separate us!" Katie wailed.

None of us reassured her. None of us told her they would keep us together. Like with the coursework, we knew they could do whatever they wanted.

"Katie, yours and Jai Li's match."

"But I want us *all* to stay together!"

"I know, sweetie, so do I," I answered.

"Tiff?" George asked.

"No, it doesn't match," she answered. Tiffany and George had finally figured out they were sweet on each other. They'd been an item for two months, give or take a day. Beanbag Guy, as I'd nicknamed him when I'd first seen him, was wonderful with Faith and adored her and Tiffany. Now, they'd be separated.

David and I would be separated.

David and I didn't sleep that night. We stayed awake talking and holding each other.

"Maybe if I don't go to sleep, tomorrow won't come."

David didn't answer me, just squeezed me closer to his side.

Morning came anyway. At eight o'clock, the seal to the POD cracked and gave way with a loud hiss. Cool air seeped through the crack around the large, circular door.

We waited for the escort to unlock the door and take us topside. The lock to the POD sounded like the dial on a safe. It spun, clicking when the correct bar and slot lined up. The door creaked when it was pulled open.

The escort was a uniformed military officer. His uniform was pressed and heavily starched, his black shoes buffed to a blinding shine.

He stepped inside. I felt like he was intruding. It was *our* space, our home. He could've at least waited to be asked inside. Or better still, he could have done his business from the corridor.

"Number A01S14," He announced. "Come with me."

Josh looked at his badge. He stood and walked to the door without saying a word. No goodbye, no wishing us well—he just left. Maybe he was as glad to be away from us as we were him. The door relocked behind him.

Thirty minutes later, another officer opened the sub-POD door. "A03S10. Two of you. Come with me."

Jai Li grabbed Katie's hand as they walked to the door. He barely let them say goodbye to us before he ushered them outside the sub-POD and re-locked the door.

They were coming for people in sequential order. George and I would be the next to leave. He and Tiffany went into one bedroom to say their goodbyes. David and I slipped into the second bedroom for the same reason.

I was crying too hard to speak. I couldn't get out the words I wanted him to hear, *needed* him to hear. The hot tears wouldn't stop. They ran in rivulets down my cheeks, falling on my shirt. My shoulders shook with the force of my sobs.

"Don't cry, Eva. Please don't cry." He wiped my tears away with the pad of his thumb.

"David." It was the only word I could manage—just his name. I hoped he could hear the things I wanted to say in that one word. I hoped he heard I loved him, that the thought of leaving him caused me physical pain. That without him the last fifteen months of my life would have been hell. Without him, the rest of my life would be worse.

A tear rolled down his cheek. He brushed it away with the back of his hand. "I can't stand this," he said through clenched teeth.

I cupped his face in my hands and pulled him to me. He kissed me gently at first, then desperately. A kiss that was permanent in its goodbye—a last kiss.

The door handle turned. I could hear the click, click, click of the lock opening before the hinges creaked open.

"No, I'm not ready," I cried. "I can't leave yet."

George walked past the bedroom door into the living area. I could hear Tiffany crying in the other bedroom. The baby fussed.

"George, wait! Don't go." Tiffany hurried down the hall after him. "They can't force you. Did we lose our freedom? Our rights, when we entered the PODs? Stay with me." She was crying so hard I couldn't understand the rest of her words.

I watched from the open bedroom door as George reached for Faith and held her tightly to him. He kissed the top of her head, carrying her with him to the POD door. "I'm sorry, Tiffany." He passed the baby back to Tiff and stepped through the door into the corridor. "I love you."

Tiffany fell to the floor in front of the circular door, crying. The soldier looked down at her impassively. "Miss, you need to move. You're blocking the exit."

This couldn't be happening. Why put us in the same sub-POD just to separate us? Why did I have to be assigned this sub-POD? If I'd been in a different one I would never have met David. I wouldn't know what I was leaving behind—my best friend, my true love. But, if I'd been assigned a different sub-POD I would never have known how strong love could be, how much one person could change your life forever.

"A23S2, follow me."

"I'll find you," David whispered between kisses.

I felt like I was in a fog. David was talking, telling me he'd find me. The soldier was yelling from the doorway. Tiffany was crying hysterically on the floor. Katie and Jai Li were gone. What'd happened to my world?

The officer checked a tablet computer. "I show two of you assigned to A23S2." His tone was growing impatient.

"She's coming," Seth answered from where he sat quietly next to Aidan on the couch, his elbows on his knees and head in his hands.

"A23S2, come with me now!" the officer yelled.

"I'll find you, Eva. I won't stop until I do," David whispered, squeezing my arms. "I'll go to every village if I have to, but I *will* find you. I swear."

He picked up my bags and carried them to the sub-POD door. He set them on the corridor floor, turning to kiss me one last time. The soldier grabbed my elbow and pulled me over the threshold. I turned toward David, reaching for him. The soldier closed and locked the door before I could give him one last hug…one final kiss…tell him I loved him one more time.

"DAVID!"

"Follow me." He walked briskly down the corridor leading to the main POD.

George put his arm around me. I'm not sure if he was comforting me, or if I was comforting him—probably both. We'd just lost people we loved, for the second time.

Life was doubly cruel.

We walked down the corridor to the main POD. From there, we entered the small elevator that would take us to ground level. I'd forgotten how slow the ride was. It seemed to take forever, crammed in the small space, my gut twisting with a mixture of dread at what I'd see when I reached the top and pain from leaving David.

"Here, you'll need these." The soldier thrust two pairs of sunglasses at us.

Stepping out of the entrance, we were blinded by the sunlight. Even the sunglasses didn't erase the burning in our eyes. When we'd adjusted to the brightness, we saw the world we'd left behind for the first time in fifteen months.

It wasn't what I remembered. Oh, the landscape was the same. It smelled the same, looked the same. But my world, the world inside my head, was missing a key element—David.

"There's your area tent. You are assigned to Area 23, Sector 2. Go to the tent and stand in line with your designated sector. Wait there for further instructions." He walked away without another word.

Above ground, everything was complete chaos. Hundreds of green army tents were set up around the POD openings. Beyond them, giant wind turbines creaked above the desert like giant pinwheels.

If I'd known where to meet David, I would have bolted, but I didn't have a clue how to find him. I couldn't stay next to the main POD opening, since the soldiers were waving away other people who'd approached. And I couldn't blend in and wait until I saw him emerge from the POD. There were too many people, and we were all being herded toward the tents anyway.

My head bowed and a heaviness filling my chest, I followed George to Area 23's tent. We found our sector's line and waited. George and I didn't speak. He put his arm around me, and I lay my head on his shoulder. We didn't need words to understand we were both hurting, or how badly we felt for the other's loss. We stood in the sweltering heat and let the torture wash over us.

It was more than two hours before another soldier told us to board an antiquated school bus, much like the one I'd ridden to the PODs. The faded, dust-covered sides looked more of a bland tan than a cheery yellow, and the inside smelled of body odor and vomit. Most people sat quietly in their seats. A few cried softly. I wanted to scream.

I sat with George, shoving my bag under the seat. A woman in uniform boarded the bus, her face unsmiling. "You have been assigned to Area 23, Sector 2. You will be assigned your jobs and living quarters upon arrival."

A girl near the front raised her hand. The officer scowled, but nodded at her. "Yes?"

"Do you know about our families? There must be survivors, right? Is there a database or a way to track dow—"

"There is no database. I regret to inform you that the only people who were not exposed to the virus were in secure facilities like the PODs."

A guy with a heavy black beard, who probably hadn't shaved since before quarantine, moved into the aisle. "The place we're going—has it been decontaminated?"

The officer nodded her head. "We now know that the virus cannot be transmitted through contact with inert materials such as wood, metal, plastic, or cloth, and the secure areas have been thoroughly cleaned and readied for your arrival. You will be safe as long as you stay in your assigned area."

I leaned forward. "Will we be able to contact people assigned to other areas?"

"The military has satellite phones in operation for contact among the areas and sectors. They are not for civilian use. We anticipate having mail delivery within two months."

I leaned back in my seat. The officer answered a few more questions before stepping off the bus, but I didn't pay attention.

Two whole months without contact with David?

The bus roared to life, black smoke billowing behind it. Slowly it began moving over the hard-packed dirt, swirling up dust and making it even harder to see anything outside the grime-caked windows. The bus wobbled and shimmied across the dirt roads, passing more wind farms and acres of solar panels. About an hour into our ride, we turned onto a paved road, where we sped up, going recklessly fast on the empty interstate. Shortly afterward I saw a sign, faded from years in the unrelenting sun and oppressive heat.

Thank you for visiting New Mexico, the Land of Enchantment.

"We were in New Mexico," I said to George.

"Yeah. I'd never been here before."

"Me, neither. I did a report on it in grade school, though." I looked through the back window at the state where I'd just spent fifteen months of my life.

It was suited for the PODs—lots of flat, uninhabited land, perfect for the solar and wind power used in the PODs.

George and I had no idea where we were going or how long it would take us to get there, so we settled in for a long trip. I twisted the lanyard around my neck before pulling the sides taut and watching my name badge spin. I was still playing with my nametag when George spoke.

"Our numbers aren't really the same, you know."

"What do you mean?"

"Next to the Sector number there's a letter. It's a lot smaller than the others. See it?"

"Yeah."

"Yours has an *E*, mine an *M*."

"Well, maybe that doesn't matter. I mean, we're going to the same sector."

"Maybe."

"Where's your eyebrow ring?"

"Hmm?"

"Your piercing—did they make you take it off?" He'd worn the same piercings since I'd first seen him. The most prominent one—a silver ring in his left eyebrow—was missing.

"Oh. I gave it to Tiffany. I wanted her to have something of mine. That's probably stupid. What does she want with some guy's used jewelry?"

"It's not stupid, George, and you weren't just some guy to her."

"I hope not. She wasn't just any girl to me."

We fell silent. I bounced up and down in the bus seat every time the wheels hit a pothole. My back and head hurt from the jostling. I tried to brace myself for the bumps, but that made my arms and shoulders ache. I gave up and let the bus throw me here and there with every pothole it ran over.

Why am I angry at Tiffany? I love Tiffany. I'm not angry...I'm jealous. She got something—something of George's to keep, to touch, to hold.

"I wish I had something of his," I whispered.

"What?" George asked.

"Of David's. I wish I had something of his. I wish I would've given him something of mine. We had to say goodbye so fast...I just didn't think."

"David did give you something. Look in the front pocket of your bag."

I scrambled to grab my duffel, cursing when it rolled across the floor out of reach. I slid out of my seat and got on all fours reaching for the bag. My finger locked around the strap and I jerked it to me. I didn't bother getting off the floor before unzipping the pocket and looking inside.

I found a piece of paper folded in half. I took it out and unfolded it with careful movements, since the bus was crashing over the potholes so hard I was afraid I'd rip it. It was a miniature version of the last painting he'd made on the POD wall. The red and black "David loves Eva" jumped off the page, dancing in front of my tear-filled eyes. I got off the floor and sat next to George, looking at the drawing, tracing the letters with my fingers.

"You dropped this." A boy behind me said, handing me a small square piece of paper.

"Thank you," I murmured, turning the card over in my hand. A small cry escaped my lips when I saw his smiling face looking at me. It was a photo of David with his sisters.

"I told him you'd like it."

I smiled at George. *I love it.* "It's too bad we didn't have a camera so everyone could have a photo." I felt bad sitting next to George with a photo of David in my hand when he didn't get one of Tiffany.

"That would've been nice," he said, "but luckily for me David is a great artist." He pulled out a drawing of Tiffany holding Faith. "David said it wasn't his best work, but I think it's great."

"It looks just like them."

"Yeah. I'm gonna miss them, Eva."

"I know. Me, too."

Chapter 15 : Home

I jolted upright in bed. I looked around the room, disoriented. When the fog of sleep cleared, memories slammed into me. I wasn't in the POD anymore. George and I had arrived in Area 23, Sector 2—otherwise known as the village of Rosewood, Tennessee—three weeks ago. I felt my stomach clench and chest tighten. David was gone, and I didn't know where he was.

The sun peeked through the slats of the window blinds, shining in my eyes. I groaned, flopping backward on the bed. I threw the quilt over my head and turned from the window.

Go away.

Sunday. I hated the weekends. I couldn't wait until Monday when I could go to work and be around people again. At least work distracted me. I could think of something other than the man I'd left behind.

But until Monday I was on my own. David wasn't here, and I didn't know how to contact George. There was no village communication system in place.

The house was too quiet and left me too much time with my ache for David…and with things that reminded me of life before the POD.

Knowing I wouldn't go back to sleep, I climbed out of bed with a sigh. I changed and pulled on my running shoes. David and I had run together on the treadmills every day in the POD. The thought pierced through my heart like a dagger—even exercising wasn't free of memories of him. I ran hard, pushing myself harder than usual, trying to push through the memories that haunted me.

Finally, Monday morning. Rainy, it was gray and overcast and I wanted to snuggle down in my bed and wrap myself in my soft quilt. But it was a workday, and I welcomed the chance to get out of my quiet house. I showered and dressed, grabbed an apple for breakfast and walked across the street to meet Nona.

The rain was slanted, the kind that slapped us in the face and soaked our clothes and hair even though we had umbrellas.

"A white shirt wasn't my best decision." I looked down at my shirt already plastered to my skin. Nona laughed.

"We have time. Run and change."

Nona was my neighbor across the street. We walked to and from work together every day. By the time she and I got to work, we were both soaked. My clothes, wet and wrinkled, stuck to my skin. My shoes made squishing noises when I walked.

Since moving to Rosewood, I'd been given a house and a job. When I'd arrived the first day, after a horrible ten-hour bus ride, I reported to intake—a converted office in the old high school. Making my way to the dust-covered counter, I waited while the person ahead of me was given his information.

"Name?" The girl behind the counter asked when it was my turn.

"Evangelina Evans." I wrung my hands, the knuckles cracking painfully.

The girl shuffled through some pages before producing a large manila envelope with my name printed across the front. My stomach churned.

Stop being a baby, Eva. Take a big breath and pull on your big girl panties.

"You'll find your address in the envelope. It also contains your employment information. You've been assigned a teaching position. Looks like English and creative writing. Your schedule and first weeks' lesson plans are in the envelope. Go out this door," she pointed to a small door on the left. "Your transport to your residence is waiting."

"Thank you." I started to walk away, clutching the envelope so tightly my fingers ached.

"Wait! You'll need these." She held out a key ring with two keys hanging from it. "You don't want to be locked out."

I smiled and took the keys, my fingers trembling. I walked slowly to the door, pushing it slightly. It glided open. A security officer waited outside. He asked my name, took my envelope, and pulled out a pink slip of paper.

"This is your address. Don't lose this paper. It's your proof of ownership."

"Ownership?" I asked.

"Of your house," he answered. "Put it somewhere safe. Give your street address to the driver."

I own a house?

I walked across the parking lot to the waiting car. "Um, I guess I'm supposed to tell you my address. It's 12 Maple Brook Lane," I said, reading it off the paperwork I was given.

He opened the car door for me and smiled. "I know just where that is. We call it the teachers' district. It's over by the elementary school, you see. I bet that's where you'll be working. Your house is close enough for you to walk to work."

He drove while he talked. By the time he'd finished telling me about the school, we'd reached my house.

My house. I own a home...they just gave it to me.

It seemed unreal. Of course, there were plenty of houses to go around, and with no banking system in place it'd be hard to keep up on mortgages. So they gave us all homes.

I was a homeowner. It was a beautiful house—yellow with white shutters and a big front porch. But it felt empty. For the last fifteen months I'd lived with nine other people. My house felt too big and too quiet without them, especially David.

Walking home after my first day at work I told Nona, "I never thought I'd be a teacher. In fact, I was sure I wouldn't be."

"Well, how'd the day turn out?"

"Really, really good."

"That's great, Eva."

As the days passed, I found that I enjoyed my job more and more. In the evenings, I read every book I could on teaching. I looked forward to school days. I taught English to the younger residents. The raffle had chosen people beginning at age twelve, so I taught kids thirteen through sixteen proper English, writing and oral communication. I also taught a creative writing course.

The work and the kids kept me busy.

Work was my escape.

Four weeks went by without word from George. Nona told me the "M" next to George's sector number meant that he lived in the Medical District—the "E" next to mine meant Education District. Since I knew he had still been in school when the virus hit, I looked for him in the medical training classes, but he was never there. With no way to find his address, I'd given up. I mourned his absence like I did for everyone else from sub-POD twenty-nine.

Early on the Monday of my fifth week in the village, a short rap against my classroom's door caused every head in the room to turn. The old wooden desk chair squeaked when I stood. Pulling open the door, I let out a squeal.

"Keep working on your papers, everyone," I told my class before stepping into the hall and hugging George.

He hugged me tightly, lifting me off the ground. "I've been looking for you since the day we got here. You know they don't have any kind of directory? It's crazy."

"How did you find me? I checked the medical classes for you."

He set me down and I studied his face, now free of metal. Small marks showed where the piercings had been, and the tattoo on his neck peeked out of his shirt collar. "Yeah, I work one month at the clinic and come to school for a month. I started my first day of classes today. Your friend Nona saw my name on the roster and asked if I knew you. When I said I did, she told me where to find you."

"Here." I grabbed a pen out of my pocket and reached for his hand, scrawling on his palm. "This is my address. Come by when you can. I have to go back in there and make sure the students aren't strangling each other. It's so good to see you, George." I kissed him quickly on the cheek before I turned to the classroom door. He grabbed my hand.

"It's good to see you too. Eva, I need to talk to you. I'll come by on Saturday if that's okay. It'll give us more time to talk."

"Saturday is great. Is everything okay?"

"Yeah, it's good. Don't worry, I'll see you Saturday." He gave my hand a squeeze before letting go. He turned, his shoes squeaking against the floor. I watched him walk away, wondering what bad news would meet me Saturday.

It was a long week. I busied myself with work, going to the various stores in town to stock up on supplies and studying my teaching textbooks at night.

The closer Saturday came, the more on edge I became. By Wednesday, the students were getting on my nerves and I snapped at them. Friday morning, I thought about calling in sick, but I didn't know the rules about missing work. Besides, I didn't want to be alone with my thoughts all day.

Saturday finally came. George hadn't told me what time he'd be over.

Hurry up, George.

I paced the rooms waiting for him. From one room to another, the bedroom to the kitchen and back again, I'd pick up the knickknacks and trinkets and rearrange them only to put them back in their original spots the next time my pacing led me to the room.

The doorbell pealed through my small house, and I jumped. I'd been looking out the front bay window, but I hadn't seen him walk up. Then I realized the doorbell had only chimed once. The bell for the front door chimed twice.

I peeked out the peephole to make sure he wasn't waiting on my front porch. When I didn't see him, I jogged to the back of the house and opened the back door.

"Hey, Eva." He gave me a hug and quick kiss as he stepped in.

"It's so good to see you. Do you want some lemonade?"

"Yeah, thanks."

"So what's up?" I demanded, handing him his drink.

"You never were one for small talk." He smiled.

I didn't smile back.

He grabbed a kitchen chair and swung it around, straddling it. He put his drink on the table, and I watched a bead of condensation run down the side of the glass. George's finger played in the liquid pooling on the table before he took a drink. The ice cubes clinked against the glass and I flinched—the sound was too loud in the room. I waited. George set the glass down and looked at me.

"I saw Seth," he said quietly.

"Really! Where?"

"He's living here now."

My heart sped up. It was hard to breathe and I had to strain to find enough air to ask my next question.

"Why?"

"The government had dispersed the POD residents evenly over the continental U.S. Hawaii and Alaska are too far away to repopulate."

"Yeah, so?" I asked, slipping into a chair across from George.

"Well, the villages were too small."

"I wondered about that. Less than fifteen hundred people makes for a really small town. It's hard to be self-sufficient."

"That's why they're combining villages. Instead of one for each state, they're combining them and keeping the majority of them on the Eastern seaboard, where it's easier to move goods to and from the villages."

"Like the first colonies."

"Yeah."

"Seth and David were in the same camp," I whispered, my heart speeding up. I rubbed my sweaty palms on my jeans. I started to ask a question, but my voice came out gravelly. Clearing my throat, I started again. "David's here?"

"No."

My heart dropped. "But you just said——"

"Seth said David left not long after they arrived at their village. He's been gone a month, looking for you."

It took me a few seconds to process the information. I stared at the wood grain of the table top, following the lines with my finger. My mind spun and blood pulsed behind my ears. David was gone. He was looking for me. My hands gripped the table so hard it hurt. The edge bit into my flesh, and my fingernails bent under the force. I stood up so fast my chair toppled backward, landing on the wood floor with a crack.

"You're telling me David is wandering around God knows where looking for me. Meanwhile, the government realizes they screwed up and made the villages too small. Our villages are combined, but because David left he doesn't know. Did I get it all?"

"Yeah."

"Isn't that just flippin' ironic?" I wanted to cry. "If David had waited a few weeks, the government would have driven him right to me."

George didn't say anything. He sat at my kitchen table, just turning his glass of lemonade around and around on the tabletop.

"Where's Seth? I want to talk with him."

"You can't," George told me. "He's in quarantine. His entire village is."

"What…why?"

"Military regs. Anyone who leaves their assigned village has a mandatory quarantine period when they arrive at a new facility. That's how I found Seth. I was working the quarantine ward."

"That doesn't make sense. What are they in quarantine for?"

George looked up at me. "The government isn't sure the virus is dead."

My chest tightened. "What do you mean? How can it still be active? There were no hosts…we were all underground." I shook my head. "No. They told us it had to be transmitted from person to person. Without a host, the virus dies."

"Yeah, in theory. But there's something else…"

I groaned and picked up my chair. What else could there possibly be? I dropped onto the chair and put my head in my hands, my fingers threading into my hair. I squeezed my eyes shut to hold in the tears that were threatening to fall. I wanted to put my hands over my ears and tell George I didn't want to hear anymore. Instead, I looked up at him. "What else?" My voice sounded deceptively normal.

"There are…survivors. Some people made it. They boarded themselves up inside their homes. Some went to isolated areas where they wouldn't be exposed to anyone else. Some were just lucky, I guess."

"Survivors? Where? How many?" *My parents, maybe?* I rubbed a hand across my face. *My dad promised he and my mom would go to the cabin on Perch Lake and wait out the virus. Maybe…*

"I don't know, Eva. I don't think the government even knows how many. I just know that anyone who comes into the village is required to stay in isolation for two weeks. Sometimes more, depending on what type of exposure they had."

"So we'll talk to Seth when he gets out of quarantine," I said.

"Well, that may be an issue. The different districts aren't supposed to have a lot of contact with each other. In fact, the only contact that's permissible is what's necessary for job completion. I can see you at school because I'm taking classes there. But I shouldn't be visiting you now. It isn't work-related."

"That's why you came to the back door."

"Yeah."

"Why?" I asked, confused.

"I don't know." He lifted his glass and took a long pull.

"Man, you're just full of good news today, aren't you, George?"

Chapter 16 : Compound

The remaining week of Seth's quarantine period crawled by. *He'd told us while we were in the POD that he excelled in math. Maybe he'll be assigned to teach and I'll be able to talk to him without fear of getting caught mingling with another district.*

I didn't know the letter on his badge. I asked George, but when he went to the clinic to ask Seth, he was escorted out because it wasn't his month for clinic duty.

We sat at a cheap table that had been made to look like wood, surrounded by mismatched chairs. Our lunch—if you could call it that—congealed on our trays. We didn't have much time to talk before we had to be back in class.

"Why are they going to so much trouble to keep people separated? Districts aren't supposed to mingle unless it's work-related; you can't enter the clinic because it's your month of classes. I don't understand. This isn't how a normal town would work."

George shook his head. "We aren't in a normal town, Eva. Nothing about this is normal."

"And what's with the curfew all of a sudden? We've lived here almost six weeks and *now* they institute a curfew?" I asked, too loudly. People at neighboring tables turned and looked at me.

"The nursing and med students have a theory, but it's just a theory. We think it has something to do with the survivors. None of the villages have allowed the survivors inside. The curfew helps keep the villagers inside so the police can monitor movement for non-residents."

"But wouldn't they just put them in quarantine, like they did Seth?"

"No, they aren't allowing them in because they don't have enough quarantine equipment to deal with all of them. I don't even think we have the proper equipment to fully protect us if one of the other villagers had the virus. I think the quarantine is just for show…to make the villagers feel safer than we actually are. If we feel like our little area is clean and virus-free, no one will want to chance contaminating it by allowing non-residents inside," George said.

The bell rang. I eased out of my chair and picked up my lunch tray. "Back to class."

"Yup. Lunch tomorrow?"

I smiled. "Sure thing."

George nodded once and walked out of the cafeteria. I stood watching him leave, tapping my fingernails against the scarred tabletop. Something he'd said nagged at me. I couldn't put the pieces together, but I was sure when I did I wasn't going to like what I saw.

That evening Nona and I took a walk. I said we needed some fresh air after being cooped up all day at work. Truthfully, I wanted to do some exploring. We walked down the sidewalk to the main street that ran through town, and then turned left. I knew approximately where the clinic was, but wasn't completely sure. I was on a mission to find it.

We walked by the park in the center of town, made especially pretty by the leaves turning colors. Bullfrogs croaked in the small pond in the park. The far-off sound of loons carried across the evening breeze.

We came to the white church I remembered from my first day in the village. I had thought it looked so beautiful, sitting tall and proud in the middle of town. Up close, it looked a far throw from beautiful. The white paint flaked from the wooden clapboards, and the cement stairs leading to the front door were crumbled and broken. The once-beautiful stained glass windows showed several cracks. It wasn't the majestic temple I remembered.

Nona and I chatted about work, talked about the unruly students, gossiped about the other teachers. We passed the grocery store, the teenager who ran it already closing up for the night. I yelled a greeting, and he smiled and waved. We continued walking through the town square. I admired the bright yellow and orange mums lining the walkways. The smell of fresh paint filled the air as we passed the library, the small building getting a much-needed facelift before opening.

"It's gonna be dark soon. We should turn back," Nona said.

"Okay, let's walk to the edge of the square and turn around there."

"Wait," she said slowly. "Are you going somewhere in particular?"

I didn't want to lie to Nona, but I couldn't tell her the truth either. She was a *by the book* person. She wouldn't have come along if she'd known where we were going.

"Why?" I asked.

"Because you have a friend who works in section M and that just happens to be where we're standing."

"George. Yeah, he works in medical, but I see him every day at school. Why would I walk all this way to see someone I'd just seen this afternoon?" I said, not really lying, but definitely not telling the truth.

"Then what are we doing standing ten feet from the clinic, Eva?"

"Honestly, I didn't know that was the clinic." At least that was the truth. The brown building looked like it used to be an elementary school. A playground sat beside it, and there was no sign labeling it as a clinic. How were people supposed to know where to go when they were ill if the stinkin' buildings weren't labeled?

"Let's check it out," I said, pulling Nona with me toward the clinic.

"We aren't supposed to be here," she said, struggling to keep up with me.

"Why not? You said it was the clinic. Isn't this where we're supposed to go if we need a doctor?"

"I don't...I guess so."

"Then come on. If they ask, we'll tell them the truth. We're curious if this is the right place to go if we get sick."

We'd walked up two steps when a voice called out behind us. "Ladies." I jumped at the booming voice, sucking in a breath to keep from screaming. Nona let out a small gasp. "IDs, please."

"Crap, Eva, I left my purse at home."

I turned around slowly. The uniformed man had a rifle unslung and pointed in our general direction. "Um, we don't have them with us."

"Regulations require that residents carry their IDs with them at all times," he said.

"Sorry, officer, we were just out for a walk. We didn't think to grab our purses." I tried to look contrite.

"Then I suggest you get back home. Next time you're out, remember to bring your IDs with you. You know those pretty little strings hanging from them? Well, those are for you to put around your neck. That way you'll never forget them."

I wanted to use the "pretty little strings" hanging from his ID and strangle him with them.

"Thank you, officer. C'mon, Eva, let's get home before we get in more trouble by missing curfew."

"Yeah, yeah, just a second. Officer? What are all those lights up the road?" I pointed down the road leading out of town. I hadn't noticed the commotion before. I was too focused on finding the clinic. But the lights had flickered on and I could see a bunch of uniformed personnel milling around.

"That's the East checkpoint."

"For what?" I asked.

"It monitors who is coming and going."

"And if I wanted to go somewhere?"

"You wouldn't. Residents aren't permitted to leave the compound."

Compound? I'd heard people refer to the small village as a *camp* before, but never a *compound*.

"Wait, what do you mean we aren't permitted to leave? Since when?"

"Since the gate went up. Go home, ladies."

"Come on, Eva. Let's go."

Nona and I didn't waste time getting home. It was getting dark and we would be breaking curfew by being out after dusk. We walked so fast we were almost jogging. It took us half the time to get home as it had to get to the clinic.

"Don't do that again, Eva."

"Nona, I really didn't know that was the clinic. I swear."

"Whatever. Next time you invite me for a walk, make sure you don't have any other motives. I don't know what's going on with the fences and the gates, and I don't want to know. I want to stay in the village. So next time you want to go on a little fact-finding mission, leave me out of it."

She walked up her driveway, her back ramrod straight, her chin in the air.

A thought occurred to me as I watched her walk away. What did she mean when she said she didn't know what was going on with the *fences*? No one had said anything about fences.

"What do you know about the gate, George?" I asked him the next afternoon at lunch. The lunchroom was buzzing with activity. Kids and faculty talked and joked at the tables next to us. No one was paying attention, so I didn't worry about anyone overhearing.

"How do you know about it?"

"I took a little stroll last night after work. I saw the gate just down the road from the clinic."

"Eva, you're gonna get in trouble. I don't know——"

"Don't tell me you don't know. You're the one person in this place who seems to know everything. And why is that?"

"I don't know about the gates, just that the MPs are supposed to check everyone's ID before they leave or come into the village."

"Compound."

"What?" He looked shocked. I couldn't tell if it was because I wasn't supposed to know that our quaint little village home was now a military compound, or if he was as surprised as I was.

"That's what the MP called it last night." I watched George's face while I talked. "But you already knew that—right, George? What else do you know that you aren't telling your *friend*? What about the fences?"

"Eva, you are so flippin' stubborn. It's gonna get you in trouble. The gates and fences are meant to keep people out."

"But the soldier said…"

"I know what he said. I'm telling you what it really means. They are trying to keep all the topside survivors out of the village. And, yes, I know the military police are calling it a compound. That's what it is. No one in, no one out. Well, that's not entirely true. The 'no one out' part is false. People can leave." He leaned in, lowering his voice. "The 'no one in' part is true. If you leave, you stay out."

"What else?"

"The fences and gates will be guarded to make sure no one sneaks in. It's to keep those that could possibly be carriers of the virus out of the vil—compound."

"Why aren't they quarantining them like the others?" I asked. "Surely they have room for one or two survivors at a time."

"Have you seen the people out there? There have to be a hundred or more and they all want in. It's not just one or two survivors. It's a mob. Besides, I told you, it's not the room in the quarantine facility. They don't have the right equipment for full quarantine—not like we had going into the PODs. It's all a show designed to create a sense of peaceful well-being. That way, when someone wants to get in the compound, people will want the police to keep them out."

"And you know this how?"

"I have a friend in security. He works at the clinic sometimes. That's the real reason they want the districts separated. They don't want people like me telling people like you what's going on."

"What do you mean by *'people like you'?*"

"People who don't need to know. I work in medical, so I see and know things—like that the virus may not be dead. My friend in security knows about things like the fence and the new entrance and exit policy. He told me things I shouldn't know and I'm telling you things you shouldn't know. They're trying to eliminate that problem by keeping us separated."

"And you're telling me now because?"

George let out a breath and pushed his lunch tray aside. Ketchup dripped from the side of his plate. He picked up his drink, crushing the cup when he realized it was empty.

"David."

Chapter 17 :
Meeting

"**D**avid? What about him?"

"I didn't tell you because David's now considered an outsider. They won't let him in, Eva. He's been out of the villages too long."

I shook my head. George couldn't know that for sure. They'd have to let him in. He was a POD survivor, not someone who'd stayed topside. "They'll let him in. Yes, they will—stop shaking your head at me, George. He'll show them his ID and they'll let him in. They might make him sit through two weeks of quarantine, but they'll let him…"

My words died when I heard the small smack of plastic hit the table in front of me. I looked down and tears formed in my eyes. George was right.

"Seth had it."

"Why would he…? Why wouldn't he take…?" I couldn't finish a thought. I kept staring at the ID badge George had placed in front of me. David's face looked up at me, his eyes meeting mine.

"He probably didn't think he'd need it again. Put it in your purse, Eva. Take it home and hide it. Or burn it. Whatever, just don't get caught with it."

"It has an *E* on it," I said quietly.

"Huh? What about it?"

"David thought he'd be working in marine biology, or Earth science. But his number has an *E* at the end. He would have worked in education. We would have worked together…lived in the same district. We could've had a life together."

George reached out and awkwardly brushed a tear off my cheek. "I'm sorry, Eva."

"Yeah, well, it is what it is." I looked up at George and tried to smile. "Um, I need to go to the restroom and splash some cold water on my face and get myself pulled together before my next class. I'll see you at lunch tomorrow?"

"I'll save you a seat," he said.

I nodded and walked away. It wasn't until later I realized I'd left David's ID badge on the table.

Three weeks passed. George and I ate lunch together every day. It was Monday of the last week of George's classes. He'd be working in the clinic for the next month. It would be almost impossible to see each other with the new security that was in place.

The police had installed two gates with checkpoints, one on each end of the main road leading in and out of town. The fence encircling the compound must have been twenty feet tall. Barbed wire twisted around the slanted top. I felt like I was in a prison yard every time I looked at it.

At each corner of the fence, and at both checkpoints, guards stood vigil, overlooking the survivors who camped outside the compound waiting for a chance to sneak in. Guards were also posted at different areas of the fencing, but they couldn't watch everything.

"Here, you forgot this." George slid something to me. He lifted his hand and I saw David's ID badge.

"Thank you," I sighed. I slid my hand under George's and took the badge. "I thought I'd lost it for good."

"Keep it someplace safe, Eva."

"Why, what's wrong?"

"He'll need it," George whispered.

"David? How am I supposed to get it to him?"

"You'll be seeing him soon. I don't know how or when yet, but Seth saw him hanging around the front gate with the other people camped out there. We'll figure out a way for you two to see each other."

David.

"Thank you." I put David's ID badge in the pocket of my jeans.

"Yeah, well, if it was Tiffany on the other side of that fence I'd want to see her. I'd risk everything to see her. Will you, Eva? Will you risk everything to see David? Because that's what you'll be doing."

"I'm not risking anything. There's nothing here I want if I can't have him."

The week passed slowly. Every day at lunch I bit my lip so I wouldn't scream at George. I wanted to know when and where I'd see David.

George didn't bring up the subject again. I knew why. Everything needed to be kept as quiet as possible. He wouldn't say anything until he knew the when and where. That didn't help my fraying nerves, however.

On Friday—his last day of class—he slipped me a note when we hugged goodbye. I wouldn't see him for a month.

"Whatever you do, don't get caught," he whispered in my ear.

That was the longest day of my life, I think. I didn't dare look at the note until I got home. I couldn't risk anyone seeing it.

My fingers shook so badly, I was afraid I would tear the paper. I read the small print…twice.

Tomorrow. Midnight. At the fence in the field at the end of your street.

Tomorrow. I'd see David tomorrow. I wanted to scream, dance around the house. My stomach had butterflies the size of birds swirling around.

Tomorrow I'll see David. My David.

Remembering George's warning, I walked to the kitchen and pulled the box of matches out of the cupboard. Striking a match, I lit the corner of the note and watched the black smoke swirl up and float away. The flames consumed the words that made me so happy, that gave me hope. When the burning yellow flames licked at my fingertips, I dropped the remnants of the paper in the sink and let it burn itself out before washing the ash down the drain.

No evidence. I can't risk getting caught. Not when I'm so close.

What do I wear? Black. Need to blend in.

I dug through my dresser looking for my black jeans and sweater. Maybe it wasn't necessary, but I was taking every precaution. I'd been warned not to get caught. I didn't know what would happen if I were caught, and I didn't want to find out.

I was ready to go at ten o'clock.

I'll brush my teeth…again. Just to be sure. Perfume? No…wait! Yes. No. It'll attract mosquitos. I don't want to be slapping at them the whole time…Are they out now? Is it too cold? Who cares?

Why am I so nervous? It's David. My David. What if he's changed? Geez, Eva, it's only been a few weeks. But still…

I tried to sit on the couch and wait, but the minutes ticked by so slowly I decided to leave early. I'd wait for him in the field, but I had to get out of the house before I went crazy.

I cringed when the hinges of the back door creaked. It was as if they knew I was doing something I shouldn't and were giving their warning. I screamed when a figure loomed over me in the dark. His hand darted out and covered my mouth.

"Geez, Eva, I told you not to get caught," George whispered.

"You scared the crap outta me. What are you doing here?"

"It's dark. I wanted to walk with you. Make sure you find him okay. Why are you leaving so early?"

"The neighborhood is dark and I was going crazy waiting. I decided to wait at the fence."

"Dammit, Eva, you can't do that! Go back inside." He pushed me through the door, closing it quietly behind him. "We set up the meeting at midnight for a reason. It wasn't just a time Seth and I drew out of a hat. It wasn't some romantic gesture."

"Then what? And don't talk to me like I'm an idiot. You didn't tell me there was a reason I should wait until midnight."

"Yeah, I know. That's one of the reasons I snuck over. Listen, Eva, this is really important. You and David will have an hour together. One hour…no more. The guards patrol the fence. Seth and I timed them all week and this is the best time for you to meet, but you can't stay for more than an hour or the guards will find you."

"I could hide—"

"There's nowhere to hide. It's a meadow. There aren't many trees around—"

"But there's a weeping willow tree. I can see it from my house." *I could hide in that if I needed to. I need more time with David. An hour? Just an hour? It's not enough.*

"You couldn't make it to the tree if you needed to. It's too far from the fence. There's some tall grass, but that's too risky. You can meet again another night, but tonight it's an hour. Okay?"

I nodded and blew out a breath, frustrated and more than a little disappointed. Part of me did think meeting David at midnight was romantic. I had visions of us lying in the grass, looking at the stars while we talked all night. Of course, I'd never admit that to George.

At eleven o'clock, most of my neighbors' lights were out. With no televisions or radios to keep them occupied, most people were in bed early. I paced the living room, twisting my fingers. My knuckles cracked painfully. Each time I passed the clock I looked at it. It didn't seem to be moving—that's how slow time was going. I didn't think it would ever be time to leave.

David. Where is he right now? Is he as excited as I am? My heart is doing weird things and a million butterflies are inside me. I swear if I open my mouth they'll fly out. Just thinking of him makes it hard to breathe.

"Are you ready?" George stood and moved toward the door. I got there first.

"I'm more than ready." I pulled the door open.

No street lamps lit the small road I lived on. The community reserved its wind power and solar energy for homes and businesses, and the dusk-to-dawn curfew made lighting the residential streets unnecessary. The distant yellow glow of the lights surrounding the front gate of the compound gave just enough light for us to see. When the time came, George and I stayed in the shadows, making our way down my road toward the field.

I could see it from my house during the day, but it seemed so far away in the dark. I was glad George was with me. During the day, the meadow was calm and soothing; birds fluttered in the sky, singing to each other. The tall grass swayed gently in the breeze. But at night it was eerie. The darkness blanketed it. I couldn't see the swaying grass, or watch the squirrels play. The trees lining the road loomed over us, their moon-cast shadows making menacing images on the ground. I wanted to shrink away from them before they snatched me up.

"I'll walk halfway with you. Then I have to get back before the guards make their sweep in my sector," George whispered when we'd made it to the edge of the field.

"Okay." My voice trembled.

We walked through the knee-high grass, holding hands so we didn't lose each other. The sliver of moon didn't give us much light.

Geez, George walks like an old man. Can he walk any slower? Hurry, hurry up!

When I was standing in the middle of a sea of inky blackness, George squeezed my hand.

"See that?"

I looked ahead and saw a faint flicker. It looked like a firefly.

"David," I whispered.

"Just walk straight, Eva. He'll light a match every so often to keep you on track, but he can't leave them lit too long, so pay attention."

I turned and kissed George on the cheek. "Thank you."

And then I was running. I ran as fast as I could toward the fence, stumbling over rocks and weeds littering the ground. I lost my footing when my shoe caught in a gopher hole. I hit the ground hard; my teeth chattered together, and the wind was knocked from my body with a grunt.

I scrambled up from the prickly weeds just in time to see another match flare and then die. He was right in front of me. I only had a few yards to go. I started running again. I ran straight to the fence, stopping just before I hit it.

I expected to see him waiting for me. But there was no one there. Panic set it. Had he left already? My mind whirred with possibilities before I heard movement in the brush.

"David," I sighed.

"You're more beautiful than I remember."

"You can't even see me," I said with a sob.

"I see you," he murmured, walking to the fence. He stuck his fingers through the gaps in the fencing and grabbed my hands through it.

There was just enough moonlight for me to make out his features. His head bent forward and met mine against the cool steel separating us. He kissed me gently, letting go of one hand to run his finger down the side of my face.

"I've missed you."

"Ha, you have no idea how much I've missed you, Eva."

"Where have you been all this time?" I asked, looking at his face in the dim light. His boyishness had been erased, replaced with ruggedness. He was still just as handsome, but...different.

"Right after I arrived at my village a group of nomads moved through the area. They were topside survivors. Until then, none of us knew there were any survivors. I left with them. We traveled looking for other survivors and other villages. About a month ago, I met up with the group I'm with now. They told me about the villages merging. I joined with them, and we've been traveling from village to village. I've been looking for you. They've been looking for their own family members."

"If you'd only waited..." I shook my head, feeling tears push behind my eyes.

"I know. If I'd only waited another week, I'd be on the other side of this fence."

"Yeah. We could've walked to work together, had lunch together every afternoon, dinner every evening—"

"Wait, what?"

"We could've had dinner together."

"No, before that. What did you say about work?"

"Oh, that reminds me. Here, you'll need this." I pushed his ID card through the holes in the fence. "George doesn't think they'll let you into the compound because you've been out of the villages for so long, but you should try showing your badge to the guards at the gate anyway."

"Eva, what did you say about work?"

"Your badge has an *E* on it. So does mine. We would have worked together. Or at least we would have lived in the same district."

"George didn't tell me that," he said quietly.

"He probably didn't know," I lied. "Half our time is gone already. Do you really want to spend the rest talking about George?" I smiled.

"No."

He reached for me again, twirling my hair through his fingers as his lips found mine. I hated that I was restrained so much. I couldn't really touch him, feel him. My fingers could only reach through the gaps in the fence so far, and it wasn't far enough. I wanted to hold him and for him to hold me. But I was happy to settle for the feel of his lips on mine.

He pulled back and looked at me with a grin. "I've missed that."

I could feel the blush heat my skin, partly from his words, but mostly from his kiss. "Me, too."

I've missed your taste. Every time you kiss me, you taste the same. I crave it.

"I've told you what I've been doing. Now it's your turn to tell me. I want to know everything you've done since I saw you last. Every second, Eva."

"I'm teaching, which shouldn't be a surprise. We kind of figured I would. What I wasn't counting on was liking it. I really love what I do."

"You were dreading it!"

"I know. It's funny how things change."

"Yeah."

I told him about my classes and students. That Nona worked with me and lived across the street. That we'd become friends. And the hour passed by before either of us was ready.

"George said he'd set up another meeting," David told me between kisses.

"I don't want to wait. Our time was up before we even began."

"I know, but this will be over soon. I promise."

Chapter 18 : Meadow

I lay in the cool grass. The prickly weeds bit into my skin, snagging my clothes. The ground was moist under me, my clothes cold and damp. But I didn't care. The only sensation that registered was David's warm fingers touching mine through the small openings in the cold steel fence that separated us.

We were silent, looking at the pitch-black sky, the stars twinkling like fireflies. It would have been a romantic night if it weren't for the circumstances—if David wasn't locked out of the prison I was in.

"Time's almost up," he murmured. "I'll see you tomorrow?"

"I'll try."

"I'll be here if you can get away. If not, we can meet the night after."

"Okay." I dreaded leaving him.

It'd been three weeks since we'd first seen each other. We'd been meeting almost every night since. George warned us it was too much, reminding us not to get caught. Just because this area of the fence was away from the gates didn't mean that people—on either side—wouldn't notice us, follow us. But knowing David was nearby was too much of a pull for me to ignore. I needed to be with him.

The nights I couldn't get away were torture. Knowing he was waiting by the fence in our meadow made it almost impossible not to sneak away, even when my neighbors could see me. But George's warning stuck in my mind, so when people were around I forced myself to stay home.

I'd missed two nights. Each night, people were walking around the neighborhood, disregarding the curfew. I worried that, if they continued staying out past curfew, I'd continue missing my time with David.

The third night was quiet, just the chirping of crickets and the far-off croak of a bullfrog breaking the silence. My neighbors weren't outside and most of the houses were dark. I walked outside and listened again. The night was still and my heart lurched. I ran nearly the entire way, stopping only when I heard him whisper my name.

"I'm sorry. People were out after curfew. The neighborhood had too much activity. I couldn't get away."

"Don't apologize, Eva. I'm just glad you're here now."

He reached out to me. I pushed my hand through the gaps in the fence and cupped his cheek. He leaned down and gently slid his lips over mine. We kissed and touched as much as the fence would allow.

"What's it like where you live?"

We sat cross-legged in the grass, our fingers threaded together. His thumb moved back and forth over the tops of my fingers. The metal of the fence was hard and bit into the side of my hand, but I barely felt it. Every nerve ending in my body focused on the feel of David's thumb caressing my fingers.

"Not as cushy as where you live." I heard the smile in his voice.

"You'll be here soon. You'll be living in the cushy house with me."

"Eva…"

In the dim moonlight, I could see that his lips were pulled down and the skin between his brows wrinkled. I didn't want to hear what he had to say. From the look on his face I knew it wouldn't be anything good.

"We'll be in the same district. Did I tell you that? All the education personnel are located in district *E*," I continued, turning my head so I didn't have to look at him.

"Yes," he whispered, "you mentioned it. Eva—"

"Even if we aren't in the same district we can find ways to see each other. I mean, we're in two totally different camps and still manage."

"I won't be allowed in the village."

I shook my head. I felt the sting of tears behind my eyes and willed them not to fall. I knew what he was saying was true. Residents of the villages were banned from contact with outsiders.

"Yes, you will. This is just a misunderstanding. Once they realize you're a POD survivor they'll let you in. You'll have to stay in quarantine, of course, but then—"

"I tried. I showed my ID at the gate today."

"You were in the PODs! They have to let you in."

"It isn't dead. The virus. It…it didn't die."

"What are you talking about? It had to! The survivors were either too far away from the infected or immune to the virus. It didn't have any hosts. George said it was just a theory that the virus wasn't dead, not a fact."

"It found a way to adapt, to mutate. It survived. I won't be allowed into the compound."

"You're wrong."

"I'm not—"

"No! You're wrong, David. They'll find a cure, put you in quarantine, something."

He tugged my hair gently. I turned my head and faced him, our faces so close I could feel his warm breath. But as close as we were, we were that far away. The fence separated us, keeping us from truly being together, from being close.

He pressed his face to the fence. I scooted closer and pressed my face against the cold, unforgiving metal, barely noticing when it pinched and poked me. He kissed me through the opening. I pushed my hand through as far as I could, grabbing his shirtfront and pulling him closer, holding him to me.

He jerked his head away, banging his hand against the crisscrossed metal. "This damn fence!"

"I told you to bring metal cutters," I said.

He laughed. "Yeah, they're on my shopping list."

The tension broken, we lapsed into a comfortable silence. Lying on our backs, watching the stars twinkle above us.

"Look, David, a shooting star." I pointed in the black sky at the golden tail of the star streaking across the darkness.

"Yeah, I see. Make a wish."

I didn't say anything. We both knew what my wish was, and we both knew it wasn't going to come true.

I walked down my driveway and made a right when I reached the sidewalk. My heart rate rose and my breathing increased, but it wasn't from the exercise. David was waiting for me. My heart raced for him.

My street ended in a cul-de-sac. Beyond that was our meadow, at least a half-mile deep and as wide as the town. At the edge was the fence—the fence that kept David out and me in. The fence that kept us apart.

David wasn't there when I got to the meeting place, and I panicked. *Maybe he was caught; maybe he was hurt; maybe…* I looked at my watch, just visible in the moonlight. Maybe I was fifteen minutes early. I sighed and sat down in the cool grass to wait. The rear of my jeans turned wet from the moist ground and I shivered from the cool autumn night.

I picked random blades of grass out of the ground and tossed them into the wind. I didn't hear him walk up.

"Hey, beautiful," he whispered.

I turned and smiled. "David." I reached toward the fence. The cold steel crisscrossed my palm, catching the edges of the moonlight. I stuck my fingers as far as I could through the metal holes. David's fingers intertwined with them.

"Sorry I'm late. Something happened…I mean, I was held up." He shrugged one shoulder, like whatever had happened wasn't important.

"What happened that made you late, David? And don't say *nothing*. I can tell something is up."

"It was nothing, really. I mean, nothing we don't normally deal with. Another band of travelers tried to grab some of our supplies."

"I don't like you being out there."

"Me neither, but it keeps me near you. Let's not waste our time talking about my living arrangements," he said with a smile.

"I brought you something." I dug through my bag. There was too much crap in it. As soon as I moved some out of my way, more fell in its place. Spying the little blue bottle, I grabbed it before everything else could swallow it. "Here. Let me know when you run out. I'll get you more."

"What are they?" he asked, sticking his fingers through the fence holes to take the bottle.

"Vitamins. They'll help…well, when your food supply… Just take them, okay?"

"I will," he promised. He took the blue bottle and stuffed it in his jacket pocket.

"I brought something else."

"You don't have to bring me things to make sure I come see you, Eva. I live to see you each night. It's the only thing that gets me through my days."

"I know. Here." I picked up the shopping bag. "It's not going to fit."

"It's okay…"

"I'll put the things through one by one."

I reached into the bag and pulled out the cans of tuna fish. They barely fit through the fence. I had to lean them each to the side and pound them through with the side of my fist until the fence gave way just a little. Next I tried to push the fresh apples and oranges through, but only the smallest would fit. Even those were hard; juice soaked my fingers from the oranges I'd shoved through the hole.

"It smells good," David said.

"Eat it. It won't keep; the skin is broken. Eat it while it's still fresh."

"I don't want to eat in front of you."

"Oh, for cryin' out loud, David. I can get them whenever I want. When's the last time you had a fresh orange?" He shrugged. "That's what I thought. Eat it."

I watched his long fingers pull the rind from the orange. He worked quickly, ripping it away. He didn't bother eating the orange one slice at a time. He held it to his mouth and bit into it like an apple, moaning when the juice spurted in his mouth and ran down his chin. I smiled, watching him eat.

"Thank you, Eva."

"No problem. I have a few more things. First, these cans."

The cans of fruit were narrower than the tuna fish cans, so they slipped through easily, plopping on the ground next to David.

"I didn't know if you had a can opener, so I got flip tops. I'll bring a can opener next time. One last thing." I took out the chocolates and pushed the small bags through the fence one at a time. David caught them as they fell. "Sweets for my sweet," I told him with a smile.

"The guy's supposed to bring the girl chocolate."

"Yeah, and there's something distinctively sexist about your comment. I'll keep track of how much candy I bring you; when this is over and we're together again, you can make it up to me. How's that?"

"Deal."

The bag emptied, I pushed it through the opening so David could use it to carry the supplies back to his camp.

"This is too much. How are you paying for this?"

"I'm not. Everything is free."

"Free?"

I nodded. "All supplies are free until everyone gets established in their jobs and a banking system can be put in place. And no one thinks twice about how much someone takes. Everyone is stocking up before we have to start paying for things. People go to the grocery store every day and fill their carts full, so a few cans of fruit and tuna and some chocolates aren't going to raise suspicion."

"I just don't want you risking anything for me. You need to stay there. If they ever caught you bringing me supplies—"

"But they haven't. Do you need any clothes? Do you have warm socks? What about thermals? The nights are starting to get colder."

"I'm good."

"Okay, I'll bring thermals tomorrow."

He laughed. "You are so stubborn. I guess thermals would be nice. It's cold at night. But I don't want you risking anything. Understand? It's important to me that you be careful when you get supplies for me. In fact, as much as I like them, I wish you wouldn't bring anything. It's too dangerous."

"Let me worry about that. I love you and I'm going to do whatever I can to make sure you have everything you need until you're with me."

"Say that again."

"I'm going to do whatever—"

"No, not that. What you said before that."

"I love you."

"I love you, too."

He held my hand through the fence. We talked for two hours, longer than we should've. But it was so hard to leave him. I thought it would get easier knowing I'd see him the next night, but it only got harder. I found myself staying longer and longer each night.

"I had a thought after you left last night."

"What about?" I asked him.

"You said you'd keep track of the candy you brought me—"

"David, I was kidding!"

"No, that wasn't what bothered me. It was when you said I could make it up to you."

"And?"

"I wouldn't have any idea what to get you. We really don't know anything about each other, Eva. And this one hour a night deal isn't cutting it—"

"Oh no," I shook my head slowly, looking at him. "We know plenty about each other. All we did in the POD was talk."

"The deal is, I'm not going to be allowed into the compound. You aren't leaving it. I think we should cut our losses and move on," he said.

Something twisted within me, strangling me from within. "Cut our losses? *Move on?* You left your camp, travelled with a bunch of nomads looking for me, risked your life, just to come here and tell me you want to *move on?* Why didn't you tell me this before now? Huh? This isn't about some freakin' candy, David."

"No, I've been thinking about it for the last week or so. The candy thing just made me more aware of how little we know about each other. We don't even know if we could have a relationship outside the POD. Everything was different there. We lived in a vacuum. Literally and figuratively sealed off from the world."

"It doesn't matter where we were! We talked. That's all we did was talk. We know each other, David. Probably better than some married couples. Our relationship worked there and it will work here."

"Whispering sweet nothings in each other's ears at night and you telling me your favorite day in school was pajama day doesn't mean we know each other."

"We shared more than that…" I stared at him. *Glared* would be a better word. My fists balled at my sides; my fingers curled so tightly they ached.

He shook his head. "It isn't going to work, Eva. And my group—the people I've been traveling with—are heading out tomorrow. They want to see if they can find other survivors, their families. And I'm...I'm going with them."

"Screw you, David," I whispered.

I turned and walked away. He didn't call out to me, even though I was praying he would realize what an ass he was being and tell me to come back. And I didn't run back to him and beg him not to give up on us, even though my feet wanted to turn around a hundred times between the fence and my house. Instead, I stumbled through the meadow, *our* meadow, the toe of my sneakers catching on the underbrush and the rocks covering the ground, as hot salty tears ran down my cheeks.

I woke the next morning, the sun shining brightly through the window blinds. I didn't remember getting home or crawling into bed. I was still dressed in my clothes from the night before, shoes and all. Thorns from the weeds were stuck in my pant legs; dried leaves hung from my shirt and littered my bed.

I crawled out of bed and peeled the dirty clothes off before showering and dressing in clean clothes. I swiped at the leaves in my bed, but they clung to the fabric. Giving up, I pulled the sheets off the bed and balled them and my dirty clothes up, carrying them all to the laundry room and dumping them on the floor.

I walked to the kitchen table and slowly sat in a chair. Tears built behind my eyes, and a huge knot lodged in my throat.

I should've known. He didn't touch me. He didn't reach for my hand through the fence or lean in for a kiss. I don't even remember him smiling. I should've seen the signs, but I didn't. He blindsided me.

The tears were coming quickly now—I let them.

I reached for a notepad and pencil and made a list. My tears dripped on the paper, turning each spot gray, the blue ink smearing.

David,

You know most of this already, but this is what you should know about me:

I like chocolate with peanut butter or caramel, but plain chocolate is great, too.

I don't like liver or Brussels sprouts—my mom made me eat both.

I love Mexican food and seafood.

I had a dog named Alex when I was a kid.

I was an only child. I'd like to have two or three kids one day.

I hate being separated from you.

I love how you taste when you kiss me.

I miss you. And I love you.

I folded the sheet of paper and stuffed it in an envelope. I'd ask George to give it to David. Or not. I wasn't sure if I cared.

That night I sat on the couch, watching the clock. I'd dreaded it all day. The time I would've been with David was going to be empty. As the clock ticked closer and closer to midnight, the more anxious I became. What if he were there waiting for me? What if he'd changed his mind?

I grabbed my tennis shoes and the letter I'd written him and ran out the door. I didn't look to see if anyone was watching me. I just ran. I didn't stop until I reached the fence. It was one minute after twelve.

He wasn't there.

Chapter 19 : Dating

I moved through my monotonous days on autopilot. At work, I sat alone at lunch. George was working his month at the clinic and Nona's lunch break was different than mine. To fill the time, I wrote letters to David. Some were short:

I hope you're well. I've been thinking about you. I miss you.

Others were long. Some were lists of things I thought he should know about me, and questions I had about him. Other times I'd tell him about my day, my thoughts on life, love, politics, religion—whatever came to mind. If I ever had the chance to give them to him, he wouldn't be able to say he didn't know me. I was there, in black and white—an open book written just for him.

I spent every day telling myself I wouldn't go to the fence. But I went to the fence every night, anyway. I'd sit on the cold ground in the prickly weeds and wait. Sometimes I'd cry until my throat burned and my eyes were swollen—and then I'd cry some more. Other times I'd get angry. I'd bang my fist on the ground and dig my nails into the soil, throwing clumps at the fence I hated. I'd curse it, kick it, grab hold of the wire and jerk it back and forth, only to lay my forehead against it and cry more tears when it didn't budge. But most nights, I stared at the stars and thought of him and what he might be doing. I prayed he was safe, had enough to eat, and was happy.

Two weeks went by. I visited our meadow every night. Every night I was alone.

It'd been four weeks since I'd last seen David, and as much as I didn't believe I would, I had started to move on. I didn't forget, but I didn't let David's leaving consume every minute of every day.

"Dinner?"

"Yup, it's my night to cook," Nona answered as we walked on the sidewalk leading to our houses. Sugar maples lined the path, their leaves brilliant with spectacular fall colors.

Nona and I had started having dinner together twice a week. One night she'd cook, and the second night I would. I started meeting my other neighbors, going out of my way to say *hi* in the mornings and make small talk when we'd see each other on the street. Nona went out of her way to meet our neighbors, too. She met a guy three houses down from her, and they'd been seeing each other for three weeks. I was jealous. His name was—cruelly—David.

In addition to her new boyfriend, Nona met everyone else in our neighborhood and knew every sordid detail of their lives. We'd sit on the wraparound porch drinking lemonade and she'd tell me stories of our scandalous neighbors.

"Jenny is pregnant—"

"Wait. Who's Jenny again?"

"Eva, keep up! She's my neighbor on the right. She's been dating Todd. You know him. He teaches math down the hall from your classroom."

"Oh, him. He's such a complainer. *'My back hurts…my irritable bowel is acting up…lunch was gross.'* He whines about everything."

"Well, it seems Jenny got tired of listening to him, at least for one night. Evidently, even though she and Todd are supposed to be engaged, the baby isn't his."

"Uh-oh."

"Big time uh-oh."

"Then who's the father?"

"I don't know."

"Wait! Nona—the woman who knows more about people than they know about themselves—doesn't know?"

She laughed. "I'm working on it."

I'd learned very quickly that, if I wanted something to stay a secret, I'd better make sure Nona didn't find out about it.

I didn't go to the fence every night anymore. I only went twice a week, just in case. But David never showed up.

The first restaurant opened in town. Although it was nothing more than a greasy burger joint, it was the talk of the town. Everyone wanted to go.

Somehow, Nona got reservations for opening night. She and David—his name still made me cringe with longing every time she said it—were going.

"You're coming with us," she told me.

I was sitting on the edge of her bed, watching her hold up outfits, scrutinizing them in the mirror.

"No. I don't want to be a third wheel. Thanks for inviting me, though."

"You won't be a third wheel. A bunch of people are coming from work." She rattled off some names. I was vaguely familiar with some of the people she mentioned.

"I don't know any of them, Nona. I'd feel out of place. They're people from your department."

"Nah, you're going. End of discussion. Eva…" She saw me open my mouth to argue and shook her head. "We've been here for a couple of months already and you don't know anyone except a handful of neighbors and teachers. You need to get out and make some friends."

"You're tired of me already?" I teased.

"Pssh, no, but I know people need more than one friend in their lives. So come on. Let's find you something cute to wear. This is the big grand opening. You have to look the part."

We walked into the small diner. It was surprisingly upscale. Linen cloths covered the tables and matching napkins were crisply folded under the silver utensils. Small vases of fresh flowers sat in the middle of the tables with candles. It was understated, but classy. I was surprised. I'd expected paper napkins and red-and-white checkered placemats.

Nona's friends were nice, but there was just one problem. They were all couples—five in all, including Nona and her David. And there was one other person who was dateless…or so it seemed. To his credit, Craig, my would-be date, seemed just as surprised at Nona's fix-up as I was…either that, or he was a really good actor.

I was ready to stab Nona with a fork.

Even so, I spent most of the time laughing at Craig's jokes, and it sure beat the heck out of sitting next to a cold, steel fence waiting for a man who'd made it clear he didn't want me in his life.

"I guess you weren't expecting me tonight," Craig said as he walked me home after dinner.

"No. I was definitely not expecting you," I agreed with a smile.

"Well, if it makes you feel any better, I wasn't expecting you, either."

"I didn't think so."

"But I'm glad Nona went behind our backs and fixed us up."

I didn't know what to say. I just smiled at him. I wasn't sure if I was glad Nona had fixed us up or not. Even though I'd had a great time with him, I wasn't over David and I didn't know if I was ready to start dating.

"I hope your silence doesn't mean you don't feel the same, because I'd like to see you again, Eva."

"I…ah…no, I mean, that sounds great. There's just one problem. There's kind of someone else."

"Ah."

"No, it's not like that. I think we're through. I just need to make sure before I do…anything…"

"Okay. I'll see you around school. We can talk later in the week?"

I let out the breath I was holding. "That'd be great."

The next morning, I didn't wait for Nona. She came by my classroom just before the first bell rang.

"Pissed at me, huh?" she asked.

"You know I am."

"Why? Craig's a nice guy. You two would be great together."

"Nona, did you think to ask me first?" I asked through clenched teeth. "I don't want to see Craig. You're right, he is a nice guy, but there's someone else."

"Really? But I've never seen you with anyone. Wait, is it that George guy?"

"I don't want to talk about it."

"It *is* him! Well, he seems nice enough, but he lives in a different district. You never get to see each other."

"It's not George."

"Then who?" she asked, her brow furrowed over her eyes.

I tapped my pen against my scarred wooden desk, glaring at her. "He's someone from my POD. And, no, he doesn't live in this district. He doesn't even live in this compound. But I'm not ready to give up on the chance we might be able to be together again when this virus thing is under control. I'm not ready to date. And if you would've asked me, I could have told you this. Now I have to tell Craig and risk hurting a really nice guy's feelings."

"I'm sorry, Eva. I didn't think to ask. I thought I was helping."

I looked over her shoulder at the white wall.

She should've asked. But she seems genuinely sorry. I can't stay mad forever—not when the only other people I know in the world are in other compounds...or God knows where.

"Don't do it again. Next time, at least ask."

"Deal. Do you want me to talk to Craig for you?"

"Nona! Didn't we just decide you were going to butt out? I'll talk with him. You stay out of things. From now on, no more secret blind dates."

She gave me a quick kiss on the cheek. "Gotcha. I'll see you after work."

"Yeah, yeah. Get out of here. My class is about to start."

"Go." It was lunch hour and George sat across from me at the fake-wood table. Trays clattered and silverware clinked together. I could hear people crunching their food at the table next to us, and boisterous laughter from a group of boys across the room. The sounds made my head pound.

"No."

"Eva, go. You said yourself he's a nice guy. You should go out again. You never know what might happen."

"Would you? If I fixed you up with one of my teacher friends, would you go?"

He didn't answer me. He looked down and drew circles on the tabletop with his finger.

"That's what I thought."

It was cold. I shivered and wrapped my coat tighter around me as I sat with my back to the fence, leaning against it. I knew he was there before he spoke. I stood and turned to face him.

"I thought you'd give up on sitting out here every night, Evangelina."

"And I thought you'd have come to your senses before now."

"Eva, you are so stubborn."

"I'd watch calling people stubborn, David. They might tell you the same thing. How do you know I've been here?"

"Because I've been here every night watching you."

"And you said nothing?"

"I thought you would give up. Have a life with someone on the other side of the fence. A real life."

"Well, David, there's one problem with your thinking. A person doesn't get to choose who they fall in love with. Fence or no fence." I sighed. This wasn't how I had imagined our reunion would go. "You lied to me. When you said you were leaving."

"Yes," he admitted.

"I didn't believe you. I knew you were still here."

"I know."

"Weeks of me sitting here. Crying over you. Hurting. And you just watched? Why? Why didn't you see that I don't want anyone else? Why didn't you come to me? And why did you decide to come out of the shadows and meet me tonight?"

"I came out to meet you tonight because I couldn't see you hurting anymore. And because you haven't been coming as much and I was afraid that you were forgetting—"

"But that's what you just said you wanted!"

"I know I said it, but I don't want it. George told me about the other guy. What's his name? Greg?"

"Craig."

"Yeah. I couldn't stand the thought of you being with him."

"You don't want me, but you don't want anyone else to be with me. Is that it, David?"

"You're half-right. I don't want anyone else to be with you. You're wrong when you say I don't want you. I *do* want you, Eva. But there's a problem with us being together. I can't give you what you want, what you need. We'll always be separated."

"You don't know that."

"So how long? How long do we wait before we realize things aren't going to change? When do we call it quits, Eva?"

"I don't know! I don't know any more than you, but I think it should be a mutual decision. We need to communicate. Tell each other what we're feeling. Our thoughts and fears.

"Look, you said you didn't feel like you knew me. So I wrote these for you," I said, pushing the stack of letters I'd written through the gaps in the fence. "Read them. Make a decision one way or another. I'll be here tomorrow night. If you don't come, I'll know it's over and I won't come back." I took a shuddering breath. "I hope I see you tomorrow, David." I turned and walked home.

I walked to the fence the next night. I didn't run. I didn't rush. I wasn't even that excited or nervous about what I'd find. I was resigned. He'd be there and I'd be happy, but there'd always be a hurt, a longing, to be together. Or he wouldn't be there and that would be another kind of hurt.

"Here." He pushed something through the chain links.

"What is it?"

"Open it. I had Seth help me get it."

I opened the bag, tipping it to catch the distant glow from the gate lights. What I saw inside made me smile, and I knew I had my David back.

"I got peanut butter and caramel because you didn't say which you liked more. I even got regular chocolate. I read your letters, Eva. I love you, too. And I want to be with you. I'll wait. We'll find a way to be together."

That's all I needed to hear. "It'll work out, David. I can feel it." I reached through the fence and pulled him into a kiss.

We fell into our old routine. We met almost every night at the fence in our meadow. We'd talk and kiss and hold hands through the fence while we looked at the stars in the inky, black sky. But an hour was never enough. I pushed it as far as I could, staying an hour and a half most nights.

It was dangerous staying longer than an hour. We couldn't risk getting caught. So to make up for the twenty-three hours a day we were forced to be apart, I continued writing him letters. Soon, he did the same for me. We'd exchange them each night. I was always excited to read his. It was like Christmas morning every day.

Sometimes we'd make up a theme for the letters we wrote. We'd each write about the same thing—like the most embarrassing day of our lives. My favorite was when we wrote about the best day of our lives. His letter had two sentences. Twelve words total:

The first time I saw you. The first time I kissed you.

Technically, those were two separate days, but I didn't care. Reading it gave me butterflies, and my stomach warmed in a way I'd never felt before.

The next morning, Nona and I were walking to work. I was chattering about something—I can't remember what—when she interrupted me.

"Where do you go every night?" she asked.

"Huh?"

"I see you leave almost every night about the same time. Where do you go?"

"I just like to get out, spend some time outdoors," I said, wondering what she knew.

"You can do that during the day."

I didn't answer. I didn't know what to say. I'd been caught. She'd seen me leaving, but did she know what I was doing when I left?

"It's pretty here," Nona said.

I let out a breath of relief that she was changing the subject. "Yeah, it is."

"It's a lot different from where I grew up."

"Where was that?" I asked.

"Arizona. I like it here. Do you like it here, Eva?"

"Yes."

"I'd hate for one of us to have to leave. I hear it's really hard living in the nomad camps."

I walked to my classroom, Nona's words still ringing in my ears.

She'd hate for one of us to have to leave.

We were sitting cross-legged on the ground facing each other. I was sticking things through the holes in the fence. He was complaining that I was bringing him too much. I was shushing him. I liked bringing him things.

In return, he'd started bringing me drawings. I loved his art. It came so naturally to him, like writing my name did to me. I kept each drawing in a scrapbook so I could look at them whenever I wanted.

After I pushed the last of the cans of fruit I had brought him through the fence, he gave me my drawing. It was beautiful. Two people, holding hands, walked along the shore of the ocean, the sun setting over the water. The sand showed bits of seaweed and the footprints of the couple as they walked barefoot through it. Shells were scattered across the shoreline, and gulls flew over the water.

"It's so beautiful."

"It's a picture of us. One day, we'll be the couple walking along the ocean shore."

We didn't hear the others until it was too late.

Chapter 20 :
Nóna

The spotlight shone bright in the dark meadow. I jumped up with a scream. It took me a millisecond to understand what was happening.

"Run!"

He looked at me, a pained expression on his face.

"David, run!"

He grabbed his things and ran into the brush. He made it to the tree line before the soldiers were able to find him again with a spotlight. I sighed, my shoulders slumping in relief. I didn't know what they would have done to him, but I knew they wouldn't let him inside the compound. They wouldn't put him in quarantine.

"Stand up and show us your hands," the man yelled through a bullhorn. How ridiculous for him to use a bullhorn—the meadow was quiet, except for the sound of the Humvee and the idiot's voice booming out.

I stood up and raised my hands so the soldier could see. A man dressed in a hazmat suit approached and used a zip tie to bind my hands. He grabbed me under the arm and pulled me roughly to the Humvee, pushing me inside.

They drove me to the clinic. There were two of them in the back with me, and they never put their guns away. My hands were slick with sweat and my heart pounded painfully, each contraction sending more and more adrenaline through my body.

The drive to the clinic seemed to take an hour, but was actually just a few short minutes. We didn't drive to the front entrance. Instead the vehicle stopped next to a large green dumpster behind the building. The smell of rotting garbage filled the air. I put my hands over my nose and mouth, trying not to gag.

The MP to my right got out first. The other jammed his elbow into the small of my back, pushing me toward the door. I slowly climbed out of the vehicle, the MP close behind me.

A single lightbulb hanging over the clinic's door provided the only light in the alley. The MPs herded me through the door to the small reception desk that faced it. The men stopped, one man's fingers biting into my arm harder than necessary.

"One resident for quarantine."

The nurse looked at the soldier who had spoken, and then at me. "It took four of them to bring you in? What's your name?" the nurse asked me. She wore green scrubs, thick latex gloves, and a facemask.

"Evangelina Evans."

"She was found fraternizing with a member in the infected zone."

"'Fraternizing'?" The nurse laughed. "You guys really like to toss your military jargon around. Tell me what happened, Evangelina."

"Call me Eva, please. One of my friends lives in the infected zone. I met him tonight and we talked through the fence. But he isn't infected," I said in a rush, "he's a POD survivor, not a topside. He lived in the same sub-POD I did. That's how we know each other."

"Okay, guys, I got her from here. Come on, Eva. Let's get you washed up for quarantine."

"But—"

"I know, sweetie. He was a POD survivor. I hear ya. But I have rules to follow. Anyone in contact with an infected zone resident has to do their stint in quarantine. Sorry."

The nurse led me down a series of hallways. The walls were dirty white and the air smelled of disinfectant. We came to an opening and I saw two shower stalls set up in the middle of the small area. It was nothing more than a fork in the road map of hallways. The opening had three hallways shooting off it, with no privacy.

"Go behind the curtain and strip. Throw your clothes into the bin, tie the bag, and set it in front of the screen. When you're done, step into stall one."

I did as she asked. Peeling my clothes off, I shivered in the cold hallway. I stuffed them into the thick biohazard garbage bag and tied it off as tightly as I could. Stepping into the shower stall, I heard her call to me.

"Brace yourself, Eva. This is gonna sting."

"I know. I remember from quarantine." I squeezed my eyes closed and waited. She was right; it did sting and it was freezing cold. I shivered uncontrollably from the cold air and the colder water.

Green foam fell from the top of the stall, covering me. It smelled of alcohol, and the blast from the water hose moved the foam around until I was covered with it. It burned my skin while the water pricked it like tiny needles.

When the torture finally ended, the nurse opened the back of the stall and pointed to a towel. I dried off before dressing in white pajama bottoms and a t-shirt. Using a ring of keys attached to her belt, she unlocked a door and waited for me to walk through before closing and locking it behind me.

Her voice came through an intercom panel. "Follow the hall and ring the buzzer next to the door. They're waiting for you."

I walked down the long white hallway, ringing the buzzer when I reached the end. The door opened and two male nurses wearing facemasks and gloves guided me to my observation room. They didn't speak. One held the door open for me. I walked through, and the door was shut with a loud click. The bolt screeched when it was pushed into place.

The observation room was a mirror image of the one I'd stayed in before entering the PODs. I sat on the bed, pulling the blanket over me. I was still shaking from the cold shower. I don't remember falling asleep. When I woke, I saw George's face through the glass.

"What the hell were you thinking, Eva? I told you two not to get caught."

"Someone turned us in."

"Who?"

"I'm not sure," I said, "but I think it was Nona. How long will I be in here?"

"Probably a month," George answered.

"A month? But I thought quarantine was a sham?"

"So did I, but I've learned a few things. The government isn't being completely honest with the survivors—what's new, right? The topside survivors aren't all virus-free. Some carry a mutated form of the virus. You aren't here to make sure you're virus-free. You're here to see if they can harvest some of the mutated virus from you."

"I don't understand," I said slowly.

"You're a human guinea pig, Eva. They're hoping you were exposed to the mutated strain so they can study it and, God willing, find a cure."

"That's a good thing, right?"

George didn't answer me. He smiled, but it didn't reach his eyes.

"I have to go. I'll try to visit tomorrow."

Chapter 21 :
Going Home

I spent six weeks locked in a glass-lined medical prison. The nurses took blood every day through a box in the wall, just like the first time I was in quarantine. The doctors were the only people who entered the room. Dressed in protective clothing that made them look like space aliens, they poked and prodded me. They never told me what they were looking for. In fact, they rarely spoke to me at all. George was right. I was a human guinea pig.

George visited when he was working at the clinic. We talked through an intercom in the thick glass surrounding the stark white room I was locked in. I asked George about David every time I saw him, but he didn't know…or he didn't want to tell me. Worrying about David was the worst part.

Nona tried to visit once, but I refused to see her. She had one of the nurses carry in a note, which she passed along with one of my meals.

…did it to protect you. I was worried for your safety…

I crumpled it and threw it on the floor.

She didn't visit again. I was surprised they had let her in to begin with. It seemed Nona had extra privileges in the compound, which explained how she knew so much about everyone. George's friend in security confirmed Nona actually worked for them. Undercover security personnel throughout the compound spied on residents and reported any suspicious behavior. Nona's job at the school was a sham. Her real job was as a snitch.

Like in quarantine before I entered the PODs, there were books inside the room to keep me occupied. Every once in a while, the nurses would send a new book through the chute with my dinner. I read all the books there—twice. No television, no music, and no book I hadn't already read. Quarantine was hell.

"Today's the day." The nurse looked younger than me and I wondered what kind of medical training she'd actually had.

"What day?" I asked, afraid I was going to endure another painful test.

"You've been given the all-clear. You're outta here."

"When?"

"Now. You don't want to stay longer, do you?"

"Ah, no. But thanks for asking."

The nurse pulled out a ring of keys and inserted one into the thick metal door. The lock clicked open and the door squeaked loudly when the nurse pulled it aside.

I hurried out of the room before they changed their minds and decided I needed to stay another six weeks.

"Where are my clothes?" I asked the girl.

"They were burned. You can wear home what you have on. Transportation will give you a ride so you don't have to walk home in pajamas."

"My other belongings?" I was afraid I already knew the answer to my question.

"Burned."

I didn't really care about my clothes, or anything else I had, for that matter. The only items I was interested in were David's photo and drawings. They must've been burned like the rest of my things.

"Go straight down this hall and out the door. Transportation is waiting to take you home. Take care, Eva."

"Thanks," I murmured.

"These are your new papers." An MP handed me an envelope as I walked out the door.

I didn't look at the papers. I just clutched the envelope and climbed into the car. I wanted to go home, take a long, hot shower, and get out of the ridiculous white pajamas.

I sat with my head resting on the back of the seat, my eyes closed. I didn't open them until I felt the car turn into my drive.

"Here you are," the driver said.

"This isn't my house. I think you have the wrong address. I live at 12 Maple Brook Lane."

"No, this is the address the MP gave me. Check your papers and make sure."

I pulled out the paperwork and scanned the documents. "183 Oakwood Drive."

"That's where we are. Do you have your keys?"

I dumped a set of keys out of the envelope. They clinked when they landed in my open palm. "Yes."

"Well, then you're right as rain."

"Thank you." I slowly got out of the car, standing in the driveway as I watched him drive away.

The house was light-brown with burgundy shutters. I missed my cheery yellow house. I fit the key in the lock and it turned. I don't know if I was relieved or disappointed that the key opened the door. I wanted to go home—to my other home.

I walked slowly inside. Something was wrong. My things weren't there. The drawing David had made wasn't hanging on the wall. The scrapbook I'd made of all the drawings he'd given me wasn't on the coffee table.

I ran down the hall to the master bedroom. The photo of him and his sisters wasn't on the bedside table. In fact, nothing of mine was in the house. There were no clothes, no food, nothing.

I made a quick call to transportation and had them drive me to and from the compound store, where I got some clothes and enough food to get me through the week. Once home, I showered and changed into jeans and a sweater. I pulled on my sneakers and ran out the door. Maple Brook Lane was two streets over from Oakwood. I'd put the key to the back door under the mat. I planned to go in, get my photo of David and his drawings and take them to the new house. I didn't particularly care which house I lived in, but I wanted my things.

I stared at the house. A bubble of plastic covered it, rippling in the breeze. A yellow notice was posted, warning residents that the house was contaminated.

"Everything you touched has to be decontaminated, including your things."

"Stay away from me, Nona."

"Eva, I know you don't think I—"

I didn't turn around. "What I think is, I trusted you. I counted you as a friend and you betrayed me. What I think is, I'm glad I was moved from this street. Now I don't have to see my betrayer every day."

She sighed. "I don't blame you for being mad. Look, I got these out of your house before I called security. I knew you wouldn't be able to come back, and I wanted to make sure you got these. I thought maybe they'd be a peace offering."

I turned, and she held out David's photo and the scrapbook. I took them and hugged them to my chest.

"Thank you, Nona. I appreciate the gesture, but it doesn't change anything. Stay away from me."

I walked back to my new house. I wasn't watching where I was going. I was staring at David's smiling face in the photo he gave me. My heart hurt with the longing to see him again.

A person knocked into me, making me stumble backward. His hand reached out to steady me.

"People are watching, Eva. Keep walking. It's too dangerous to meet, but he's still here."

Seth walked by me and disappeared around the corner.

David. David is still here.

It'd been three weeks since the day I was released from quarantine, the day when I'd seen Seth. I was back to work. And things were back to normal, except I kept waiting to hear from Seth or George about meeting with David.

It was finally George's first day back to school after clinic duty.

"When?"

"I don't know," he answered.

"Why? It's been nine weeks. They've forgotten about us by now. Besides, we can find a new meeting place."

"Too dangerous. He's still here, Eva. When things cool off, you'll get to see him."

I pushed my lunch tray away with a frustrated sigh. "How do you know?"

"I see him at the front gate every day."

"The front gate," I said quietly, a plan brewing in my mind, one I was sure I'd regret later. But at that moment all I could think of was being with David again, and this time there'd be no steel fence separating us.

Chapter 22 : Together

Some people in the crowd screamed for the guards to open the gates. A few homemade picket signs waved and bobbed in the sea of bodies, but most of the hundreds of people outside the gates stood or sat in silent vigil, lines of suffering showing in their gaunt faces.

The MPs stood in a line in front of the fence, their guns aimed at the people trying to get into the compound. A truck pulled up to the gate, and the crowd reacted, surging to its feet and pressing in. An occasional *pop, pop, pop* was heard when an MP fired his riot gun at someone getting too close to the fence or the truck. The rubber bullets gave people one heck of a jolt.

I saw him on the other side of the gate, standing silently in the midst of the crowd. People bumped and shoved him, jostling him while they fought their way closer to the opening outer gate. He looked at me and smiled. I didn't return it. I watched him. He never took his eyes off me. They widened the moment he realized what I was going to do, because I wasn't looking for a way in.

I was looking for a way out.

I stood behind the inside gate, separated from the outer gate and the mob by a large, open area. Several MPs in riot gear stood guard just beyond the inner gate, watching the crowd. Additional soldiers were within the compound, and the weapons they carried didn't look like the kind that shot rubber ammunition.

David watched me, his eyes pleading. "Evangelina!" he yelled. I could barely hear him over the shouts of the people swarming around him.

I walked to the inside gate and pushed the tall door. The hinges groaned. I grunted as the heavy door dragged through the dirt and gravel. The metal clanged against a large rock, vibrating with the impact.

"Eva, don't!" I heard David yell. I turned and leaned against the gate, closing it behind me. The latch came down with a loud clang. Dust stirred up by the crowd billowed around me like a fog. I put my hand over my face to protect it.

Turning to the closest guard, I pointed to David on the other side of the gate. "Let him in."

The MP clutched his rifle across his chest. "Miss, you aren't supposed to be out here."

"Let him in," I said again.

"He's in the infected area. Go back to the compound," he ordered. He swung the rifle barrel around, not quite pointing it at me.

I looked at David and smiled. A look of relief washed over his face, and I knew he'd mistaken my smile as a sign I would return to the compound.

"He's not a top-side survivor. He was in the PODs. He's not infected." My eyes never left David's face.

"He's in the infected zone. No one comes through that gate without proper authorization. He doesn't have the required paperwork, he doesn't get in."

"Fine."

I turned toward the gate, hesitating for just an instant. Was I ready to give up what I'd built in the compound? My little house, my friends, my job?

Yes. For David—yes.

I walked slowly at first, and then I ran. I ran between two guards, hitting one in the shoulder. I stumbled forward toward the gate, hitting the wire mesh so hard it knocked the breath from my lungs. David reached his hand through and cupped my face.

These damn fences! If he can't be on this side, I want to be on that side.

"Eva, what the hell are you doing? Go back."

"I can't," I said, out of breath. "I don't want to."

"Miss, step away from the fence," a voice over a loudspeaker warned.

People in the crowd pushed against David, pressing their faces against the fence, screaming at me to open the gate and let them through.

"Eva, don't be stupid. Go back," David insisted.

I shook my head. *Don't make me go back, David. I need to be with you.*

One of the MPs approached, pointing his weapon at me while still keeping his distance from the outer fence. "Go back," he ordered.

Pleading filled David's voice. "Listen to him. Go—stay where it's safe."

"No! I want to be with you!"

I can't go back, David. This isn't how it's supposed to be. There isn't supposed to be a fence between us.

I ran down the length of the fence to where a crossbar held the metal-plated gate closed. I tried to lift it free. It was heavy—I could barely move it. I huffed, pushing with everything I had. One bar, one gate was all that separated us.

David.

"Step away from the gate," the voice over the loudspeaker said again.

MPs ran toward me, their words unintelligible as they shouted over each other. The shouts from the sea of people on the other side of the gate grew frantic, begging me to open the gate for them.

I looked over my shoulder. The MPs were closing in, their guns drawn. For a brief second, I wondered what I was doing. Why was I risking my life?

"Go back!" David yelled.

"No!"

I looked into his gray eyes and knew. He was the reason I was giving up what the compound offered. David—I didn't want to be without him a day longer.

I belong with you.

I smiled at him through the openings of the fence. "It's okay, David."

Pushing the bar as hard as I could, I got it just above the brackets before letting go. It fell to the ground with a thud, and dust rained down around us. I didn't wait, I didn't think—I just pushed as hard as I could on the edge of the gate. It opened just enough for me to squeeze through. I struggled through the small opening, stumbling out the other side. My hand against the dusty ground, I balanced myself, looking frantically for David.

"It's open!" someone in the crowd shouted, causing the mob to descend on the opening. They pulled the gate open and shoved their way through. I waded through the people pushing into the compound, making my way to where I'd last seen David.

"Eva, are you crazy?" he yelled, grabbing me in his arms.

"I can't stay in there, David. Not without you."

"You shouldn't have done it."

"It's done." I buried my face in David's shirt.

He tipped my head up and gave me a deep kiss. "You should have stayed." He held me, smoothing my hair down my back. "It was safe there—you were safe. It's dangerous out here."

Chapter 23: The Camp

Something woke me. I couldn't see anything, so I held my breath, listening. I grabbed the flashlight next to me, but I didn't turn it on. I sat in the pitch-black tent—a simple tarp strung between two trees that sheltered a single bedroll—and listened.

I heard it again. The crack of twigs, the rustling of leaves. It wasn't from inside the survivors' camp; it came from the woods.

The tarp made a crinkling sound as it moved. I jumped and inhaled sharply.

"Shh," David warned.

"What is it?" I whispered when he moved closer.

"I don't know." I had to strain to hear him, but I could hear the lie in his voice. "Just stay still and don't turn the flashlight on."

A twig snapped close to the tent. It sounded like it was right next to the plastic tarp.

Then it happened. All hell broke loose.

Screams, along with the drumbeat of running feet, came from all over the camp. The tent was ripped away from the trees and a huge man stood over us, a baseball bat raised above his head.

David grabbed my arm and jerked me from the bed. He blocked the blow with his arm, grunting in pain when the bat connected. He wound his hand around the wooden bat, twisting it from the man's grasp before he swung the bat hard, hitting the man's knee. The man fell across the tent.

David jerked me up and pushed me out of the plastic that pooled around our feet. My shoe caught on something and I fell, smacking against the hard ground. David didn't stop. He pulled me from the tent. Holding my hand, he ran, swinging the bat at anyone who got in our way.

A frenzy of people ran without direction, screaming and cursing. A shelter made of tree branches crashed into a campfire, sending flames into the air and brightening the night. The firelight revealed more men like the one who'd barged into my tent. Tall and broad—easily twice the size of a normal man—they chased the people of the camp, scattering supplies and tearing down the shelters.

David pulled me behind him. I stumbled over rocks and tree roots, trying to keep up with his long strides. We ran toward a circle of men from the camp, nearly two dozen in all. They stood with their backs to each other, the women inside the ring. David pushed through them, putting me inside the protective circle.

A large boom rang out next to me and I screamed. More deafening explosions filled the air as the men shot at those raiding the camp. I put my hands over my ears as shot after shot rang out, until the invaders were dead or had retreated back into the woods.

When it was over, most of them lay on the ground in pools of their own blood. Those who weren't dead were shot and killed. The men of the camp left no survivors.

I stood in the middle of camp, looking at the still, twisted bodies, at red blood dripping from blue tarps and pooling on the ground below.

Oh, no, no. This is wrong on so many levels. And I'm about to puke from all this blood—or I might pass out. I haven't decided yet.

A man lay dying in front of me, his hand outstretched toward me. I bent down, reaching for his hand. David grabbed me before I could touch him.

"Don't touch the blood," he said.

I watched in horror as a man from our camp walked up to the dying man and shot him once in the head. He turned and looked grimly at David.

"It's getting worse," he said, stopping to reload.

"David, what just happened?" My voice rasped. "That man just shot him. He just killed him right in front of us!"

"They're other survivors, Eva. They were raiding our supplies. We have to defend what's ours or we starve."

"No," I shook my head. "They weren't here for supplies. They would have snuck in, taken what they wanted, and left. They were attacking us."

"You're gonna have to tell her," the man who'd shot the dying man told David.

"Stay out of this, Devlin."

Devlin looked menacing with a shotgun propped on his shoulder. "She needs to know."

David blew out a frustrated breath. "This is what I didn't want you to see. This is why I wanted you to stay in the compound, even though it killed me to be away from you. These people, the men who raided the camp tonight. They're infected with the mutated virus, and it's done something to them. Don't touch their blood, Evangelina."

"And whatever you do, don't get bit," Devlin said, walking away.

David nodded. "Don't get bit."

Chapter 24: Infected

"What don't I know?"

"A lot," he answered.

"I gathered as much when the giant crazy-man was standing over us with a baseball bat. What's going on, David?"

He wrapped the hem of my t-shirt around his finger, bent down, and leaned his forehead against my shoulder. I reached up and ran my hands through his dark hair.

"I didn't want you out here, Eva. I didn't want this for you. The virus didn't die like scientists hoped it would."

I gently pushed him from me, looking in his eyes. "Are you saying those were topsiders?"

"Yeah, those were topsiders infected with a mutated strain of the original virus. But not all topsiders are infected. Everyone in this camp is clean, as far as we know."

The sun peeked over the horizon, turning the sky a brilliant shade of blue, streaked in pinks and oranges. Shadows from the trees fell across the ground in front of us.

David sat silently next to me, lost in his thoughts, the skin between his eyebrows furrowed. He threw stones at the trees, the small thuds barely audible over the light breeze blowing the autumn leaves from their branches.

"What are they, David? I mean, it's obvious they're human. But they're something else, too. The virus has changed them somehow, hasn't it?"

"Yeah. Devlin thinks the virus has affected their brains, rewiring them. He's the closest thing we have to a doctor. He was in medical school before the virus hit. He says it's sort of like rabies—the infected have lost all reasoning. They've reverted back to an animal state, living purely on instinct—hunting by smell, mostly. They can't even speak—just grunts and screams. And they avoid coming out in daylight—we think their eyes might be over-sensitized, or maybe it's their skin."

"They're odd-looking," I said, remembering bits and pieces of the attack. The people had been huge, towering over David, who was easily six feet tall. Their skin was pale and crisscrossed with prominent blue veins. "What's with the blood?"

"Huh?"

"You told me not to touch the blood. What is it about their blood?"

"It stings when you touch it. Like a bee sting, only more painful. We aren't sure if that's one way the virus is transmitted; so far, we don't think anyone has been infected just by contact with their blood."

"Their bite, right? That's the way you know it's transmitted. You and Devlin warned me not to get bitten last night."

"Yeah, their bite injects the virus. It can either kill or infect. We aren't sure how it works." He picked up a handful of pebbles and threw it at the trees. The rocks made little *pops* when they hit the tree trunks, and the breeze blew loose dirt back in our faces. I rubbed my eyes with the palm of my hands to rid them of the grit.

"And what's their prey?"

He looked at me, his gray eyes boring into mine. "Last night, *we* were."

"Cannibals?"

"No," he reached out and tucked a strand of my hair behind my ear. He dropped his hand with a sigh. "Opportunists. They eat whatever is easiest. Us, livestock, dogs, cats, whatever. They don't care, as long as it's alive. Now they know we're here. We'll have to move camp today. We'd have to anyway, because of all the blood."

I stood and walked to the trees, leaning my back against a large tree trunk. I stared at the ground between my feet. It was littered with brittle pine needles and fallen leaves, smelling of rotting leaves below.

"I'm sorry, Eva. You shouldn't have to live like this. You should've stayed—"

"Stop it! No one should have to live like this. Stop treating me like I'm some kind of porcelain doll that's gonna break under the least amount of pressure. Geez, David."

His mouth twisted as he tried to hide a grin. He failed and chuckled. "I should have known. Eva the Great—strong, feisty, and too damn stubborn for your own good."

"I just don't want to be babied."

"I know."

"I can't believe what you risked each night."

"What do you mean?"

"When you came to see me at the fence. You walked alone every night. You were so vulnerable to them. I can't believe you did that!" I smacked his arm.

"Ow," he laughed. I didn't laugh in return. I was just realizing how much danger he'd been in. How hard life had been for him over the past months.

He threaded his fingers through my hair. "I would have done anything to see you, Eva. The infected didn't scare me. Not seeing you again did."

I cupped his face with my hand.

"So beautiful," he murmured, lowering his lips to mine. He kissed me long and slow, his tongue sliding over my lips and gliding with mine. His hands roamed across my body, under the hem of my shirt and up my bare back. Fingers closed over the clasp of my bra. My breath stuck in my throat. He broke the kiss and took a step back, smiling ruefully at me.

"David," I said quietly.

"Hmm?"

"When we get supplies today, promise me we'll get a toothbrush and toothpaste."

He laughed loudly in the morning's quiet. Birds squawked, and small animals scurried away from the sound, leaves rustling quietly as they made their way through the underbrush.

It was the laugh I remembered—a carefree laugh—one I'd missed for so many weeks. The one I'd left the safety of the compound to hear again.

We packed up what was salvageable in the camp. The tents were ripped and unusable and most of the water was gone, running like mini-rivers across the ground.

"What now?"

"We walk to the next town and see if there's a Wal-Mart or sporting goods store that hasn't been looted, so we can get some supplies," David said.

I stood in the small clearing and looked around. Everyone was packing up their supplies in hiker backpacks. Tin pots and cups clanged as people tied them to their packs. Fabric rustled as it slid into the canvas bags.

"Why do we walk?" I asked no one in particular.

"Huh?" A small girl shrugged on a pack twice the size she was. It was weird being around people so much younger than me—most people in the compound had been around my age, with the exception of some of the military and medical people.

"Why are we walking to the next town?"

She looked at me like I'd lost my mind, and then rolled her eyes. "Because we can't fly."

"I meant, why don't you use cars? There must be plenty around."

"No gas," Devlin answered. "The pumps need electricity to work. When we find a car, we use it until the gas runs out. Then we ditch it." He grinned. "That's when the walking comes in."

"Funny."

"We'll be able to pick up a car when we get to town," David said.

"And then someone hotwires it. Who's that mastermind?" David and Devlin both grinned. "Never mind. I don't want to know."

When the camp was packed up, we began the long, arduous trek to the next town. Many members of the camp stumbled and tripped on the broken asphalt, their heavy packs making them unstable.

I shielded my eyes from the grit and grime our feet kicked up. As the hours passed, everyone's faces became streaked with dirt. Our hair filled with dust and pieces of leaves.

The evening sun was starting to dim when we saw buildings in the distance. Everyone let out a sigh of relief. We found a small motel and settled into the rooms, excited at the possibility of warm beds—a huge step up, even without working electricity or heat, from our makeshift tents.

"We'll stay the night here, grab our supplies in the morning, and move on," David told me.

"David, why don't we just stay here? There are stores, the motel—"

He shook his head. "Staying here would be like a neon sign pointed right to us. We need to get our supplies and get out. The towns are the first place the infected hunt. We found that out the hard way."

I nodded, deciding I didn't want to know what'd happened. Judging from the night before, I had a pretty good idea.

"You and Jessica will stay in this room. Devlin and I will be in the adjoining room."

"Wait! You're not staying here with me?"

"I'll be right next door," he said.

"I just thought—"

"I'll be right next door."

"Oh. Okay." I watched him walk through the adjoining room's door. "Don't close it all the way."

He smiled, leaving the door slightly ajar.

I woke sometime during the night. It was impossible to know the time. The room was too black to make out the numbers on my watch. The moon was only a sliver, not giving the room any light.

I climbed out of bed, shivering when the cold air hit me, and walked toward the bathroom. My arm outstretched, feeling for a wall to use as a guide. My toe found the corner of the wall before my hand did, and I had to bite my lip to keep from crying out. I followed the wall around the corner and to the bathroom.

Walking back to bed, I stopped short. I heard something outside. Memories of the night before crashed through my mind. I didn't want to be in the room alone. Jessica was nice, but she was young and small—no match for the strength of a giant.

I held my breath, listening. I heard the noise again—a quiet thud.

"Jessica?" I whispered. Her even breathing and soft snores told me she was asleep.

I walked along the walls, using them as guides until I found the door to the adjoining room. I pushed it open, cringing when the hinges squeaked loudly in the stillness. I froze, listening again. The only thing I heard was crickets and then the distant rumble of thunder.

Maybe it'll rain tonight, take the edge off the dry, dusty air.

I stepped forward, waving my outstretched hand back and forth as I felt for the beds. I knew Devlin was sleeping in the bed closest to the door, David in the one by the bathroom. When I found David's bed I crawled under the sheets. He moaned and mumbled something before rolling over, giving me room to lie next to him. I snuggled against his back, listening for the noise. I didn't hear it again and I slowly drifted to sleep, curled up next to David's warmth.

The morning sunlight shone between the hotel room's drapes. I groaned and rolled over. I wasn't ready to wake up. The bed was warm and I hadn't gotten enough sleep during the night, spending most of it listening for sounds that weren't there.

"Eva," David murmured close to my ear. He smelled of soap, and the hair tickling my ear was damp.

I jumped and sat up in bed. "David!" I'd planned to wake up and get back to my room before he woke. That way, he would never have known I was scared and had crawled into bed with him.

"Good morning," he said with a grin. "What are you doing in my bed? Should I start calling you Goldilocks?"

"I'm sorry, I thought I heard something last night and... well, I didn't want to be alone." I shrugged.

"You probably heard one of the guys keeping watch."

"Oh." I hadn't thought of that. "How long have I been asleep?"

"About two hours or so, I'd guess. There was enough water in the pipes to fill the sink, so you can sponge off. I got it ready for you."

"Thanks."

I started to get out of bed when David reached out and grabbed my arm. He gently pulled me to him. He looked at my face, his eyes roaming until they found my mouth. He ran his thumb across my lower lip; my tongue darted out to moisten it. I watched his eyes darken, never looking away from my lips. He bent his head forward and kissed me.

His lips felt soft but firm as they moved over mine. His tongue tasted minty when it dipped between my lips. It was sensual and sexy, and I sighed with pleasure. He groaned at the sound and put his hand on the small of my back, pulling me closer to him.

I threaded my fingers through his damp hair, kissing him deeper. I slid my hands down his back and pulled his t-shirt up, running my fingernails softly up and down his back. Our kisses moved from mouths to other parts of the body—I pulled his t-shirt over his head, letting it flutter from my fingers and land on the floor next to the bed. I was running my hands up his chest and kissing his neck when he grabbed my arms and pushed me away.

I looked up at him with wide eyes. "What's wrong?"

"Eva…don't…I…we aren't alone."

"Oh." I wasn't thinking about anything other than David and the way his touch made my insides warm. I *definitely* wasn't thinking about anyone else.

"I need a shower. A cold one. A very, very cold one," he muttered.

I laughed. "Well, I guess you'll have to suffer, Romeo. There's no running water."

He looked at me seriously. "I want to."

"Um, it's okay, David. I understand," I said with a smile. His need to stop before things became too intense—that was one of his ways of caring for me. It made me feel as good as hearing his groans of pleasure. I wasn't sure which made me feel better.

"I just want you to know—"

"I know. Me, too," I told him. "Now quit seducing me and let me go wash up."

He grinned. "Always joking."

"Yeah, well, I've learned not to take life too seriously. We don't know how long we have. We may as well make it fun while we can."

"I'll meet you outside."

"You're not waiting for me? I don't want to be alone."

"Hell's bells, Evangelina. Are you trying to torture me?"

I grinned. "Maybe a little."

David and I met the others outside for breakfast. I looked around and frowned. It was like there were two camps. The women scurried about on one side while the men stood around talking and laughing on the other side. The women fussed over the breakfast, stirring the grits in a pot hanging from a stand over the fire, and then hurrying to the other side of the camp carrying bowls of grits and cups of coffee to the guys and bringing back their empty cups and bowls to wash. Only when every man and boy had a full bowl and cup did the women dish out some of the nasty grits for themselves, finding a place to sit and gulp down their breakfast before the men decided it was time to start breaking down the camp.

I watched in disgust. It was like the clock had rolled back a century and the women's only job was to take care of the men.

"Eva! Are you okay?" Jessica skipped over to me.

"Yeah. Why?"

"You weren't around when I woke up. I thought maybe you weren't feeling well and went out for some fresh air. You shouldn't do that, you know. We need to stay with the group—safety in numbers."

"I didn't wander off. I was with David." She studied me and I squirmed under her gaze.

"So you're the one."

"One what?"

"The reason David isn't interested in any of the other girls," she said with a smile. "They've all given it a try. He's nice and funny and gorgeous. But he wasn't interested."

"Oh," I didn't know what to say. On the inside I was jumping up and down for joy. On the outside I tried to look calm. I didn't want to seem like I was gloating, but secretly that's exactly what I was doing.

"I can see why he likes you," she said.

"What? Why?"

"You're nice and really pretty. I like your hair. It shimmers like gold when you stand in the sunlight. You make a good pair."

"Um, thank you." I could feel the heat of the blush covering my face.

I stayed on the women's side of the camp eating a bowl of bland grits. Jessica introduced me to the other "womenfolk." Many were my age, some a little older, with a few who might've been in their thirties—the topsiders hadn't been age-selected like those of us from the PODs. Although everyone in our group of survivors was healthy enough to keep up on day-long hikes, the oldest survivors were in their early to mid-fifties. While I talked with the women, I couldn't help stealing glances at David. He stood with his hands on his hips, his jeans riding low, talking to the other guys. Now and then he'd look over his shoulder at me and grin.

Breakfast over, the women bustled about, gathering bowls and utensils. The bowls clanged together as they scrubbed the hardening food from the sides.

A man who looked to be in his late twenties, with a ruddy complexion and red hair, kicked sand over the fire; smoke billowed out, stinging my eyes.

"Dang it, Roy! I done told ya I'd do it. Now you smoked us all out!"

"Woman, that's why we don't go helping you none," Roy called over his shoulder with a grin.

"I ain't got any use for yer help," the woman muttered, gathering dishes and walking away.

"That's Judy," Jessica whispered. "She and Roy have a thing for each other. At least, that's what Devlin says. But Roy and Judy don't know it yet."

I laughed. "Who's going to tell them?"

Jessica shrugged. "Not me. I've got my own love life to sort out."

"Oh?" I tried to hide a grin.

"Yeah. His name's Chris. He's that one." She pointed to a teenaged boy with shaggy blond hair wearing a rock band t-shirt. He looked over and smiled at Jessica. She blushed and giggled. "Devlin says I'm too young for a boyfriend. I tell him that's okay 'cuz Chris and I aren't boyfriend and girlfriend."

"No? Then what are you?"

"Soulmates," she sighed, waving her fingers at Chris. He dipped his head and smiled, a small blush coloring his cheeks. "I'm going to go see if he got enough to eat." Jessica skipped to Chris. I watched her cross the divide between the women's side of the camp and the men's.

"Are you ready to go shopping?" David asked, walking toward me.

"Are we going together, or are we segregated? The womenfolk shopping in one area while the strong, manly menfolk shop in another?"

He laughed. "I guess it does look like the women are segregated from the men. But it's just how it turned out. We fell into a routine and it stuck."

"Whatever. But I'll tell you right now, I'm not washing anyone else's dishes but my own. Well, maybe yours, if you ask right."

"You're going to start a women's lib movement in the camp? That'll really throw everyone for a loop." He chuckled.

"No, that'll throw you guys for a loop. It'll be a nice change of pace for the girls. They'll thank me for it."

A stuffed bear met us at the entrance of the sporting goods store, holding a "welcome" sign. Canoes and kayaks hung from the ceiling.

"Too bad we can't find a river and float away," I said, staring at the boats.

David grinned. "I'm just glad this one hasn't been looted. Most of the ones near the major highways have been stripped bare."

Tents were set up for display in the middle of the store. I looked them over, choosing a four-person tent with windows on the sides.

"It's too big, Eva," David whispered in my ear, his breath tickling my skin.

"I'm just dreaming of having a mansion instead of a bungalow."

David chuckled.

We grabbed some one-man tents and bedrolls. I found the backpacks and picked one big enough to hold the supplies I thought we'd need. When I put it on, it was so big and bulky I stumbled backward. Chris—who seemed to go wherever Jessica went—reached out to steady me.

"Maybe you need a size smaller." He patted the pack. "You won't be able to stand once it's full of supplies."

"Yeah, I think you're right." I took the smaller pack he held out for me. "Thanks."

My pack in place, I looked around the store and found David and Devlin at a gun counter, filling their packs with ammunition. I walked over and looked in the glass gun cases. Shotguns lined the wall behind me; I knew a shotgun would be too big for me to handle, and I didn't know anything about them. But the handguns didn't look too complicated. In fact, they looked like the handguns I'd seen on television.

I walked around the gun case and pulled the door—it was locked. I grabbed a shotgun Devlin had left lying on the case and used the wooden butt to break the glass. Brushing away the shards of glass with my sleeve, I reached in and grabbed a medium-sized gun. It fit my hand just right and looked easy enough to work. I looked it over. I immediately found the lever that let the thing the bullets loaded into drop out.

Not hard at all.

"What are you doing?" Devlin asked.

I thrust my hand out, showing him the gun. "I need bullets for this."

"No you don't," he said.

"Why?"

"Because we take care of that kind of stuff."

"You mean the guys form a circle and shoot at the infected while the girls stand around inside the circle like a bunch of ninnies."

"Eva," David said quietly.

"I got news for both of you. I'm not standing around doing nothing. I want something to protect myself with. Now what kind of bullets do I need for this?"

I thought Devlin would argue. But I saw him purse his lips to hide a grin. He looked at David and said, "Feisty. Sure you can handle her?"

I scowled. "I don't need *handling*."

David rolled his eyes. "Give her the bullets."

Gun and bullets safely tucked away in my pack, I patted it and winked at David. As I walked away, I grabbed a pink pocket knife and jammed it in my pocket.

"What do you need that for?" David sighed.

"You never know." I smiled. "Besides, it's pink."

He snorted. "Well, that makes sense."

Our next stop was a general store. It had everything from clothes to car batteries. I grabbed three days' worth of clothing. That's all that would fit in my pack. I also found a box of powdered milk and some canned meat. I shoved it all in my pack, the zipper skipping when I tried to pull it shut.

"Are you going to be able to walk with that?" Jessica asked.

"I hope so. Help me put it on?"

"Sure."

She put one strap over my arm and then the other. I staggered a few steps backward, leaning precariously against a counter. Jessica giggled. Chris reached out to steady me. Once I got used to the weight and bulkiness, I was able to balance myself enough to carry the pack without falling on my butt. Jessica and Chris wandered away to fill their own packs.

"Are you sure you can carry all that, Eva? You don't have to fill your pack so full," David murmured behind me. His breath made my hair move, tickling the side of my neck. I turned my head and kissed him. I didn't stop until Jessica came around the corner talking to me. I sighed and turned to listen to what was so important she needed to interrupt my mind-numbing kiss with David.

It seemed I'd made a friend in Jessica. She followed me around and chattered away. I liked it. It'd been a while since I had a girlfriend to talk to. Jessica reminded me of Katie—a bittersweet connection.

We left the store and found two cargo vans parked outside near the loading bays. Devlin broke a window on each, reaching in to unlock the doors. He climbed into the front seat of one and pulled down the sun visor.

"Of course. They're never in the visor. Things on television are always easier," he muttered.

He jammed a screwdriver into the steering column and pried away the plastic covering; it cracked as it came loose. Devlin pulled out a tangle of colored wires, bending two until they broke in half. Ripping away the plastic sheathing, he twisted two of the wires together and flicked a third wire across them. The van roared to life. He repeated the process on the second van.

"These should get us to the next town. They might not be very comfortable to sit in, though. Jessica, run into the store and grab some pillows and blankets. They'll help cushion the back and make the ride a little easier."

We made it to the next town before running out of gas and found a small motel to spend the night in, making a fire next to the near-empty shell of the swimming pool.

"Show me how to work this, David." I pulled out my gun after we'd finished dinner.

"You don't need that. Give it to me," he said, reaching for the gun.

"I probably won't need it, but I'm keeping it."

"Eva, the men—"

"The men, the men. I don't care about the men and their super-inflated egos. You guys probably will be able to keep all us poor, helpless *womenfolk* safe, but I'm not taking a chance. After seeing those things, I think we all need guns. This isn't some western movie where we all run around in our frilly petticoats and Sunday bonnets."

He grinned. "Can't you take anything seriously?"

"I am taking this seriously. We all need to know how to protect ourselves."

"So your idea of protection is putting a gun in the hands of someone like Jessica? She's twelve, Eva!"

"Boys are taught to hunt at that age. If she's taught how to properly handle one, I don't see why she shouldn't have a gun. Women are just as capable as men when it comes to hunting."

"Evangelina..."

"David." I glared at him.

"Fine. Go grab some of the pop cans left over from dinner."

I ran to the area around the fire and picked up the Coke cans littering the ground, jogging back to David.

"First lesson. Don't run with a loaded gun."

I rolled my eyes. "I'm not a total fool. The safety's on."

David walked a short distance into the forest. Twigs snapped when he stepped on them, and his movement stirred up the smell of rotting leaves and wet dirt. He balanced the cans along a fallen log before turning and walking back to me. It was already getting dark. The inside of the forest was nearly black. The trees were so thick, the moon's rays didn't reach the ground. I had to strain to see the cans.

"These are your sights. Line up the can here," he pointed. "Don't put your finger around the trigger, just extend it along the side of the gun until you're ready to shoot. When you shoot, keep your shoulders relaxed and make sure your hips and shoulders are square to the target. Wrap this hand," he picked up the hand not holding the gun and kissed it softly, "around the gun grip to help steady the gun. Make sure you are making contact on all four corners of the gun. The higher you grip, the steadier it will be. Both thumbs should be pointing at the target. Use your thumb to click the safety off, place the tip of your finger on the trigger, look straight at the target and aim dead center. Your sight should be crystal clear—the can slightly out-of-focus. Gently, but firmly, pull the trigger." He stepped back. "Okay, give it a whirl."

I took my time aiming at the first can, the red color barely visible. The can in my sight, I released the safety and fired… and missed by yards. I aimed and fired at the pop cans until I had to reload the magazine. I had missed every time.

I reloaded, surprised I could do it without David's help. I guess all the television I'd watched was paying off after all. I extended my arms, relaxed my shoulders, placed the tip of my index finger on the trigger, and pulled. My bullet grazed the side of the can, knocking it over. That gave me the incentive to keep trying.

My next shot missed, but the third connected with the can, blowing it up and off the log. I smiled at David.

"Not bad," he said.

I emptied my magazine again, hitting all but one of the cans. By the time I reloaded, the forest was too dark for me to see and we stopped for the night.

"Are you sure you've never fired a gun before?" David asked as we walked back to the motel.

"That was my first time."

"Then you're either a quick learner or you have a natural talent. Either way, you did good."

"Thanks," I said. *Told you so.*

He stopped on the road in front of the motel. I turned to look at him. He threaded his fingers through mine and gently pulled me to him. He leaned down and his lips moved over mine in a gentle caress. He lifted his head and looked at me. He started to say something, but stopped and kissed me quickly.

"You're amazing," he whispered.

"You're not so bad yourself, David."

He smiled and held my hand while we walked across the street.

The smell of stale cigarette smoke and body odor smacked me in the face when he opened the door to my room. The walls were covered in chipped fake-wood paneling, and the two double beds' quilts were threadbare and stained. I tried not to think about what the stains were.

"This must be what the Ritz looks like," I said.

We walked in; the foul odor got worse and I wrinkled my nose. He smiled and kissed the tip. "You look so cute when you do that."

Reaching around his head to the back of his neck, I pulled him toward me. He came willingly, closing the door behind us. His kisses trailed down the side of my neck and over my collarbone. I sighed in pleasure. I walked backward into the room until the bed hit the back of my knees, my lips never leaving David's.

We fell onto the bed, our lips and hands roaming over each other. I opened his shirt and trailed my hands down his chest, across his belly to the light dusting of hair that disappeared under his waistband.

He pushed my shirt above my head, trailing feather-light kisses across my chest, his tongue following the lacy edge of my bra. He reached under me to unhook my bra. I undid the button of his jeans, reaching for the zipper.

And Jessica opened the door.

Breathless, David rolled off me, throwing his arm over his eyes. I slipped my t-shirt back over my head, a blush creeping across my face.

"I guess I should have knocked, huh?" she said, flouncing into the room and jumping on the bed next to us.

"Gee, honey," I arched a brow at David, "didn't you lock the door?"

He groaned. "My mind was on other things."

I woke up when I felt the bed sag beside me. I didn't look—I knew it was David. He snuggled behind me, wrapping his arm around my waist. He didn't say anything. I drifted into a peaceful sleep, knowing David was close.

He was gone when I woke. It was still black outside, with a pale dusting of moonlight outlining the window. I sat up in bed, the springs in the old mattress squeaking.

"Shh," David said from somewhere in the room.

Chapter 25 : Banned

"What's wrong?" I whispered.

"Dunno," I heard Devlin answer.

"What are you doing in here?"

"David was in here. I thought it was a party."

"Well, you weren't invited," I said, hearing David chuckle.

"Damn. Jessica, wake up."

Jessica jumped out of bed, the headboard knocking against the wall.

"Be quiet!" Devlin whispered.

I reached slowly for my pack. The zipper scraped loudly in the silent room. I reached in the little compartment and took out my gun and extra magazines. I knew what was about to happen. We could stay quiet all we wanted. They still knew we were here. They could smell us.

"What are they doing?" Devlin asked David.

"Too dark to tell. It looks like they're standing in the road."

"They're gonna rush us."

"Yep," David said. "Here they come."

I heard the grunts as the infected ran toward the motel. I screamed when one jumped through the window. The glass shattered, splinters flying toward my face. I shielded my eyes with one hand.

He lay on the floor next to David, a charcoal outline in the moonlight. He—it—was so still I was sure it was dead, until it grunted, the glass clinking as it tried to stand. David pushed the infected man's head to the floor with his shotgun, firing one shot into its skull.

Blood and brain matter sprayed through the room, burning when it hit my arm.

Another man tried to climb through the window. This time, it was Devlin's gun that fired. More infected yanked at the door. It shuddered, the doorknob jangling when they tried to push their way through.

"You get the door, David. I'll take the window," Devlin said.

"Heard that."

Five figures swarmed the window, pushing and clawing at each other to get through. I loaded my gun and extended my arms like David had showed me. I flipped the safety off, aimed at one of the infected climbing through the window and... froze.

I couldn't bring myself to pull the trigger. David seemed to sense my hesitation and shouted at me. "They aren't rational human beings, Eva! They'll kill you in a second, without thought or remorse."

I nodded in the darkness and took aim. I fired my shot, hitting a woman climbing through the window. They were coming so fast Devlin was having a hard time keeping up with them. I fired again, grazing a man. He screamed in pain and anger, shoving the person beside him out of the way as he climbed halfway through the window. I finished the job—one bullet through the forehead.

I could hear the faint sound of gunfire—*pop, pop, pop*—from other parts of the motel. I knew the others in our camp were in the middle of their own fights.

The door to the room gave way, and a surge of infected fell forward. Devlin turned to help David. I covered the window. Each body that tried to come in, I shot. I tried not to think of them as human. Whatever they were, they weren't human anymore.

Their numbers depleted, the infected disappeared into the darkened forest just as the sun peeked over the horizon.

Stunned, I looked around the room. Blood dripped from the walls; a mound of dead lay in front of the door and window. I was covered in gore. My hair dripped blood onto my shoulders; my arms stung where glass had become imbedded in them, my blood mixing with the infected blood.

"David."

He turned and looked at me. I spread my arms, looking down at myself, letting him see the amount of blood covering me, drying on my skin.

"Go wash up, Eva."

I did what he said. I didn't ask why and I didn't voice my fear. If blood was how the virus was transmitted, I'd just been exposed to the infection.

I came out of the bathroom a little while later. I'd washed my hair in the cold remnants of water left in the pipes and scrubbed the blood from my body before dressing in clean clothes. I started to walk by the bed when I saw movement out of the corner of my eye. Jessica was huddled between the wall and bed, her knees pulled to her chest, her hands over her ears.

I reached out and touched her arm. She screamed and jumped up, running to Devlin.

"It's okay, little one. It's over," Devlin reassured her in a soft, soothing voice.

I looked at David. "She's his half-sister," he told me.

"Oh."

David walked over to me, reaching for my hand. I jerked away from him.

"You shouldn't touch me, David."

"Why not?"

"I was just covered in their blood. I could be infected. You shouldn't be around me," I whispered, scared of becoming one of the monsters we'd just seen.

"No one's been infected by just touching their blood. We've all gotten blood on us. You're fine." David reached for me.

"Hold out your arms, Eva," Devlin said.

I held my arms out in front of me. My eyes never left David's face. I knew something was wrong the second David looked at the cuts covering my arms. His face turned ashen, and his shoulders sagged.

"She's right," Devlin said. "If their blood got into one of those cuts she's at risk of infection."

My heart froze at the confirmation. *Infected—like those no-longer-people who just attacked us. Becoming one of them…*

"She's fine," David insisted.

"You know the rules, David. We can't bend them for her just because she's your girlfriend. The rules are in place to protect everyone. They can't be changed for one person."

"Wh…what rules?"

"You have to be segregated from the camp for a week. In a week we'll know if you've been infected. If not, you come back and everything is fine. If you are…well, let's just hope you're not," Devlin said.

"You're going to leave me?" I asked, my voice rising in panic.

"No!" David yelled. I jumped at the hard tone. "You just have to stay away from the camp, but you'll follow us. We won't leave you behind. You'll just have to be separated from the camp. You'll eat separately, bunk separately and, if we find some cars, you drive alone. But you stay with us."

I was put in a hotel room by myself. David sat outside the door talking to me for most of the day. The camp members decided to stay another night at the hotel. It was risky. The infected knew we were there, but we needed time to figure out where our next stop would be.

Dinner was left outside my hotel room door. David moved away from the door when I opened it and took my plate. When I was back in the room, he sat at the door again.

"How will I know?"

"I'm not sure, Eva. I don't know how it feels."

"Outward signs. Things you can see. What are they?"

"First you develop a rash—large, red splotches with red dots through it. But that doesn't really mean much. People develop rashes all the time out here—poison ivy, poison oak. There are a hundred different things that could give a person a rash. So we don't really think a person is infected because of that. Besides, your skin is already irritated from their blood burning it."

"Yeah," I whispered, "it did burn." I looked at my arms. They were red where the infecteds' blood had stung my skin. It would be impossible to tell if I developed a rash there. I pulled up the leg of my jeans and looked at my legs. No rash. Yet.

"I'm sorry."

"What else? What should I look for?"

When will I know? Will I feel myself losing control? Will I know I'm losing my mind?

"Changes in your veins. When blue veins start showing all over, we're pretty sure a person is infected. But it's the last sign that tells us. The person's gums turn blue. That's how we'll know. Your gums will turn blue."

I didn't remember seeing blue gums on the infected. Of course, I had tried not to get too close. But I did remember the blue veins crisscrossing their bodies. The skin looked almost translucent in the moonlight and the blue veins were like neon road maps.

"I never liked the color blue."

"Still joking around, huh, Eva?" I could hear the smile in his voice.

I want his laugh, his voice, to be the last thing I hear.

"Yeah, well, there isn't anything else to do. The television doesn't work."

He laughed, and the sound warmed me.

"Whatever happens, I want you to know, I don't regret it," I told him, my voice thick. "I only have one regret."

He was quiet. I didn't think he was going to answer. Finally he asked, "What's your regret?"

"That I didn't kiss you one more time."

We left the next day. Devlin found two trucks and a car for us to use. The camp members piled into the two trucks. Some crammed into the cabs. The rest huddled in the beds. I was given the car to use. It was a small compact car, but it felt big and empty all by myself.

We drove three hours before stopping in another little town. We found a gas station that had ten full gas cans sitting inside the office. After raiding the gas station's small store, the camp members grabbed the fuel, filling the gas tanks and putting the rest in the back of one of the trucks. When everyone was safely back in their vehicles, I was allowed out of the car to use the bathroom and grab something to eat.

I pulled the handle to open the car door, the hinges sticking when I tried to swing it open. I shoved the door with my shoulder; it finally gave way and I stepped out, stretching up to the sky as far as I could. It felt good to get out of the small car that was filled with ancient burger wrappers and other trash.

"Just shove it out," David told me when he saw how cluttered with litter the car was.

I gathered the junk and stuffed it in a trashcan on my way inside. I walked around back and did what I had to do before going inside and finding something to eat and drink. Turning to leave, something lying on the counter caught my eye.

The counter was grimy. The laminate was gray with a thick layer of dirt. The paper on top was a glaring white spot in the filth. I walked toward it and smiled. David had laid out some chocolates; under them, he'd slid a note telling me he loved me. I grabbed the chocolates and stuffed them in my shoulder bag for later. I picked up the note and carefully folded it before slipping it in my bag next to the candy. As I walked out of the store, my eyes searched for David. I smiled when I found him, patting my bag to let him know I found his gift. He winked and grinned.

Between the gas still in the tanks and what we'd found at the station, there was enough to last for the day. Devlin thought it would be safer if we kept moving. So we drove until we ran out of gas. Unfortunately, we didn't make it to the next town, which meant we had to bunk outside. I had to stay well away from the others. As I set up my tent and unrolled my bedding, I saw David setting up his tent as close to mine as was allowed. I smiled.

"Goodnight," I called.

"Sweet dreams, Evangelina."

It was the third day of my quarantine. I was changing clothes in the small hotel we'd found when I saw something that made my heart go cold.

They were all over my calves—large splotches with red dots.

I lifted my shirt and inhaled sharply. The rash was on my stomach, too. I walked across the room and sat down, my back against the door. It creaked and the knob rattled.

"Good morning, Evangelina," David murmured on the other side of the door.

"Hi, David. How was your night?" I was surprised at how normal my voice sounded. My insides were shaking like jelly.

We talked about what the members of the camp were doing. Jessica was mad because she had to stay with one of the other girls in the camp. She liked staying with me. David talked about what would happen when we made it to a safe compound. "There's supposed to be one in California. That's where we're going. They let topsiders in. They're supposed to have a nice little compound, like the one you lived in."

We talked about the compound most of the morning and afternoon—what we would do, where we would live, the possibility that family and friends would be there.

I didn't mention the rash.

On day five of my quarantine, we had to sleep outside again. We didn't have working vehicles and had been traveling on foot for two days. Stopping for the night, even if it meant bunking on the hard ground, was a relief.

The rash had spread to my back and arms. Thankfully, the weather was cool and I could wear long sleeves.

Blue veins were visible on the undersides of my wrists, around my ankles and the tops of my feet. I couldn't remember if I'd had them before or not.

I didn't tell David.

On day seven, I had to be checked for signs of infection before I would be allowed to go back to the camp.

"Rash?" a man, I couldn't remember his name, asked.

"Yes."

"Let us see," he demanded.

I lifted up my pant leg and showed the red splotches, feeling my heart thudding hard as I did.

"Fine. Blue veins?"

"I'm not sure." I cringed when they raised their guns, pointing them at me. "Um…I think I had them before…"

I held out my wrists and showed the blue veins running just under the skin.

"Are those the only ones?" Chris asked.

I shook my head. I pulled up my pant leg and showed them my feet and ankles.

"That all?"

"Yes."

Chris lowered his gun, letting the barrel rest on the ground, and smiled at me. "She's good to go, guys."

"Eva, look at me," David said quietly. "Open your mouth."

I opened my mouth, lifting my lips up with my fingers so everyone could get a good look. My gums were pink. Not blue. They were normal.

"She's fine," Devlin said with a smile. "C'mon, Eva."

I walked right into David's arms. He held me and I cried. I wasn't sure why I was crying. I suppose it was stress. I'd been so worried during that week of quarantine. I'd analyzed every little thing I did, every little thing on my body. David held me, massaging my back and neck.

"Why didn't you tell me about the rash?"

"I didn't want you to worry," I said.

"Eva, you don't always have to be the strong one. It's okay to be scared. It's okay to let other people help you. I wish you would have told me."

"I'm sorry. I didn't see any sense in both of us worrying. David? What would've happened if I'd been infected?"

"It doesn't matter. You're not."

I had a feeling I knew the answer. I'd known as soon as they'd aimed their guns at me.

Chapter 26 : Chris

They came again that night. The moon was large and bright in the sky. I was awake, listening to the snores and whispers of the others in the camp. David was asleep in the tent beside me.

The air smelled of smoke. The fire's dying embers glowed a yellowish-orange. The dying fire left the camp cold and I shivered, sinking lower in my sleeping bag.

I heard it over the rustling fabric of my bag moving across the nylon tent—a far-off snap of a twig, the sound unmistakable. I held my breath and waited. If it were a single animal, it would walk through, twigs breaking occasionally as it took a step. If it were a group of animals or people, twigs would break in different areas, moving steadily toward the camp. The second snap was louder than the first, closer. And then I heard it and I knew. A third snap, to the left of the first, followed closely by the rustling of underbrush in front of the camp. Didn't the man standing watch hear it? I didn't have time to think about it.

I reached slowly out of my tent and grabbed David's hand. He squeezed my fingers softly in answer. He had heard the noises, too. Jessica's tent was on the opposite side of David's, Devlin's tent next to hers. The sound of the shotgun gliding against the floor of the tent was barely audible.

David let go of my hand and I panicked. The blood rushed behind my ears, making it impossible to hear. I couldn't breathe. Fear squeezed my chest, and cold sweat beaded on my back. Not so soon after I was allowed back in.

My hand moved back and forth against the hard ground, searching for David. I heard the clink of metal against metal and realized he'd grabbed his shotgun from his pack. He reached out and grabbed my hand again. A shotgun in his left and my hand in his right, he waited.

I slowly moved my right hand down my side, feeling for my backpack. Unzipping the small side pocket, I pulled out my handgun.

The noises in the forest were getting closer.

"Roll over," David whispered so quietly I had to strain to hear. "There's one right behind us. Roll on your back and get ready to fire."

I rolled to my back, extending my arms as I clicked off the safety. I waited. It seemed like hours, but was probably just a few seconds. The large shadow loomed over my tent. It raised its arms above its head—and I fired. The man crumpled, half on the ground behind my tent and half across my legs.

I furiously kicked, freeing my legs from the weight of the man I'd just shot. My tent fell around me; I felt like I was trapped in a net. David reached in and pulled me free.

The shot alerted the others to the danger lurking in the trees. They scrambled from their tents, the men carrying their guns, the women huddled behind them.

The infected rushed the camp. Screaming and grunting, they ran toward us, weapons raised over their heads. Devlin's gun rang out. The smell of acrid smoke filled the air. Banshee screams assaulted my ears.

Three men went toward Devlin, and five more came in behind our tents. David's gun echoed Devlin's as shots thundered. I heard Jessica crying in her tent. I reached down and wrenched her up by her arm. Not waiting for her to get her balance, I dragged her to the center of the circle the men were forming, the girls cowering inside. Throwing her inside with the others, I turned and stood next to two camp members, my gun aimed at the trees.

David and Devlin ran behind Jessica and me, taking their places in the circle. David stood next to me.

"Get in the circle!"

"No." I was surprised at how calm I'd become.

"Dammit, Eva! Get in the circle where it's safe."

I didn't answer him. More infected were swarming the camp. I fired my gun—*pop, pop, pop*—and felt a sense of empowerment each time I saw my bullets make contact with our attackers.

That sense waned when I saw a guy get hit in the head by one of the infected's weapons. He crumpled to the ground. The man standing next to him shot the infected man towering over him. The injured man—no, not a man, a boy, no more than sixteen—lay on the ground, dark blood pooling around his head. My stomach heaved.

I backed into the circle and ran to him. He was already dead. I grabbed his gun, cocked the lever like I had seen the other men doing, and shot. The blast knocked me backward. I fired again; this time, expecting the jolt, I was able to stand my ground.

I turned and looked at the girls standing in the middle of the circle, doing nothing to protect themselves.

"Fight!" I screamed. They stared at me. "Fight or die." I held out my handgun. A young girl grabbed it and took a place in the circle, firing on the infected. I used the shotgun, watching the infected advance on the camp, seeing their blue veins shimmer against their pale skin when they came into the circle of the firelight, hearing their grunts and screams as they tried to make it past our gunfire.

I also watched the men next to me, trying to learn how to reload the gun. Chris grabbed the gun from my hands and quickly showed me how to reload. He threw it back to me and took aim at an infected woman who'd wandered too close to our circle. She snarled at him, her blue gums grotesque against her white teeth.

The fight lasted more than an hour. The infected came one after another, pushing each other out of the way in an attempt to reach us. When their group was depleted, the survivors melted back into the tree line, disappearing through the darkened forest.

"What the…Evangelina, what did you think you were doing?" David yelled.

"Fighting. The same as you."

"I told you to stay inside the circle," he yelled louder.

"I know what you said. I don't remember agreeing to it."

Standing toe-to-toe, he looked down at me, his gray eyes shimmering in the pale moonlight—angry eyes.

Out of nowhere, he grabbed a handful of my hair and jerked my head back before kissing me hard. Pulling his face back just far enough that our noses touched, he stared into my eyes. "You scared the crap outta me," he whispered, lowering his lips to mine, taking them gently, caressing them.

His hand let go of my hair and cupped my face. I stretched my arms around his neck, leaning into him, forgetting about the carnage that lay around us. I focused only on David.

At the sound of a giggle, I opened one eye. Jessica stood next to David and me. "Devlin said to tell you guys to get a room."

David groaned and cursed under his breath, letting me go.

I looked around the destroyed camp. "You know, I could be teaching English right now."

David laughed. "Always with the jokes."

I wasn't joking.

Life outside the compound was much harder than I'd anticipated. Not for the first time, I found myself wondering if leaving the compound had been the right thing to do. Then, as always, I looked at David and I knew. Yes. I was where I was supposed to be—where David was.

PODs

The morning sun was just beginning to rise, the black sky turning purple and then cerulean. Puffy cotton-ball clouds dotted the blue. It was beautiful…until you looked down.

At our feet lay the bodies of the dead infected. Blood seeped across the hard-packed earth; body parts lay in unnatural positions.

Two camp members had been killed during the night—the boy who'd been standing next to me and another who'd been caught before he'd had a chance to make it to the protective circle. The camp felt their loss deeply.

I helped clean the remains for burial. I wiped their cold bodies with a damp rag, the blood smearing over their unnaturally white skin. The water turned pink from it, dripping on the ground like bloody teardrops. When we'd finished cleaning the blood and gore from the bodies, we dressed them in clean clothes and the two men were gently laid on their bedrolls.

David held my hand tightly as each camp member walked by the bodies and silently said goodbye. Some of us had silent tears rolling down our cheeks. Others sniffled quietly. One girl cried loudly as she said goodbye to her dead brother—the only family she'd had left.

When the ceremony was over, the bodies were gently wrapped in their bedrolls and buried. A small cross carved in the tree hanging over their graves marked their final resting places.

"I need to talk to you," Devlin told David.

"What's up?"

"Alone."

"Whatever it is, you can say it in front of Eva."

Devlin looked at me. "I don't want Jessica to know."

"Sure. I won't say anything," I promised.

"It looks like someone's been bit."

My heart did a nosedive. "Oh, no." I covered my mouth with my hand.

David stood ramrod straight. His jaw worked, tightening and untightening. He ran his hand through his hair and looked at Devlin.

"Who?"

Devlin opened his mouth, and then closed it. Staring at the ground, he kicked at it with the toe of his shoe. "Dammit."

Tears filled my eyes. "Oh, no. It's not Jessica?"

"No, it's not Jessica. It's Chris," Devlin whispered.

"Chris. Jessica's friend?" I asked.

The boy Jessica called her 'soulmate.' The boy who helped me pick out a backpack the first morning I was with the group. The sweet kid who showed me how to reload a shotgun last night. No. This is going to devastate Jessica. And...what will happen to Chris?

"Yeah."

"Oh." I couldn't say anything else. A lump had lodged itself in my throat. It felt as though it was growing, making it impossible to speak, cutting off the air to my lungs.

He's only thirteen.

David had remained silent—his face hard, a look I'd never seen. He was always so open, so friendly. I'd never seen him look stone-cold. A shiver ran up my spine.

"Do we quarantine him?" David asked, looking around the camp.

The members were gathering the gear that hadn't been damaged in the attack. Their voices carried on the breeze. If I listened closely, I could pick out pieces of conversations. Tin plates and cups clanged together as they were shoved in a bag. The embers of the fire were doused with water, creating a smoke plume that burned my eyes. Across the camp, Jessica helped one of the other girls take down tents. They were laughing and talking, looking almost like normal kids—almost.

I tried to find Chris in the bustle of activity. He wasn't there. My eyes scanned the perimeter of the campsite. I found him sitting on a tree stump, rubbing his arm and watching the rest of the people pack up the camp.

"No." Devlin's voice pulled me back to the conversation.

"No? What are you talking about?" I asked.

"No, we don't quarantine him," David said quietly.

Something lurched in my chest. "Hey, you said everyone was quarantined. It's a bad move not to remove him from the rest of the camp until we know for sure he isn't infected. Besides, the wound on his arm might not be from a bite, anyway. He'll be back making googly eyes at Jessica in a week."

David and Devlin stared at me, their faces hard and unreadable.

"He's already showing signs," Devlin said, looking at David. "He knows it, too."

"What do you mean? I thought it didn't show up this early?"

"It does when it's a bite, Eva. A bite injects the virus directly into the bloodstream. The virus is spreading through his body quickly. He'll show advanced symptoms in less than twenty-four hours. He'll be completely transformed in two days." Devlin jammed his fingers through his hair.

"Who?" David asked.

"I can't. If it was anyone else...but this is Jessica's friend. She thinks they're boyfriend and girlfriend. There's no way I can...I can't have that hanging between us. She'd never forgive me."

Birds sang in the trees. The soft swaying of the pines in the autumn breeze whispered through the air. Remnants of breakfast and smoke from the dead fire scented the air. It seemed so serene. But the conversation was morbid.

"I guess—"

"No, David."

"Eva, someone has to."

"Not you. I don't know what's going on, but I think I have a pretty good idea. Not you." I couldn't imagine looking at him the same way if he did what I feared was going to happen to Chris.

"Juan?" Devlin asked.

"Yeah. Juan will do a good job," David agreed. "I'll talk to him. You talk to Chris."

"Eva? Would you distract Jessica?" Devlin started to turn away.

"Sure, but wait," I called. "What's happening?"

David cupped the side of my face with one hand, laying the other on the small of my back. He kissed me softly, just a whisper against my lips. "Please don't ask too many questions, Evangelina," he murmured before dropping his hand and walking away.

What was I supposed to do? How was I going to explain where Chris and Juan were going if Jessica saw them leave?

I wasn't even sure *I* understood what was happening. What would I tell Jessica?

I watched as the two young men walked away, their shoes squishing in the thin layer of mud and stirring up the smell of rotting leaves. Alone in the small clearing at the side of the campsite, I wondered how they could talk about doing something so vile like it was something that happened regularly.

Although, maybe it did.

Chapter 27 :
The Walk

I watched David from across the camp. His posture was stiff, the look on his face grim. His shoulder leaned against a tree, with his thumb hooked through the belt loop on his jeans. He was gorgeous, but he wasn't my David.

Since Devlin's news that Chris had been bitten, David's demeanor had shown me that he didn't like what was going to happen. And that's how I knew. Two would walk away from camp today. One would come back.

He turned and his eyes searched me out. He tried to smile, but it looked forced. He walked to me and folded me in his arms, laying his cheek on the top of my head.

"He's going to kill Chris, isn't he?" I whispered.

"What happened to not asking too many questions?" His breath ruffled my hair.

"You asked, but I don't remember agreeing. What's going to happen?"

"No, they aren't going to kill him. Not today." He dropped his arms from around me. My body shivered from the loss of his warmth. He pulled back and looked at me, running his finger down the side of my face. Dropping his hand, he sighed. "Geez, Eva, why do you have to know every little morsel of information? I don't want you to have to worry about things like this," he said, running his fingers through his hair, the morning light making the dark strands look like shimmering silk.

"Why? Because I'm a girl? I don't need protection, David. I need answers."

"And that's another thing. Why do you always assume I don't tell you something because you're a girl? I don't tell you the ugly truth of life out here because I love you and I don't want the ugliness to touch you. I want you to be safe, to be happy."

"What?" I asked quietly.

"I want you to be——"

"Not that part."

"I love you. I think I have since the day you first entered the POD. I knew I did the morning I kissed you. I still know I do because I'd lay down my life for you here and now."

"I love you back," I said with a smile. "But your declaration of undying devotion didn't do its job."

"What job?"

"You didn't distract me enough to forget about what's going on. I want to know, David. I *need* to know."

"Fine." His voice was clipped.

"Don't get pissy with me, either."

"Juan and Chris will stay behind when we leave today. Juan will watch Chris, and if he shows additional signs of infection, he'll do what needs to be done. Chris wants it that way. None of us wants…the alternative." He looked up and swallowed hard. "If Chris is symptom-free, they'll follow us and we'll meet them in the next town. He'll do his week in isolation and everything will be fine."

"So I'm right. Juan's gonna kill him," I whispered.

"No, you're wrong. You couldn't be more wrong," David told me. I looked at him, confused. "He's going to kill an infected person. If the virus was injected when Chris was bitten he'll turn into one of them. He won't be Chris any more. It's no different than you shooting one of them when they attack the camp."

I flinched at his words. I did shoot them when they attacked us. I didn't let myself think of them as human. They were just monsters. And that's what Chris would become. David was right. None of us wanted that. If it were me, I'd want them to do the same thing.

I thought frantically, searching for another way. But I couldn't find one and my heart ached for Chris. *He was a nice person.* My heart broke for Jessica. *Her first love.* Not for the first time, I wondered how in the hell the world had gotten so screwed up.

The group started toward the next town. Jessica and I walked side by side; she was chattering like always. I was trying not to think about what was happening with Juan and Chris. Instead, I was thinking of what to say to Jessica when she noticed Chris wasn't with the group.

David didn't walk with me. We decided his presence would only highlight the fact that Chris wasn't with Jessica. So David and Devlin walked behind the rest of the camp members.

The day was sunny. I had to squint to see anything around me. The path we took was a narrow trail through a pasture. I could hear the far off bark of a dog.

"Look, Eva." Jessica pointed to a tree branch.

I jumped, startled by her excited squeal. "What?"

"See that bird? Isn't it pretty? The blue is so deep."

"Yeah, um, it is pretty." I tried to smile. "I think it's a bluebird, but I'm not sure."

"Chris will know. He loves watching the birds. He carries a journal that lists every type of bird he's seen, the date he saw it, and the place. It's probably a bluebird, or maybe a blue jay."

"Well, I'm sure he's seen a bluebird before." I tried to change the subject when Jessica butted in.

"Where *is* Chris?" Jessica looked around the group. "I don't see him."

"I'm sure he's up there. I saw him just a little while ago." I used the toe of my sneaker to dig into the ground as we walked.

She stopped and stood on her tiptoes, looking for Chris in the sea of people.

"Jessica, you won't see him if he's in front."

She turned to me, her face pale. "They took him, didn't they?"

"Who?" I asked.

"The cut on his arm. He told me how he got it, but—they took him anyway."

I didn't answer. I didn't know how to answer.

"I'll take that as a *yes*." She turned and ran toward Devlin.

"Jessica! Wait!" I called, jogging to catch up to her.

"Who?" she shouted at Devlin.

He didn't answer right away. He stared at the ground before looking up at me through his eyelashes.

"I'm sorry. She figured it out."

"It's okay, Eva. I knew she would." He looked at Jessica, his face filled with compassion. "Juan."

"You should have told me," she yelled. Other group members turned and stared. "It's nothing. He scraped it on a tree when he was gathering wood for the fire. That's all."

"Then he'll be back tomorrow."

Jessica turned and walked away, her back straight, chin lifted in the air. She tried to look angry, but her fear showed through, even though she tried to hide it. I walked silently beside her for a few steps before she turned to me.

"Get away from me. You knew. You knew, and you didn't tell me. Some friend you are."

I stopped walking, watching her pull ahead of me.

"She'll be fine." David came up behind me and kissed the back of my neck. It sent a shiver down my spine. He took my hand and threaded his fingers through mine, pulling me gently along with him.

"I hope so," I said. I didn't think so.

Juan met us at the town around dinnertime. When I saw him walking toward us, my heart sank, and I couldn't catch my breath. I dropped the bowl I was dishing stew into; it clanged loudly against the pavement. Gravy splattered on my jeans and vegetables scattered across the ground.

Chris wasn't with him.

When Jessica saw him, tears filled her eyes. She ran into the little motel room, slamming and locking the door behind her. She stayed in the room the rest of the night and most of the morning. She didn't come out until the group was ready to leave.

She looked from Devlin to me, turned, and moved back to walk behind another group. She didn't speak.

We made camp at the end of the day. It was a beautiful evening—the sky was clear, just turning a purplish black. The stars were already emerging as bats fluttered in the sky.

The campsite was just a small clearing in a wooded area. A fire burned in the middle; people were setting up tents around it. I froze at the sound of Juan's low voice from the tree line just beyond where I was setting up my tent. "Jessica, Devlin asked me to talk to you. Said you needed to hear it from me. The wound on Chris's arm wasn't from gathering wood. It was a bite."

The light from the campfire barely touched their faces among the trees. The cool metal of the tent pole bit into the palms of my hands, and I said a silent prayer that what Juan was telling her would give her peace. I had to strain to hear him over the crickets and cicadas buzzing. Watching them out of the corner of my eye, I tried not to look like I was eavesdropping, which was exactly what I was doing.

When he didn't get an answer, Juan continued. "He told me he knew it was a bite. He also knew what he was going to turn into."

"You're wrong," Jessica bit out, her voice cold.

"He was already showing signs. The rash, the blue veins… they were there."

She shook her head. "No, you're wrong."

"Jessica, he asked me to do it. He knew what was happening and he didn't want to become one of them. He asked me to do it before he could hurt anyone. He said to tell you he was sorry he didn't say goodbye."

Tears ran down Jessica's face, catching the light from the fire. Mucus and saliva trickled from her nose and mouth. She didn't care. She sobbed, repeating, "You were wrong," at Juan, over and over.

I went over to her and took her hand. She turned and sagged against me, crying. I held her silently, smoothing the hair down her back, letting her cry. We sank down to the forest floor, our backs against the wide trunk of a tree.

"They're wrong, right, Eva?"

"No, honey, they're not. I'm sorry."

I held her while she cried, my shirt damp with her tears. She sobbed until she was so exhausted that she fell asleep on my shoulder.

Devlin carried her to her tent and placed her blankets gently over her.

"She'll be fine," he said, almost to himself. "She'll be fine." He looked at me and I gave him a sad smile.

Will she? Will any of us?

The clinking of metal woke me. I listened. David's breathing was quick and shallow in the tent next to me. Gone were his soft snores. From somewhere in the camp I heard the click of a gun being cocked.

It was beginning again and I braced myself. I heard the grunting first, followed by banshee screams as the infected descended on our campsite.

By dawn, we'd lost two more camp members. One had been mauled by one of the infected attackers. The other walked into the woods and took his own life when he realized he'd been bitten on the ankle.

We packed quickly when the attack was over. We didn't even take the time needed to bury our dead. The infected were following too closely behind us, and we were still on foot. We needed to get some ground between us and them.

The afternoon was wet. Thunder rolled in the sky and cold, fat raindrops pelted us. We splashed through puddles and mud, going as fast as we were able in the horrible weather. Some of the group ditched their heavy, waterlogged packs so they could keep up with the rest.

The wind howled. It whipped through the trees, ripping the autumn leaves from the branches. The rain beat them into the muddy ground. I looked up, shielding my eyes from the rain. Gray clouds churned above us and lightning spread like jagged fingers across the sky. I prayed we'd come to a town so we could get out of the storm.

I dropped my head and wiped the rainwater from my eyes with my hands. My head facing to the side, I saw it—just a flash of color among the otherwise dark trees.

"David?"

"Yeah?" We were walking right next to each other but had to yell to be heard over the wind and rain.

"Do they only attack at night?"

He stopped abruptly. I skidded in the mud when I stopped and turned to face him. "Usually, but not always," he said slowly. "Why?"

I put my lips close to his ear. "I think they're in the trees. I saw a flash of yellow."

David whistled to Devlin. He didn't look back at us. He nodded his head once and reached behind him for his shotgun. That created a domino effect. Everyone tensed. Without stopping, people grabbed their guns, and the unarmed group members made their way inside the formation. The men—and the few women who were armed—encircled them.

We walked faster. The cold rain made it almost impossible to see into the darkened forest. The roaring wind made it impossible to hear. We could only wait.

We walked another half-mile, maybe more, before it happened. A group emerged from the trees in front of us, another group behind us. Their white skin seemed to glow in the dim light, the blue veins even more visible. They stood silently, blocking our path. Seconds ticked by, and with each one the tension in our group rose.

Then it started.

The screaming came first. Then they ran toward us, weapons raised. The shotgun blasts echoed through the trees. I watched numbly as the infected in front fell in the mud. Their blood mixed with the rain and pooled on the ground. The other attackers jumped over the dead and continued running at us. Some tripped and fell over the bodies sprawled in the mud. That seemed to infuriate them and they screamed and snarled as they advanced.

"Eva!" David shouted.

I turned to him and froze at the look on his face. He wasn't looking at me. He was looking over my shoulder. I didn't need to turn around to know what he saw. It seemed to happen in slow motion. David raised his gun. I whirled around. The infected man lurched toward me. David fired and the eerily white-skinned man fell, his club knocking my gun from my hands. The weapon landed yards away—in the middle of the oncoming attack.

I didn't have time to think. Behind my attacker was another infected just as eager as the first to reach me. I was unarmed. I looked around frantically, searching for something I could use as a weapon. I grabbed the dead man's club and swung it at the infected's head, screaming with the effort. The club connected with her head with a sickening crunch. She crumpled to the ground. I stared at her for a beat, praying she was dead. I didn't have time to defend myself from her again. There was already another taking her place.

He advanced slowly toward me with a guttural scream. I raised my club and readied myself. He lurched and I swung... missing him. I stumbled and fell. On my hands and knees in the cold mud, I looked to David. He was fighting off a group of infected behind us. The bulky man lurch toward me again. I screamed and braced myself for the impact of the tree branch he carried.

His body jerked and fell in front of me, spraying mud across my face. I raised my arm and wiped it over my eyes. I looked across the group and saw Devlin, his gun aimed in my direction. I nodded my thanks. He swung the tip of his shotgun toward the center of the group, where the unarmed group members huddled together. I scrambled off the muddy ground and grabbed the bat, making my way to the center of the circle.

Jessica ran to me. I held her close. I couldn't hear her over the rain and vicious fight, but I felt her body shake with sobs. We huddled together until the fight was over.

I screamed when I felt big hands grab my arms. Someone swung me around and crushed me against him. "You scared the crap outta me!"

"David." I fisted my hand in the front of his jacket.

"What the hell were you thinking, swinging a bat around like a lunatic?" He pulled back and looked at me.

"That I'd better do something before one of them got me," I snapped.

I heard a chuckle and looked to my side. Devlin was checking the fallen infected, making sure there were no survivors. I smiled at him as he passed by. "Thank you."

"Anytime."

"No, not anytime. No time. Because she's not going to do that again. From now on, you stay inside the circle where it's safe."

"David, you are blowing—"

"You could've been killed!"

"You could've been, too," I answered calmly.

"Inside the circle."

"No."

"Eva, so help me…"

"The inside of that circle isn't safe. Their numbers are growing and ours are weakening. The only way for us to be safe is to teach each other how to fight, and then watch each other's backs."

"She's right." I jumped at the loud blast that followed Devlin's words. He'd found a survivor and put a bullet through its head. *We don't leave survivors.*

"Don't encourage her."

Devlin chuckled before he fired another shot. "I gotta say, Eva. You don't fight like a girl. I saw you take one out with that club. Very badass."

"What a sexist comment." I grinned. "But I'm going to overlook it since you saved my life today."

"Gee, thanks." He laughed. I watched over my shoulder as he walked away.

"Evangelina…"

I turned to David. He fisted his hand in my wet hair and pulled my head to his, kissing me hard. His mouth moved over mine, claiming it as his own. His warm tongue darted between my cold lips and I shivered at the sensation. He felt so good. So vital, alive.

His kiss eased into a slow caress. His hand dropped from my hair. He pushed my pack off my back. It splashed mud and water over our legs when it hit the ground. David ripped the zipper down on my hoodie and put his hands inside. They roamed over me, leaving trails of fire everywhere he touched.

He lifted his head and his gray eyes bored into mine. "Are you hurt?" His hands still moved over me.

"No."

"Are you sure?"

"Why? Are you asking because you're worried about me or because you're worried I might turn into one of them?"

And he was off. "How could you even say that? I'm worried about you...only you...I can't believe you would even think that I wasn't..."

I laughed, picking up my pack and slipping into it.

"Stop joking around, Eva. This is serious."

Laughing harder, I turned and walked toward the group. David stalked at my heels, stopping only to shoot a surviving infected Devlin had missed.

We stopped for the night early. The rain hadn't let up and everyone was tired from fighting not once, but twice, in twenty-four hours. After a quick dinner, we pitched our tents and realized our problem. A lot of our tents had been destroyed in the fight the night before. We had twice as many people as we had tents. So we did what we did with everything else. We shared.

"Jessica and Eva can share—"

"No," David interrupted.

I looked at David, and then at Devlin. He raised one eyebrow at David and smiled. "Okay, new plan. Jessica and I'll share a tent and you and Eva can share. Good?"

"Yeah."

I snuggled close to David that night, listening to the raindrops hit the tent. I was cold and he felt warm. "Do you feel better?" I whispered.

"Better than what?"

"You were all wound up earlier. You seemed irritated at me."

"I feel better. It's just that…you scared me and, well, it didn't seem to sink into your thick skull how close you were to dying today."

"It sunk in."

"Don't do it again, Evangelina. Just stay inside the circle and be safe—"

"I told you, inside the circle isn't safe. It just gives an illusion of safety. I'm gonna do what I need to. You and Devlin can't keep everyone safe, David. We all have to learn to fight together. Or…"

"Or what?"

"We fight together or we die together."

David pulled me gently to my back. He leaned over me, looking at me with his silvery eyes. "You're so pig-headed."

"I know."

He dipped his head and kissed me gently, rubbing the fingers of one hand up and down my arm. I framed his face with my hands and lifted my head to deepen his kiss. Our tongues glided together, and our hands roamed over each other, pushing clothing and blankets out of our way.

My lips made their way down the column of his neck and across his shoulder. I inhaled his scent and smiled. It was heaven in David's arms. Even in that godforsaken place, hunted by monsters, I found heaven in David. Peace. Happiness. Love. That's what David gave me and I took it all greedily.

When more clothes were pooling around us than covering us, when the blankets had long been cast aside, when our kisses had moved from mouths to other areas and our hands had roamed over each other's bodies, hesitating at secret places, David stopped.

"Not here, Eva."

"I know."

"I want to be with you somewhere nice. Somewhere clean and safe. Somewhere I can see all of you."

I smiled and slipped into his sweatshirt. It draped around me like a blanket and smelled of him. Scooting down, I snuggled against him. He wrapped his arms around me and I felt myself being pulled toward the peaceful cocoon of sleep.

Maybe they won't attack again.

I was wrong.

Chapter 28 :
Full Circle

We walked four days before we came to another town, where we scavenged the stores to replace our desperately low supplies. The infected had attacked our camp every night. They followed us from camp to camp, and we were exhausted from the constant battles. With every attack, our energy and supplies dwindled. Our tents were ruined, and our water supply was depleted, as the infected destroyed many of the containers in the commotion of the fight.

"This is a quick stop." Devlin scanned the buildings for motion as we drew closer. "Restock our supplies and find vehicles, so we can put as much distance between us and the infected as possible. We'll split up to get everything before nightfall. David, take a group for equipment. Juan, find food. I'll go for the vehicles."

We found a sporting goods store that hadn't been looted— the first we'd come across in weeks. David wrapped a sweatshirt around his arm and jammed it against the glass. Nothing.

He laughed. "They made this stuff seem so easy on television."

He pulled back his elbow and jammed it against the glass a second time. It shattered and pieces of glass bounced on the ground with a clang, shards flying around our feet.

"Damn, that hurt."

"Did you cut yourself?" I unwound the shirt from his arm, searching for blood.

He winced. "No, I hit my funny bone." He reached through and unlocked the door. The glass crunched under our feet as our group entered. "Tents, sleeping bags, snake bite kits, matches, water purification tablets, canteens, and ammo."

"Let's get the stuff and get out of here. It's starting to get dark and I don't want to be hanging around," I said.

We grabbed what we needed and carried it to the vans Devlin had found.

We were in and out of town in less than an hour. Driving down the road, I blew out a breath of relief. Maybe, just maybe, we'd get a full night's rest without another attack.

We drove three hours before the first van ran out of gas. The people from that vehicle climbed into one of the remaining two. Between supplies and people, we were wedged in, every inch of space taken.

I sat on David's lap, my back against the wall of the van, his arm around my waist. His thumb moved back and forth over my side under my t-shirt. That was the only body part he could move. People were crammed everywhere. The armrest jammed painfully into my back, and Juan sat on my feet. Every part of my body hurt, but there were two reasons I didn't mind. First, David was touching me. Every spare inch of space he could, he pressed against me. And second, we were driving away from the group of infected that had been hunting us. Every mile we drove crammed into that van, smelling each other's body odor and rancid breath, we got farther away from them. And that made the trip almost blissful.

I turned my head and looked at David. His silver-gray eyes twinkled in the waning sunlight streaming through the windshield. He smiled at me and tapped my side with his thumb. I moved slightly, painfully toward him. I was able to move just far enough before something stopped me. But it was all right, because what stopped me were David's lips.

I kissed him slowly, my tongue parting his lips and gliding inside. He moaned and strained his head forward to deepen the kiss, his thumb pushing into my side to bring me closer.

"Get a room," Juan said.

I pulled back, a red-hot blush creeping across my face. I'd been lost in David, and how his lips felt against mine, so I'd forgotten we had an audience.

"Man, if you had someone like her sitting on your lap, you wouldn't care if you were at the Waldorf or in a van that smelled like a locker room. You'd kiss her whenever and wherever you had the chance." David smirked.

"Yeah, yeah," Juan muttered.

Two hours after the first van ran out of gas, the second ran out. The third and final van had less than a quarter tank. Our ride was over. We couldn't all fit in one van; even if we could, there wasn't enough gas to get us very far.

We fell out of the van when the doors opened, the fresh air hitting us in the face. I inhaled deeply, stretching to soothe my aching muscles. David ran his fingers across my belly where my t-shirt rode up. It tickled in a way I'd only read about.

"Come here." He pulled me to him. "We have some unfinished business," he whispered against my lips. His eyes found mine before he started kissing me slowly, deeply. One hand cupped the back of my neck and he trailed his fingers down the length of my spine. His touch made my head spin and the feel of his lips sliding over mine, of his hands on me, made my knees weak. I leaned further into him.

His hand traveled up my back, underneath my shirt, and I sighed with pleasure. The kiss deepened as his mouth moved over mine, his tongue dipping between my lips…

"Aw, c'mon you two. We've got work to do," Devlin complained. "Eva, leave him alone so we can get these tents out of the van and set up."

I laughed and let my arms drop from around David's neck.

"I'll be back," David promised.

David set up our tent like he did every night. We curled together while we slept. Well, while he slept. I couldn't. I tried, telling myself we were far enough away. The infected weren't anywhere near us. But my brain wouldn't stop whirring. What if there was another group in the area? What if the sentry dozed off again and they were able to sneak up on us? What if…? A million scenarios ran through my mind. I spent the night listening for any sound, anything that seemed out of place.

So much for getting a good night's sleep.

We walked for two days. The temperature was rising, and there was more flat, sandy land than lush green forest around us. We had made it to the panhandle of Texas. We found three more vehicles in Shamrock and drove until we ran out of gas somewhere in New Mexico.

That's when I saw it.

It was off in the distance. I had to strain to see, but it was there—hundreds of green army tents, with wind turbines in the distance.

"David, look." I pointed down a dirt-covered road.

"Devlin, turn down this road. I want to check something out," David called.

We walked down the road, tripping over ruts and slipping in the stone-filled dirt. Our feet made the dust billow around us. I shaded my eyes with my hand to keep the grit out of them.

"Next store we stop at, remind me to get goggles," I muttered.

It took most of the day to get to the tents. "We're wasting time, David. We need to go back to the main road," Devlin called.

"It'll be worth the extra trip."

"It better be," a redhead named Margie complained. I shot her a dirty look. She seemed to like David a little too much, which meant I disliked her a lot.

We walked over a mound of red sand and Devlin whistled. "What are they doing out here?"

"They're the tents the army set up when we exited the PODs. A tent for each area. The POD entrance is in the middle of them. There should be supplies and beds," David said, his hand shielding his eyes from the sun and sand as he looked at the tents ahead.

"There'll be showers," I sighed. I couldn't get to the PODs fast enough. A shower—I hadn't had one in weeks.

"How do you know there'll be water?" Devlin asked.

"The PODs had to be self-sufficient, right, Eva? Look at all those windmills. They generate electricity," Jessica said.

"Yep. The water system was completely contained. As long as we use it carefully we should have plenty. Tonight, we can all have nice, long showers."

We picked up our pace, moving as fast as we could while bogged down by our gear. The wind whipped around us. Sand blew painfully against my face. Tumbleweeds bounced across the ground.

"Welcome to the southwest," David muttered.

The entrance to the elevator we'd used, back when we'd entered the POD the first time, was deserted and locked down with a code. We found an emergency access hatch close by, set into a cement square. David wiped the sand and grit off the hatch. "Doesn't look like anyone's been here."

"The way the sand is blowing, you wouldn't be able to tell," I said through the red bandana Roy had given me to tie around my face. Only my eyes were uncovered. I must've looked like an outlaw in an old western movie.

"Well, the only way to know is to open it up and see. C'mon, Devlin. Give me a hand." A few blows with an axe usually used on firewood broke off the padlock. The hinges creaked loudly when David and Devlin pulled open the hatch. The thick metal door hit the sandy ground with a thud.

We peered down into the opening. Narrow passages led away from the hatch, disappearing into the dark in four directions, and a circle of dim light showed a ladder that led downward.

"It sounds quiet down there."

"Yeah, let's go." I stood and took a single step before David grabbed me by the waist and lifted me away from the POD opening.

"We'll go first." He pointed at Devlin and Juan.

"Oh, 'cuz a girl can't look around an empty tin can. Yeah, okay. Go first, David." I turned and walked to the nearest tent and sat on a bench. Jessica followed me.

"Guys are a pain sometimes, huh?" she said. "Devlin is such a control freak, it's unreal."

"He's your brother. He's supposed to be a pain." I put my arm around her and pulled her into a hug. "How are you doing?"

"Good. I mean, well, you know. I'm good."

I smiled at her, smoothing her hair out of her face. "I'm always around if you need to talk."

"Thanks."

David strode over to where we sat. "It looks all clear."

"Good. Let's go take that shower," I said, standing.

"Do we get to use the elevator?" Jessica asked.

"It's locked down—there's a keypad. Maybe the code's written down somewhere in the POD—keep an eye out. Right now, we get to jump through the hatch into a small passageway and then climb down the ladder." I remembered seeing the ladders on the schematic of the entire POD I'd memorized in quarantine.

"That sounds fun! I'll race you, Eva," Jessica called over her shoulder, already running toward the POD opening.

David easily caught up to me and grabbed me around the waist, lifting me off the ground so Jessica could run by and get into the POD first. She giggled as she ran by, waving her fingers at me.

"Cheater!" I called after her, laughing. David put me down, turning me around by the shoulders to look at him. "You're a cheater, too. Picking me up so Jessica could win."

"Yeah, but I had ulterior motives," he whispered, lowering his lips to mine.

He put his hands on my waist, just under my shirt. His touch sent jolts of electricity through me. I touched my tingling lips with the tips of my fingers. They were swollen from his kiss.

"What? Did I do something wrong?" he asked, a look of confusion on his face.

"No," I whispered, "I think you did something very, very right. That's the problem." I turned and walked to the POD entrance as the last of our group lowered themselves inside.

"That explains everything." He snatched up his gear and followed me down into the POD, pulling the hatch closed after him. It shut with a loud clang that echoed through the metal halls. The internal locking wheel screeched when David turned it, sealing the hatch.

We were safely locked in. I hoped we were the only ones inside.

"It's weird being down here again." I looked around the main room of the POD.

"It isn't very pretty down here." Jessica wrinkled her nose.

"The sub-PODs are prettier inside. C'mon. I'll show you."

Jessica and I walked the circular room until we came to sub-POD 29. I stopped at the end of the corridor and stared. I don't know what I was expecting to see.

It's so different without Tiffany's smiling face and Seth and Aidan playing cards and George in his beanbag. Katie should be painting the walls and Jai Li practicing her English…it's too quiet.

"Was this your sub-POD, Eva?"

I smiled and nodded. "Mm-hmm."

"Sub-POD 29," she read the sign. "What's this?" She pointed at the red and white striped box next to the sub-POD door.

"I don't know. The information we got never mentioned it." I looked closer. The metal box around the lever had a glass door; it looked like something that would hold a fire alarm. I read the label above the lever. "'Main Shut-Off—29.' Oh my…" The lever was how people in the main POD cut off a sub-POD. That was how they'd cut off Cam's POD, how they'd cut off David's friend's POD. "David?"

"Let's go get that shower, huh?" David said. Jessica bounded ahead of us down the grate-floored corridor.

"I wondered how they did it." I looked at the air, water and electrical lines running through the large box below the lever.

"Now we know."

Chapter 29 :
The Vote

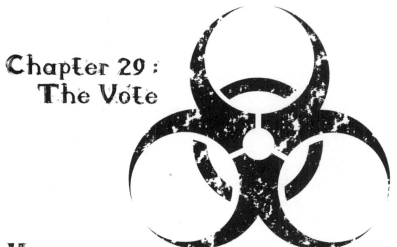

"How are you going to make it through the desert?" David asked.

"The same way we've made it this far," Devlin answered.

"We're only just into New Mexico, barely past the panhandle of Texas, and already the heat is horrid. The towns are further and further apart. You don't know when, or if, you'll find a town for supplies. Stay here. We have food and shelter." He gestured at the people assembled in one of the greenhouses, which was large enough to hold the several hundred researchers and medical personnel who'd lived in the main POD for more than a year. "It's a perfect set-up. We stay until another group moves through. They can join us, or whoever wants can leave with them."

I looked around at the faces of the others we'd been travelling with. In the three days we'd been down in the POD, people had cleaned up and gotten some rest, but many still looked weary, exhausted from the constant travelling and fights with the infected. Others were shaking their heads—the ones who were convinced there was a safe compound in California and that's where they wanted to be.

The greenhouse was thick with humidity, making it hard to breathe. I felt sweat slide down my spine; our faces were slick with it. The thick, glass domes above looked foggy with condensation, giving the room a filtered look, like looking through a piece of opaque plastic.

The air smelled of ripe, lush fruit, but the vegetable gardens were overgrown and needed work. The smell of decaying plant life tickled our noses, blending with the sweet smell of the fruit trees.

Water dripped from rain chains into tanks, collecting the extra moisture for re-use.

We could live here indefinitely if we wanted to. The POD latched from the inside; the infected couldn't get in. The gardens offered a constant supply of fruits and vegetables, and occasional hunting trips could supplement our diet. It seemed like the perfect set-up. David and I knew it could work. We'd even moved back into our old sub-POD. Jessica and Devlin had joined us there.

"We'll vote on it," Devlin decided. "Secret ballot, majority rules. Everyone go talk it over with your family or significant other. We'll meet in the main POD for dinner and vote afterward."

David and I headed back to our sub-POD after the discussion in the garden. Jessica ran ahead of us on the metal walkway. Her footsteps clanged loudly. We pulled back, letting her run ahead.

"They won't stay," I said.

"Probably not."

"And you?" I bit my lip as I waited for his answer.

"Whatever you want, Eva."

"That's not fair. It's not fair to put the decision on me."

"I'm not." When he saw the argument coming, he added, "I know where I want to be. With you. Whether that's here or in California makes no difference to me. So whatever you want is what I want."

"I don't know what I want. We could make it work here. But if there's a chance there is a compound in California it would be a much easier life. We may even have family or friends there. Crap, I don't know."

"What's holding you back from California?" Devlin asked behind us.

The sound of his voice startled me and I jumped. "Don't sneak up on people like that, Devlin. I don't have anything against California. I'm just not sure what you've been told is entirely true. I lived in a compound. They didn't let topsiders in. In fact, David is a POD survivor and they wouldn't even let him back in once he'd left."

"But the government compounds are in the east."

"Yes, that's what we've been told. Do you trust everything the government tells you?"

He didn't answer. He nodded his head and brushed past David and me, following Jessica into the sub-POD.

We gathered for dinner that evening in the main POD's cafeteria, where we found canned meats and vegetables. I helped the others open the cans, and the overpowering smell made my stomach turn. The little sausages felt spongy when I lifted them from the can. I put my hand over my mouth to keep from gagging.

I wasn't hungry. I didn't want to see or smell the food. I was worried about the vote after our meal. With people's emotions running so high, it was probably going to get ugly.

After a strangely silent meal, Devlin stood up. "I couldn't find enough pens to go around, so, one by one, everyone needs to walk to the front, write down your vote, and place the paper in the box."

He went first. The pen scratching against the paper was the only sound in the room—no one even seemed to breathe. He ripped the paper from the tablet, folded it neatly, and placed it in the box.

Jessica stood to vote. "Sit down," Devlin ordered. "My vote goes for you, too."

"The hell it does!"

"Jessica, sit down. And don't curse."

"I'll stop cursing when you stop being a horse's ass," she said through clenched teeth. She shoved her way past Devlin and wrote down her vote, tossing it in the box with a defiant stare.

I had to cover my mouth with my hand to keep from laughing out loud.

One by one, each member of the group silently walked to the front and cast a vote. Chairs squealed against the floor as each person stood, making me cringe. The pen scratching against the paper, and the sound when they ripped their page off the tablet, seemed too loud in the quiet room.

A knot twisted in my stomach. With each vote, it grew tighter and tighter until it became painful.

David and I were the last to vote. I stood and walked slowly to the front of the room. I still didn't know what my vote was going to be. I was hoping I'd have some great epiphany on my way to the voting box. I didn't.

"What's your vote?" David had asked on our way to dinner.

"I don't know."

"You don't know, or you won't tell me?"

"I don't know."

And standing in front of the box filled with the other members' votes, looking down at the pen placed neatly next to the tablet, I still didn't know.

I picked up the pen. It felt heavy in my hand. I bent forward and wrote one word across the sheet. Laying the pen on the table, I ripped the page from the tablet, giving myself a paper cut. A drop of blood formed on the side of my index finger. "Damn. That's never a good sign," I murmured, placing my vote into the box.

David stood and walked to me. His hand grabbed mine. "What'd you write, Evangelina?" I looked in his gray eyes and realized how deeply I loved him. More than anything, I wanted his vote to match mine, but I didn't tell him what I'd written. He needed to vote his way. I needed to vote mine. I shook my head and kept walking, our fingers gently falling away from each other's.

David was the last to enter his ballot. Devlin shook the box, mixing up the papers. Then he began reading them.

"Stay. Stay. Stay. Stay."

Murmurs filled the room. Some people smiled. Others grew frustrated. It was easy to pick out who had voted what.

"Leave. Stay. Leave. Leave. Leave." The murmurs grew louder. Some people's faces turned red as each dissenting vote was called. Others were wide-eyed with worry.

It's too close.

I looked at Jessica. She stared at Devlin, biting her fingernails. Juan sat next to her, his knee bouncing up and down.

"Leave. Leave. Leave. Leave." Juan's knee bounced. Jessica chewed.

So far there were five stays and eight leaves. It was going to be close.

When all the votes were read and counted—twice—twenty-one had voted to stay. Sixteen had voted to leave.

A large fist banged against a tabletop. I jumped, inhaling sharply. David lay his hand on my knee.

"You can't make us stay." A thick-necked man named Jacob banged the table again. "I don't give a rat's ass what the majority voted. If I want to leave, I'm gonna." His voice shook with anger.

"Yeah, what are you gonna do? Put guards at the hatch? Keep us here like prisoners?" Margie yelled.

David stood up. "Obviously, no one is going to stop anyone who wants to leave. But no one is going to force someone to leave if they want to stay. If the sixteen want to leave…then they should go."

"And what was your vote, David? I want to see a show of hands. Who voted to leave?" a kid in a Yankees t-shirt demanded.

"That defeats the purpose of a secret ballot, Dan."

"Screw the secret ballot. Who voted to leave?"

A sprinkling of hands rose—Margie, Dan, Jacob and his girlfriend, and a few others. The rest of the group sat silently, their hands in their lap.

"Cowards," Jacob yelled.

"It doesn't make a difference what anyone voted." Juan stood up so fast his chair fell backward on the floor. "If you want to leave, Jacob, then get out. Go now. But stop your bullying. Some people want to abide by the majority vote. That takes more courage than having a temper tantrum like a toddler."

Jacob fisted his hands at his side. His face was red; a vein throbbed in the side of his neck. I drew back, afraid he was going to make the argument physical, but he slowly sat back down in his chair. A muscle in his jaw jumped as he glared at the group.

Later that evening, Jacob, his girlfriend, and three others grabbed their gear and left. I said a prayer that they'd be okay. I knew they probably wouldn't be. They'd be no match against a group of infected.

The next morning I woke to an empty bedroom. I walked down the hall to the kitchen for a drink of water, peeking in David's room when I walked by. He was lying in bed on his stomach, one arm curled above his head, the other hanging off the bed. His face was turned from me, but I could tell by his breathing he was asleep. I looked around the bedroom; Devlin was gone. David and I were the only people in the sub-POD. I felt a stirring in my stomach. I didn't know if it was good or bad to be alone with David.

I had just gotten dressed after my shower when I heard David moving around. I sat at the small bathroom vanity, brushing my hair.

"Love that smell."

"What smell?"

"Your hair. I love how it smells after you shower. Peaches."

I smiled at him. "I found some of the shampoo I left behind."

He didn't smile back. His eyes roamed over my face, landing on my lips. He walked to me, gently pulling me up so I was standing in front of him.

"David, I..."

His lips covered mine. He kissed me gently at first, quickly growing insistent, fevered. He wanted more, and I wanted to give it to him.

His hands slipped under my shirt, caressing my skin. I moaned with pleasure, making him more brazen in his exploration. Our lips never left each other's as we stumbled backward into the girls' bedroom. We fell across the first bed we found.

Our hands explored each other, roaming over each other's body. Our kisses moved from our lips downward as David kissed my neck, pushing my t-shirt up and over my head. I pulled at his; he reached over his shoulder and yanked it off. My hands moved over his bare skin. I kissed his neck, across his shoulders and down his chest. He groaned, grabbing my hands and pinning them above my head.

His mouth covered mine, our tongues gliding against each other. His touch warmed my skin, my breathing increased, and warmth built in my stomach.

David kissed up one side of my neck, to my mouth and down the other side. He laid soft, feathery kisses across my collarbone, down to my bra, following the fabric's outline with his mouth. I arched my back, reaching for him, wanting more.

He let go of my hands and ran his fingertips down my naked side. I shivered, goosebumps covering my body. His hands became bolder in response, his mouth following his hands. He kissed everywhere he touched. I threaded my fingers through his hair.

His fingers shook as he reached for the zipper of my jeans, and that's when it happened. The rational side of my brain screamed at me, damn it to Hades and back.

"David," I whispered.

"Hmm?" His lips never stopped moving over my skin, leaving trails of heat wherever he touched.

"Do you have something?"

He froze. Slowly he lifted his head and looked at me. "Eva…I can't…I thought you…"

"I should've had another shot over a month ago—we can't risk it."

He bowed his head and cursed violently under his breath. He looked at me. "No."

"We have to stop."

He cupped my face with his hand and kissed me gently. He ran his fingers through my hair, his lips moving over mine, his tongue dipping between my lips. I had to concentrate to form a coherent thought.

"David. We can't."

He rolled over and sat on the side of the bed. His feet spread, elbows on his knees, he rested his head in his hands.

I pulled my t-shirt back over my head. Moving behind him, I kissed across his bare shoulders, moving up to his ear. "I want to."

"I know," he murmured. "But we can't take the chance."

"A baby wouldn't be a good thing right now. As much as I want to…"

"I want you, too, Eva. But you're right. You're right," he repeated, as if to make himself believe it.

I handed him his shirt and he slipped it on. "I need to, um, I'm going to take a walk around the POD. Make sure everything is working okay." He moved toward the door.

"Okay."

"I gotta go. I'll be back."

"It's okay, David."

He made a face. I think it was supposed to be a smile, but it looked more like a grimace.

I watched him leave. "Crap, Eva," I muttered. *Why'd I have to open my big mouth? I could be in David's arms right now—where it*

Michelle Pickett

feels like Heaven and there is no one else, just David and the way his hands feel on my body.

Chapter 30 : Found

It'd been a week since we'd arrived at the PODs—a blissful, almost carefree week. Each person fell into a routine. Jessica and I worked in the gardens every morning. David and Devlin did minor repairs around the main and sub-PODs. A few people took turns cooking, and some cleaned and did laundry for the camp. Some of the men—and a couple of the women—went hunting every day. Everything was working fine...until that day.

The hunting party was coming in for the day. They climbed down the long ladder, their boots raining red dirt on the floor below.

"What'dya get today?" Judy, who was serving as one of the cooks, asked. "Rabbit? Maybe a stray cow?"

"No cows, but we got these." Juan held up what looked like several long ropes. The odor of blood and meat filled the air.

I plugged my nose and looked up at what he was holding. "You're kidding, right?"

"Nah, them's good eatin'," Roy, one of the hunters, assured me.

"I'm not eating that," Jessica said.

"Well, I'm sure as anything not cookin' 'em." Judy grimaced and took a step back. "I don't have no use for those, dead or alive. Alive, especially."

David walked up behind me, nuzzling the back of my neck. I swatted him away, still discussing the fate of my dinner. "We'll eat what they brought," I told Jessica. I held my hand over my mouth and nose and tried not to gag from the smell and the thought of eating what Juan was holding.

David nibbled on my ear before whispering, "Yum."

"David, I know I taste good, but what the hell are we gonna do about the rattlesnakes Juan thinks we're eating for dinner?"

His laughter filled the small space. "I *was* talking about the rattlesnake. Them's good eatin' huh, Roy?"

"That's what I told 'er."

"I just became a vegetarian." Jessica half-ran down the metal corridor to the gardens, Devlin's chuckle following her.

"Roy, I don't know how to cook rattlesnake." Judy frowned at the day's catch again. "What's the matter with your thick head, bringing in those foul things?"

Roy grabbed the snakes from Juan's hand. They swung back and forth, their scaly bodies bouncing against each other as Roy hurried to catch up to Judy. "I can show you. My maw made rattlesnake all the time. These're—"

"Yeah, I heard you the first time. Them's good eatin'."

The sound of forks and spoons scraping against the china plates that night at dinner told me most people agreed with Roy.

David and I were on our way back to our sub-POD after dinner when I heard it—a dull thumping. I stopped and cocked my head, not exactly sure what I was hearing or where it was coming from.

The sound got louder, becoming a clang of metal hitting metal.

"David?"

"I hear it."

"Of course you hear it. You're standing right under it. Only a person who needed a hearing aid couldn't hear that."

"Always with the jokes."

"Is the hatch latched?"

"I don't know. Juan, Roy and the others were the last people in. I can't remember if they locked it or not."

I strained my memory. All I could see were the snakes swinging back and forth, their slimy, headless bodies bumping into each other as Juan bounded down the ladder into the POD. I couldn't remember seeing if anyone had turned the wheel that locked the hatch.

"No." Juan's voice startled me and I jumped, grabbing David's arm.

Devlin ran around the corner, sliding across the metal grating. He placed his hand on the floor to steady himself. Standing, he looked from Juan to David. "It's not locked?"

"No. I don't think any of us threw the bolt," Juan answered.

David grabbed the metal sides of the ladder and swung himself up, climbing the rungs two at a time. He made it to the top just as the hinges of the hatch squealed open. He grabbed the wheel on the hatch, jerking it down. The person outside howled when their fingers got caught in the opening. David tried to hold it closed long enough to lock it, fighting whoever was pulling from the outside. He hitched one foot under a rung on the ladder. Using both hands and all his weight, he pulled the hatch down and spun the wheel quickly, locking the door. Three purple, swollen fingers fell from the hatch, bouncing against the metal grate before one fell through an opening to the level below.

Still staring at the fingers lying on the floor at my feet, I felt someone tap me on the shoulder. I turned, but no one was there. My stomach lurched when I realized what it was. I slowly took a step to the side, not looking at the blood drops on my shoulder.

"Fun's over," David said.

Jumping from the bottom rung of the ladder, he took his shirt off and covered my shoulders. He rubbed his thumb gently across my cheek. When he pulled it away, I saw the blood. Wiping my face with the back of my hand, I felt the warm, sticky liquid smear.

Ah, it stings! "They've found us," I whispered, staring at the blood.

"I knew we should have moved on when we had the chance," a boy named Robbie yelled.

"No one was keeping you here!" I shouted back.

"He's right. We should've left." That was from Margie—oh, how I hated that girl. Well, not her, exactly, just her fascination with David. I wished *she'd* left.

The group had spent the better part of an hour arguing. Our shouts reverberated against the metal walls of the cafeteria where we'd just shared a peaceful dinner. They echoed in my ears, giving me a splitting headache.

Other than my outburst at Robbie, I sat silently, my hands fisted in my lap.

How quickly people change. A few hours ago, when they were shoveling a nice hot dinner into their mouths, they weren't complaining about staying. Last night, when they were sleeping in soft, warm beds, no one was screaming that it was a bad idea to lock ourselves away in the POD. This morning, when they showered and dressed in clean clothes—a luxury they hadn't had in months—they didn't think twice about their decision. But now it's a different story altogether. Now the infected have found us and they need someone to blame. And they're placing the blame squarely on David and Devlin.

I was tired of hearing their complaints. I was fed up with hearing them refuse to take responsibility for their own decisions. I was pissed that David and Devlin were the targets of their ill-placed wrath.

I stood up so fast my chair fell, bouncing against the linoleum floor. My fist came down so hard on the tabletop it hurt. "Shut. Up!"

The room was blanketed in silence. Everyone stared at me. Some looked defiant, others shocked.

"I am so sick of hearing you complain about your decision to stay! And it *was* your decision. If you recall, we voted. The majority of you wanted to stay. Those of you who didn't could've left with Jacob and the others. But you didn't. So stop blaming others for your choices and start thinking of ways to protect ourselves and our community."

"Hell's bells, Eva," David murmured. "You sure know how to quiet a room."

I righted my chair, setting it down with a hard smack against the floor. With a huff I sat down, folding my arms in front of me. I looked up and saw Robbie staring at me, his face hard, his expression cold. I raised my eyebrows at him, waiting for his response. He blinked first, looking down at the table.

"We need to stop arguing and start deciding how we're going to deal with the infected now that they've found the PODs," Devlin said.

"The guns and ammo are in the storage locker off the main hall. We should be armed anytime we go outside," Roy said.

"No shit, Sherlock," Robbie muttered.

"You can leave, you know," I snapped.

Robbie stood, glaring at me. "You know, Eva, you think you're—"

"Watch it," David warned.

Robbie sat down, cursing under his breath. I didn't hear everything he said. I just saw the people sitting next to him scoot their chairs away. Not even his closest friends wanted to be associated with him.

"No one leaves the POD alone. We stay in groups of at least five or more, and everyone is armed," Devlin said. "The hatch stays locked except when a hunting party is out. When the hatch is unlocked, we post two armed guards next to it, and all residents are aware that the hatch is open so they can be ready to defend the community, if needed." He let out a heavy sigh. "We need to find a way to know if the infected are waiting for us to emerge. We don't want to open the hatch if they're up there, staking it out. Any ideas?"

Murmurs filled the room, and Robbie raised his hand tentatively.

I rolled my eyes. "Here we go again," I whispered to David. He looked at me with a resigned smile.

"We could attach a mirror on the end of a small pole, like an antenna or somethin'. Then we could stick it out and move it around. We'd see if anyone was lurking around up there. You know, like the ones they showed in police movies and stuff."

I looked at David in surprise. *Robbie the complainer actually had a decent idea?*

David shrugged. "That's a good idea, but we'd have to open the hatch. One person couldn't look around and hold the hatch shut at the same time."

"Two people could go up. One to look and one to hold the hatch," Robbie said.

David shook his head. "No. Not enough room."

"Yeah, there's plenty of room," Robbie argued. "One in the passageway and one on the ladder."

"The hatch is too high for someone in the passageway to reach. And the ladder's too narrow for two people," David said with a frustrated sigh.

"Well, you got any better ideas, hotshot?"

The room filled with heated debate. I leaned back and closed my eyes. Robbie had a good idea in theory, but in practice it just wasn't gonna work.

"What if we built a platform?" Jessica said, so quietly the crowd nearly drowned her out.

"What?" David asked.

"What if we built a platform? Then two people could be up there at a time—three, if the platform was big enough. There are all kinds of tables around. There's a dozen in here we aren't using. We find a way to attach them—"

"There's chains and other stuff in the maintenance room," one boy said.

"Yeah, I've seen them." Devlin nodded and smiled. "We attach a table at the hatch opening and cut out a hole big enough for us to get through when we go up and down the ladder. Before anyone leaves, one person can crack the hatch open just wide enough to get a mirror through while the other person holds the hatch, ready to pull it closed and lock it if there are any infected waiting on the other side. It might just work."

"It's gonna have to. It's the best idea we've got," I said.

That night, David and I lay on the living room floor. We'd piled pillows and blankets around to soften the hard floor under the brown carpet. The room was dark. The only light came from the green glow of the clock hanging on the wall. I was nestled in the crook of David's arm, his cheek against the top of my head. Devlin snored loudly from one of the bedrooms, and Jessica slept soundly in the other down the hall.

"Do you want to leave?"

"I don't know. I'm not sure we'd be going anywhere any safer than we are here," he answered.

"You don't think there's a compound in California?"

"There might be. If there is, I don't think it'll let people like us inside. We've been out too long."

"I've been wondering something. How long does the virus last?"

"What'dya mean?" David's breath moved my hair, tickling me.

"Well, the first strain killed people pretty quickly. When they starting showing symptoms like fever and muscle aches, they only had another five days, max, before their internal organs shut down and they were dead. I wonder—how long does the mutated strain lasts before it kills its host? Another thing—I don't think the infected are as dumb as we think they are."

David pulled back. Turning on a small flashlight, he looked at me. "What are you getting at?"

I swallowed hard. What I was thinking wasn't going to make him happy. "How'd they find us, David? The hatch isn't easy to see. And even if they did see it, you said they hunt based on smell."

"So?"

"So, they can't smell through three feet of metal."

"Maybe they followed the hunters back."

"I thought of that," I said. "But they came too long after the hunters came back. Their smell would have been gone by then. The wind and the sand blowing would have masked it."

"I'm still not following you, Eva. What are you trying to tell me?"

"Well, we're all pretty sure that Jacob and the other four who left with him are toast, right? What if one of them brought the infected to us? What if it wasn't the group of infected that was following us before? I mean, they couldn't have caught up to us so quickly, and besides, they've probably found another group of people to torment and forgot all about us. What if the infected outside the PODs *are* Jacob and the others?"

"I'm pretty sure she's right," Devlin said. I jumped at the sound of his voice piercing the darkness.

"Would you stop sneaking up on people? It freaks me out," I said, relaxing against David.

"Sorry," he said absently. "I've wondered about the lifespan of an infected person, too. I've never been able to do a head count, we've always been kinda busy when they visited our camps," he said ruefully, "but I've never seen the same person more than a few times."

"So, the virus has a lifespan. It kills the host just like the strain before it," David said. "So the first strain killed in five days. Let's say this strain doubles that and kills in ten. We've been here a week. We haven't seen any infected in more than ten days. That group should be dead.

"Jacob and his group left five days ago. If they were infected the night they left, they'd be three days into their sickness—"

"Wait, why three days?" I asked.

"It takes two for the virus to take over after a bite. They waited until they saw a hunting party, followed them back to the POD, and tried to attack. They knew if they could get down here they could pick us off one by one." David tapped his finger against his lips. "Yeah. Yeah, that fits. I never thought they were capable of reason. It seemed like they were just hunting, but if this is Jacob's group, then we're dealing with a whole new set of trouble."

"Hey, what are you two doing up so late, anyway?"

"Privacy, man," David said, like it should be obvious.

Devlin's laughter filled the room. "You've got food, water, shelter, and you're safe. The one thing you ain't gonna get is privacy." He chuckled and walked to the kitchen. Banging around, he grabbed an apple and walked past us, whistling. "G'night."

"So, you think it's Jacob and the others?"

"I don't know, Eva, but I know how we'll find out."

"Yeah. And it isn't the way I want to."

The next day the hunting party didn't go out. Devlin told the group what our thoughts were on the life of the virus and the possibility that it was Jacob and his group outside. Surprisingly, there were no outburst of anger, no fits of rage, just a few murmurs of disbelief, of disgust, and of worry. People listened to what Devlin had to say, and then went about their daily routines inside the POD.

A group of the guys took apart and reassembled a table near the hatch opening as had been discussed, passing it up through the ladder hole in pieces. It took nearly all day, but the idea worked. A chain had been looped through a handle on the hatch and threaded through a winch Roy had found in one of the maintenance areas. If the hatch was pulled open, one person would hold the winch, pulling the chain tight and keeping the hatch in place. The second person would throw the deadbolt, preventing the people outside from opening it.

"Looks like your idea is going to work, Jessica," I said. We were on our way to the kitchen, carrying baskets full of ripe apples from the greenhouse. Then I heard David, his easy laughter filling the small space above me. He was crouched up on the table near the hatch, looking over the mirrored device Robbie had made.

"It looks like a mirror a dentist would use."

"Nah, man." Robbie grabbed for the mirror. "It's like one a military sniper or somebody would use,"

"Yeah—a dentist-military-sniper." David handed the long device to Robbie, who hung it on a hook next to the hatch. Everything was in place for the next time anyone left the POD.

I smiled listening to him, my eyes drinking him in. It wasn't often I could stare without him catching me. I liked watching him without him knowing it. He had an easygoing way about him—calm and secure, but smart and aware at the same time. He was comfortable in his own skin—self-assured, but not cocky. And gorgeous, with that dark hair and those gray eyes, like no one else's.

"...told me if it was Jacob—you're not listening to me!" Jessica whined.

"Sorry. Jacob what?"

"He's good-looking, huh? Is that why you like him so much?"

"David?"

Jessica nodded, looking up at him.

"No. I mean, yes, he's good-looking, but that's not the only reason I like him. He's sweet and smart and funny. I like being with him."

A loud bang sounded behind me when David hurled himself down from the ladder. I jumped, apples flying out of my basket and rolling around the corridor. He planted a quick kiss on my lips before gathering the apples and tossing them back into the basket.

"That goes double for me," he said with a smirk.

I rolled my eyes and looked at Jessica. "Did I mention he's a pain in the rear, too?"

She giggled and looked at David. He smiled and winked at her, taking a large bite out of one of the apples, wiping the juice from his mouth with the back of his hand.

"What about Jacob, Jessica?" David asked.

"I'm not really supposed to tell anyone. I was just telling Eva because I knew she'd keep my secret."

"Jessica, we can't have secrets down here," I said. "It's important that we all be honest with each other. That's the only way for us to stay safe."

"Well, some of the people—" She lowered her voice and rushed on. "—are worried, if it's Jacob and the others out there, they won't be able to kill them."

"Ah. I wouldn't worry about it. Whoever's out there is infected. They aren't the same people anymore. People shouldn't have any trouble defending themselves," David told her, giving her a reassuring smile. But when she gave him a hug, the look he gave me over her head was full of concern, and my gut tightened.

What if Jacob's friends aren't able to do what is necessary? If they hesitate, they'll put us all in danger.

After dinner we heard it again. The banging on the hatch grew louder, and the wheel turned back and forth as they tried to open it. David and Devlin climbed the ladder.

"What are you doing?" I yelled. "Are you insane?"

"We need to know. We'll open the hatch just far enough to get the mirror out and have a little looksee." Devlin smiled down at me.

Horror filled my voice. "David! Don't open that hatch. It's putting us all in danger if you open it when you know they're out there."

More people joined us. Roy brushed past me and grabbed the ladder. Swinging himself up, he took the rungs two at a time.

"Thank goodness," I breathed. "Grab that mirror thingy out of his hands and talk some sense into him, Roy."

"Oh, I'm not talking him down, Eva. I'm helping Devlin hold the hatch."

"You're all insane!"

The group of us watched as they opened the hatch a crack. David slid the mirror out of the opening. He turned it around in a slow circle. My heartbeat thudded in my ears, and I couldn't breathe. Every second that hatch stayed open, we were in danger—*David* was in danger.

It seemed like it took forever for him to pull the mirror back into the POD. Just as he was lowering it through the opening, someone on the other side grabbed it and pulled it back through the crack. David jerked it down, not letting go. The person above jerked it up again.

"Let go," I yelled. "Shut the hatch!"

With one last jerk, David freed the mirror from the person—thing—and the force sent him flying across the table. Roy and Devlin pulled the latch closed, cranked the wheel, and locked the deadbolt.

They climbed down the ladder. David inspected the mirror, while I inspected him.

"Are you hurt?" I asked, pulling up his shirtsleeve. Any scratch, any bite, and he was susceptible to the virus. He'd have to do a week in quarantine...or worse.

"No."

"Did they scratch you? Let me see your hands." I looked at the palm of each hand, turning them over to examine the backs. They looked clean. I didn't see any scratches, cuts or—God forbid—bites.

"The mirror looks okay," he said to no one in particular.

"The mirror? The mirror! You're worried about the mirror? You could've been scratched or bitten! You could have been infected, David, and you're worried about the mirror? You're insane!"

"Probably," he agreed.

"Well?" someone asked.

"It's Jacob." David still examined the mirror, turning it this way and that.

Everyone began talking at once. The sound echoed in the metal room and made my head hurt. If it was Jacob, that meant the infected were able to reason, to problem solve. If it was Jacob, he knew our routines.

"Evangelina," David called over the noise. "Was Jacob with us the day we went to the greenhouse?"

"I don't know."

Devlin looked at David and they broke into a run, weaving around poles and doorframes on their way to the greenhouse. Their shoes clanged against the metal, and the suspended walkway swung. I trailed behind them, holding on to the side railings to keep my balance.

"What's up?" Roy panted, out of breath. His belly heaved as he gulped in air.

"The greenhouse is glass!" David yelled.

"David!" I shouted. Stopping and bending over, I tried to catch my breath, holding my sides with my hands. "It's not just glass."

He slowed to a jog, letting me catch up. "What do you mean?"

"It's bulletproof. Hail and wind won't penetrate it. A tree could fall on it and it wouldn't do anything. It's thick and strong. He won't be able to get through."

"How do you know?"

"I actually read the information given to the POD residents," I said.

David rolled his eyes. "But how much can he see? People are working in there every day. How much of our routine is he monitoring through that glass?"

"None," I said. "It's covered in condensation. He can't see in; we can't see out. The greenhouse is safe."

"Evangelina, nothing is safe."

Chapter 31 :
Leaving

"**I** don't want you to work in there tomorrow." David's chest rose under my head, and he wrapped a strand of my hair around his finger.

"Okay. I don't want you to go to work, either. I want to stay in this sub-POD all day and all night. I want to spend every second with you to make sure you're safe. I want to talk with you, laugh with you, and make plans about what we're going to do when this is all over. But I'm not going to get what I want, am I? You'll go to work, do your job, contribute to the community. You won't stay with me all day. Am I right?"

"Yes."

"Well, then, we'll both know what it's like not to get what we want. I'm not staying here tomorrow and letting someone else do my job. The greenhouse is my responsibility. If it's Jacob out there, who cares? If not him, it'd be someone else. There's always going to be infected."

"But Jacob knows—"

"So?"

"I want you to be safe."

"David." I sighed, running my fingers through his hair and pulling his lips to mine. "I am safe."

"No, you're out here in this godforsaken place. Back where we started, only this time the POD isn't offering a new beginning like we were promised. This time the POD offers only a place to hide from the infected—from people who are infected by the very thing the POD was supposed to shield us from." His words got louder as he talked, faster and faster. "You should've stayed at the compound, Eva. You were safe there. You could've had a life—"

"David! Stop it. I'm right where I want to be. I made the decision to leave the compound. Me. And knowing what I know now, I'd do it again, because there was one thing the compound didn't have. You."

He reached around my waist and lifted me off his chest. Shifting our positions, he angled himself over me. "You're so stubborn."

I smiled. "That's what you like about me."

"No. That's what I love about you, Evangelina Mae." He smoothed wisps of hair away from my face, looking down at me. I arched my back, grazing my lips across his. "It's also what I hate about you."

I drew back from him, his words like a blow. "Hate? That's a strong word, David." I pushed him off me and sat up. His arm snaked around my waist, holding me in place. He leaned his head against my back.

"Okay, maybe not 'hate', exactly, but it frustrates me beyond belief. Eva, you could have had anything, everything, if you'd only stayed at the compound. If I'd only been stronger and stayed away, you would have forgotten—moved on. You wouldn't be here hiding and waiting for…"

"What, David?"

"The end."

I turned and cupped his face with my hand. "Don't give up on me, David. I'm not waiting for the end of anything except the damned virus. And you're wrong. I couldn't have had anything and everything at the compound. I couldn't have had you—the one thing I want in this world was the one thing the compound couldn't give me. And I wouldn't have forgotten. That's why I sat in the middle of the meadow on the cold, wet ground night after night. Because I couldn't forget. I didn't want to. I was petrified you had. Terrified that you'd left me. Crushed that it was so easy for you to leave. And I still wonder how, out of all the girls in all the PODs, I got so lucky."

David snorted a laugh. He took my hand in his and turned it over, doodling with his finger on my palm. "Yeah, lucky. I'm not sure that's how I'd describe it."

I shrugged. "Well, whatever you want to call it, me and my stubborn streak are happy with the choices we've made."

David leaned forward and touched his lips to mine. He pulled back and looked me in the eyes. "I love you, Eva. If anything happens to you I'll never be able to forgive myself."

"I know, David. I love you, too." I pulled him down to the floor, wrapping my arms around his neck, kissing him deeply as our hands roamed each other's bodies.

His trembling fingers fumbled with the top button of my pajama top. I placed my hands over his and slowly undid each button, his eyes fixated on my fingers. I stopped just above my breasts, watching him. His heart beat hard and fast against my chest.

I reached out and pushed up his shirt, caressing the skin beneath. He muttered an oath and bent his head to kiss me, gently at first, and then deeper. Harder. Demanding. One hand tangled in my hair, and he tipped my head back to expose my neck, and I gasped. He trailed warm, moist kisses from my mouth, across my jaw, and down the side of my throat.

One hand reached under my shirt and skimmed across my bare belly; my muscles contracted and goosebumps covered my skin. I moaned and he gritted his teeth, his jaw tightening. His other hand drifted from my hair; moving down, he pushed my shirt over one shoulder, his lips following his fingers—moving lower. From my shoulder to my collarbone, and still lower. From soft kisses grazing over my collarbone to my chest. From my chest still lower, kissing between my breasts through my nightshirt. His hand reached for the next button…I knew I should stop him. We were passing the point where neither of us would be able to stop. I knew there was a reason we shouldn't be doing this, but my mind wouldn't focus on anything but what David was doing with his tongue as it trailed lower and lower…

"You guys are still up?"

"Dammit, Jessica," David whispered through clenched teeth.

I yanked my shirt back over my shoulders and buttoned up the front before she saw anything she—or David—shouldn't see.

"Yeah," My voice came out breathless. "What are you doing?"

"I needed a drink. Do you feel okay, Eva? Your cheeks are all red and you're breathing funny." Her eyes danced with suppressed glee.

David smirked. I glared at him before looking at Jessica. "I'm fine. It's just a little hot in here."

"Really? I think it's cold," she smirked. "I think being in the POD is getting to you." Jessica walked back down the hall toward the bedroom.

"Something's getting to me," David murmured, kissing the hollow behind my ear.

"Me, too," I said with a laugh. His kisses tickled in all the right—but very wrong—places. He reached for the buttons on my shirt, and I tossed his shirt at him.

"Fun's over, huh?"

"Yes."

"Tomorrow I'm getting a cup for the bathroom," he muttered.

"What?"

"A cup for the bathroom. Then she won't have to come out here for a drink of water."

"Quiet down out there, you two. Some of us are trying to sleep," Devlin yelled from the bedroom, before chuckling.

"No privacy. None."

"That's a good thing, David. No privacy means no babies."

"It means no fun, is what it means."

I laughed at his grumbling.

The next morning I was working in the gardens in the greenhouse. Something clanged above me and I jumped. Looking up, I strained to see through the foggy glass.

It couldn't be them. They stayed away during the day—we figured the sun was uncomfortable for them. The only time I'd seen them in daytime, it had been overcast and raining. So it never entered my mind to be afraid.

Judy figured it out first. She stood and, without a word, ran down the slippery walkway to the doors leading to the main portion of the POD. I watched her go, still listening to the strange clanging on the roof of the greenhouse.

"I told you to stay outta here, Eva," David yelled, running into the greenhouse.

"What are you talking about?"

"Them." He pointed at the domed ceiling.

"The sounds?"

"Judy's right, them's people up there," Roy drawled, squinting at the ceiling. "Jacob and his friends, I'd wager."

I looked at the glass-covered ceiling and shielded my eyes from the sunlight. I couldn't make out the faces of the people—the sun was at their backs and condensation coated the glass. But human-shaped shadows hulked over the glass, looking down at us as we looked back at them.

Another loud bang reverberated through the huge room and I jumped. "Oh!"

"I want everyone outta here now," David ordered.

"No."

"Eva—"

"They aren't going to break that glass with a few hits of a baseball bat—"

"Nah, that there looks to be a tree trunk," Roy said, another crash sounding. I could almost picture him chewing on a piece of straw with the way he drawled each word, like it was just another typical day in Dead Possum Hollow—or wherever he'd said he was from.

"A tree trunk?" I asked.

"Yup. Not too big, mind ya. But big enough."

"Satisfied? Let's go." David grabbed my arm and pulled me toward the door. I jerked free.

"I'm not finished with what I need to get done. They aren't getting in here. I don't care if all five of them have tree trunks—"

"They do," Roy interrupted.

Not helping, Roy! I wanted to scream at him to shut up.

"It doesn't matter. That glass is too strong for them to do any damage." I knelt down in the moist, black soil and continued to weed rows of carrots.

"Eva," David sighed, easing himself down next to me. "What do I need to do to help? The sooner we get this done, the sooner you'll leave, right?"

"Yes, dear." I smiled at him.

They were waiting that afternoon when the hunting party opened the hatch. A boy named Tyler reached too far out with the mirror, and one of the infected bit him on the hand. We all knew what needed to be done—even he seemed resigned to the fact.

"We can do the quarantine, or you can leave," Devlin said.

He was younger than me, maybe fifteen or sixteen, with blond hair, blue eyes, and a smattering of freckles across his nose. Tall and lanky, his arms and legs seemed too big for his frame, like he hadn't grown into them yet.

It's funny—I'd never called him by name. We said *good morning* at breakfast and *hi* when we'd pass each other in the halls during the day, but I'd never really spoken with him. It seemed like such a waste. I'd miss him. I'd mourn for him. But

I hadn't taken the time to get to know him when it would've mattered. After the bite nothing mattered, except how we'd protect ourselves from him.

He wanted Devlin to do it. They walked silently to his sub-POD—the others who'd been staying in there with him grabbed their things and moved into other quarters. He had enough food and water for two days—the smell of fruit and vegetable soup filled the corridor. After that, we'd know. He'd either be allowed back in the community, or the sub-POD would remain locked. It had just become a quarantine facility—and probably a tomb.

Tyler wouldn't be coming out of the sub-POD, not alive. A bite was a death sentence. We all knew it. Two days later, it was obvious he was infected. The sub-POD was disconnected from the main POD. The metal of the corridor screeched as the passageway was crushed, the sound so loud I covered my ears. Squeezing my eyes shut, I tried to squeeze out the knowledge that another one of us had been lost.

We waited a week before attempting to send the hunting party out again. There was no sign of Jacob or the others that had left with him. We assumed the virus had killed them and it was all clear. We were right that they were dead. We were wrong that we were in the clear.

Juan was on watch that day. He sat on the table under the hatch. The winch held the hatch in place, open just enough so Juan could see out, but not enough that anyone—or anything—could get in.

David sat on the table with him. They played cards while they waited for the hunters to return. Their laughter drifted into the cafeteria, where I was helping clean up from lunch.

"They're telling 'em today," Hannah, a girl not much older than me, said.

"Who?" I asked her.

"Juan and your David. They're really going at it." Hannah smiled.

"They seem to be into the card game, that's for sure."

"Hun, that ain't got nothin' to do with cards. They're going on about something. Probly some dirty jokes or your David's telling tales about y'all."

I could feel the red-hot blush color my cheeks. She smiled and winked. I wasn't sure what it meant, but it embarrassed me even more.

"David!" I yelled, walking into the main junction of corridors where the hatch was located.

"Yeah?" He peered over the side of the table, still laughing at something Juan had said.

I wasn't sure what I was going to say next. It didn't matter because all hell broke loose and thoughts of dirty jokes flew out of my mind.

"Open the hatch!" I heard someone yelling.

Juan reached over to let the winch free. David's hand snaked out and grabbed Juan's wrist.

"Tommy? Where's everyone else?" David called.

"Roy's coming behind me. Everyone else is dead."

Dead. Dead. Dead. The word echoed in my mind. *How can they be dead? We haven't seen Jacob and his gang in more than a day.*

Since we'd first seen them above the greenhouse, they'd been a constant fixture around the POD. No one could go in or out. They were there waiting for the hatch to open—for any little mistake they could exploit. But they hadn't been around for almost two days.

I climbed a few rungs up the ladder, high enough that I could see out the gap of the hatch opening, but not high enough to be in the way. I saw Roy running toward the POD. The red sand churned around him like he was caught in a tornado. It was impossible to see if anyone—anything—was following him.

"Open the hatch, Juan!" Roy wheezed.

Juan looked at David, his hand reaching for the winch. David shook his head once. "Not yet," he whispered. "Take your shirts off and hold out your hands," David called through the gap.

"We don't have time—"

"Then shut up and do it quickly!" I flinched at the harshness of David's tone.

Through the crack I saw their shirts drop to the sandy ground. "Is there anyone behind you?" David asked.

"No."

David nodded and Juan released the lever on the winch, loosening the hatch enough for the men to climb through. The table creaked under their weight. I climbed down the ladder. Roy and the other hunter followed me down to the main POD floor, David and Juan close behind.

Once down, David looked at the two men. "Strip."

I averted my eyes. I tried to leave, but the men were blocking the way to my sub-POD. I tried to push through, but all four men ignored me. So I stood with my back to the stripping hunters and looked at David instead. I didn't like what I saw. His face was hard, menacing. "Turn around slowly."

I could hear their feet shuffle against the floor as they turned. "Lift one foot. The other. Raise both arms and show me your hands. Do you know of any scratches, cuts, or bites that I can't see?"

"No," the men said in unison.

"Okay, get dressed and meet us in the cafeteria." David grabbed my hand and gently pulled me to his side.

"What's up?" Devlin asked when we entered the cafeteria.

"The hunting party was attacked." David ran his hand down his face and blew out a breath.

"Everyone get back okay?"

"No."

Devlin nodded his head, running his fingers through his dark hair. "Who?"

"Roy and Tommy made it back."

"That's all?" Devlin asked, dropping his hand.

"Yeah."

Devlin looked over David's shoulder. The men had followed us into the cafeteria, their faces grim.

"Where's everyone else?" Devlin asked.

"Dead." Tommy sounded almost as if he was in a trance.

"How?"

"There was a group of infected waiting between the tents when we came back from the hunt. We weren't expecting them...I mean, we haven't seen Jacob in almost two days...we were sure it was clear. They picked us off one by one."

"Jacob?" Juan asked. I jumped at the sound of his voice behind me.

"No, Jacob and the others weren't with them. This was a new group." Roy's face remained tomato-red from the run to the POD.

"C'mon, Roy. Let's get you something cold to drink." I took his hand, pulling him with me.

David held my other hand. I pulled away, but he didn't let go. I looked up at him and smiled. "It's okay," I whispered. He drew me to him, kissing me softly on the lips before letting go, our threaded fingers falling away slowly. Roy followed close behind me, still holding my hand.

"If it wasn't Jacob's group, then who was it?" Devlin asked behind me.

"I don't know," Tommy said.

"A group of nomads moving through that Jacob and the others attacked, or maybe an entirely new group of infected moving through looking for food. What difference does it make?" David asked.

"We aren't safe here," Judy whispered. She handed Roy a cup of cold water.

"We're as safe as we can get," I answered.

"I don't want to," Jessica whined.

Her voice carried up the walkway as I was coming back to the sub-POD from the gardens.

"Too bad," Devlin said, his voice hard. "I've made up my mind."

"So? I have a mind, too. And my mind's made up. I'm not leaving."

"Yes, you are."

"I'll stay with the others," she said.

"The others are leaving."

"Everyone?"

"I think so." I could hear the lie in Devlin's voice and wondered if Jessica could, too.

"What'dya mean, *you think so?*"

"We haven't talked to Eva and David yet."

"Why? You all had a meeting without them? Without me? You made decisions that will affect us all without letting everyone have their say?"

"It doesn't matter what your say is. You're my sister and you're staying with me. As for Eva and David, they think the PODs are the answer. I don't think they'll want to leave."

"We would've liked a say, Devlin," I said quietly, stepping into the living area.

"Ah, Eva, you weren't supposed to—"

My hands tightened into fists. "What? I wasn't supposed to find out?"

His cheeks colored. "No, we were all going to tell you together. You weren't supposed to find out this way."

"When were you gonna tell us? When you were packing to leave?"

"Um…"

"Don't bother." I turned to leave and ran into David's chest. I looked up at him. A vein throbbed in the side of his neck, the tendons tight along his jaw. "David, you scared me."

He didn't speak. At first I didn't think he'd acknowledge me. Then he looked down and smiled. "Sorry. C'mon. I think we need to talk."

He took my hand and pulled me behind him. I had to jog to keep up with his long strides. "Is the greenhouse empty?"

"Yes."

"Good." We made our way through the metal corridors, our feet clanging against the grates. We passed through the main portion of the POD and I could hear people in the cafeteria talking. I looked at them as we passed. They averted their eyes. David didn't stop. He kept walking straight to the gardens, pulling me behind him.

The hot, humid air overwhelmed me. Sweat broke out across my face. The hiss of sprinklers came from somewhere deeper in the greenhouse. The sun streamed through the glass ceiling, giving David's hair a shining hint of red.

I sat on the damp walkway. The trees loomed over me like a green umbrella, shielding me from the drops of water falling around us. David stood with his back to me, one hand in his hip pocket, the other rubbing the spot between his eyes.

"You knew," I said.

"I guessed."

"Guessed?"

"I've heard some people rumbling about going to California to look for their families. I figured it was only a matter of time before some of them left."

"Some."

"Yeah." He dropped his hand and turned. Crouching down in front of me, his gray eyes looked into mine. "What do you want to do, Eva? Stay or go?"

"I don't know. Who's planning to stay?"

"I think they're all going."

"*All?* Are you kidding?" He shook his head. "Oh. I wasn't expecting that." I drummed my fingers on my lower lip, looking around. The trees were heavy with fruit. The vegetable plants were growing, leafing out nicely. The sound of water dripping from the rain chains played like gentle percussion throughout the large room.

With the gardens providing food and water, and the wind and solar power, why would people want to risk leaving the

POD for a compound that most likely didn't exist? And even if it *did* exist, they probably wouldn't be allowed to enter.

"Do you think we could keep this place up by ourselves?" I asked him.

"I think we'd have as good a shot keeping it up alone as we would out there running from infected every day and night."

"I guess."

"What, Eva?"

"What if they're right? What if there's a compound out there for topsiders?"

"If you want to go with them, you just have to say the word and I'll start packing."

"What do you want?" I asked, holding my breath.

"I want what you want, Eva."

"I hate that."

"Well, it's true." He gave a humorless laugh.

I glared at him. "I hate it when you leave the decision to me! It involves both of us. We should decide together."

"We are. You're deciding what you want to do. I've already made my decision."

"Lemme guess, you've decided to do whatever I want to do," I said.

"Yep."

"Fine. Let's go get dinner over with so we can get this figured out."

I stood and took one last look at the gardens I'd toiled over for weeks. It was beautiful there, peaceful. Everything the outside world wasn't.

What was I supposed to decide? Maybe there *was* a compound in California and maybe we'd be allowed inside. Maybe. There definitely were infected and we'd definitely run into some. Definitely.

Should David and I leave the safety of the PODs for a chance at a normal life in California, or stay in the PODs for a chance at a life at all?

I knew my decision.

PODs

Dinner was tense, the conversations strained by the many things not being said. The clattering of silverware sounded garish in the room that was usually filled with friendly banter. The potato soup, normally one of my favorites, stuck in my throat no matter how hard I tried to swallow it down. No one met my eyes.

I threw down my spoon. It clanged across the table, bouncing onto the tiled floor. I couldn't stand it anymore.

"Let's just get it over with. Who's staying?" I called out, waiting for a show of hands. None came. "No one, huh? No one is staying where you know you'll have fresh food, water, and warm beds to sleep in every night? You'd give that up for a place that may not even exist?"

"And you'd stay here and give up the chance at seeing your family again?" Robbie asked from across the room.

I looked into Devlin's face, seeing a flash of shame in his eyes. "My family is dead," I said quietly. "And it's likely yours are, too. If the first wave of the virus didn't kill them, the mutated strain did. If they lived through that, the infected have probably killed them by now. Either way, it isn't likely that you'll see them again. Wouldn't they want you to stay in a place where you're safe? Where you could build a life?"

"I have to know, Eva. Even if it means getting to California and finding there's no compound after all. I have to know," Devlin murmured, "Winter is almost over. When the spring and summer hit it'll be too hot for us to travel through the desert. We either leave now or wait a year. I can't wait that long."

"And you'd risk Jessica?" David asked.

Devlin shrugged.

"Are you...are you coming, Eva?" Jessica's voice quivered.

"No."

They left the next morning.

Chapter 32: The End

David and I waited two weeks—giving time for the infected to leave or die—before we attempted to leave the POD on our own.

"How are we gonna know if they're in the POD when we come back?" I asked David.

"This." He held up a toothpick before inserting it in the small gap between the unlocked hatch door and the frame of the POD. "If this is gone, we know someone, or something, has been here. It's small enough not to draw attention. No one should see it. If it's still here when we get back, we can be reasonably sure no one has disturbed the hatch."

"Sounds good," I said.

"That's it?"

"What?"

"It '*sounds good*' is all you have to say?" he asked.

"Oh, okay, how's this? David, your plan is genius. You're a genius. I'm in awe of your problem-solving skills. Better?"

"A simple 'that's a great plan, David' would've been enough," he muttered.

I laughed and kissed his cheek.

We started our hunt. We were looking for rabbits, but David said if we found a rattlesnake or two we'd take them. I didn't agree to that.

The sun was brutal. Even in the early morning hours it beat down on us with an oppressive heat. We walked for two hours and never saw another living thing—except for some bugs and a few scorpions, none of which I was putting in my mouth. I'd live on the fruit and vegetables the gardens provided before I ate a scorpion.

David wasn't an experienced hunter. That made two of us. When the sun was directly above us and the wind blew the sand in our eyes and mouths, we decided to call it quits and go back to the POD.

"We'll wait until dusk and try again," David told me, removing the toothpick from where he left it and opening the hatch for me.

I heard scratching first, and then the banging started. The hatch didn't move when they hit it, but the noise was unbearable. The clanging of the metal door was ear-piercing and made my breath hitch in my throat. My hands started to shake and I mentally checked off everything David and I had done after we returned to the POD.

David opened the hatch for me and I climbed down onto the small ramp leading to the ladder next to the elevator. I waited for David to climb through the hatch and I grabbed the wheel, pulling the door closed after him...then what did I do? Did I turn it to bolt it? I don't remember turning the wheel.

Cold sweat slithered down my spine. "They're at the hatch," I whispered. "David, I don't think I locked it. They don't usually come out during the day, and we were going back out. I don't think I locked it when we came in! I don't think it's locked!"

"It's okay. They won't be able to get in the sub-POD."

"David! We won't be able to get out. Even if they can't find which sub-POD we're in, they can stay in the main POD and wait us out. There's no other way for us to get out of here."

They clanged against the hatch at a deafening rate. One after another they hit the door…*bang…bang…bang*. Every time one of them hit, my stomach lurched painfully. Bile rose in the back of my throat, burning it.

If they get in here, we're trapped. Dead. dinner…or worse. We'll be turned into them, a fate worse than death. I'd rather they killed me.

David stood looking at the floor. He was silent so long I didn't think he was going to answer me. I was just about to shake him and scream at him to do something—anything—when he looked up, his face grim.

"You're right. We need to check the hatch. I'll climb up the ladder and—"

"Like hell you will!" I grabbed his arm when he moved toward the ladder. "If it's unlocked, they could open it any second. You aren't going to be sitting up there when they do. No way."

He gestured around the POD. "Well, we can't stay here, Eva."

"No kidding." My voice shook and cracked when I talked. "Let's move before they get that hatch open."

"Okay, but we should set a trap first." He grabbed the meat out of the sub-POD freezer, leftovers from the last hunting party before Devlin and the rest left the PODs. "Come on, Eva. We have to move fast. Grab the meat—as much as you can carry."

We ran down the corridor to the main POD, leaving a trail of meat behind us. I could hear the infected scurrying above the hatch, looking for a way in.

The scraping and pounding got louder the closer we got to the entrance to the main POD. I stopped and looked at David.

"Eva, come on!"

"Do you think they're this stupid? That they'll follow a trail of dead meat? It's frozen, David! You told me they like living animals."

"We don't have anything living to bait a trap with. Get moving."

"Yes, we do," I whispered.

I yanked my small pocketknife out of my jeans pocket. I turned and ran down the corridor back to the entrance of the sub-POD. My fingers shook, bobbing up and down as I ran. I could barely get the small blade open.

I heard David curse and run after me.

"Go back, David. I'll be right behind you."

I slid to a stop in front of the sub-POD door, my shoes squeaking loudly against the metal floor. Without giving myself time to think, I plunged the knife into my arm. Warm, sticky blood gushed from the wound. It trailed down my arm and dripped off my fingertips, forming a small pool at my feet. I walked as slowly as I dared back to where David stood.

"What the hell, Eva?"

I shrugged. "Fresh meat. Here, give me your shirt. I need to wrap my arm. I can't bleed on the floor any more. It'll lead them right to us." He pulled his shirt over his head and wrapped it tightly around my arm. "Let's find a storage locker or somewhere to hide."

"No. Your scent will lead them right to you. You have to get as far away from this corridor as possible. We only want them to smell the blood on the floor, not on your arm."

"Where then?"

"One of the sub-PODs on the other side of the main POD. You can hide in one of the bedroom closets. When they follow your blood trail to the sub-POD, I'll lock them in. Then I'll come back and get you."

I shook my head. "No—"

"Yes. You can't be out here. You're bleeding too badly. Look, you've almost bled through my shirt. Take your shirt off."

"Why David, are you getting fresh with me?" My voice trembled and my teeth chattered.

Why are my teeth chattering? Is it shock? Fear? Both? Do I care? No. Pay attention, Eva.

"C'mon, Eva, be serious," David said.

"Geez, you can't take a joke."

He reached forward and ripped open the front of my t-shirt. Standing in just my bra and jeans, I watched him tie my shirt around my arm, pulling it tight. I could almost feel the blood seeping through the fabric of David's shirt and into mine.

"Okay, let's find you a sub-POD."

"No."

"We don't have time for your stubborn streak, Eva. Let's go."

He pulled on my good arm. I jerked away from him.

"I'm not leaving you here to fight them alone."

"Well, you can't stay. C'mon."

I followed him down the hall. Our shoes made dull thuds against the framework of the walkway. The metal shimmied and shook, scraping against the wall. The sound gave me chills.

The infected banged at the POD, their clubs—baseball bats? tree branches?—bouncing off the hatch, which rattled with every impact. My heart beat painfully in my chest. It was hard to take a breath.

"David, the greenhouse! We can go into the greenhouse and watch them through the glass door. When they enter the corridor, we can lock them in."

"No."

"What do you mean *no*?"

"You can't go out there with your arm. The greenhouse is a good place to hide. There are a lot of different smells inside to mask the smell of your blood, but if you come out they'll smell your wound. You have to stay inside the greenhouse."

I nodded once. We ran to the greenhouse, pulling the heavy glass door closed behind us.

"Listen, Eva. When I leave, I want you to lock this door. Don't unlock it until you see me."

"Okay," I said, my voice strained.

We huddled down next to the stack of weeding baskets and hand tools we'd left by the door, hoping its shadow would hide our silhouettes. David used his hand to wipe away a small area of condensation—just big enough that we could look through.

"The banging stopped," I whispered. "Maybe they left." Then I heard it. The unmistakable sound of the hatch hinges creaking open. "Oh. I guess not." My insides shook. "David?"

"Yeah?"

"Kiss me."

He put his finger under my chin and lifted my face upward toward his. He touched his lips softly to mine. He pulled back and smoothed some hair from my face, pushing it behind my ear.

"I'm scared," I said, barely a whisper.

"I know, Eva. I am, too." He kissed me again, stopping when we heard the first grunt in the main POD.

"How ironic would it be if we died in the very place that was supposed to save us?" I let out a half-hysterical giggle.

Feet shuffled down the ladder. We could hear the grunts and groans, and then the screams of the infected echoed against the metal walls.

Through the wiped spot in the condensation, I watched the first man step off the ladder. His weapon—it looked to be a two-by-four—bounced along the metal floor grating as he dragged it across the room. Another, and then another, and another came down the ladder—seventeen in all. Some were unarmed, but most had bats or clubs of some kind.

"There are so many."

"Mm-hmm," David said.

"What are you thinking?" I turned to look at him, pulling his face to me so I could see his eyes.

"I'm hoping they take your bait."

The group of infected wandered around the large room in the main POD. Occasionally they'd disappear into other rooms, but always returned to the main room. I held my breath. My chest hurt from lack of oxygen.

Through the foggy glass we watched as one of the infected came closer to the glass door of the greenhouse. David and I slid back, away from the glass. The blood rushed behind my ears so loudly that I almost couldn't hear the infected rattling the door. It grunted and groaned with the effort.

I put my hands over my mouth to hold in any sound. Pulling my knees to my chest and laying my head on them, I faced the door and watched the infected look for a way inside. David wrapped his arms around me, squeezing me to him.

The infected pulled at the door, which shimmied in response. It pulled harder. The door clanged, moving against the metal doorjamb. The infected raised its weapon—a tire iron.

It's gonna hit the glass.

I leaned into David, grabbing his arms. *We're dead. If it breaks the glass…*

Please, please, please don't break.

It pulled back, ready to swing.

Just go away…go away!

Something caught its attention. It turned its head and dropped its arms, mid-swing. The tire iron connected with the glass with a small tap. The infected turned and shuffled away.

I felt David let out a breath. The room spun around me. I didn't feel as though I could breathe. It was as if I'd held my breath so long my body had forgotten how.

"Eva," David whispered, shaking me gently. I dropped my hands from my mouth and gulped in a huge lungful of air. "That was too close."

"Yeah. They've been here too long. They aren't falling for it, David." An edge of panic crept into my voice.

"Look." He nodded his head at the sub-POD entry. "They found it. That's what drew the infected away from the greenhouse door."

The group congregated at the opening of the sub-POD. A few of them took tentative steps into the corridor. When nothing happened, they ventured further inside. Others followed. Soon they were all in the corridor, visible as a collection of shuffling, dark shadows.

"I have to go now. I need to collapse it before they get to the end of the blood trail."

I nodded. I couldn't trust my voice to speak. A tear escaped my eye. David brushed it away with the pad of his thumb. He kissed me quickly and slipped out the door.

I watched him move across the room toward the sub-POD. My gaze moved from David to the opening and back again. Through the foggy glass, I saw the moment we had a problem.

As David moved toward the sub-POD corridor, an infected man turned, his pale face eerie in the dark corridor. He watched David for a millisecond before running down the corridor toward him. David started sprinting for the opening. My heart raced as I watched the two men running toward each other. "Run, run, run," I whispered. My hands slick with sweat, I balled them into fists, my fingernails digging painfully into my palms.

David was almost to the sub-POD corridor. All he needed to do was pull the red lever, and the corridor would collapse, killing the infected inside. He reached the metal box containing the shut-off lever. The infected man was nearly to the end of the corridor.

David pulled his elbow back and jammed it through the glass door of the box. He reached for the lever. The infected man reached out of the corridor for him. David's fingers wrapped around the lever. The infected man's hand grabbed for David's arm.

"Screw this." I jumped up, grabbed a garden spade, and was out of the greenhouse before I gave myself time to think.

I heard the lever click into place when David pulled it. The sound of the metal collapsing was deafening. The screams of the infected pierced my ears—like they were in a Coke can someone was crushing between their hands.

"David?" I called.

"Eva! Get in the greenhouse and lock the door."

He got out. The infected man wasn't in the corridor. He got out before the doors closed.

I walked around the ladder. I saw David standing beside the lever, his right hand still gripping it. I walked closer. The infected man stood in front of David. Drool dripped from its mouth, and it made soft snorts and grunts. A grotesque smile showed blue gums against yellowing teeth.

David.

I reached over and tore the shirts from my arm, making sure the blood was still flowing enough to attract the infected man's attention. It didn't take long. I'd barely dropped the shirts on the floor when his head snapped in my direction. The blood ran down my arm.

"Come on," I yelled. I shook my arm, sending droplets of blood through the air. The infected man ran toward me, a scream on his lips.

David yelled, "Eva!"

I love you. Trust me. I have this.

The man rushed me.

When he was close enough that I could smell his body odor and the stench of rotting meat on his breath, I lifted my other arm and plunged the garden spade into the side of his neck. Blood spurted from the wound, running down the man's arm and chest, spraying across the room and down my arm. The man's screams turned to gurgled cries. He stood in front of me, his hands at his throat, looking in my eyes for what seemed like minutes before his body crumpled. His blood flowed through the grates in the floor, dripping onto the metal floor beneath.

Then David was on me. Squeezing me hard against him. Whispering in my ear.

"Don't ever do something so wildly stupid again, Eva!" David whispered. "Why would you do that?"

You needed me.

"I love you, Evangelina Mae. More than anything." His lips were on mine before I could answer him, so I let my kiss answer for me.

I love you, too.

"Are you okay?" I scanned him with my eyes, ran over his body with my hands, making sure he was all right.

"Yeah. I'm fine. Let's get you cleaned up." David grabbed some towels from the kitchen. He wet one and quickly wiped the infected's blood off my arm, drying me with the second.

"That stuff really stings." I bit my bottom lip while David wiped the blood away.

"Yeah, it does. I think I got all it off." David threw the towels on the floor. "We can't stay here, Eva. If this group found the PODs, there'll be others. We have to move."

We raced up the emergency ladder toward the hatch leading outside. David reached up to push it open; I laid my hand on his arm. He looked at me, raising an eyebrow.

"Are you sure?"

"No," he said with a crooked grin.

"Well, that makes me feel better," I said, letting my hand fall from his arm.

He started to lift the hatch. "Wait!" I whispered.

"What?"

"Kiss me," I said, looking in his silvery-gray eyes.

His hand fell from the hatch and threaded through my hair, pulling my head gently back. He angled his mouth over mine and grazed my lips with his. I moaned when his tongue dipped between my lips, caressing mine. He lifted his head too soon and studied my face so long I felt a blush creep across it.

"My beautiful Evangelina."

I smiled and kissed him in answer. If we opened the hatch and found another group of infected waiting, I wanted the last thing I remembered to be the feel of David's lips against mine, his hands on my body.

Pulling my mouth from his, I smiled up at him. "Ready."

"I'll go up first. If there are any infected, you close and lock the hatch behind me."

"No."

"Hell's bells, Eva!"

"If there are infected up there, you know as well as I do that they'll wait for me to surface. I can't stay down here indefinitely, David. We go up together."

"Another camp might move through. You could join up with them."

"They'd never make it through. You know that. We go up together."

"You're so stubborn," he huffed.

He pushed the hatch open, the hinges groaning in protest. It hit the ground hard. Sand billowed around us, smacking us in the face and cutting off our vision.

The dust cloud began to clear and I saw feet standing just yards from the hatch. I listened for the groans and growls of the infected, and braced myself for their attack.

As the dust cloud rose above the people, I gasped. David and I slowly raised our hands above our heads. The two dozen ominous black barrels aimed at our heads were even scarier than the infected I'd expected to see.

"Lower your weapons," a man's voice boomed through a megaphone.

We watched the men dressed in military fatigues slowly lower the guns.

"Step out of the POD," Megaphone Man ordered.

David and I slowly climbed out of the hatch. Three soldiers rushed forward, pushing us to our knees.

"Open your mouth," one yelled.

Shaking, I opened my mouth, careful to show my gums. I saw David do the same.

"They're clean," one of the soldiers called out.

"Of course they are, you idiot. Look at her arm. It's bleeding all over the place. If he was infected, he'd have gnawed it off by now," another soldier called out, motioning toward David.

"Where are the group of infected we saw enter the POD, the ones we've been tracking?"

"Crushed in a sub-POD corridor," David said.

"You were able to take down more than a dozen infected by yourselves?"

"Well, they weren't the smartest kids in class. It was easy to trick them," I said, wrapping my arms around myself to cover the fact that I was standing in the middle of the desert, in nothing but my bra and jeans, with an army looking at me. David held out an arm and pushed me gently behind him.

The soldier closest to me pursed his lips to hide a grin.

"Let's go. Load them in the back of the truck."

"Here." A soldier threw a shirt at David, who caught it one-handed. "Figure she'll want that."

"Thanks." David turned and held it while I slipped my arms in; he then pulled it gently over my head before kissing my forehead gently.

"Let's go!" Megaphone Man yelled, breaking the moment.

"Where are we going?" I asked the soldier—the name on his chest read "Perkins"—when he helped me into the back of the truck. While a medic cleaned and wrapped my arm in a bandage, Perkins handed David an extra shirt to wear.

"The compound. You'll receive your inoculation and do some time in quarantine."

"Inoculation?" David and I asked in unison.

"Yeah. Haven't you heard? There's an immunization. As long as a person gets it before they're infected, they're good to go."

I looked up at David. The billowing sand stuck to his face and hair. He smiled at me, his white teeth gleaming against his dirty face.

"We made it," he whispered.

The bumps and ruts in the road made the truck lurch. I slid from one side of the bench to the other, bumping into David and the guy sitting next to me.

We drove for hours. The heat in the back of the truck was stifling. Sweat covered my face and dripped from my hair. The shirt Perkins had given me stuck to my back.

When we finally pulled up to the compound gates, I was exhausted. I was actually looking forward to the cool quarantine room.

A soldier opened the back of the vehicle. "Welcome to Area Twenty-Three, Sector Two."

"Home sweet home," I whispered.

We were herded through the back entrance of the clinic, past the same green dumpster I'd seen the last time I'd been quarantined. It still reeked of rotting food, and flies and bees buzzed around it.

We were silent as we followed the soldiers through the door of the clinic. The metal door swung shut with a loud clang. We stood at the same sign-in desk that I had seen so many weeks before. But the same girl wasn't sitting behind it.

"George!"

"Hey ya, Eva. Back for more?"

"Yeah, I couldn't stay away."

"Hey, man," George said to David. "Glad to see you're safe."

"Hey, George."

"Okay, let's get you guys showered off and into your rooms."

David followed George to his sanitizing shower, and I followed a young female nurse to mine. The cold water felt good after the long, hot truck ride. I didn't even mind the stinging spray or foam disinfectant that poured over me.

After the shower I dressed in the standard white pajama bottoms and t-shirt. A young doctor stitched the cut on my arm before I followed the nurse to get the required immunizations. No one had mentioned that the inoculation wasn't one shot, but three. Like most people, I still didn't much like getting shots. But I'd never been more happy feeling the needles break my skin and slide inside, pushing in the serum that would protect me—and those around me—from the brain-altering virus that had claimed so many.

After the immunizations were administered, the nurse told me all the possible side effects and complications that might arise, which included nausea, vomiting, bleeding gums, diarrhea and debilitating headaches.

Sounds like a bucketload of fun.

I followed the young nurse into the hall of quarantine rooms and saw George standing next to an empty room.

"Here you go, Eva. Your master suite."

"Gee, thanks, George. How long do I have the pleasure of staying at the Hotel Quarantine?"

"Six weeks."

I groaned.

"But I think I have something that may cheer you up." George pointed to the room next to mine.

"David," I whispered, placing my hand against the glass. He placed his over mine on the other side of the glass wall separating us.

"Here. I managed to pilfer these for you two lovebirds." George handed me a pen and note pad. "The glass is too thick to hear each other without screaming, but you can use those to write love notes back and forth." He grinned.

"Thank you. Speaking of love notes…?"

His grin widened. "Yeah. I've seen Tiffany. She arrived seven weeks ago—just finished her quarantine. And you won't believe how big Faith has gotten."

"They're good?" I asked around a lump in my throat. Hot tears pressed against the backs of my eyes.

"They're great, Eva. She'll be waiting to see you when you're outta here."

"I can't wait to see them. What about Katie and the others?" I wiped my tears on the back of my hand. George handed me a tissue.

"Seth is still here. I haven't heard about anyone else."

"Miss?" the nurse said, motioning me into the room.

"I'll stop by when I can," George said. "Enjoy your stay." He chuckled as he walked away.

I looked at David through the glass. He was writing something in his notebook. When he'd finished, he held it up to the glass.

I love you.

I love you, too, I answered.

Will you marry me?

I stared at the question. He had to ask? I'd risked everything to be with him and he had to ask if I'd spend the rest of my life with him? *What a dolt.*

Yes, I wrote. **But I want a big diamond. I hear they're free now, you know.**

I watched him laugh. He held his note pad to the window. *Always joking.*

I smiled.

Acknowledgements

After writing a novel, editing, revising and rewriting that novel, writing the acknowledgements page should be easy. That isn't the case, however. While writing is a solitary process, the business of producing a book is a collaborative effort.

First, to my husband, thank you for understanding my need to write and for sharing me with my imaginary friends. Your support, encouragement, and praise have been instrumental. Without your unending support I wouldn't be able to do what I love. Thank you for being my sounding board. I love you.

To my kids, thank you for helping me remember how to play and visit the wonderful places and people of my imagination. Evan, your monsters, zombies, and weapons are wicked! Thank you for your many ideas and drawings to help me visualize them. Aleigha and Alana, thank you for telling everyone your mommy is a writer. You are the best publicists I could have. In the world of words there will never be enough to express how much the three of you are loved.

To my parents, thank you for teaching me to go after my dreams. Dad, I wish you were here to share this with me. I hope I made you proud. You were a wonderful man and a better dad. I am proud to be your Mac—you're forever in my heart. Thank you for instilling your work ethic in me. Mom, you're the best critique partner I could have—brutally honest, but always with enough praise to ease the sting, you're exactly what I need. I love you both and am so thankful that you are my parents.

Kate Kaynak, it's hard to find words to express how grateful I am for you. Thank you for taking a chance on me and PODs. You always made me feel as though PODs was as important to you as it was to me. You poured your time and talent into _our_ project, making it shine. You are an editor extraordinaire! Warm, thoughtful, and always encouraging, you make working with you a joy. With everything you do, I swear you're superhuman! It's been an honor calling you my publisher and editor and I hope I'm blessed enough to work with you again and again in the future. Your dedication, hard work and encouragement have helped so many authors realize their dream of publication. I'm proud to say I'm a Spencer Hill Press author.

The team at Spencer Hill Press, you rock! You are a group of extremely talented individuals and I'm so grateful that you shared your talent with me and PODs. Kate and Danielle Ellison, your ideas and insights were epic. I loved them all and they made PODs a stronger story. To my editors, Kate Kaynak, Danielle Ellison, Rich "The Closer" Storrs, Shira Lipkin, and Kathryn Radzik—wow! What can I say about what you do? Combing over every word, period, comma and run-on sentence is exacting and exhausting work. It takes a special person to put so much detailed effort into a project. Thank you. You made PODs sparkle. I'd been told by authors at different publishing houses that editing was a nightmare. I guess I'm lucky. You made editing a joy. Thanks also to Rebecca Mancini, my foreign and film rights agent, and to Kendra Saunders, my publicity and marketing coordinator, for everything you have done to get the word out.

The wonderful bloggers who featured PODs on their blogs, you have no idea how instrumental you are in an author's, and a book's, success. Author interviews, book spotlights, cover reveals, virtual blog tours, blog hops and memes such as Waiting on Wednesday, Swoon Thursday and Six Sentence Sunday, to name just a few, are appreciated by me, and a multitude of other authors. It takes a great deal of time to keep up a blog.

Thank you for giving some of your time to PODs. I'm forever indebted to you.

Professor Arnold, of Baker College, you were the only instructor in my school career who encouraged my writing. You told me I had talent and always gave the most encouraging comments on each of my writing assignments. You recognized how shy and reluctant I was to have people read my writing, so you never made me wait for a grade, always passing me my assignment first so I didn't sit and bite my fingernails to the quick! And when you *gave* me my first "A" in an English course, you made a point to tell me that you didn't give me anything—I earned it. You probably didn't know how much you touched my life. Thank you for being the outstanding professor that you are. There would be no PODs if it wasn't for your encouragement. It started with you, and for that I'll be eternally grateful.

I've saved the best for last. As I've written this acknowledgement page, my mind has wandered to ways I can word my next thank you. Unfortunately, I wasn't granted a great epiphany. All I can say is my biggest thank you goes to my readers. I am truly honored and blessed that you chose to spend your time reading PODs. I'm continually amazed and humbled by your excitement and support. There are no words to express my thanks and gratitude. I hope we will share many more worlds and adventures together in the future.

All my best and happy reading,

A very thankful Michelle